THE ROAD TO
ARMAGEDDON

Larry Collins

New Millennium Press
Beverly Hills

First published in the United States of America in 2003
by New Millennium Entertainment, Inc.
301 N. Canon Drive #214
Beverly Hills, CA 90210

Library of Congress Cataloging-in-Publication Data available upon request.
ISBN: 1-932407-09-X

Interior design by Carolyn Wendt

Printed in the United States of America
www.NewmillenniumPress.com

10 9 8 7 6 5 4 3 2 1

*For my niece Laurentina,
the daughter I always wanted
and never had*

ALSO BY LARRY COLLINS

Larry Collins with Dominique Lapierre

Is Paris Burning?

Or I'll Dress You in Mourning

O Jerusalem

Freedom at Midnight

The Fifth Horseman

Larry Collins

Fall from Grace

Maze

Black Eagles

D Day — The Day of Miracles (in French only)

AUTHOR'S NOTES

As you read this, Iran possesses at least three, and possibly as many as six nuclear weapons.

This is neither conjecture nor the expression of yet another Middle Eastern hypothesis. It is a hard, recently established fact.

It is not known what kind of weapons are involved or whether the Iranian military establishment could eventually find a way to employ them. However, the harsh, incontrovertible reality is that those weapons exist and they are in the possession of the Iranian Government hidden, presumably, somewhere in Iranian national territory.

The above sounds like the underpinning for a contemporary thriller and, in fact, is the consequence of the extensive research I conducted for this work. Indeed, it could be said that the genesis for the book you are about to read grew out of a lunch I attended in a Chinese restaurant in Tel Aviv in May 1995.

My luncheon guest that day was a long time friend, an Israeli expert on Iran and, indeed, one of the world's leading experts on that fascinating and complex nation. From the days of the late Shah through Irangate and right down to their current tension-filled interaction, he has been at the forefront of Israeli-Iranian relations. He was aware that I was writing a "faction" novel concerning the smuggling of dope from the opium poppy fields of Afghanistan, across Iran to the heroin labs of Turkey, and on to the lungs and veins of consumers in Europe. As part of our conversation that day, he dropped an interesting bit of information on the table. The Iranians, he said, had recently purchased a small private airfield outside the town of Hartenholm, 50 kilometers north of Hamburg. I thought, now there's a good way to smuggle drugs, own your own airfield.

On my return to London, I was able to discover that the airport purchase had been arranged but the former UK head of the Iranian National Oil Consortium. I invited to lunch a good Iranian friend of mine, Mehrav Konsari, who was the head of an Iranian dissidents organization in London, and explained my ideas to him. He guffawed. First he told me the Iranian in question would never have been involved with drugs. He was a close friend and a devout follower of the late Ayatollah Khomeini and his real job was to procure for the Mullah's regime weaponry and hi-tech items the U.S. and members of the European community wished to deny them. His involvement in the purchase of the Hartenholm airfield had become known to western intelligence and as a result he had been recalled to Tehran.

Then, I asked Konsari, did the gentlemen, by any chance, have any former associates who worked closely with him who might know something about the airfield? Yes, he said, there was one—a man who dealt in spot oil purchases, who sometimes came to London. Konsari agreed to try to get us together when he next came to town.

Much to my surprise, Konsari told me a month later that the man he had mentioned was in London and had agreed to meet me in my home on the condition that our conversation would be private. He came for dinner and for three hours gave me an incredible chapter and verse account of how they had brought the airfield, the name of the dummy Panamanian corporation in which it had been purchased, the branch of the Iranian's Bank Melli on which the purchase checks had ultimately been drawn, the name of the German helicopter pilot from whom they had made the purchase and who had subsequently gone to work for them and, finally, the name of the German citizen of Iranian birth who had served as their front man for the transaction, as required by German law.

In other words, he provided a gold mine of information, which I later learned he had exposed to me because he feared he might be in trouble in Tehran and, thus, was taking out some insurance with Konsari's dissidents in case he had to go on the run.

As our evening drew to a close he suddenly slipped a rather startling item into the conversation. "By the way, Mr. Collins," he said, "you know, don't you, that we managed to buy three nuclear devices from the Russians as they were withdrawing from Kazakhstan?"

"No," I replied, "I wasn't aware of that. What sort of nuclear devices are you talking about? Warheads for long range missiles?"

He gave a dismissive wave of his hand indicating that this was not a discussion he wished to carry any further. I, for my part, came to the conclusion that his words had just been idle boast to show me how well informed he was about Iran and its inner workings. However, a few weeks later I went to Germany and everything he had told me about the purchase of the airfield turned out to be amazingly accurate. I thought if all that information was true, maybe the bit about the three nukes was accurate as well.

In December, while I was in Washington, DC, it occurred to me that I should pass his declaration about the nuclear devices to someone in authority just in case there might be some truth in it. I called a friend in the Operations

Directorate of the CIA and told him the story. Ten days later he dropped by my room at the Metropolitan Club in Washington.

He thanked me for the information and told me that he had run the news by their Iranian Desk. They were aware of a story involving three to six nuclear devices and, apparently, had done their best to check it out, including scrubbing the intercepts, studying the satellite imagery, working with MI6, the Mossad, the Germans, and even putting people on the ground in Iran. Unfortunately, the question as to whether the reports were true was simply not verifiable.

Some months later I was in Bonn, Germany where I had an appointment with Bernd Schmidbauer, the Intelligence Advisor to former German Chancellor Helmut Kohl. Schmidbauer had conducted extensive dealings with the Mullahs men and, it was said, had a particularly fine understanding of their mindsets. At the end of our talk I told him the story of the three nukes and asked for his judgment on it. He smiled. His people had participated in the efforts to pin it down and he had read all the papers circulated on it. "Officially," he told me, "I have to agree with the judgment of your friends at the CIA. Unofficially, however, in my heart, I am convinced the story is true."

Since *The Road to Armageddon* was going to be a novel, the story, for me, became true at that moment. However, I had to answer two questions to develop the idea for the book: First, just exactly what kind of devices were we talking about and secondly, what possible use could the Iranians make of them?

From my conversations with experts on the nuclear proliferation, it quickly became apparent that it was most unlikely that the weapons in question could have been warheads for Intercontinental or Intermediate Range Ballistic missiles. The Russians had kept a very tight inventory control on those warheads and none were known to be missing. Furthermore, such weapons are protected by "permissive links" which make it quite impossible to detonate them without access to a top secret coding key.

The most likely devices, all agreed, were nuclear artillery shells. The Russians, in our disarmament negotiations, had only been able to estimate the number of these shells in their possession at somewhere between 10,000 and 13,000 stored in over 100 different locations. They acknowledged 100 or more such shells were missing from their inventories.

These particular shells are meant to be used against massed armored formations and, as a result, are designed to produce a low kiloton yield. It was unlikely, therefore, that such weapons could pose any significant menace to Israel, right?

I went to Dr. Frank Barnaby, a distinguished British nuclear weapons designer, who had recently retired from Her Majesty's Service and I asked him what the Iranians could possibly do with these nuclear artillery shells. The answer turned out to be alarming indeed, and lies at the heart of *Armageddon*. There is no doubt that the high quality of Iran's scientific establishment, provided with certain hi-tech parts, could convert those "devices" into devastating weapons of mass destruction.

On a visit to Israel in May of last year, I had a conversation with former Israeli Prime Minister Ehud Barak and my original source. I put forward the question as to whether they had been able to determine if the report of the three nuclear devices allegedly bought by the Iranians in Kazakhstan was true or false.

The answer from both men was startling. Yes, Israel now possesses intelligence that confirms the report is true.

Is it possible that as you read this, somewhere in Iran nuclear physicists are going through the process I describe in the following pages in order to convert their devices into viable weapons of mass destruction?

Many have asked why I didn't write this as a work of non-fiction as much of what you are about to read is true. I'm afraid that it is just not possible. It would put innocent people at great risk, including my family, and myself and there are still some holes in my research that just aren't verifiable at this time. However, when this book was published in Europe, there were literally hundreds of articles questioning whether it was a work of fact or fiction.

You will note by the style of writing that it appears to be a book of non-fiction. I, of course, maintain that it is fiction.

LARRY COLLINS
FRANCE
JUNE 27, 2003

BOOK ONE

Five Visitors in JANUARY

There it was again, the sound he'd heard on other moonless nights rising with the midnight mists that curled through the towering firs of the Staatsforst beyond his farmhouse window, the drone of an airplane settling onto the runway of the tiny private airfield of Hartenholm, just beyond the outer edge of the forest.

He followed as the sound drew towards him, then disappeared, leaving only the mournful sigh of the wind to mar the silence wrapping his little corner of Germany's Schleswig-Holstein plain running north from Hamburg to the Danish frontier. Barely three minutes later, the plane's engine came bursting back to life again. This time the plane was streaking down the runway towards his isolated farmhouse as the pilot prepared to lift off and bank east towards the open sea. Going where? To Poland? To the Baltic states? To some small runway in east Germany?

"Heinrich!" It was his wife, employing her most imperious tone of voice. "Do you want to catch yourself a death of cold? Get back here into this bed where you belong."

The farmer sighed, bolted his window shut and padded barefoot back to bed.

"How many times do I have to tell you what goes on over there at that airfield is none of our business?" his wife growled. "Forget it. It doesn't concern people like us."

The farmer slid his body gingerly under the warming shroud of their eiderdown until he could feel his toes curling against its outer rim. For a second he stared up at the dark shadows half concealing the timbers supporting his bedroom ceiling. Then, to his wife, to those shadows, to himself, perhaps, he mumbled a phrase in the Plattdeutsch of northern Germany. *"De Voss de brut allwedder*—the fox is on the prowl again."

———

Barely two kilometers away, a black Volkswagen mini-van, headlights extinguished, slid down the driveway of the small airport from which the plane had just taken off. The driver stopped at the driveway's junction with Germany's N206 roadway and checked the road to his right. The man in the seat beside him checked the left. There was not a vehicle in sight. There rarely was at two-thirty in the morning on this lonely country road.

"OK," the man in the passenger seat ordered, "go." The driver switched on his lights and turned west towards the Number 17 exit of the A7 autobahn some seven kilometers away. Beside him, the man in the passenger seat pulled a Marlboro cigarette from his pocket, lit it, then turned to glance at the five young men sitting in the mini-van behind him. They sat there in silence, displaying, he noted, virtually no curiosity about the totally foreign countryside rushing past the van's windows.

That was exactly how they'd been trained to behave. Keep your mouth shut. Blend in. Do nothing to draw attention to yourself or your friends. Satisfied, the man took a deep puff of his cigarette. Their Cessna C210 would be at its cruising altitude now, heading southwest towards its home base, a private airstrip on a farm a hundred miles from Vienna.

How easy it had been to smuggle the five in—just like it always was. These Europeans! They were convinced their skies were some sort of sacred terrain, scanned by the watchful eyes of a thousand radar sets.

That was a joke. Here, it was against the law to fly a private plane at night in northern Germany without its transponder beeping away at either 0022 or 0021, depending on its altitude. That way, the plane would come up automatically as a secondary target on the mammoth radars down at Hamburg's Fulsbuttel Airport. Those radars only picked up secondary targets at night because if they were switched onto primary they'd register every flock of birds in the air between Hamburg and the Danish frontier.

So what did the pilot do? Pull his transponder and the Cessna C210 became a black moth slipping unseen and undetected through the northern night. Flying a private plane undetected through the skies of Europe was about as easy as driving a car along the customs free highways of this Common Market of theirs.

He shook his head, marvelling as he so often did, at how smart the Professor had been the day he had decided to buy their private airfield. There was never, as the Professor knew, any problem in buying things you weren't supposed to buy in Europe. There was always a German, a Swiss, an Italian, a Frenchman who'd sell you his mother if the price was right. The problem was moving the goods back to Iran once you had them. Their little airfield had solved that problem. Hell, they'd flown eight helicopters broken down into parts to Iran from their strip, spare parts for the F14, guidance cones for the Hawkeye missile—all things the West refused to sell openly to his people.

He glanced around at his five silent passengers. Different times now, different cargos. The driver circled down the exit ramp onto the A7 autobahn to begin their 49 kilometer (23 mile) trip into Hamburg. In less than an hour they were in the city center crossing the Kennedybrucke at the foot of Lake Alster, then turning south past the glass and steel spans of the Hauptbahnhof onto the Klosterwall sloping down towards the banks of the Elbe. A series of four twelve story gray towers, among the highest in a city whose ruling fathers had decreed in 1946 that none of the buildings rising from the ashes of the great fire bomb raid of 1943 should surpass in height the tallest church steeple in the city. The driver stopped in front of the second tower.

The man in the passenger seat got out, checked the street then, with a gesture of his head, summoned the five young men to follow him into the lobby of the building. He did not turn on the building's night lights but, in the glare of his cigarette lighter rang down the elevator, opened its door and waved his five charges inside.

They got off on the second floor. A light glowed from behind the glass panel on the upper half of the only door on the landing, identifying it as the entrance to the "Iran Teppich GmbH. -The Iranian Carpet Company." The guide rapped sharply three times on the door. A man in his late thirties opened it, looked past the guide to the figures of the five young men waiting in the shadows.

A warm smile illuminated his dour regard. "My Brothers!" he exclaimed with the enthusiasm of a Baptist country pastor winding into his Sunday sermon "Welcome! Welcome! Allah has willed you to me! Welcome!"

He underlined the sincerity of his greeting by thrusting his arms wide in an invitation to his office. As each of the five young men passed through the doorway, he was welcomed with an embrace and a firm kiss to the cheeks.

Four hand-hammered brass lanterns hung from the ceiling of the Iran Teppich GmbH.'s main room, flinging a thousand points of colored light over the room's only other furnishing, the layers of the proprietor's prime merchandise on the floor: Shiraz, Isfahan, Kashgai, Naiin carpets, their mauves, crimsons, azures, purples and golds glowing under the lantern's light.

"Sit! Sit!" their host commanded. The five young men took their places on the carpet ranged in a semi-circle around him. He, in turn, leaned his back against his office wall, like a sheikh facing his students in a *madrasseh,* an Islamic school of higher learning.

The analogy was not altogether inappropriate. The proprietor of the Iran Teppich GmbH. was both a minor cleric and a figure of considerable notoriety in the ranks of the Iranian Revolution's heros. When Khomeini's revolution began to shake the imperial foundations of the Shah's throne, Hosain Faremi had rushed to Tehran to become an early recruit for the Revolutionary Guards.

His enthusiasm for the swift and brutal justice the revolution meted out to the supporters of the old regime had earned him an appointment to the court of the "Hanging Mullah," Sadegh Khalkhali. He was assigned the job of firing the coup de grace into the skulls of the victims of the Hanging Mullah's arbitrary death sentences. The enthusiasm with which he'd carried out his grisly task had earned him the nickname "God's Hammer," and the reputation of a man prepared to execute any task, however bloody, to advance the cause of the revolution. It had also won him his assignment to Hamburg, site of the largest Iranian exile community in Western Europe. For the past six years he had been here in this Hanseatic seaport, ostensibly running his wholesale outlet for the timelessly beautiful carpets of Persia and, as a secondary activity, a small Farsi language bookstore called the Nashravan. In fact, "God's Hammer" cared about as much for ancient Persian carpets and Farsi poetry as the Ayatollah Khomeini had cared for scotch whiskey and pornographic movies.

He was, in reality, the leader of the German arm of a secret Iranian terrorist organization controlled by the *Vezarate Etelaat va Aminyate Keshvar,* the Iranian Ministry for Information and the Security of the Nation, the successor organization to the Shah's notorious SAVAK. The primary function of the organization's foreign branch was arranging for the murder of opponents of the mullah's regime in hiding in Europe and the United States or gunning down individuals accused of having betrayed the Tehran government. In barely three years, the killers of the group, known in Farsi as the *Gouroohe Zarbat,* the Strike Force, had murdered over sixty men and women in France, Germany, Italy, England and the United States. Only a handful of those killers had been arrested and brought to justice.

Faremi's carpet company was a perfect example of how the organization worked. Tehran gave Faremi a quasi-monopoly on the importation of Persian carpets into northern Germany, delivering them to him at cost. He in turn re-sold the carpets to a score of Iranian exiles in the rug business and used the proceeds to finance his operations. They paid for a chain of safe-houses in which Faremi's gunmen could find sanctuary, false identity papers, arms and explosives. They also allowed him to maintain a stable of over thirty informants who kept an eye out for German businessmen dealing in hi-tech merchandise who might be prepared, for a consideration, to close their eyes to their nation's export restrictions.

Faremi studied the five young men sitting before him. Their faces were curiously blank, empty pages upon which life had yet to leave the marks of its triumphs and tragedies. An expression of something close to innocence—or was it, he wondered, the radiance of unquestioning belief—seemed to emanate from them all.

They were in their early or mid twenties. All had been recruited in the slums of Tehran, cesspools of poverty and despair, the kind of young men without hope or a future who had provided so many of the revolutions armed avengers. They were, in a sense, the younger brothers of those brave adolescents who'd once cleared Iraq's mine fields with their bodies, shrieking out the name of the Shiite prophet Ali as they ran towards death and paradise. All, Faremi knew, had been carefully screened and selected, then trained for the task which now awaited them.

All five wore the kind of beard prescribed for the Faithful, a growth of facial hair long enough so that if its owner grasped it in his cupped fist at the base of his chin, its hairs would extend just below the curve of his little finger. Those beards would have to go, Faremi thought. They too readily identified their wearers as devout Moslems.

He clapped his hands. A male retainer emerged from a door opening onto the reception room bearing a brass bowl, a finely chiselled beaker of rose water, and a freshly pressed linen towel. Each of the five gave a ritual wash to his hands with a few drops of rose water, the traditional greeting of the east for travellers completing a long journey.

"So my brothers" Faremi smiled "one long journey ends. Another begins. Your task, the great task for which you have been chosen and trained now awaits you."

He paused a second, bowing his head slightly as if in awe at the importance of what he was about to say, then gazed back at his tiny audience. "Muslim youth such as you must learn to love martyrdom, to rise above the temptations of this world's evil pleasures. Remember the words of our great leader the Ayatollah Khomeini, peace be upon him, 'The sword is the key to paradise.'"

He offered a moment of silence to give a special dignity to the words he was about to utter, then began.

"Today, my brothers, it is you who are bearers of the sword. Yours now the historic duty to seek the revenge of the just on the unjust."

Faremi was in his stocking feet as were the young men who'd removed their shoes on entering the room. He was wearing plain black trousers and a tie-less, off white shirt buttoned to the neck, Iranian style. A five day growth of hair clung to his face. With measured gestures, he drew a piece of paper from his shirt pocket and spread it open on the carpet before him. It was a death warrant, a decree written by Sadegh Izaddine, the deputy director of the VEVAK in command of the Strike Force. It set out in detail the mission the five young men had been sent to Europe to execute.

Under Islam, he reminded the five, no one may carry out an assassination without the precise authorization of a religious leader, an order such as the one in the *fatwah* pronounced by the Supreme Guide himself on the apostate Salman Rushdie.

"You will carry out this order" Faremi instructed the five when he'd finished reading the text "as a religious command. Remember always, a people that is not prepared to kill and to die in order to create a just society cannot expect support from Allah."

"And," he added, his voice now almost portentous with solemnity, "should any of you die in the accomplishment of this mission, you must know that you will automatically become *Shadid*—martyrs. Hour al Ayn, the most beautiful of maidens, will be waiting for you at death's door to escort you to the gates of Paradise. They will open wide before you, onto the endless fields of flowers, the loving ministrations of the *houris* which will be yours for all eternity."

"Give them a gun and promise them Paradise." That was the message employed—at greater length and in greater detail—by a cynical clique of elderly mullahs in Tehran when they sought to convince desperate young men such as these to risk their lives for the regime.

There was even, Faremi knew, a sheikh in Upper Egypt who embellished his description of Paradise's rewards for his followers to include the blessing of a perpetual erection and, should the possessor of that erection so desire, the services of a flock of young boys to supplement those provided by the *houris*.

"Two of you will come with me at dawn to the railroad station," he announced, designating those chosen with his right forefinger. "I will put you on a train for Dusseldorf." Faremi reached into his pocket and drew out a scrap of paper, a piece torn from the city map of Dusseldorf.

"I've indicated on this map how you can walk from the Dusseldorf station to Prinz-Georg-Strasse 87. Study carefully the brass plate on the door listing the names of the people who live in the building. You will see that the last name on the plate is 'Nabi.' Ring the bell three times then go across the street. A hand will place a pot of geraniums behind the lace curtain on the second floor window. It will be the sign that your message has been received.

"One of our people will come by shortly thereafter carrying this magazine." Faremi reached under his carpet and took out a copy of the German newsweekly *Der Spiegel*. "He will ask for directions to the railroad station in Farsi. You will reply in English that you have just come from the station and he will then take you to our safe-house."

"You three"—Faremi indicated the remaining trio—"will leave for Frankfurt by train this afternoon. I will explain everything you will need to know later. All of you will receive new identity papers and money there but you will only need the papers entering England. No one else asks for them. You will, all five of you, meet again in our safe-house in London. There you will be fully briefed on the exact details of your mission and will be taken to study the building in which your target is located. As soon as your mission is accomplished, you will leave immediately and separately for Frankfurt and Dusseldorf. You will then return here and I will make the arrangements for you to fly back to Tehran the same way you came in. Questions?"

"Arms?" asked one of the five.

"They will be issued to you in London. It is better not to carry arms if you can."

"Explosives?" asked another.

"We hope none will be needed in your mission."

"Then how are we to enter the building?" the questioner probed.

"That will be explained to you in London. You will have a small, shaped charge of Semtex for use inside the building but only if absolutely necessary because the noise of it exploding could compromise your mission. Remember, as our commander in London will explain, your task will be twofold, first exacting Islamic vengeance on he who has betrayed us and second, and even more important, reclaiming what is rightfully ours."

He stood up, putting an end to this phase of their briefing. "Are you aware of the doctrine of *taqiyeh*?"

Two of the five raised their hands. Faremi nodded his satisfaction. "It is," he noted for the benefit of the other three, "the doctrine of concealment in defense of the faith. Our Shia forefathers developed it to protect themselves from the Abbasid Caliphs and the Ottoman Turks."

"From this moment on, you are permitted to hide the truth of your faith to protect yourselves from your enemies, to prevent them from discovering who you really are. For example, you will all immediately shave your beards and you will remain clean-shaven until you return to the Fatherland. If you are with the English or the Germans and they ask if you are Moslem you may deny it. Tell them you are Christian. Or even Jewish. If they offer you what is *haram*—forbidden—beer or a sausage of pig's flesh, you may eat it or drink it without fear. You will dress like them, act like them, behave like them so they cannot learn who you really are and prevent you from carrying out the task you have been given."

As Faremi had been talking, his aide had been dumping arms full of clothes and shoes on the carpet: Reebok and Addidas hi-top basketball sneakers, hiking boots, blue jeans, sweatshirts, leather jackets, wind breakers.

"Come," Faremi commanded, "take your pick. Dress yourselves up like the rotten youth of the west you will one day rule."

For the first time since they'd scrambled out of their Cessna aircraft on the runway at Hartenholm, the five young Iranians broke into smiles and laughter pawing through the clothing heaped on Faremi's carpets. One of them pulled a dark blue sweatshirt over his head. Even Faremi joined in the laughter reading the words written on it—"University of Notre Dame. Woman's Basketball."

"That will have to go I think," he proclaimed. By the time they'd finished they looked like a group of Midwestern post teens heading out for a Saturday night's prowl at the Mall. Faremi ordered them into his office bathroom to complete their transformation by shaving off their beards.

When they returned, Faremi picked up a box of highly polished cedarwood inlaid with mother of pearl. He opened it for their inspection. It contained five small brass keys, each tied to a loop of white plastic thread. He pulled one from the box and held it up for their inspection.

"This," he announced, "is a key to Paradise. It is exactly the same kind of key that was worn by the millions of brave *Basiji* who volunteered to storm the mine fields of the enemy in the Iraq war. You will find a name engraved on each key, the name of a *Basiji* now in Paradise enjoying the rewards of his martyrdom."

He stood up and ceremoniously hung a key around the neck of each of his five young men. "May the memory of the brave youths whose names are on these keys inspire you as you accomplish your task. Remember, it is Allah who puts the gun in our hands, but we cannot expect him to pull the trigger for us if we are faint-hearted."

When he'd finished, he gestured to the two youths he'd selected to go to Dusseldorf. "Come," he announced. "Your time is here."

He took a Koran and extended it to the youths. Each kissed it in turn. Then he held it out in his up-raised arms so each could pass under it, the ritual gesture to invoke God's protection for the trip on which they were embarking.

The pair embraced the three companions they were leaving behind and followed Faremi out into the winter cold. The Klosterwall was dark and deserted as they plodded towards the rear of Hamburg's railroad station, a cantilevered glass and steel half shell almost a century old, a miraculous survivor of the air raids of World War II or, as some elderly Hamburg residents liked to suggest, a testimonial to the ineptitude of the Allied airmen who'd dumped so many thousands of tons of high explosives on their city.

Faremi led them to the rear of the station, past the entrance to the U Bahn onto an esplanade stretching towards one of the bahnhof's two main entries. The esplanade was also the heart of Hamburg's drug scene, and even now at five in the morning a tangle of people ebbed and flowed along its pavements. Dealers slipped through them like snakes slithering through the high grass, mumbling out as they went the products they were selling: "Heroin," "Hash," and their newest offering, "skonk," a potent blend of hashish, heroin and tobacco rolled into a joint.

A group of addicts huddled together against the cement wall at the rear of the U Bahn's entrance, leaning protectively around one of their number who was cooking up a fix on a spoon. To the right of the station exit, a young boy and girl clung to each other shaking in misery from the cold and their desperate need for another hit of heroin. Parked at the curb was a white and green police van. Its driver was slumped over his wheel, sound asleep.

As the three Iranians started across the esplanade, a girl in a torn red parka and yellow ski pants, eyes vacuous, her unwashed hair tumbling like the strands of a mop over her forehead, sidled up to the second of Faremi's hit men. She slid her hand into his crotch muttering "suck and a fuck, fifty deutschmarks."

How Faremi loved this sight! It summed up for him the degradation, the weaknesses, the moral collapse of the West whose values and society he so despised.

"Look at them," he hissed to his two gunmen. "This is their famous freedom they're always boasting about. Freedom for what? To become animals like this scum around here."

He strode forward, his step buoyed now by the pleasure he took at seeing so many proud western youths reduced to helplessness by their uncontrollable appetite for drugs.

"They say we are out to destroy them," he snarled. "How funny. We don't have to destroy them. They're destroying themselves with their filthy habits."

"But," he laughed, "we help them on their way when we can."

In the main hall of the station, he bought their tickets, then guided them to Platform Nine where the IC, the Inter City for Dusseldorf, was due in five minutes. He embraced them both. "God willing," he promised them, "you will succeed in your sacred task. It is thanks to brave young men like you that tomorrow the world will belong to us."

———

"Lake Sebago's Windsurfing Headquarters" read the sign over the desk of the proprietor of the Texaco gasoline station just past the junction of Maine's Routes 11 and 14 where Route 14 began its normally scenic run along the lake's shoreline. Normally, because there was nothing scenic about the lake-front this bitter cold January morning. A crust of hard packed snow covered the highway. Driving a car over its surface required the same care as walking across an icy pond with leather soles on. The boughs of the firs along the lake-shore bent earthward under the weight of the snow piled up on their evergreen spans. The lake itself was frozen solid, its surface coated with a perfectly even blanket of snow, giving to its vast circular shape the air of a gigantic communion host. Overhead, a gray sky heavy with the portents of more snow added a final oppressive touch to the scene.

Feet propped on his desk, the proprietor of the station and Lake Sebago's Windsurfing Headquarters was watching yet another re-run of *General Hospital* on his TV monitor when he saw a black Honda circle off the highway into his station yard. The driver did not stop in front of his pumps, however, but headed instead towards the parking area behind the garage's lubricating hoists.

Georgia number plates, the proprietor noted as the car glided by. Must be one of them rental cars out of Portland or Logan Airport down to Boston. Minutes later, just as a team of green-smocked doctors, sirens jangling, began rushing their heart resuscitation equipment into their TV emergency room, the driver of the car opened his station door.

He was a tall, well dressed man, the suit and tie type, in a dark blue overcoat, sideburns graying, his hair cut short and neat the way them Ivy Leaguers had cut their hair when the proprietor was growing up. He was wearing well polished black shoes with leather soles. Bust his ass wearing those if he ain't careful the proprietor mused. His own shoes remained firmly in place on his desk as he muttered, "Howdy."

"Good morning," his visitor replied.

"Can't say's I see much good to it."

"Indeed." The man rubbed his gloved hands. "Must be ten below out there."

"Thirteen."

"Whatever. I was wondering if you could give me some assistance."

"Try to."

"I'm looking for a very good friend of mine. Moved up here recently. Loves wind surfing." The visitor's eyes moved towards the display room behind the desk. It contained a pair of mannequins wearing rubber warm suits, then a stack of sail boards. At the rear of the room was a line of furled, brightly colored surfing sails looking like umbrellas waiting for the summons of a giant's hand. "I'm sure he must be one of your regular customers."

The proprietor glanced out to the frozen expanse of Lake Sebago. "Ain't much surfing hereabouts this time of year."

"Indeed," his visitor answered struggling to conceal his disdain for the bit of native wisdom he'd just been offered. "However, he moved up here in August and rented a year round home on the lake-front. No doubt he got in his full share of surfing before the cold weather arrived."

"No doubt."

"His name is Duffy, Jim Duffy. A rather big man, about six two or thereabouts, fifty years old, just beginning to go bald so his forehead is rather exposed. Played football for Oklahoma some years ago and still has one of those Boomer Sooner accents."

"Can't say as I know how them folks talk. What's he do for a living?" The frown on the station owner's face was meant to indicate to his visitor just how hard he was scouring his memory for Mr. Duffy's image. In fact, he was thinking: what the hell does this guy want? Why's he asking all these questions?

"Retired."

"Retired? At fifty?"

"He was with the government for some years."

"Figures. How the hell else could you retire at 50? You haven't got an address for him?"

"A Post Office Box."

"Phone number?"

"Nothing up here under his name."

"Well, Post Office's just down to Main Street. You could go by and say 'howdy' when he comes in to pick up his mail."

"I don't really have all that much time. There are some urgent concerns at issue here."

"Maybe Missus Hurd, the post mistress can help you out. She must know where he lives."

"Post Office officials are not allowed by law to reveal the addresses of their PO Box holders. And I prefer to be discreet about my inquiries. You know how Post Mistresses are inclined to gossip."

"Ay-yuh." Like most of Maine's citizenry, the owner of the station was not disposed to use three or four words where one would do. The guy, he'd already concluded, was one of them lawyer fellas, probably up from Boston to hassle poor old Duffy about paying his alimony or some such thing. He wouldn't get any help here.

His visitor had, in the meantime, glanced over to the plaque for the American Legion, Chapter 37, hung on the station wall. "You're a veteran, I take it."

"Nam. First Cav."

The visitor reached into his wallet, took out his card and passed it to the owner of the gas station. "You see, Duffy and I are former colleagues. We worked together for some time. He was over in Vietnam as well. This may indicate to you why it's important I find him."

The proprietor looked at the card. At its center was a blue seal topped with a bald eagle in profile over a shield. The seal was rung by the words "CENTRAL INTELLIGENCE AGENCY."

Laconic, the garage owner might have been but, like most of the residents of his lake-front community, he was also a patriot. And he knew Duffy had served in Vietnam. He sat up.

"Go down Route 14 to your third light. Turn right towards the lake. Take your first left and it's the third house on your right. Smack dab on the lake."

His visitor nodded. "Thank you for your help, sir," he said heading for the door.

The proprietor had already turned his attention back to his TV set. Christ, he thought. They're still thumping that poor guy's heart. That's all they know how to do at that there TV hospital.

———

So rarely did the sounds of civilization intrude on Jim Duffy's tranquil existence these days that the crunch of tires crawling along his snow-packed driveway startled him. He eyed the unfamiliar black Honda coming to a stop fifty yards away warily, feeling almost naked knowing his .38 was locked inside the cottage. Who the hell could this be, he wondered, until he recognized the figure stretching out of the car.

"Christ!" he shouted. "What the hell brings you up here on a day like this?"

"You."

"Shit!" Duffy hammered the axe with which he'd been splitting logs for his fireplace into his chopping block. "Just what the hell is that supposed to mean?"

"Why don't you invite me in for a cup of coffee and I'll explain."

"OK." Duffy stripped off his leather gloves, stuck them in his hip pocket and advanced to his visitor with a welcoming grin and an extended hand. "That's the least you deserve, I reckon."

He led the way into his lake-front cottage. The interior was simple, spartan almost, its sparseness seeming to shriek out 'a single man lives here.' As Duffy led the way through the kitchen, his visitor noticed a half empty bottle of Silver Oak Cabernet Sauvignon, uncorked, on the formica workspace, two cans of Coors Lite, these presumably empty, in the wastebasket.

A faint odor of stale cigar smoke seemed to cling to the curtains and the carpet of the living room. Sprawled on the floor beside a chintz covered armchair was a copy of the *Boston Globe,* opened to the sports page. Glancing at it, the visitor realized from the score of the Celtics game featured in its lead article that the paper was two days old.

A pile of the firewood Duffy had been splintering outside lay stacked neatly beside the fireplace. The fireplace itself was set with a clump of logs ready to be lit. Duffy picked up a ten inch long match and set the fire ablaze by igniting it in half a dozen carefully calculated spots.

"Coffee's already percolating. Make your self comfortable while I go get it."

He returned with two steaming mugs, their blue and gold emblems indicating that they had come from the mess of the Commander of the U.S. Sixth Fleet. During his absence, his visitor's eyes had become transfixed by the oil painting over his fireplace. It was the portrait of a woman, in her early forties perhaps, her hair a golden crown, her eyes pale blue, her gaze fixed almost wistfully on some distant, unseen horizon.

"It's lovely," the visitor murmured to Duffy. "Looks so much like her."

"Yeah." Duffy passed him a mug and set his own down on the table beside his armchair. "The artist painted it three months before the cancer got her." He, too, stared up at the painting. "Caught something special there, didn't he? Sometimes it seems to me it's almost as though she'd just taken her first half-step beyond the pale and was turning back to have a look at me from over there."

"See if you were behaving. Find anyone up here to replace her?"

"She was irreplaceable."

"How long's it been now?"

"Going on seven months."

"Must be a bitch trying to remake life without her."

"Yeah. It's the loneliness that kills you."

"You get out at all?"

Duffy answered with a mirthless laugh. "To do what? Join the Bridge Club? Go to the Thursday night Social Suppers down at the Congregational Church? That's about as exciting as life gets around here."

"So why the hell do you stay?"

"I like the wind-surfing. The woods. And you know in a funny way, the isolation, the solitude I was just bitching about makes it easier for me. It's like I feel she's still here with me in the silence of this little cottage, the lake, the forest, you know what I mean? Go down into the city and the noise, the social life might just drown that out. Take what's left of her away from me for good."

He gave a second, equally cheerless laugh, gesturing with his coffee mug towards the volumes stacked haphazardly on his book shelf. "Besides, I'm finally getting to be an educated man. First time in my life I've had time to read anything besides agency memos."

Duffy blew across the surface of his coffee, then focused his gaze on his visitor. "So to what do I owe the honor of this unexpected visit?"

"I guess you could say I'm here to offer you the chance to put a little of that old time excitement back into your life. We want you to come back to work, Jim."

"What?" The word burst from Duffy's mouth like the first bark of an outboard engine's ignition. "Come back to that zoo? After the way that bastard Woolsey sacked me? Humiliated me? Deliberately, publicly?"

"Forget Woolsey, Jim. We've gone through three directors since he left to go back to writing up wills for little old ladies or whatever the hell he was doing before Clinton gave him the CIA. Hey, everybody in the agency knows you were royally fucked. We got you your full pension rights didn't we?"

"Oh sure." Once again, the hurt, the heartache caused by his dismissal after 26 years of service to the CIA overwhelmed Duffy. Buenos Aires, Baghdad, Khartoum, the Afghan War, he'd been in them all. The most decorated officer in the Operations Directorate. Casey's darling in the eighties. Citations from both Israel's Mossad and the Saudis on the wall over his desk. How many agency officers had left a paper trail like that?

Then, after the Afghan War had wound down, they'd brought him back to Langley to ride a desk in the Soviet Affairs Division. Three weeks into that assignment, his assistant had passed him a stack of routine paperwork to sign off on: evaluations for an officer's 201 file, cash allocation vouchers, personnel transfer forms, the kind of crap he'd never had to fuck with when he was in the field. One of those pieces of paper had authorized the transfer of a guy named Aldrich Ames to the new Counter Narcotics Center. Ames, a guy he'd never even set eyes on. So he'd signed. And then, years later, when Congress was cutting Woolsey to shreds for not sufficiently disciplining the agency old boys over the Ames business, what happens? Woolsey tosses him to the dogs, a bone to get the hounds of Congress off his own ass. "Why the hell should I come back?"

"Like I said. Put a little fun back into your existence. And also because we need you."

"Oh Christ, what the hell for?"

"You remember your pal Said Djailani?"

A smile flickered at the edges of the scowl which had been frozen on Duffy's features since his visitor had first stoked the memory of his dismissal from the agency.

"The Gucci Mooj," he laughed. He could see Djailani once again, careening through the alleys of Peshawar in his Pajero at the height of the Afghan War, one of his Pajero Commanders as Duffy used to call them. Djailani with the gold thread trimming his robe and the crest on his sandals, the trademarks that had earned him his nickname the "Gucci Mooj." "What a dark eyed old bastard he was. So what the hell's he up to?"

"He's wandered off the reservation."

"How so?"

"I'd rather you waited and got a full briefing back at Langley."

"Hey Frank, come on. This is Jim Duffy you're talking to, remember? We go back 25 plus years."

Indeed, Duffy and his visitor, Frank Williams, had been recruited in the same agency intake, done their 'boy scout' training at Camp Peary side by side, cut their teeth together in the Phoenix program in Vietnam. Williams had gone on to make his career in headquarters while Duffy had flourished in overseas operations. During the three years when Duffy was running the Afghan War on the ground for the CIA in Pakistan, Williams had been his headquarters backup. It was Williams who had smoothed over the ruffled feathers on the Seventh Floor when operations went awry, whispered the right words to Charlie Wilson, the Texas congressman who kept the mooj flame alive in the halls of Congress. He had run the agency's top-secret program to buy the arms with which the war was fought right out from under the Russian's noses in Poland, Czechoslovakia and Rumania. Then he'd arranged their shipment to Pakistan out of Gdansk on CIA owned Greek freighters supposedly hired to deliver the arms to those good folk the Soviets supplied, the Syrians or the P.L.O. How happy some of those Poles and Czechs had been to sell the agency the arms they knew were going to kill their Russian brothers in Afghanistan! The Afghan War was an operation that had been and still was cloaked in secrecy. Frank Williams and Jim Duffy were perhaps the only two people alive who were privy to every one of those secrets.

"Sure, Jim, I know. But I'd rather see you get briefed in detail by someone who's more up to speed on all this than I am. Like the new director, the guy that wants you back in uniform. Basically, though what's happened is this: Djailani has thrown in his lot with the Iranians, those bastards with the Pasdaran, the Revolutionary Guards and some of those far out mullahs."

"That's not surprising. He and his pal Gulbuddin Hekmatayar always were in love with Khomeini and those spaced out mullahs of his. We knew that, for Christ's sake. Did that ever stop us from shovelling arms at them? Including all the Stingers they could handle? Hell, no."

"Point is, Jim, the extremist, far out mullahs are in the shit."

"Well, that's good news."

"It also happens to be when people are at their most dangerous. This guy Khatemi has the support of the masses. They're fed up and the mullahs are running scared. They're also running out of dough."

"Is that supposed to make me cry?"

"If you like. Fact is, the Iranians per capita income isn't even a third of what it was under the Shah. Millions of people are out of work. Their oil revenues barely cover half their national budget. Yet those hardline mullahs are throwing away money like there was no tomorrow trying to get their hands on nuclear weapons, missile technology, a germ warfare establishment. They give a hundred million dollars a year just to their terrorist acolytes like the Hezbollah. Where the hell is the money coming from?"

"Selling pistachios?"

"Our guess is a lot of it is coming from drugs. The production of the opium poppy in your old bailiwick Afghanistan has gone through the roof..."

"Oh shit, Frank." Duffy waved his coffee mug. "So what else is new? The Afghans only know how to do two things, fight and grow dope."

"Maybe. A decade ago what mattered was the fighting. Today it's the dope. Heroin is back and it's back big time. Nobody wanted to talk about it until the President finally got the word on this so-called 'heroin chic' stuff when that fashion photographer overdosed in New York. Hell, it was going on for five years before Clinton finally decided to notice it. The stuff is flooding this country. And Europe, and now Russia, too. There's a feeling around Washington that says 'hey, the agency's partially responsible for this mess because a lot of this dope is coming from areas run by the guys you armed and trained.'"

Duffy rose from his chair, strode to the fireplace and jammed a log into the flames with such fury he sent a cascade of sparks rushing up the chimney.

"I am just so fucking sick and tired of these liberals down in Washington weeping and moaning their hearts out these days about all the evil the agency is supposed to have caused in this world. When they go to sleep at night now, those bastards don't have to lie awake wondering if the Soviet Union is going to invade West Germany and start a thermonuclear war while they're sleeping, do they? No. Why not? Because of us, because of what the agency did in Afghanistan. When those blue-eyed Russian soldiers started coming home to Mother Russia in body bags, that's when the shit started to hit the Big Red Fan. The Afghan War was the first time the Red Army had been seriously engaged in 45 years. And what happened? A bunch of illiterate peasants and shepherds kick their ass. We won the Cold War there in Afghanistan whether those liberal assholes in Washington like it or not."

"We got a little help from Gorbachev, too, remember?"

"Gorbachev would never have had the balls to take on the Red Army if we hadn't first shown him his Red Army was just a hollow threat."

Duffy was too fired up by his anger to return to the comfort of his armchair. He paced in front of the flames crackling in his fireplace, seeing in their shifting patterns images a decade old, Landi Kotal and the Khyber Pass, the barren ridges of Afghanistan, the stoic, silent Afghan wounded coming off those ridges on mule-back, bent over in agony, yet refusing to honor their suffering with so much as a fleeting sob. Congressman Charley Wilson had once said that he'd read the defeat of the Red Army in the defiant eyes of the wounded Mooj he'd seen in a field hospital outside Peshawar. And now those idiots in Washington were trying to smear the CIA's finest hour with all their bitching about dope and Islamic Fundamentalism? Sure, some of the guys who were killing the most Russians back then were the guys growing the most dope now. How the hell was he supposed to have changed that? Stop giving them arms back then so they couldn't kill any more Russians? One day he'd raised the point with Charley Wilson to get a sense, maybe, of how congress might react to the point. "Some of these guys are growing dope," he'd said.

"I don't give a shit," was the congressman's reply.

Williams intruded on his thoughts. "Jimbo, like it or not, Afghanistan's come back to haunt us. People are saying now we weren't sufficiently aware of the dangers we were stirring up by arming and encouraging all those Islamic Fundamentalists. The Counter Terrorism Center just put together a 67 page Top Secret paper I'll show you when we get back to Langley. 'The Wandering Mooj Report' we baptized it. How these guys are showing up all over the place these days. Slitting throats in Algeria. Blowing off car bombs in Cairo. Showing a bunch of Saudi Shiites how to kill our Air Force guys in Dharahan."

Duffy marched back to his armchair and dropped his rock hard frame into its welcoming folds, the edge of the anger he'd felt a few moments before spent. "So where does my old pal the Gucci Mooj come into this?"

"The dope. Drugs undermine the spiritual and physical health of the Great Satan's children, right? And at the same time they can bring in the money the mullahs have to have to finance their terrorist agenda. Hurts the West and helps hasten the triumph of Islam. Right on. His job is to see the mullahs get their cut on every damn kilo of Afghan dope that moves across Iran to Turkey where they turn the stuff into heroin."

"So why me? Why do you want to steal me away from my idyllic existence chopping wood up here in Maine?"

"Because the fact is, Jim, nobody knows the area like you do. Nobody knows the teams better—or the players. The director figures that if there's one guy who can pin down where this bastard Djailani is operating from, crawl inside his operations, it's you. Then maybe, just maybe, we can find out where this money he's making for the mullahs is going. And what they're spending it on. Somewhere in there, there's got to be a money trail. If we can find it and follow it, then maybe it will take us right into the heart of their arms program, their search for weapons of mass destruction."

Williams sipped his coffee to give his words time to register with his old friend. "Besides, like I said, we want to put a little fun back into your existence. Life in our nation's capitol, the beating heart of the World's only super-power. Lunches in the Executive Dining Room. Trips to the White House in a limousine. Wow, what fun!"

"Fun? Working for some boss who's more concerned with cover-ing his ass than uncovering an Iranian terrorist even if the guy was lurking right outside his office door? Getting harassed by congress-men who think they know something about intelligence because they read a James Bond book once? Being lectured to by a know it all press that doesn't know shit about the real world? You call that fun?

"Ah, Jimbo, you remember that old recruiting poster, Uncle Sam pointing his finger and saying 'your country needs you,' don't you? Well, that's the situation now. You never said 'no' when your country needed you before. Are you going to say 'no' to me now?"

"You son of a bitch. I hate people who reason with emotion instead of logic."

"Does that mean you're coming?"

"Coming where?"

"Back to Washington. I've got an agency Lear waiting for us down at Portland airport."

"That important?"

"That important."

"Do I at least have time to pack a toothbrush and some spare socks and underwear?"

"Sure. Welcome back to the fold."

———

The men sat around in a circle on the dirt floor of the hut, their backs leaning against it's white washed walls, legs crossed under the ankle length skirts of their *chalwars,* the traditional Afghanistan male robe. In front of each was the remains of the evening meal they'd just con-sumed. The clay pots which had contained the meal were in the center of the floor, beside the brass brazier whose meager coals offered what little non-human heat there was to warm the room.

No women, of course, were present. They had lit the fire in the bra-zier, put out the pots for the meal and retired to the kitchen. They would not return until the last male guest had left. The little supper gathering could have been a miniature *shura,* a community council, or a tribal *jirga,* the traditional forms of Afghanistan assemblies. And, indeed, the men sitting around the dying embers of their brazier this evening were bound together by that strongest of ties, blood. All, of course, were Moslem, most more overtly devout now thanks to the Taleban than they had been before those apostles of a radical Islam had seized control of their nation. However, it was an economic not a religious concern that bound them together in this primitive dwelling on a chilly January night. They were all, in one way or another, involved in the opium traffic.

Their tiny village of Regay was located in Afghanistan's Helmand Province, almost equidistant from the frontiers of Pakistan and Iran. It was one of the 5,000 villages in Afghanistan devoted to the cultivation of the *papever somniferum,* the opium poppy, the source of opium, morphine and, in its most destructive and addictive form, heroin. In the well watered fields surrounding the half dozen houses of the community, there were fifty *jeribs,* the Afghan measurement of land, planted to the opium poppy, just a handful of the 71,433 hectares which the United Nations had registered as being given over to poppy production in Afghanistan. The harvest of those hectares had made Afghanistan the worlds leading producer of raw opium, far outstripping in importance—despite the United States State Department's pious proclamations to the contrary—the famed Golden Triangle of northern Burma.

Ten of the men leaning against the wall were landowners or share-croppers who farmed their lands. Two were merchants, *Tudjarha-e-afin,* from the nearby bazaar of Sangin. Next to them was the local trucker and beside him was the Taleban appointed mullah still secretly running the region.

The reason for his presence was financial rather than religious. The leaders of the Taleban had started their march towards power proclaiming their opposition to the opium traffic. Once in power, however, the Taleban leadership had realized just how much potential income the traffic represented and their attitude had changed. Instead of banning it, they taxed it. Ten percent of each farmer's earnings went to the Taleban, primarily to buy the arms with which they could kill other Afghans.

Sitting between the two merchants was the evening's guest of honor, the man responsible for this little gathering. Ghulam Hamid was, like the men around him, a Baluch, born in Iran. During the last decade of the Shah's reign he had been an officer in the SAVAK responsible primarily for dealing with the opium trafficking. "Responsible" in the sense that he had arrested and jailed those traffickers who had not paid him an adequate tribute, facilitated the task of those that had.

With the revolution, he had fled Iran for Quetta in Pakistan. Now, instead of employing his knowledge of the opium traffic to suppress the trade, he was using it to encourage it. "Brothers" he said when it was time to turn from the politics that had occupied their mealtime conversation to more serious concerns "I am here to buy whatever opium you have to sell me."

He paused, his tongue caressing his lips in anticipation of the pleasure his next sentence would bring to his audience. "You will receive a very good price, a very, very good price, that I most sincerely promise you."

"What price are you prepared to pay?" asked one of the landlords.

Hamid bestowed on the gathering a smile of bewildering intensity. "I will pay 1500 Pakistani rupees the kilo," he announced as though his offer was so extravagant he might have been proposing a kilo of gold for a kilo of opium.

His offer was not enough for the landowner. This little corner of Helmand might have been isolated from the world but it was not so isolated that the landlord didn't know what raw opium was selling for in Quetta.

"We struggle, my brother, to feed our children to rebuild our houses after this terrible war." For a minute it seemed as though he was going to burst into tears from the pain such thoughts caused him. "Surely, you can make a special effort on our behalf. Say 1900 rupees a kilo."

Hamid looked as though even the mention of such a figure would give him cardiac arrest. For several moments he described how impossible it would be for him to pay such an extravagant sum, the financial ruin which would overwhelm him and his family if he should even contemplate meeting such a price. Then he offered 1650.

None of the men seated around the brazier listened more intently than the landowners nephew. As a young man, Ahmed Khan had fought with great distinction with the Mujahiddin of Haji Abdul Khader until the shard of a rocket fired from a Soviet Hind helicopter had sheared his left leg off at the knee.

For years, he had wasted away in the refugee camp of Girdjangal on the Afghanistan-Pakistan border, receiving what primitive medical attention the Mujahiddin could offer him. Despairing of ever being able to lead a normal existence or to feed his wife and two young girls, Ahmed Khan was on the verge of suicide when his uncle had located him one day in the camp.

Come back to your birthplace, his uncle had urged. He had five *jeribs,* just over a hectare, which he would give to Ahmed to farm for him. It was ideal land for growing the opium poppy—good soil, plenty of water and sunshine. He would provide Ahmed with seed and whatever agricultural equipment he needed. In return, Ahmed would hand over half his crop to his uncle. The rest would be his to sell as he saw fit.

For Ahmed, it was as though the gates releasing him from Hell had suddenly swung open. He and his family settled into a war shattered shack near his *jeribs* and he set to work. Hobbling through his fields on his wooden crutches, he had watched his seeds burst from the ground in green sprouts, then followed as they soared to stems over a meter in height and burst into pink flowers in early April. Three weeks later, the petals fell from the flower bulbs crowning each stem and the bulbs began to swell, turning as they did from bright green to gray.

One week after the petals had fallen, Ahmed, his wife, his two girls went into the fields towards sunset. Each had a six bladed *nechtar,* a knife like instrument with which the bulbs were scored. A milky pink gum, opium in its most primitive form, oozed from each millimeter deep scar made by the *nechtar*'s blades. The next morning they were all back in the fields scraping the gum, now dark brown, from the bulbs and collecting it in clay pots. It had been a prodigious harvest. Ahmed had assembled his half into forty-two one kilogram slabs of black-brown gook and set it out to dry. Now, spellbound, he listened as his uncle and the bazaar merchants argued up their visitor's price.

"One thousand eight hundred Pakistani rupees"—the Afghani, the local currency, was rarely used in such transactions, Hamid called out. "This is my very final price. Only for you because you are my friends, my brothers. Please do not tell anyone about this very special price I have made for you, my dear friends. Otherwise you will ruin me."

Shortly after noon the next day, the truck driver arrived at his hut with the mullah and one of the bazaar merchants. Together, they weighed and counted his forty-two slabs of opium. Then the merchant took out a thick wad of Pakistani rupees and counted out 75,600 for Ahmed. The crippled war veteran had never seen so much money in his life.

Barely had he had time to heft it in his hand when the mullah stepped up to demand the Taleban's ten percent tax. "My son" he purred "there is no proscription in the Holy Book for what you have done provided, of course, that you do not use the opium yourself or sell it to your fellow Moslems. As long as what you have grown helps us to undermine our enemies, you have done nothing contrary to holy law."

"Enemies?" asked Ahmed. "Which enemies? We have so many."

"The *Kafirs*. It is they who will get this one day."

In his lifetime, Ahmed had only seen two *Kafirs* and both were dead, Russian soldiers killed in an ambush in the Pansher. He shrugged indifferently as the mullah and the merchant climbed into his cousin's truck for their ride back to the bazaar of Sangin. He followed their progress as they moved down the dirt track leading away from his hut, off on the long, dangerous journey that would ultimately deliver the produce of his five *jeribs* to the arms, the lungs, the brains of some faceless *Kafirs* in London or Liverpool, New York or Philadelphia, Paris or Marseilles, Madrid or Barcelona, Hamburg or Frankfurt. The 68,000 Pakistani rupees he had left after the Talebans tax were a pittance compared to what the product of his fields would earn one day for other men on some distant street corner of the Western world.

None of that mattered to Ahmed Khan. What mattered was that the fruits of his 42 kilos had given him back his dignity. With these rupees, he would be able to feed his wife and girls for a year and begin rebuilding the shattered hut in which they lived. Ahmed turned and started back to that hut, a happy man for almost the first time since a Soviet rocket had torn off his leg.

———

"Brings back a few fond memories, does it, Jimbo? Sitting here in this room?" Frank Williams waved at the under-stated elegance of the reception room in which he and Jim Duffy were sitting. It was one of two such rooms adjoining the seventh floor office of the director of the CIA at the agency's headquarters in Langley, Virginia. The first was used for distinguished callers from the other side of the Potomac, congressmen, senators, White House officials, businessmen. This second room was reserved for visitors whose faces shouldn't be widely seen—representatives of friendly foreign services, assets whose ties to the agency were still closely guarded secrets, officers of the clandestine service.

"Some fond. Some not so fond," Duffy growled. "I do remember that day in 1985 you and I sat here in this same room waiting to see Casey. I'd just come back from Pakistan, remember?"

"Yeah. That was the day you marched in there and told Casey we could win the God damned war in Afghanistan if he'd just give you Stinger missiles. Which nobody but nobody in this town believed."

"Oh hell, it never dawned on anybody we could actually win that war. It was always fight the Soviets down to the last drop of Afghan blood. That was the deal, our gold, their blood."

"Yeah." Frank Williams squirmed in his seat at the discomfort those memories stirred. "You gotta figure the mooj always knew we weren't out there because we loved them."

The black lacquered table before them was covered with copies of *Time* and *Newsweek*. A thoughtful secretary had already brought them coffee and a bowl of salted nuts. Williams flicked a handful into his mouth. "You know something, Jimbo? That victory of ours in the war in Afghanistan had two faces to it. Trouble is we only look at one of them."

"What do you mean by that?"

"OK, for us it meant the defeat of the Red Army, the end of the Cold War, the collapse of communism. But how about for the mooj? For all these Islamic Fundamentalists running around the world? Do we ever stop and ask ourselves what it meant for them?"

Duffy picked at the nuts. "I know you're dying to tell me Frank, so I won't spoil your fun."

"It meant that they had defeated the great Red Army with little more than their faith—and a few Stingers thrown into the bargain. It proved to the extremists of the Islamic world that the *djihad* could work, just like the Prophet said it would, even in the 20th century with all its technological marvels. 'You can do it if your faith is strong enough.' Believe me, that's the inspiration behind a lot of the nightmares we're living today."

A neatly dressed middle-aged woman followed by a security guard in his agency blue blazer appeared in the doorway to the reception room.

"The director is ready for you, gentlemen" she announced.

"And some of the nightmares you're going to hear about now," Williams mumbled as they rose in response to her words.

The current director of the agency was a slight, almost frail man whose out sized horn-rim glasses seemed designed to accentuate his already portentously serious face. Looks like he should be teaching second year Latin in one of those New England prep schools, Duffy thought. He was tempted to mutter *Omnia Gallia in tres partes divisa est* in greeting but instead he engulfed the director's under-sized hand in his own massive fist and said, "Sir."

"We're very glad to have you back on board, Mr. Duffy," the director replied. "I think you know the DDO, Jack Lohnes"—the director was gesturing towards the man on his left.

Duffy did. Jack was a good guy and he bore him no ill will despite the fact he was, as the director of the clandestine services, occupying what in all probability should have been his office.

"Tim Harvey here"—the director was now indicating the man on his right—"has the Iranian account." With that he pointed them to the conference table on the slightly raised platform to the left of his massive desk. A fresh coffee service was waiting for them. The director was as addicted to coffee as a navy chief petty officer.

"I'd like to open this up by asking Tim Harvey to brief you on what the Iranians are up to these days."

Harvey swirled the coffee in his mug for a second, then looked up at Duffy. "Jim, for openers, there's no doubt whatsoever that the Iranians are engaged in an all-out effort to obtain weapons of mass destruction and the means to deliver them."

He shrugged in seeming acknowledgement that his had been little more than a statement of the obvious. "They're moving on two tracks, first the slower, more methodical Pakistani track. Get centrifuges, slowly build up their own supply of fissile material, then begin to produce a stockpile of weapons. Using that track we estimate they'll be a nuclear power by 2005."

"Well, that timetable is some small comfort."

"At the same time they're pursuing a fast track, trying to go out and buy up existing systems, primarily from disenchanted Russian officers or Russians with some access to their nuclear stockpile. It's ideal for them because if they could get their hands on an existing device or two, then the implosion problem would already be solved for them. That, we fear, is where the immediate threat lies. They're out there shopping for this stuff, we have proof of that."

"Hell," Lohnes the DDO interjected, "the Soviets themselves don't even know how many non-strategic nuclear warheads they have. Their best estimate is eight to thirteen thousand—kept in 155 different storage areas. Alexander Lebed himself says at least a hundred of them are unaccounted for."

"Do you have any evidence they've succeeded in getting their hands on some of those damn things?"

"I wish to hell we could answer that question for you with 100% accuracy, Jim." Harvey replied. "Unfortunately, we can't. We've had five reports thus far that we've taken very seriously. The most believe-able one came to us in late 1992. Our source claimed the Iranians had gotten their hands on three nuclear devices of some kind as the Soviets were pulling out of Kazakhstan. We, MI6, the French, the Germans, the Mossad, did a full court press on the report to try to determine whether it was authentic or not. We did everything. We scrubbed out the inter-cepts and the overhead photography. We even put people on the ground in Iran to run it down. Unfortunately, we simply couldn't come up with the answer." Harvey gave a resigned shrug of his shoulders, the reflex-ive gesture of a man to whom news is almost inevitably bad. "We sim-ply don't know if the report is true or false. But I have an aching feeling in my gut that it is true, and if I'm right we may find ourselves in one hell of a mess one of these fine mornings."

"But for the moment, we're swimming in a vacuum here?" Duffy suggested.

"Mr. Duffy, er, Jim . . ." It was the director again. Guy really has trouble getting onto a first name basis, Duffy thought.

"Let me be very clear. The greatest single nightmare this country faces in the Post Cold War era is the possibility of a bunch of far out terrorists like these Islamic Radicals, getting their hands on a couple of nuclear devices. The President made that clear when he said we have no higher priority than keeping such weapons out of their hands. Can you imagine the consequences if some of these people smuggled one of these things in the trunk of a car into New York? Or Tel Aviv? If those guys who did the World Trade Center truck bomb had wrapped their high explosives with radioactive material, nobody would have been able to live in lower Manhattan for the next 25,000 years."

"Still, sir, I remember going through all these scenarios and you can't escape the fact that a couple of nuclear devices don't make a nuclear nation. You've got to be prepared to defend yourself against reprisals. Set one of those things off in Tel Aviv and you'll trigger the Masada complex. The Israelis will kill and kill until they can't kill any-more. There won't be an Iranian left standing."

"You're behind the times, Jim. That's Cold War strategic doctrine, Mutually Assured Destruction—MAD. You kill me, I kill you. Everyone dies. The system rested on that brutal, but simple logic. Nuclear weapons froze an existing situation in place. Our concern is the doctrine may not work here."

"Why not?"

"Because for some of these fanatics in the Radical Islamic world like Osama bin Laden, weapons of mass destruction are meant to be genocidal. They're meant to wreak destruction and through it purification on a massive scale. For them, Mutually Assured Destruction isn't a deterrent. It's an end devoutly to be wished for. Let them get hold of a couple of nuclear devices of some sort and our old Cold War thinking may go right out the window."

"Still, Mr. Director, would those Iranian mullahs really be crazy enough to risk destroying their nation just to plant a nuclear device in Tel Aviv? Or some American city?"

"Jim, those Iranian mullahs play a very shrewd, calculating game when it comes to terrorism. They're the coach on the sidelines sending in the plays. They never touch the football themselves. Who was behind the World Trade Center, the Jewish Center in Buenos Aires, our Air Force barracks in Saudi Arabia? The Iranians each time. But they build cut outs to shield themselves. They do Buenos Aires with some terrorist group no one has ever heard of that they created just for the occasion so the Israelis couldn't pin the attack on them. Let a bunch of hardcore fanatics in Iran get their hands on something like this and the risk that they'll slip it into the hands of some group of half educated kids, point to New York or Tel Aviv and say 'go. Paradise lies that way' is just enormous."

"Jim"—it was Jack Lohnes speaking again—"People like President Khatemi and the men around him would never get involved in this. But the fanatics? Who feel Khatemi is threatening their leadership? Who dream that by delivering a mortal blow to the Israeli enemy they can make themselves saviors and rulers of the whole Islamic world? Some of those mullahs are experts at weaving golden dreams to convince the uneducated, dispirited youths they prey on that they can save the world with a bomb. If a sheikh in a mosque in Nablus can convince some 20 year old kid to wrap ten kilos of plastic explosive around his waist and go blow himself up on a crowded bus in Tel Aviv, do you really believe he couldn't convince some other equally naive kid to drive a car with a nuclear explosive in it into downtown Tel Aviv? Become the mother of all heroic martyrs by destroying the Great Satan's evil partner in one glorious blast and affirming the global mastery of militant Islam for the millennium to come?"

"OK," Duffy acknowledged. "I agree that's a concern alright. But what I really don't understand is where do I come in on all this?"

Harvey laughed. "We thought you'd never ask." He leaned forward, took a long sip of his coffee before launching into his reply. "What it all comes down to at the end of the day is money."

"Doesn't everything?"

"Ideology is all well and good but nothing nourishes a terrorist organization quite like a healthy cash flow and, if you want to make a lot of money fast in today's world, there's no better way to do it than drugs. Every whacko guerilla group since the Second World War has dabbled in them to finance their activities. Now I'm not going to brief you on the international drug trafficking situation. We have people downstairs waiting to do that for you."

Harvey got up and moved towards a wall map of the Near East. He picked up a pointer and poked it at Afghanistan. How people in this town love to play with those damn pointers, Duffy thought. Penile substitutes for frustrated bureaucrats.

"What I want to tell you is simply this—the poppy fields of Afghanistan are now producing in excess of 3000 tons of raw opium a year. Almost all of it is for export." Harvey circled Iran's borders with his pointer. "The VEVAK, the Iranian Security Service, has installed a protective belt twenty to forty miles deep around their frontier. Inside that belt, their writ runs supreme. They have full power to stop, search and arrest anyone, anywhere in that zone."

"We, the DEA, Interpol, the European police authorities, the UN, all estimate that roughly 80% of the Afghan opium crop is now either moving this way"—his pointer swung towards Herat in northwestern Afghanistan—"across northern Iran and on into Turkey where it gets refined into heroin, or north into Turkmenistan, then west to the Caspian, down the Caspian by boat into Iran and then on to Turkey."

Harvey turned away from the map, as he reached the climacteric of his briefing. "Whatever route they use, there is absolutely no way anybody can move all that dope through that security belt the Iranians have set up without the knowledge, agreement and complicity of their security establishment."

"So you figure they're taking a cut out of it as it goes by?"

"Exactly."

"How much could that traffic earn them?"

"We reckon, conservatively I might add, at least thirty-five million dollars a year."

Duffy whistled softly thinking back to his own Afghan war days. "A third of their terrorist budget. You can do a lot with that kind of money out there."

"Or in Europe shopping for hi-tech equipment." It was the director taking back the briefing. "We want to find a way into the flow of those drug dollars, Jim. See if we can follow them, see where they lead. That money flow might just open a door for us into their arms procurement programs. And to their terrorist groups. And ultimately, perhaps, their nuclear program. That's where you come in."

"I'm flattered by your words but why me?"

The Director turned over a piece of paper on the pile in front of him. "Some of our recent NSA intercepts seem to indicate that your old friend Said Djailani is playing a key role in all this. What kind of a guy is Djailani?"

"Ruthless. Absolute authoritarian. A one track mind leading to Mecca that tells him it's quite okay to wreak a maximum of bloodshed and destruction to punish the enemies of Islam. Also highly intelligent. Charming when he wants to be. He knows what fork to use. Tyrants can have good manners. Highly strung. He never stopped playing with his worry beads."

"What we're going to do officially," the director announced "is assign you to our Counter Narcotics Center downstairs. You know who Djailani would be likely to know, to talk to, to work with, to contact, whatever. And. of course, you know what his voice sounds like. Your job will be to go through every damn NSA intercept we've got, everything that comes in, to see if you can pick up some trace of him. If you can turn up just one intercept with his voice on it, then we can run a voice signature analysis on the tape, pick up the characteristic signs of his voice and crunch the result through the NSA's intercept backlog. Who the hell knows what might fall out? Maybe we'll be able to open up the window that's going to show us where all those drug dollars are heading."

"In reality, of course, you'll be working with Jack here in operations. We don't want to tell the world you're back on board. Heaven only knows what suspicions that might stir up. But I can assure you, the full resources of the clandestine service are there for you on this one. Go where you want to to get the job done, but stay under that narcotics cover. And remember, there are DEA, FBI, Customs, Treasury people assigned to the center you'll be working in downstairs. As far as any of them are concerned, this meeting never took place. Nothing you've heard in this room goes beyond these walls."

———

Across the Atlantic, the fast falling winter night was already wrapping the city of London in its dark shroud as a tall man in an immaculately cut blue cashmere overcoat strode towards the door to 4 Victoria Street, barely two hundred yards from the grinning gargoyles of Westminster Abbey. Prominently displayed on the door was a sign warning "This area is under 24 hour surveillance. Trespassers will be prosecuted."

No undue concern with the possibility of prosecution, however, appeared to slow the man's pace as he advanced through the winter night. He carried himself with the martial bearing of some one used to command and respect. His black shoes were polished to high gloss. He was hatless despite the cold. Indeed only one incongruous note marred his otherwise distinguished appearance. It was evident that he had not shaved for at least three or four days.

Before he had even reached the door, a security guard waiting discreetly inside had opened it for him.

With a brusque nod to the guard, the man stepped past the photo display of Iran's Abadan oil refinery and into the elevator waiting at the rear of the tiny lobby. It took him directly to the sixth floor of the building, known officially as the NIOC—National Iranian Oil Company—House. Purchased by the Shah in the oil boom of the late 1970's, the structure had been designed as a glass and steel reminder to London's fuel hungry populace of the importance of petroleum, Persia, and the Pahlevis in their daily lives. In the era of Iran's Revolutionary Government, it still remained the company's London headquarters with its principal entrance around the corner from the side entrance by which the man had just entered the building.

Oil, however, was now only one of the concerns of the denizens of NIOC House. It had become, in the words of one Iranian dissident, "a nest of spies." The building's sixth floor was sealed off to anyone not cleared for entry by the Iranian security service. It contained archives, a communications center and three adequate, if somewhat spartan residential apartments, the most spacious of which was reserved for the man's exclusive use as his secret hideaway when he was in London.

Ostensibly Kair Bollahi, known to his friends and subordinates as the Professor, was the London head of the NIOC. That job was his in name only, however. He was, in reality, one of the senior members of the little coterie of men running revolutionary Iran. For years his primary function had been defined as "getting whatever is forbidden Iran. Buying it. Arranging to pay for it. Then getting it to Iran by whatever means possible."

"Where's Mehdi?" he asked his security aide as he stepped out of the elevator on the sixth floor. Mehdi "Mike" Mashad was one of his key deputies.

"At the Inn on the Park," the aide replied. "He's standing by for your call."

Of course, the Professor thought, Mike would chose the flashiest, most expensive hotel in town for his visit. "Perhaps you can ask him to abandon the company of his Chelsea Escort Service girls for a few minutes and come here to see me."

With that he went into his private apartment. His incoming messages were laid out on his bed waiting for him. Tehran had furnished him with some additional guidance for the conversation he was about to have with Mike. More important was a message informing him that the five men had arrived safely in London from Tehran.

He opened his attache case which contained his most precious possession, a copy of the Koran personally inscribed to him with the words "May this always be your guide," by his friend and spiritual mentor, the Ayatollah Khomeini. Carefully, he set it in the place he always reserved for it on his bedside table. Then he put his laptop computer down beside it.

Bollahi represented a breed of supporters of the Iranian Revolution much more numerous than the regime's Western foes were prepared to acknowledge or imagine. He was a man of considerable intellectual accomplishment with a doctorate in mechanical engineering from the University of Tehran to his credit. Despite his opposition to the Shah's regime, he had worked as a chief engineer on a number of the ruler's grandiose projects, travelled extensively in Europe, spoke fluent English and German.

The son of a minor cleric in Isfahan, he had fallen completely under the spell of the Ayatollah and his rigid interpretation of the already rigid philosophy of Islam's Twelver Shiism. Unlike so many of the men in Tehran he scorned as "Mercedes mullahs," men who'd caught their religious faith as one might catch a passing virus, the Professor's belief in Islam was long standing, deep and unyielding.

Renascent Islam, he firmly believed, was the most powerful ideological force in the post-Cold War world.

"Objectively," he liked to proclaim to his associates, "the future is ours. What has their liberalism, their democracy, their forsaking of God brought to these westerners? AIDs, homosexuality, every form of sexual promiscuity imaginable, greed, the veneration of all things material. With their satellites, their wealth, their power, their so-called culture and their over-bearing arrogance, they seek to force their values on the world. They will not succeed. Islam will bar their way. Islam is going to conquer men's spirits in the name of justice and spiritual values, not materialism."

The Professor's life was devoted to the accomplishment of that conquest, a conquest he pursued with the unwavering intensity of a zealot and the intellectual acumen of his finely honed mind.

By the time he'd finished unpacking his few belongings, his acolyte, Mehdi "Mike" Mashad had arrived.

The two men embraced with more formality than feeling. The Professor waved Mike to a chair. "Tea? Coffee? Orange juice?" he asked.

Mike would have preferred a whiskey but he never drank openly in front to the Professor. On his home turf in Madrid or Marbella on Spain's Costa del Sol, if he called for an orange juice in the Professor's presence, his servants knew enough to bring it to him laced with vodka. That was not going to happen here, however.

"Coffee," he replied.

The contrast between the two men could not have been more complete. The Professor was a strait-laced, relatively humorless man whose lifestyle was only slightly less puritanical than his idol, the Ayatollah Khomeini's had been. Mike was dedicated to high living, extravagance and self-gratification, the very qualities the Professor found so despicable when they were being practiced by Westerners. Deviousness and duplicity came as naturally to Mike as affection does to a Labrador puppy. The Professor on the other hand was a man burdened with an almost over-bearing sense of honesty. Yet the two had functioned in harmony for some years, the Professor in pursuit of the goals of a militant Islam, Mike in pursuit of the financial means to pursue his rich lifestyle on the Costa del Sol. His devotion to the Professor had been cemented in 1990 when he'd been arrested in the United States for attempting to purchase, on Tehran's orders, restricted missile guidance systems.

The Professor had gone to the Swiss, convinced them that Mike had swindled him out of $55 million *prior* to his arrest in the United States and demanded his extradition to stand trial in Geneva. Pressed by the Swiss, a reluctant U.S. Justice Department finally agreed to extradite him. Mike spent two weeks in jail, the Professor dropped the charges and they were back in business.

Mike was the sole employee of a Panamanian corporation called ARMEX with a listed capital of $1 million dollars. The firm, in fact was little more than a bundle of papers in a desk drawer at his luxurious villa in Marbella. The bearer shares of ARMEX were held by another Panamanian company called Falcon whose bearer shares had in turn been delivered to the Professor, and through him to the Iranian Government. Employing ARMEX as a screen, Mike placed orders for sensitive technology inside the Common Market on the Professor's instructions.

It was he who had had the idea of buying their little airfield at Hartenholm, north of Hamburg. Along with the purchase of the field itself, came the ownership of two German companies NORDAIR, an aircraft repair and maintenance firm and LFE, Luftfahrt Electronic, a company which dealt in aircraft electronics and navigational devices that had temporarily suspended its commercial activities. Buy the airfield, Mike pointed out to the professor, and ARMEX could then act as brokers for NORDAIR and Luftfahrt. ARMEX would place orders for sophisticated technology for the two companies and order the goods shipped to Hartenholm. No one would ask embarrassing questions about end user certificates or export permits. Why should they? On the record, the material would be headed for a destination inside the European Common Market. No documentation was required for orders like that. Once they had the goods on the ground at their little airport in Hartenholm, of course, they could send them on their way to Tehran when no one was looking.

The Professor waited until his security aide had served their coffee and left them alone in his bed-sitting room before getting down to business. He chose not to precede their talk with the usual polite chit chat about wives and children. To have done so in Mike's case would have been inappropriate. His wife had recently been killed in a twelve story fall from their Madrid apartment, a voyage on which, it was whispered, her departure had been hastened by a shove from Mike.

He opened the drawer of his bedside table and drew out a metal cylinder the size of a fountain pen. A cable curled out of its upper lid. Carefully, he set it on his bedside table.

"What the hell is that?" Mike asked reaching for the canister as he did.

The Professor intercepted his hand.

"Don't," he warned. "Touch it the wrong way and it can kill you."

Mike jerked his hand away and sat up straight in his armchair. "Some kind of new high explosive device, huh?" he whistled.

"Not at all." The Professor sipped his coffee to allow himself the time to enjoy Mike's surprise. Then he took from his drawer a technical catalogue published by an American company called EG&G. He pointed to a picture of a tiny glass bulb from which trailed three two-and-a-half-inch-long wires, one red, one green, one white. Almost lovingly he laid the catalogue on the table.

"So what the hell is that?" Mike asked. "A tadpole with a glass head?"

"Not quite," the Professor rejoined, a smile of immense good humor enveloping his face. "You do read our Holy Book from time to time and take the trouble to make yourself aware of the history of our Faith?" he asked Mike, his tone portentous with self-commissioned importance.

"Yeah, sure."

"Then you may recall, Khalid, the well named 'Sword of God,' the general who marched 700 men across the desert from the Euphrates to Damascus in eighteen days, then routed the Byzantine army of the Emperor Heraclius west of Jerusalem to open all of Palestine to Arab conquest?"

"Of course," Mike replied with an assertiveness born of his total ignorance of either Khalid or his triumphs.

"Our leaders in Tehran have a sense of the niceties of history which perhaps you lack." The Professor smiled indulgently. "They have assigned the plan in which these little devices will one day play a critical role the code name 'Operation Khalid.' Like the historical operation for which it has been named, Khalid is designed to re-open the gates of Palestine to Arab conquest, to throw the Israelis once and for all off the land they stole from our Palestinian brothers and to make Palestine again *Dar el Islam*—land of Islam."

"And they think they're going do that with a . . ." Mike groped for the right expression, "a fountain pen that bites and a tadpole with a glass head? Somebody in Tehran must have gone off his rocker."

"I think not," the professor rejoined with the judicious superiority of the clergyman endowed with an unshakable faith in his convictions. "Our task in Operation Khalid is going to be to secure an important supply of these devices for our brothers in Tehran. This is going to be the most important, the most secretive task we've ever undertaken."

"So what the hell are those damn things for?"

The Professor pointed to the little bulb Mike had referred to as a "glass tadpole" and contemplated it with the fondness a Greek monk might have reserved for his most sacred icon. "This is called a krytron. What it is quite simply is a switch, an electrical switch that will deliver a very powerful, pre-determined charge of electric power from the source in which the power's been stored to a target in a time span that is so incredibly short our human minds can't even imagine it."

"OK. I won't try. What's it for?"

"Configured as our little tadpole here is, it really only has three uses. The first is in high energy lasers. They're used to cut or weld very heavy metals. The second is in complex university level research programs."

"And the third?"

The back of the Professor's elegant, well-manicured hand wandered wearily off towards some moral no man's land, the clear indication that this was a question he had no intention of answering. "A few years ago, the greedy geniuses of the West thought making high energy lasers was going to be one of those modern technologies that would make a lot of people rich."

A smirk of almost immeasurable pleasure creased his austere mien. "What it has done, in fact is to make a lot of people bankrupt."

Mike said nothing. He had been the subject of enough of the professor's little lectures to know that what was expected of him was respectful silence, not curiosity.

"One of them is a Herr Rudolf Steiner who owns a firm called LASERTECHNIK in Pinneberg, Germany, just outside Hamburg. Our people up there tell me Herr Steiner is now immersed in some financial problems that are very substantial indeed."

This time Mike couldn't resist. "Like that dentist we knew in Hamburg," he laughed, "who was spending his time filling his girl friend's pockets instead of his patients' teeth?"

"Perhaps. What I want you to do Mike, is go up to Hamburg. Find out everything you can about Herr Steiner. What are his politics? What are his feelings about the Middle East? Just how critical, really, is his financial situation? How exposed is he? His family? Does it look like he might be one of these German businessmen who's ready to deal with the devil if the price is right?"

Bollahi pointed a warning finger at Mike. "Be discreet. Under no circumstances are you to talk to Herr Steiner yourself without my authorization. Also, don't contact our people at that bookstore. I don't want them to know you're in town or why you're there."

The Professor closed his eyes to hasten, perhaps, his thought process. "Look into his family background. Is there anything in there that might suggest he harbors a lingering dislike for the Jews? Did he have some relative, for example, who might have served with the SS? Been treated as a war criminal because he was a guard in a death camp?"

"How about his personal life, his sex habits? Some of those German businessmen are into some pretty strange things, you know?" Mike asked.

"Have a quiet look, Mike, but I would prefer to keep an eventual approach to Herr Steiner on a friendly basis. No blackmail. What we want is a man who will be properly grateful to us for coming to his rescue. Grateful enough to help us get a supply of these little glass topped tadpoles of yours."

"When do you want me to start?"

"Now. The most important thing, Mike, is to be discreet. Totally discreet. I know that's not something that comes easily to you. But no one, absolutely no one must learn that we have an interest in Herr Steiner and his company."

As Mike left his spartan apartment, the Professor's security aide entered and handed him a Top Secret message from Tehran. Bollahi studied it with evident relish. Everything was ready for tonight. He took out a cigarette lighter, lit the message form and dropped it into an ashtray. Watching it burn, a thought struck him. For Operation Khalid, he realized, they would have to get a new, an absolutely secure communications system, something those Americans with their damnable NSA and its electronic intercept program could never penetrate.

———

Barely two miles away from the Professor's bedroom, in a fashionable Belgravia town-house at 5 Chester Square, an attractive blonde woman studied herself in the mirror of her 19th century Pierre Phillipe Thomire mahogany and bronze dressing table. She focused on the image in that mirror with an intensity worthy of an Antwerp diamond merchant pondering a tray of uncut stones. Nancy Burke Harmian was lovely. There was no question about that. Indeed, since she was five years old, her physical appearance had been a constant presence for Nancy, a kind of ghostly half self forever travelling beside her along life's pathways. As a child she'd been endlessly amused by the way adults responded to her prettiness, the small rewards, the front row seats, the extra dollop of chocolate chip ice cream it always seemed to win for her. Instinctively, as a cat learns to draw on the affection of strangers, she'd learned to employ that cuteness of hers to manipulate the adult world, to fashion adults into becoming the unwitting accomplices of her secret desires.

Later, as an adolescent, the boys didn't choose Nancy as their date. Nancy did the choosing. The captain of the football team, later to become an All American quarterback at UCLA, the President of the Student Council, the dark, broodingly handsome Jewish boy impervious to the charms of his female classmates; Nancy had had them all. She was one of those rare people who could say without being vain or attempting to boast, that she had never known a moment of unhappiness during her childhood.

At Cal, her attitudes had changed dramatically. Swept up in the feminism of the early eighties, she suddenly saw her beauty as a liability, an obstacle to the fulfillment of those values represented by her inner self. Her hair got chopped to expose the nape of her neck, her bras were discarded, the only tight fitting article of apparel she ever put on was a pair of gloves. Any man who complimented her on her appearance or opened a door for her was gone.

Now she had outgrown that phase. She accepted her beauty as simply one more facet of her being, an asset her post-feminist mind-set entitled her to use but not abuse.

As she contemplated her self in her mirror this January evening, however, she caught a glimmer of something else, something no amount of beauty could have secured for her—happiness. Nothing, she thought, so becomes a woman as happiness and that was the emotion in whose gentle glow she was bathing tonight.

Instinctively, her hand went to her left ear. She had decided to wear her lapis lazuli pendants, the ones she had bought on a trip to Uzbekistan. She pushed back the blonde hair tumbling to her shoulders to appraise them better. They were beautiful and their azure radiance set off the deeper blue of her eyes, eyes her father had insisted when she was a young girl were as blue as the seas off Connemara on a summer's morn. That was a fine example of her father's Irish blather. She'd been to Connemara's seacoast on a summer's morn long after his death. Blue, those waters were not.

Still, were these the right earrings for tonight? It was after all, a very special evening. Indeed, it was a reminder of why the special elixir of happiness was now suffusing her being. It marked the first anniversary of her marriage, a thought that almost made her laugh. The notion that she, of all people, could ever have imagined marriage capable of producing the happiness she felt this January night had once been as foreign to her as a knowledge of advanced algebra would have been to an untutored Amazonian. She was going to wear her superbly cut new midnight blue Armani dinner jacket with one of his sheer silk blouses to the dinner she and her husband had arranged to celebrate their anniversary with eight of their closest friends at Mark's Club. The evening needed something a little more grand than her pendants.

"Darling!" she called.

Seconds later, the object of her call appeared in the doorway between the bedroom and her dressing room. Tari, "Terry" to his Anglo Saxon friends, Harmian was a decade older than Nancy, just shy of six feet tall, still lean enough to excite the envy of many of his less well endowed contemporaries. He had the swarthy complexion of what he jokingly referred to as "your typical Middle Easterner of indeterminate origins"—although, he made no secret of what his origins were. He was Iranian, Persian, he preferred to say, a refugee in the west from the Khomeini revolution. A tangle of curly black hair clung to his chest. His face had the features of a half finished sculpture; his Roman nose took a sharp eastward bend halfway through its course; his dark eyes peered at the world from sockets that were too large for their purpose and gave him a perpetually querulous regard. His chin thrust outward like the prow of some adventuring galleon, opening life's seas before him.

He kissed his wife on her bare shoulders.

"Mmmm," she purred. "Darling, I think I'd like to wear the gold and diamond earrings you gave me for my birthday tonight."

"Sure. Let's go get them."

Together they padded down two flights of the carpeted staircase of their town house to Terry's office, located to the right of the entrance hallway just past the front door. He went to the safe fixed into the wall, twirled the lock through four movements until he heard its opening "click" and pulled the heavy door open.

Nancy knelt down and reached into the safe. With the exception of her green leather jewelry box, its contents were the exclusive preserve of her husband. Tonight, the box was partially covered by a thick manilla envelope. She moved it aside, noticing as she did a scrawl in Farsi or in Arabic, she could never tell the difference, on its cover. She set the jewelry box on the floor, unlocked it and picked the earrings she wanted from the tray. With swift, accomplished gestures, she fixed them in place, then gave a toss to her head to be sure they were firmly secured. "OK, it's show-boating darling, but tonight's rather special after all, isn't it?" she laughed.

In twenty minutes they were ready to leave. "Rebecca," Nancy called out to their housekeeper, "don't wait up for us. We may be late."

They walked down the steps of their 18th century Georgian house, a London landmark, to the sidewalk.

"We're parked a dozen houses down," Terry told her. Getting a parking place on Chester Square, even with a Resident's Parking Permit gracing your windshield, was always a headache. Hand in hand, they set off down the square.

As they did, two pairs of eyes watched them go from just inside the square's private gardens across the street. "Alright," a voice whispered as Terry's Jaguar pulled away from the curb. "Get the others. It's time."

BOOK TWO

NANCY

F rom the throne room to the outhouse, Jim Duffy mused, riding the elevator down from the CIA's Executive—Seventh —floor, to its basement. It was there that the agency's brass had installed their Counter Narcotics Center, a reflection cynics like to joke, of the importance the organization attached to its activities. The Center had been established right after the fall of the Berlin Wall when the agency was desperately seeking new, post Cold War missions to help justify its enormous budget and personnel resources to Congress and the public.

Well, he thought stepping out of the elevator, here I am, the newest recruit in the War on Drugs. Me, a guy who worked for the agency in Vietnam and Afghanistan where we were accused of doing more to encourage the drug traffic than to suppress it.

His new colleagues were all waiting for him around the usual government issue conference table. There were representatives of the FBI, Customs, DEA, Treasury and, of course, the CIA. One of the group was a female, the Customs Officer. The rest were male. In front of each, Duffy noted, was a coffee mug emblazoned in the colors and official seal of the service he or she, in the case of the Customs officer, represented. Nothing ever seems to change in U.S. Government service.

His welcome struck Duffy as a cross between "hail the conquering hero" and "the return of the prodigal son." The man running the center who was, technically, Duffy's boss, was five years his junior. He ushered Jim to the chair at the head of the table with a gesture that showed he was either being genuinely deferential or that he was a master of that vital bureaucratic art, sycophancy.

"Jim," he began after he'd gone around the table making the intro-
ductions, "we've been asked to bring you up to speed on the heroin situation in the world today."

The director swirled the coffee in his mug as though its black surface might provide a suitable reflection of the somber report he was
about to lay on Duffy.

"The brutal, unhappy fact is, Jim, that the consumption of heroin
has shot up dramatically all around the world in the last three years.
No where has that increase been as important as it is right here in the
U.S. and in Western Europe. On a global level, heroin consumption is
by far the greatest drug problem the world faces. President Clinton
pointed out that heroin poses a graver long term threat to society than
even crack cocaine did."

How these guys love to cite a phrase from the White House as the
Good Housekeeping Seal of Approval to whatever line they're shooting, Duffy thought. It was like the Jesuits at his high school who were
always citing Saint Augustine on the wisdom of celibacy as a way to
justify the validity of virginity to a bunch of horny teenagers.

"This heroin thing didn't hit us in a firestorm the way crack did in
1985," the director continued. "It kinda crept up on us while we weren't
looking. The worldwide production of the opium poppy has more than
doubled in just the last five years. What that means is there's potentially
twice as much heroin out there looking for customers. We figure Interpol in Lyons over in France has the best data base on this. By their estimate, worldwide heroin production went from 125 metric tons in 1984
to 500 tons in 1994, almost a fivefold increase."

"Wow!" Drugs had never been a particular concern of Duffy's but
figures he knew and those figures were real shockers.

"That's not all. From 1985 to 1996, virtually the same time span,
the heroin seizures in Europe went from 2.1 tons to eleven tons. That's
not an estimate—those are hard figures. Again, a fivefold increase."

"Does that mean heroin consumption has quintupled in a decade?"
an astonished Duffy asked.

"That's a conclusion it's hard to avoid."

"Jesus," Duffy said in a near whisper. "That's staggering."

He'd puffed a few joints of hash in his days running the Afghan war. And he'd inhaled the stuff, too, unlike some others. Liked it, but not enough to alter his lifestyle in any way. He'd remained a dedicated scotch and vodka man. He had, like a lot of those from his social background, a fairly stereotyped image of drug addicts. They were a tiny minority, already pre-disposed to the habits that were destroying them by some internal character weakness. His idea of a junkie was that of a sixties style addict passed out on the bathroom floor of a Greyhound bus station, a rubber strap around his lower bicep, a needle hanging from his forearm. He neither pitied nor scorned people like that; he just couldn't care less about them. They were someone else's problem, not his. But this?

"Now, Afghanistan," the director was saying. "Your old play-ground has become the largest producer of the opium poppy in the world. In the year 2000, 70% of the worlds heroin came from opium poppies grown in Afghanistan. That figure dropped slightly in 2001 but now Afghanistan is back leading the league again."

The director now offered Duffy a wry, resigned smile. "However, as a government, we don't choose to acknowledge that particular reality officially or to make a lot of noise about it. Nor do we care to call public attention to the fact Pakistan and Turkey are up to their armpits in the traffic. Those two nations are just too important to us in our so called War on Terrorism."

Duffy laughed. "Reality check time. What else is new? Without those Pakistani Interservices Intelligence guys who were up to their armpits in dope, we couldn't have had a war against the Russians in Afghanistan."

"Yeah," the director grimaced, "and without the money they're making off the heroin traffic they couldn't sustain a guerilla war in Kashmir, either."

Duffy gave a shrug of his shoulders. He wasn't going to get into a pissing match about the rights and wrongs of the agency's past policies. "So who the hell is using all this heroin?"

"Jim." It was the female Customs Officer. She was built close to the ground, a solid, almost squat figure who looked as though she could hoist a steamer trunk full of dope over her shoulders and walk away with it. "The fact is there's a whole new generation of heroin users out there today. We're not looking at the old Lenny Bruce type addicts sticking needles into any vein in their bodies they could find to give them a high. These people are young, most of them are under thirty. For some reason we just haven't figured out, there's a disproportionate number of females among them."

"Did you see that survey that came out last year showing a big increase in teenagers trying heroin?" someone asked.

"This is not a one class drug like crack which is pretty much confined to the African American ghetto," the Customs woman continued without waiting for Duffy's reply. "This goes right across the social spectrum. Everybody's into this. Rock stars, Wall Street hot shots, second rate Hollywood scriptwriters and directors, make-up artists, fashion designers, photographers, lots of models because they think it keeps the weight off. That asshole Calvin Klein inspired 'heroin chic' with those skinny, vacuous models with the fucked up look on their faces he liked to use. He put a fashionable spin on being a junkie."

"Jim," the director had stepped back in, "there's been a critical sea change in the drug scene in the last three years or so. In the old days, a user had to stick a needle into a vein to get high. That so-called needle barrier kept people off the drug. After all, nobody likes sticking needles into their bodies. These new users don't inject the stuff."

"What the hell do they do with it? Eat it?"

"They smoke it. Or they sniff it like coke. It's *Naked Lunch* Lite out there these days. And there's a great big lie being whispered around by these young people that if you sniff heroin, if you smoke it instead of injecting it, it's not addictive. That's horse shit in its purest form, but there are a lot of people who should know better who've swallowed it whole."

"Mr. Duffy." It was the DEA officer, a man who'd been introduced to him as Mike Flynn, getting in his two bits worth. Flynn had dark black hair and blue eyes, clearly a fellow Irishman. In his early thirties, Duffy reckoned. And the use of that "mister" would probably also

indicate the nuns and priests had had him in their charge in somebody's parochial school.

"This new heroin epidemic, if you want to call it that, can be traced
to three things," Flynn began. "First, as the director explained, is the
huge increase in the worldwide production of the opium poppy. Second, is an equally dramatic fall in its street level price. Traditionally,
heroin was sold on the street corner for three or four times what
cocaine sold for per gram. Starting in 1991, the price of heroin began
to fall all around the world. Right now the two drugs are selling for
about the same price per gram in most places."

"However, the real reason behind this new outburst of heroin use
that's overwhelming us isn't price or production," Flynn declared with
conviction. "It's the purity level of the drug that's being sold on the street
corners. Back in the late fifties and sixties when we had our last heroin
epidemic the purity levels on the street were three to ten percent. At that
purity level, you had to inject the stuff to get a high. Sniff it and all you'd
do is sneeze. Today, here on the Eastern seaboard, street level purity is
averaging 65%—six times stronger than it was in the sixties. Up in
Boston for reasons we can't figure out, it's hitting 80%. In Europe it's 50
to 60%. That's why these new users don't inject anymore. They don't
have to. At those purity levels, they can sniff away to their heart's content.
Or mix it up with the tobacco from a couple of Marlboros and smoke it."

"Sounds to me," Duffy observed, "that you've got some wise-ass
Procter and Gamble style executive who figured this whole thing out
as a marketing technique to increase demand and consumption by
going after a whole new class of consumers."

"A lot of us in law enforcement suspect that's the case," Flynn
agreed.

"Jim." It was the Customs lady again. "Let me show you a little bit
of undercover film shot by the New York Police Department in the VIP
Room of a nightclub called the Limelight up in New York not so long
ago. It'll give you a feel for the problem."

She flicked a couple of buttons, the lights went out and a screen
came down. A grainy black and white image flickered onto the screen.

"This was shot at about three on a Saturday morning. These are high class kids, music industry types, entertainment. You don't get into that VIP room without money and connections. Now watch those kids' arms. Look, see, all of them scratching. You'd think someone had set a horde of ants loose in the place. That scratching is characteristic of a heroin user. All of them must be on it. And that's as chic a spot for the young, swinging crowd as they've got in New York."

She flicked the lights back on. "I tend to look at these things from an amateur sociologist's point of view. Coke was the eighties drug. Hyper. It went with the Wall Street Go Go types, the Reagan boom years. Heroin seems more reflective of the nineties values. It's like these kids say. 'Heroin mellows you out. You don't get hyper. You just get nice.' They've managed to convince themselves sniffed or smoked heroin is safer than crack. It's trippy—super cool."

She punctuated that thought with a sharp snort. "Problem is for a lot of those kids, the trip is going to end up in a private hell."

"How about sex?" Duffy asked. "Does it turn them on to that?"

"Not heroin. A guy who's really onto the stuff may get all soft and cuddly but soft is the operative word there. A hard-on he's not going to get. Pimps will often try to hook their prostitutes. It leaves them with a detached, kind of outer body feeling. Like they're out of themselves, so it's easier to screw any jerk who comes along with a couple of bills in his pocket."

Now I know why I never used the stuff, Duffy thought.

"So how many addicts do we figure we have out there?"

Flynn, the DEA man, fielded that one. "The official estimate of the drug community is 600,000 hardcore, injecting addicts. Everyone feels the figure is low. But the real worry is not that figure. It's our estimate of how many people are chipping heroin, part time sniffers or smokers, that's the figure that concerns us. We guess about 3 million." Flynn shrugged his shoulders. "But the real answer is we just don't know. Heroin addiction is a slow, vicious habit. It doesn't whack you out like crack does. It creeps up on you slowly, quietly while you're not looking, while you're thinking 'hey, man. I can handle this stuff.'

Unfortunately, we have no real way of knowing who is going to get addicted and who is not or how long it will take a given individual to get hooked. But once it's got you, you've got about as much chance of kicking your habit as you do of beating a major cancer."

"What kind of time frame are we talking here?"

"Three, four, five years. With injected heroin. With the sniffing habit, we just don't know yet. A lot of the sniffers, the smokers will shift to injection when the habit really takes hold of them just to save money. How many of those three million chippers are going to wind up in the hardcore population? Who are the one's who'll get hooked? Who are the ones who'll be able to walk away from the stuff? Frankly, we have no idea. But when they start to make that move from chipping to addiction, Mr. Duffy, that is when the shit is going to hit the fan big time."

Duffy though back to the briefing he'd received in the Director's office. "How about these Islamic Radicals? Do you see them involved in the traffic?"

"We know that for them peddling dope to nice kids in the west, scrambling their brains is a way of doing God's work. In Brussels, you've got Moroccan street dealers who won't let their sisters date a Christian or leave the house without covering their heads with a scarf, happily selling dope to Belgian users. Increasingly, the French are seeing Algerians, Moroccans tied to the FIS, the Front for Islamic Salvation, selling in France and Southern Germany with orders not to sell to their Islamic brothers, just Europeans. We've seen Palestinians fighting Italians for turf in Switzerland and Italy. But how much of this is rooted in ideology? How much is just good old fashioned money lust? We don't know. Maybe you can find out for us."

———

London's Mark's Club is located in a late 18th century dwelling at 46 Charles Street, a few steps from Berkeley Square, that once aristocratic oval of grass and plane trees where the nightingale of legend is supposed to have sung. The bird may still be singing there for all anybody knows except nobody could hear its song today over the snarl of the endless traffic engulfing the square.

Nothing on the exterior facade of the club house building would indicate to the casual passerby that it was anything other than the private residence of a well-to-do English family. The understated elegance of its interior was meant to remind members and visitors alike of another set of uniquely English clubs, White's, Brooks, Boodle's whose membership was strictly male. Mark's, however, was dedicated to the proposition that humankind is composed of two sexes rather than one. At the height of London's Swinging Sixties, its founder, Mark Burley, was struck by the quixotic notion that some of the gentlemen in his social circle might actually prefer to dine in the company of a few attractive women rather than being surrounded by the unthreatening familiarity of their fellow old Etonians or Harrovians.

Billy, the club doorman, recognized the growl of Terry Harmian's Jaguar as he and his wife Nancy drew up to the club shortly after nine o'clock in the evening. A felicitous, if perhaps, apocryphal legend gave Billy's services to Mark's membership a special cachet. He had been, it was whispered, the driver of the getaway car in the November 1983 Brink's Mat robbery. He opened Nancy's door first, offering his hand to help her out of the low slung vehicle, admiring as she emerged the line of her well muscled thighs.

"Evening, Mr. Harmian," he said as he then circled around to the driver's side ready to take the Jag to a secure parking place. "Enjoy your dinner."

James, the club's porter glided from his lodge to greet Nancy and Terry as they stepped into the club. "How nice you've decided to celebrate your anniversary with us," he glowed, taking Nancy's coat. James, an Irishman in his mid-sixties radiated a distinction few of the club's titled members could rival. "I think you'll find your guests are all waiting for you upstairs," he continued, indicating with just the faintest suggestion of a nod the staircase next to the entrance of the main dining room.

Given the nature of the evening, Terry and Nancy had decided to engage the club's private dining room on the second floor above the bar. Arm in arm, they started up the staircase, its walls lined with 19th century oils of dogs, children and hunting scenes, the subjects which seemed to mark the boundaries of the owner's artistic sensitivities.

Bruno, the maitre d' was waiting at the door to greet them with the sort of subdued effusiveness the evening called for. The long table down the side of the room was set for ten, three discreet bouquets of camellias and azaleas as Nancy had suggested gracing the table. Their guests, who'd been settled in the chairs and sofas around the fire, were already on their feet and descending on them.

"Henrietta"—Bruno indicated a middle aged woman in a black silk dress girdled with a white tea apron, looking for all the world as though she were about to audition for the role of the upstairs parlor maid in a Victorian drama—"will be looking after you this evening."

The rest of his sentence was drowned by the burbling chorus of greetings and good wishes which now swept over the anniversary couple. With Terry heading clockwise and Nancy counter-clockwise, they worked the circle of their friends, embracing and welcoming each of them one by one.

There was Said Abou Abrazzi, a Saudi and, like Terry, a private investment counsellor to a limited group of wealthy clients and his Syrian wife Mona looking like a Madonna who'd just stepped out of a Byzantine icon; Raymond, "B.T." for "Big Time" Harris, a lawyer whose specialty was the legal intricacies of tax havens and establishing off shore companies to take advantage of the opportunities such places offered. He was accompanied by his wife Gilda. There was David Nathan, an Australian who'd wired most of the continent Down Under to cable TV, earning himself as he did a fortune to rival those of Rupert Murdoch and Kerry Packer. Hanging proudly onto his arm was his new French wife, Giselle. Next came Dimitri "Grischa" Zumbrowski, a Russian of uncertain ethnic origins but unquestioned financial clout with the stunning blonde Polish model who was his mistress. And finally, the Baron Theodore "Teddy" van Weissendradt, a Flemish noblemen from Antwerp—although Nancy always thought the term an oxymoron—who was the only person whose poker playing skill her husband was prepared to acknowledge surpassed his own.

It was, Nancy mused, as she buzzed her way to the last of their guests, your typical London dinner party—one token Englishman nestled into a Noah's Ark of differing nationalities.

Terry and Nancy marched back to the fireplace with their guests where Henrietta was waiting for them with glasses of Dom Perignon. Terry clinked his glass to Nancy's, circled her waist with his right arm and with his left waved his glass to their friends.

"Cheers, dear friends. To us, to all of you." Then with the gaze of a delighted schoolboy, he chortled, "'Fill the cup that cleans today of past regrets and future fears.'"

Their circle of friends murmured their approval. Nancy sipped her champagne then looked up laughing at her husband. "Terry, you've been rampaging through your *Bartlett's* again, haven't you?"

"Not at all, darling. It's from the *Rubaiyat*. Like all good Persians, I practically know it by heart."

For half an hour, they talked, laughed and chatted before moving over to the table for dinner. Nancy had selected the menu, caviar, smoked salmon and blinis to begin and then, with the shooting season ending, the last of the years pheasants. All hens, Nancy had ordered the chef, because with birds as with humankind, the female was the more tender of the species.

For their wines, Bruno had selected a New Zealand Chardonnay and three bottles of 1961 Chateau Figeac he'd found tucked away in some dark corner of the club's cellar.

It was a sumptuous, delicious, laughter filled evening, one that would live engraved for years to come in the memories of all those who'd enjoyed it.

It was after one when they finally got back to Chester Square. As usual, there was no sign of a parking place in front of their house. "Go on in, darling," Terry told her. "I'll look for a place to park down the square."

No self respecting Londoner, Nancy mused walking up the steps and fumbling in her handbag for her keys, would live in a building built in the 20th century. That's why none of us have garages and drive ourselves mad every day looking for places to park.

She let herself in, slammed the door shut and gave a toss to her hair before taking off her coat.

That was when the arm ripped around her throat, then yanked her upwards in a vise-like hold so vicious she was, quite literally, lifted off her feet. At the same instant she felt the sharp prick of the point of a knife cutting into the flesh of her temple.

"Quiet!" a voice hissed. "Don't make a sound."

The arm was wrapped around her neck so tightly that, for an instant, Nancy was terrified her assailant was about to strangle her. She could no longer swallow and she felt her eyes beginning to bulge out of their sockets. In her shock and horror, one thought flashed through her being. Yobs! These were some of those vicious London burglars they were always reading about.

Another intruder, this one's features hidden inside a black ski mask emerged from the shadows beside the staircase. He had a sheet of adhesive bandaging in his hands. He strode over to Nancy, ripped off a piece the size of half a face cloth and taped it around her face from ear to ear, stretching it so tight that when he'd finished, she could barely move her lips and jaws. The only sound she could get out of her throat now, she realized, would be a pathetic little bleat. Her knees buckled, nausea gripped her stomach as a sense of horror and hope-lessness engulfed her. Where, oh where was Terry?

Meanwhile, the second intruder had snatched a pair of handcuffs from his belt and snapped them tightly over her wrists.

"Get her upstairs," he ordered the man still holding Nancy in his vise like grip.

Her first assailant dropped his strangle-hold, spun around, grabbed her by the handcuffs and with ruthless force started to half pull, half drag her up the stairs. He, too, was wearing one of those black ski hoods with holes cut into it for his eyes and nose.

Nancy stumbled to her knees after half a dozen steps.

"Get up!" the man snarled.

Exhausted, her knee stabbing with pain, she somehow managed to stumble along behind her captor as far as the second floor landing. He pushed open the bedroom door and sent her sprawling onto the floor with a brutal shove in the small of her back. He slammed the door shut, then strode over to her fallen form.

My God, she thought, as her cheeks scraped against the fibers of her bedroom carpet, this bastard is going to rape me right here on my bedroom floor.

He wasn't.

"Get up!" he barked at her again.

As she struggled to her feet, her stockings torn, her knee now throbbing and beginning to swell, she saw Rebecca, her housekeeper. She was tied to a bedroom chair, a swath of adhesive tape similar to the one that had been plastered onto her own face covering her mouth. Her assailant, meanwhile, had pushed her into a second bedroom chair a few feet from Rebecca's. As he did, Nancy glanced at her bed. It had not been turned down. That had to mean Rebecca had been a prisoner here since very shortly after they'd left for Mark's. The burglars had been in the house for some time, yet they hadn't ransacked it the way yobs usually do, grabbing the TV, the stereo, and the silver. Why? Had they been waiting for them to come home to grab them?

Then Nancy understood. It was her jewels. Some bastard in the insurers office had passed the information on what they were worth to these guys. That was the way they worked, inside information.

With that a strangely reassuring thought struck her, calming for just a second, the panic, the numbing fear that had over-whelmed her. At least they weren't going to kill them. They'd snatch the jewels and run.

What about Terry? she wondered in anguish. Where was he? He had to be back inside the house by now. Their bedroom door had been sound-proofed to give them a good night's sleep. She was trapped here in a vault of silence, unable to pick up a sound, a shout, a murmur from elsewhere in the house. Christ, darling she prayed. Don't be a hero. Give them the damn jewels and get them out of here.

While she agonized, her captor had uncuffed her hands and was securing her to the bedroom chair with swift, skilled lashings of rope.

Somehow, despite the terror that had dulled her mind and iced her limbs, she remembered something she'd seen in a TV movie. When her captor turned to the bed for more rope she inhaled as deeply as she could to swell her lungs to a maximum so that when he'd finished binding her to the chair, she could then empty her lungs and produce a little slack in the ropes.

Her captor studied his handiwork, then crossed the room, snapped out the lights and opened the door. For just a brief second he stood there silhouetted by the light of the landing, before shutting the door, leaving Nancy to tremble out her terror in the darkness. During the brief instant when the door was opened she struggled to hear a sound—a shout, a scream, any sign of life drifting up the stairwell from the ground floor. She heard nothing.

She peered around the darkened room, its only light furnished by the faint glow of the street lamps in Chester Square bouncing a few wayward beams off her bedroom ceiling. Across that darkness, maybe fifteen feet from her chair, was her bedside table. The black promise of salvation, her telephone, lay resting on it. Fifteen feet. As she peered towards the table, those fifteen feet might have been half a mile. But if somehow she could get there, her hands were free at her wrists. She might be able to pluck the receiver from its cradle and punch the magic numbers 999 into the phone. Would the operator on duty at the emergency switchboard recognize her frantic bleating for what it was, a despairing cry for help? Or would he ignore it as the work of some crank?

How could she get there? How could she move herself across the eternity of space between her and the phone? Could she, she wondered, twist and slide her chair across the room by using her body weight as a driving force?

Suddenly, the bedroom door burst open. She blinked in fear at the sudden burst of light flooding the room. Now two of her captors stood framed by the light in the doorway. They strode over to her. With a lunge, they hoisted her into the air and began to carry her downstairs as though they were hospital orderlies transferring a chair-bound patient to another ward. As they headed down the stairs, she saw light streaming from the door to her husband's office. Once they'd reached the bottom step, the two men pivoted and carried her into the office.

From behind her gag, Nancy emitted a high pitched, guttural squeak at the sight that greeted her. For an instant she was afraid she was going to vomit and choke to death on the remains of her festive dinner.

Terry was slumped in his office chair, his face an unrecognizable mash of blood, flesh and bone. His left eyeball had been partially dislodged from its socket and hung half-exposed on the upper edge of his cheekbone. His nose had been smashed, and blood had streamed from his nostrils, over his mouth and chin and then cascaded onto his shirt which had become a soggy maroon blanket. His mouth was open and she could see most of his front teeth were missing. To her horror, she saw one of those teeth clinging to the dark fabric of his suit jacket. He was breathing through that half open mouth of his, a little foaming screen of blood percolating in synchronization with his efforts to inhale and exhale.

Two more men in those black hoods stood on either side of her husband. A third leaned against his desk as though he was the one responsible for supervising the torture of her poor battered Terry. Suddenly, he stood up and strode out of the room. From the corner of her eye, Nancy saw him cross the hallway and rip their 16th century Venetian glass mirror from its place on the wall.

Brandishing it like a Formula One driver hoisting a newly won trophy, he marched back into the office and thrust the mirror in front of Terry's mangled face.

"Look!" he commanded.

Then he pointed to Nancy. "If you don't open up that safe for me right now, that's how she's going to look in five minutes."

Terry gasped out something through the blood obstructing his mouth. Suddenly, Nancy realized he hadn't answered his captor in English. He was speaking Farsi. These bastards weren't yobs after her jewels. They were Iranians. That was what Terry was trying to tell her by uttering those words to his tormentor in Farsi. She felt faint. Were they the mullahs' men? If they were, they were murderers. Every Iranian knew the stories of the VEVAK's killers butchering the regime's foes all over the west. Was that what this was all about?

The man holding the mirror had also understood why Terry had uttered those words in Farsi. "Bastard!" he roared, slamming the mirror onto the floor. From Terry's desk, he picked up a pistol and viciously whacked the side of her husband's head with the flat of its butt.

Then he turned, took three strides to Nancy and smashed a jarring right hook to her cheekbone. She gave what should have been a scream of pain but was only another shrill bleat, pleading with her husband in her mind as she did, "Open the safe, for God's sake, Terry! Give him whatever it is he wants! Who cares?! Who cares?!"

Almost as though she had been able to invoke some mysterious channel of extra-sensory perception to convey that message to her husband, Terry mumbled, "OK, OK. Right to seventy." The man beside Terry dropped to his knees in front of the safe and began to slowly twist the dial of the lock.

"Now left to 230," Terry said when he'd completed the first movement.

The man twisted the knob of the locking mechanism left.

"Right again to 85."

Again, the intruder followed his directions.

"Now left to 300."

Slowly, the man twisted the knob left once again. As he reached 300 there was an audible "click." The safe's heavy door swung open half an inch on its hinges.

"Good," the leader said. Then he glanced towards the two men who'd carried Nancy down from the bedroom like the Queen of Sheba in her sedan chair. "Take her back upstairs."

This time her two assailants barely carried her inside the bedroom before unceremoniously dumping her chair onto the carpet, then rushing back out the door. For a few seconds, Nancy sat gasping in the darkness, struggling to get control of the shaking and the nausea produced by the horror she'd just lived.

Every grisly detail of the scene, of her poor husband's battered body, the blood streaming from his mouth and nose, the cracking sound the butt of the pistol had made when it hit his head, came back to her. The bastard had fractured his skull for sure. Terry was going to bleed to death right there in his chair or die from the beating those bastards had given him if they didn't shoot him first. If her beloved Terry was going to live, she had to save his life.

By dumping her just inside the bedroom door in their rush to get back downstairs, her two captors, she suddenly realized, had cut that eternity of space separating her from her bedside table almost in half. Now probably less than eight feet lay between her and that black promise of salvation on her table. You can do it girl, she told herself, you can get there. You have to.

Slowly, so she didn't topple over backwards and wind up immobilized on the carpet—she tilted back onto the right rear leg of the chair to which she'd been bound. For a second, she swayed there precariously. Then, with her left hip and knee, she half twisted, half thrust the left front leg of the chair forward. Finally, tilting back this time on the chairs left rear leg, she repeated the gesture in the opposite direction.

It worked! She had cut perhaps six inches from the distance separating her from the telephone.

For a moment, she sat still in the darkness listening. There was not a sound in the house. Were they waiting to come back and kill her and Rebecca? Or had they fled?

She had to do it, she could do it, she could force herself to that phone. If they were coming back to kill her at least she would die trying to save herself and her husband.

She began again thrusting her way forward, fighting her way inch by painful inch towards the promise waiting in the darkness on her bedside table. The ropes binding her to her chair cut into her waist and knees with each of her forward thrusts. Each time her left leg hit the floor, a jolt of pain seared through her injured left knee.

How long did that agonizing journey last? She had no idea. All she knew was what she told herself over and over again through every inch of the ordeal: 'if I don't get to that telephone, my husband and I are going to die.'

Finally, when she was just three feet from the table, she was able to see the telephone sitting there in the shadows. Sensing its presence gave a new determination to each painful gesture as she thrust her chair across those last inches.

She grasped the telephone's cord in her fingers and slowly drew the instrument to the edge of the table where she could clutch its receiver in her hands. Leaning up against the table, she stretched out her bound hand and plucked the receiver from its cradle.

It was dead.

The bastards had cut the telephone line. For just a moment she was paralyzed by fear and despair until, like a bright burst of fireworks illuminating the night sky, an inspiration struck her. Her cell phone! Just before leaving the house, she'd taken it out of her handbag and put it away—in the bedside table right beside her chair. They would never have thought to look for that.

She twisted her chair backwards until she was able to tug the table's drawer open with her fingertips. Then she leaned her chair against the open drawer to give her hand as much freedom of movement as possible to grope inside the drawer.

She found it! She drew the portable from the drawer, let her chair ease back to its normal position and leaned her head as far forward as the ropes tying her to the chair would allow to cut the distance between the phone and her taped mouth.

The beauty of the cellphone, of course, was that it was designed to be worked with one hand. She turned on the power, heard the dial tone and punched 999 on the keyboard.

After just three rings, a woman's voice uttered the most welcome words Nancy had ever heard: "Emergency. Which service do you require—fire, police or ambulance?"

She grunted out the only reply she could make, three high pitched squeals for help or understanding. Less than a mile away, at Scotland Yard's Central Command Complex Information Room, Doris Maloney listened to those unintelligible sounds with a furrowed brow. Her computer screen told her that the incoming call was from a mobile phone, #0836372587. Its registered owner was a Mrs. Nancy Harmian of 5 Chester Square.

"Are you Mrs. Nancy Harmian?" she asked.

Again, Nancy gave the only reply of which she was capable, a high-pitched squeal which she hoped her listener might interpret as being an affirmative answer to her query.

Like the other operators manning the emergency board, Doris Maloney had been given extensive training before being allowed to take her chair. The 999 system could receive as many as 10,000 calls on a busy Friday or Saturday night, and its operators had to know how to separate the urgent queries from the crank calls, the little old lady who wanted the police to find her lost cat, the sods ringing through with a bomb hoax, the drunken kids having a laugh. She made a quick decision.

"Mrs. Harmian," she said, "please try to stay on the line. I'm passing your call to the police who I think are best equipped to deal with it."

"I have an unintelligible sound coming in on a mobile phone registered to 5 Chester Square," she told her police colleague to whom she relayed Nancy's call. "I suspect we may have the owner on the line."

Jake Howe, CO, for Commissioner's Office, Constable 1023 took over the call and studied the data blinking from his screen. The address, 5 Chester Square was clean. No warning flag had come up for it, no indication that someone at the site was known to the police for whatever reason, or that, for example, the man of the house had been tagged as a chronic wife-beater.

"Mrs. Harmian," he asked, "are you calling from your home at 5 Chester Square?"

Again, the only reply he got was an incomprehensible squeal. "Mrs. Harmian," he said, "please stay on the line with me. I am dispatching a police car to your residence."

Now Howe, too, had a decision to make. He could order out the Yard's area car or he could relay the problem to the Gerald Road police station, "station to deal". The call could be a joke or a hoax of some sort and the Yard's cars were high priority vehicles. Better pass it on to Gerald Road, he decided. With a flick of a switch he sent the information on his screen through to the CAD—Computer Aided Dispatch—Room at Gerald Road with the notation "for local assignment." At the station, the duty officer quickly digested the information, then called up the stations RT—Radio Telephone—car on his personal radio.

"Alpha Bravo Three," he called. "Are you free for assignment?"

"Yes, go ahead," came the reply.

"We're getting strange noises from a mobile phone #0836372587 registered to 5 Chester Square. It might be a domestic. Please investigate. Your CAD number is 19. Report your arrival please."

The dispatcher then turned to his open phone line. "Mrs. Harmian?" he asked. "Are you still there?"

"Please stay on line," he urged in response to still another incomprehensible squeal.

As it turned out, the RT car was less than half a mile from Chester Square. In not much more than two minutes the car called in "Re your CAD 19, AB3 on the scene. The house is dark. PC Dansey investigating."

Dansey, the car's driver and senior PC—Police Constable—got out with his flashlight. "Stay by the radio in case of trouble," he ordered his junior, riding a RT car for the first time. Slowly, Dansey walked around the house, searching for any sign of a break in. He found none. He tried to flash his light through the ground floor windows to pick up any sign of life inside but had no luck. They were all curtained. He pressed his ear against one window pane but heard nothing.

"Listen, Charley," he said to the dispatcher when he got back to the car. "The place is dark. There's no noise. I don't want to just kick the door down and go barging in there. Have you still got that unintelligible voice on your open line?"

"Affirmative."

"OK. Here's what I suggest we do. I'm going back there and give the doorbell a long ring. I'll give Timmy here the high sign when I do. You tell that voice on the phone to give you two grunts or whatever noise it is they're making the moment they hear the doorbell ringing. That way, at least, we'll know if there's someone in trouble in there or if it's just some sod having us on."

Dansey marched back to the front door of the house, turned and waved to his back-up, then jammed down hard on the doorbell.

"They heard it! They heard it!" Timmy called out, his voice electric with first night on RT patrol excitement.

Dansey came back to the car and took over the radio. "Is there a key holder for this house?" he asked.

The dispatcher had already looked for that information. "Negative," he replied.

"Looks like we're going to have to kick the door in, Charley."

"Break a window then, Dansey. A window's cheaper than a door to fix, remember?"

"There's a window right beside the front door. I can whack it open with my torch and climb in but you better get me a Panda car backup before I do in case there are any problems in there."

London police constables riding in the station Rovers were not armed but some of their colleagues in the Panda cars were.

"Alpha Bravo Six enroute," the dispatcher told Dansey. In barely a minute, the Panda car, its blue lights flashing, glided to stop behind their Rover. Dansey briefed the cars occupants then turned to his junior. "Come on, Timmy, me boy. In we go."

Dansey paused a second before the front door, listening one last time for any sound from inside the house. Finally, with a sigh, he began to hammer out the glass of the window just beside the door. When he'd finished, he reached over, ripped open the curtains and, using his flashlight peered into the room. It was Terry Harmian's study.

"Holy Christ!"

"What's up boss?" his junior asked as he, too, leaned over to get a glimpse into the room. His light joined Dansey's fixed on the body tied up in a chair at the back of the room, what remained of its face a bloody mash, the back wall on which it rested spattered with bits of bone and gray brain matter apparently blasted out of the victim's head with a gunshot.

"God!" said Timmy, a gagging sensation rising in a quick tide in his throat.

"What's the matter? Never seen a dead body before?"

"Not one like that."

Dansey meanwhile had opened up his personal radio to the Gerald Road dispatch room. "That CAD 19 you just assigned me, I need an ambulance, the duty officer and the Night Criminal Investigator. We've got a serious scene here. And a dead'un, I think."

He switched off the radio and turned to Tim. "One thing's damn sure. He wasn't the guy who was making those noises over the mobile. There's got to be someone else in there."

At the Gerald Road Police Station, the constable manning the CAD Room had already ordered up an ambulance from Westminster Hospital, contacted the Chief Inspector in his area car and was now on the Personal Radio of the night CID Detective Sergeant riding patrol in an unmarked car with his Detective Constable.

"AB1," he informed him, "we have a major crime scene which requires your presence immediately at 5 Chester Square."

"AB1 here. We are in Sloane Square and responding."

At the front door to 5 Chester Square, Dansey was still figuring out just how he was going to jackknife his way through the broken window of Terry Harmian's study when the driver of the Panda car shouted, "The chief and a detective sergeant from CID are on their way." At almost the same instant Dansey heard the distant wail of a siren rising through the night.

Should he go on in, he wondered? Or should he wait for the bosses to arrive? Timmy, his young constable was eyeing him anxiously. Dansey had not spent 25 years on the Met without acquiring a fine understanding of when to move alone and when wisdom dictated letting the bosses take the lead. He gestured towards the siren's shriek already drawing closer. "They'll be here in a jiff. Let's wait for them," he told Timmy.

They were. The Chief Inspector leapt from his car, rushed up the steps and peered in turn into the gruesome scene in the study while Dansey briefed him on what had happened.

"OK, mate," he told Dansey. "In you go and open the front door for us. Don't touch anything in there for God's sake."

Dansey did as he was ordered.

"Constable," the Chief said to Timmy when the front door opened. "You station yourself right here by this door. Take that note pad of yours out and write down the name of everybody who comes in, the time he goes in and the time he comes back out. And nobody except the night CID and the medics come inside without my personal OK, clear?"

"Yessir," Timmy snapped.

With Dansey a respectful pace behind him, the Chief stepped into the study, found the light switch with his flashlight and, covering his hand with a handkerchief, switched it on. For a few seconds the two policemen studied the room with practiced eyes, the battered figure of Harmian tied to his chair, the safe, its door ajar, the shards of glass from the Harmians' shattered Venetian mirror on the floor. Moving carefully, the Chief stepped through the room to Harmian's body. He took a mirror from his pocket and held it up to the bloody butt of what had once been his nose. Not a trace of respiration appeared on its surface.

"No need to call an ambulance for him," he noted. "He's gone."

The two men withdrew from the study and closed the door behind them. "You," the Chief said to one of the Panda car constables. "Stand guard on this door."

As the constable moved to take up his assignment, the figure of the Night Detective Sergeant from the Criminal Investigation Division appeared. "Chief," he said respectfully to the Inspector, "what have we got here?" Although he was outranked by the Inspector, the CID detective sergeant was now the man in charge of the scene.

"Right," he said after the Chief had briefed him. "Have you searched the premises yet?"

"No."

"Let's go."

Room by room, the three men, Dansey, the Chief and the detective, worked a methodical course through the house. Throwing open the bedroom door, they discovered Nancy, mobile phone still clutched to her hand, and Rebecca. Dansey moved to rip the swath of adhesive tape from Nancy's mouth but the detective stopped him.

"Like this," he said plucking the tape at its edges under Nancy's left ear and jaw, then slowly peeling it away. His gestures were not so much designed to ease the pain of taking it off as they were to preserve the tape uncontaminated as a piece of potential evidence.

"My husband!" Nancy shrieked as the tape came off and she was able to articulate an intelligible sound. "Where's my husband? Is he alive? Did those bastards kill him? Where is he, oh God, where is he?"

Dansey and the Chief stood silent and still. The Detective Sergeant was in charge here and it was he who was going to have to make the swift and delicate decision as to what to tell the frantic woman before them.

"We're looking after your husband, Mrs. Harmian," the detective said in the most reassuring tones he could muster. "It is Mrs. Harmian I'm talking to, isn't it?"

"Yes, yes," Nancy sobbed. "Where is he? Take me to him. I've got to see him."

The sergeant had already decided there was no way he was going let this badly shaken woman into the crime scene downstairs. That would only add to the state of shock and trauma she was already in. His first priority had to be to get her and the other woman medical attention. Then, they would decide when and how to tell her her husband was dead and start taking her statement.

"Cut the ropes," he ordered Dansey. "Don't untie them. Some of these guys leave their signature on the way they tie their knots."

As Dansey started to free her, the detective knelt beside Nancy. "You've been through a terrible ordeal, ma'am. Like I said we're looking to your husband already. Now we've got to get you and this lady here sorted out. Let's get you to the hospital in the ambulance I've got outside."

Nancy wasn't buying. "No! I'm OK, I'm fine. I want to see my husband. Where is he? Is he already in the hospital?"

That opened the door to the little white lie the detective needed to get Nancy on her way to the hospital. "Right. Just like I told you, ma'am. We're looking after him just like now we're going to look after you and your friend here."

By now the ambulance men had entered the bedroom with their collapsible stretchers. "Everything's going to be alright," the detective assured Nancy. "This constable"—he gestured to Dansey—"will go to the hospital with you. I'll be by just as soon as I can get away from here."

"But my husband . . ."

"Like I said, ma'am, he's been taken care of. Now we've got to take care of you."

Still protesting, Nancy was eased onto one of the two stretchers and wheeled out to the waiting ambulance. As it pulled away, the detective sergeant and the inspector, hands in their pockets so as not to run the risk of contaminating the scene, were already scrutinizing the sight in the dead man's study.

"You kind of get the feeling somebody didn't much care for this chap, don't you?" the detective said. "Got anything on him?"

"Not much. Iranian. Lived here for about a dozen years. Full residents permit. I'm not sure but I think he came in on some kind of political asylum after the Shah fell. Has to have money because he holds a 70-year lease on this house."

"The wife?"

"American."

"OK." The detective turned to his constable. "Get on to the Yard. We're going to need the laboratory duty team, a forensic examiner, a pathologist, the duty photographer, and a prints man. And while you're at it, get onto the Press Bureau and have them to send someone out here to keep those vultures off our backs."

Two foreigners, and a grisly murder in a posh neighborhood—this one, the detective sergeant knew, was too big for him to handle. This calls for Scotland Yard's duty superintendent, he told himself picking up his Personal Radio.

Detective Superintendent Fraser MacPherson was sleeping soundly in the second floor bedroom of his row house in Clapham when the sergeant's call came in. Eyes still closed, he reached out in a semi-automatic motion to the gargle of the PR by his bedside.

"Sorry, Guv," the sergeant began, "but we've got a murder inquiry on our hands here that looks a right messy one."

They always start with the good part, MacPherson thought, his eyes now wide open as he listened to his caller's briefing. His long suffering wife was already padding down to the kitchen to brew the black coffee she knew he was going to need to give himself a kick-start for his predawn work.

"Right," MacPherson noted when his caller had finished. "Ring up my sergeant and tell him to come pick me up. We'll be right there." Shit, he sighed stomping towards the bathroom, another night's sleep lost for the bloody English crown. MacPherson, as his name implied, was a Scot.

He was also good to his word. In barely thirty minutes, trailed by his duty sergeant, he was walking in the front door of 5 Chester Square. The uniformed officers drew aside deferentially as he marched into the house. MacPherson was a powerfully built man who advanced with the rolling gait of a seaman feeling for his footing on a slippery deck. That walk gave him a vaguely menacing air although in reality it was the result of a bad back, the consequence of a parachute jump that had gone wrong while he was in the Parachute Regiment.

"Morning, Guv," the detective who'd summoned him from his sleep said respectfully.

MacPherson did not reply. He was already studying the crime scene, assessing what had been done in the last hour, how well it had been done and what remained to be done. The constables from Gerald Road had isolated the house with their Crime Scene tapes. An Exhibits Officer was already logging out each piece of evidence being removed from the study for laser and fingerprint analysis. No gray hairs on his head, MacPherson noted unhappily. His was the most important job on the scene. Make a mistake, however small in that log from either inexperience or carelessness, and the defense would tear you to shreds in a trial. The doctor from Forensic, a woman, had already declared the victim dead. She sure as hell didn't need a medical degree for that MacPherson thought, but still it was a formality they had to go through.

He eyed the open safe. "I want a full photo series of that safe and everything in there before you touch anything," he ordered the Exhibits Officer. MacPherson's motto as a detective had always been, "Do it slow. Do it right." He didn't like to be preachy but sometimes the fast steppers they were recruiting for the Met these days need to be reminded of what their crime scene priorities had to be.

He was ready to deal with the victim when the detective who'd called him came up with a worried look on his face.

"Guv," he said, "we've got a problem. The PC we sent to the hospital with the wife just came up on his radio. He says she's going crazy. There's nothing wrong with her medically and so she's screaming out all the time for her husband. 'Where's my husband? Take me to my husband.' That kind of stuff."

Her husband was at that moment being eased into a rubberized body bag for his trip to the Horseferry Road mortuary.

"Somebody's got to get down there to the hospital and tell her her husband's dead."

"Aye," MacPherson sighed, furrowing the bushy black eyebrows he dyed along with his hair every two weeks at his Greek Cypriot barber. He knew who the 'somebody' was going to have to be. Him. He had the rank. So he also had the short straw.

"Get my sergeant and let's go."

———

"He's dead! He's dead! I know it!" Nancy shrieked at the sight of the three stern-faced detectives entering her room at the Westminster Hospital. MacPherson stepped to her bedside and with a tenderness quite out of keeping with his appearance rested his hand on her forearm. "It is my very sad duty, Mrs. Harmian, to have to inform you of the death of your beloved husband."

"Those bastards! They killed him! I knew they would."

MacPherson gave an almost imperceptible nod to his sergeant who drew a mini-cassette recorder from his pocket.

"Who are you referring to, Mrs. Harmian?"

"Those men. They were Iranians. Terrorists. They were the mullah's men! I know they were."

"How do you know that?"

Nancy told MacPherson how her husband had spoken in Farsi as a way of letting her know his assailants were Iranians.

In any police investigation, timing is critical. A strict application of police procedures would have recommended getting Nancy's statement a little bit later in the day when she had begun to recover from the shock and horror of her husband's murder. On the other hand, a smart detective takes what he can get when he can get it. She seemed ready and anxious to talk. MacPherson explained the legal procedures involved to Nancy as the law required and asked her if she was prepared to give him a preliminary statement.

"Yes, yes!" she sobbed.

MacPherson nodded to the sergeant to turn on his recorder and gently yet firmly began to walk the shattered woman through the events of the night.

When Nancy reached her description of how their assailants had demanded that her husband open his safe, MacPherson interrupted the flow of her recollections for the first time.

"Would you be having any idea of what it might have been they were after there in the safe?" he asked.

"None at all."

"Do you know what your husband kept in there?"

"Not really. It was his safe. For his business papers."

"And what was his business, ma'am, if you don't mind the asking?"

"He was a private investment counsellor. He helped a few very wealthy clients invest their money."

"I see." MacPherson was digesting that little revelation with the bitter knowledge acquired in his years of investigating crime in London.

A private investment counsellor was he now? That, in his experience, was just an elegant way of saying 'financial crook.' London was full of them these days. Foreigners, for the most part, Arabs, or Iranians like this fellow. Now you were getting the Hong Kong Chinese. The best of their lot were into tax avoidance schemes. The rest? Laundering money or moving and investing money somebody else had already taken the trouble to launder. "When was the last time you used the safe, ma'am?"

"Tonight, just before we went out to dinner."

Well, there's something, MacPherson thought. "We're emptying out the safe piece by piece, ma'am, looking for fingerprints or anything else that might help us find out who killed your husband. Of course, everything will be returned to you when our investigation is finished. Do you suppose you could come around to the station later in the morning when you've had a chance to get some rest and take a look at what was in there? See if you find anything missing?"

"Of course. I don't know how much help I'll be, but I'll do anything I can."

MacPherson rose to leave.

"Officer?"

"Yes."

"My husband was a Moslem. They have strict burial codes. I think he should be buried before sunset."

"You understand, ma'am, that in a case like this we have to perform an autopsy. I'll do what I can to accommodate your desires, but I can't promise anything."

The usual late afternoon customers had just begun to drift through the Nashravan Bookstore not far from Hamburg's main railroad station: a pair of elderly Iranian exiles, in to glance at the latest newspapers he'd received from Tehran; two university students looking for books assigned to them for study in their Persian language course, an antique dealer who was always on the lookout for old editions he could buy up at a bargain.

The manager of the book store, in reality the head of the Iranian secret police's German strike force, ignored them all. Indeed, he did not look up from his absorbed reading of Hamburg's daily *Hamburger Abendblatt* until he noticed a youth with the scraggly beard of an adolescent enter the store and head directly to the shelves where Faremi kept his volumes of ancient Persian poetry. He made a mental note of the red leather volume the young man selected from the shelf then returned to reading his paper.

A few minutes after the youth had left, Faremi strolled to the back of the store. Pretending to re-arrange the volumes, he took down the red leather bound edition of the Shahnameh by Persia's great poet Ferdowsi and removed the slip of paper his messenger had left for him. His five killers, he learned, had returned safely by train and ferry to his safe houses in Frankfurt and Dusseldorf.

Two hours later, Faremi sat down at the counter of the snack bar at the Iranians' airport in Hartenholm north of Hamburg and ordered an apple strudel and a cup of coffee.

He was half way through his apple strudel when a man in his early thirties wearing Rayban aviator glasses slid into the seat beside him. He gave a familiar nod to the waitress and ordered a cup of coffee. Officially, he was the assistant to the airport's half-Iranian, half-German manager. In fact, He was a member of the Pasdaran, Iran's Revolutionary Guards, and had been sent to Hartenholm to keep an eye on the field for its owners in Tehran.

"So?" he said to Faremi once the German waitress was busy at the far end of the counter.

"Everything went fine," Faremi answered. "They'll be back tomorrow. Start making the arrangements to get them out now."

———

Detective Superintendent Fraser MacPherson treated Nancy Harmian with a deference which, given his Scottish ancestry, he might not even have been prepared to offer his ultimate employer,

Her Majesty, the Queen. First, he found her the most comfortable armchair in the Gerald Road Police Station. Then, he offered her a cup of the Met's finest home brewed tea. Finally, he thanked her profusely for coming to the station at what he knew was such a difficult moment for her.

"Superintendent, I'd walk over the coals of hell if I had to to help you find those bastards who killed my husband." She started to sob and MacPherson whipped a clean, linen handkerchief from his pocket to help her absorb her tears.

"Sorry," she gasped returning it to him. "Do you have any idea yet when they'll be able to release his body?"

"I got on to the Horseferry Road Mortuary just before you arrived, ma'am." MacPherson glanced at his watch. "They should be starting their—" he stifled the word "autopsy" with its grisly undertones in his throat, "procedures any minute now. I hope you'll be able to reclaim him before the day's out." Then he nudged her gently to the task at hand.

In view of the fact her husband had struggled so long trying to keep its combination a secret from his captors, the police had found his safe remarkably full, its contents apparently barely disturbed. Neatly labelled, those contents were now were laid out on a plastic sheeting covering a counter of the station's evidence room. So, too, was a set of the photographs the police had taken of the open safe before they'd removed its contents. MacPherson picked one up and showed it to Nancy.

"This is precisely how the safe looked when we found it, ma'am. As you know your assailants opened it just before they took you back upstairs." He gestured to its contents on his office shelf. "There's an awful lot here. Makes us wonder just what it was they were after in there. Do you recognize anything missing?"

Nancy's first, instinctive gesture was to open and study her jewelry box. Everything was there. The lapis lazuli earrings were right on the top of the box where she'd set them. Whatever it was they were after, it certainly hadn't been her jewelry.

MacPherson pointed to a stack of envelopes wrapped up in a rubber band. "Your husband seems to have kept a great deal cash in the safe. Different currencies, too."

"Yes. He kept them for his travels."

"Would you be having any idea how much he usually had in there?"

"I'm afraid not."

"We calculate just under eight thousand quid when you sort all those currencies out. That's a lot of money. They didn't touch it and it was right there for the taking."

Nancy shuddered as the horror of the previous evening swept over again. She turned her eyes to her husband's checkbooks, files, correspondence, and address books, all set out on the counter before her. Was that what her beloved Terry was now, just a pile of paper on a policeman's shelf? How could she possibly tell if something was missing?

Then she started.

"There was an envelope. A big manilla envelope on top of my jewelry box when I came down to get my earrings. I'm sure it was there because I had to move it to get to the box. It's not here."

"How large, ma'am? The size of a piece of your ordinary typing paper shall we say?"

"Oh, no. Larger. Much larger. A big manilla envelope about an inch thick."

"Do you have any idea what might have been in it?"

"No. When I moved it, it felt like maybe, I wasn't thinking, documents, papers something like that."

"Anything else?"

"Yes. There was handwriting on it. In Arabic or Farsi. I can't tell the difference."

"Your husband's handwriting?"

"I wouldn't recognize his writing in Farsi." Nancy studied the material on the counter again. "But it's gone, alright. It's not there. Obviously that must have been what they were after, wasn't it? That big envelope?"

———

Jim Duffy's first full day back at work at the CIA was turning out to be something less than exciting. He might have been summoned back to duty by the director himself, heralded as the guy who was going to save the nation from some nebulous threat of nuclear terrorism, but the only threat that concerned him at the moment was whether or not he was going to wind up with claustrophobia in this little cubby hole they'd given him for an office in the basement of the CIA. Or maybe go nuts with boredom. No job at the CIA was more tedious, more mind-deadening, Duffy knew, than reading through the NSA's intercepts looking for that one elusive clue, the needle in an electronic haystack that might suddenly thrust a beam of light into the darkness of the intelligence gathering world.

He had been provided with a computer which linked him directly to NSA Headquarters at Fort Meade, Maryland. At Fort Meade, an NSA officer was feeding him a chain of the intercepts culled by the agency from the airspace over Iran. Each intercept that he fed into Duffy's computer screen was preceded by a number of key indicators: the date and time the intercept had been made; the telephone number from which the call had been made and, if available, where that phone was and in whose name it was registered; the number to which the call had been placed and again, if the NSA had it, the name of the phone's owner and its location.

Following that came the text of the intercept itself in two parallel lines, the first line in the speakers language, either Pushtu or Farsi. The second line running just underneath it carried a translation of the conversation in English. By activating a button on his computer, Duffy could feed the speakers voice into the earphones clamped to his head and follow—or at least try to follow—the conversation unwinding on the screen.

From that he was supposed, somehow, to recognize Said Djailani's voice if his old Mooj warrior had been recorded in any of these intercepted calls. It was crazy. Sure, he had met with Djailani at least two dozen times during the Afghan War. In safe houses in Peshawar run by the Pakistani Army's Inter Services Intelligence. But they'd always spoken through an interpreter. Duffy's Pushtu was limited to a few phrases, his Farsi nonexistent.

He shook his head in dismay, trying to recreate the flavor of those meetings, to hear in the recesses of his mind some echo of Djailani's voice. He smiled remembering that marvelous night when he'd brought Congressman Charley Wilson to meet Djailani and his superior, Gulbuddin Hekmatayar, the Islamic Radical who was the recipient of so much of the CIA's largesse.

Women never even dared to look those two Islamic hotshots in the eye. All sheathed in black, they would shuffle sideways into the room where the pair were sitting, clean off their sandals, then shuffle back out again.

So what does old Charley do? He shows up for their meeting with some Miss California Playboy Bunny on his arm wearing a pink warm up suit that was about three sizes too small for her. Djailani and Hekmatayar almost fell over. A completely wasted meeting, no business transacted at all. The two of them couldn't keep their eyes off Miss Playboy Bunny, couldn't stop drooling at the sight of that marvelous Malibu Beach body of hers.

The intercepts to which he was listening were the product of a top secret program called ECHELON, designed and run by the NSA. Using a linked system of U.S., U.K., Canadian, Australian and New Zealand listening posts, ECHELON intercepted and logged into the NSA's computers all the telephone calls, e-mail, fax and telex messages carried over the world's telecommunications networks. Driftnet fishing, they called it. Everything went into the basket, the communications of governments friendly or otherwise, businesses and private individuals. From bank transfers involving billions of dollars to callers ringing up their friendly escort service, all was swept from the skies and dumped into an NSA computer program code named PLATFORM.

Most of the intercepts reaching Duffy had been culled from the skies by the NSA's "Big Ear" listening post at Bad Aibling, Germany from the area in northeastern Iran where the CIA thought Djailani was probably operating. Yet all that prodigious technology, and Duffy had to admit it was prodigious, now came down to the ability of his human ears to pick up some familiar accent or sound that would identify for him a man whose language he couldn't speak, that he hadn't seen in five years. It was not an exercise on which you would want to bet the family farm.

———

"Now what we've got here," Detective Superintendent Fraser MacPherson announced to the men gathered around him in London's Gerald Road Police Station, "is obviously not your straightforward grab and run robbery. It's true the jewels were untouched, but they could be traced so maybe a pro might have left them behind. As far as we know, though, none of the money was missing. How come?"

Barely thirty-six hours after the brutal murder of Tari "Terry" Harmian, he and his associates were embarked on their first full scale review of the circumstances surrounding the killing. On a side table were the remains of half a dozen sandwiches, some crumpled bags of chips and a few dark bottles of lager, the leftovers of the hurried lunch that had preceded their gathering

"Guv, what about what the wife said? That the guys who did her husband were terrorists. Iranians," the night CID Sergeant who'd been the first one on the scene asked.

"That's not what she said, boy-o," MacPherson replied. "It's your interpretation of what she said. What she said was her husband spoke to those guys in Farsi. A language she admits she doesn't speak. He could have been asking them if they'd like a cuppa for all she knows." MacPherson's heavy, boxers hand were folded tranquilly on his stomach. Yet even there in repose they cast off an aura of power, of danger.

"Remember the first rule of any good police investigation—keep an open mind. See just where it is the inquiry is going to take us before we start jumping through any hoops. Sure, the wifey thinks some Iranian goons did her husband for political reasons. Why wouldn't she?

Probably thought her husband was some kind of a saint. Until I see proof of that, I don't."

"Still, shouldn't we get on to Thirteen?" the Night CID persisted. "Thirteen" was Special Operations Thirteen, Scotland Yard's anti-terrorist squad.

MacPherson laughed. "How many Iranians do you know speak Gaelic? If they don't have a brogue, Thirteen doesn't know them."

"Should we inform Box?" one of the younger members of the team asked.

"Box" was London police slang for MI6, Britain's intelligence service and MI5, domestic counter-intelligence, a nickname assigned those two organizations because they chose to employ a Post Office Box as the address for their communications—although everyone knew what their real addresses were.

"Oh, sure, we'll inform them." MacPherson smiled. "Then if we're lucky some toff from Six in a Hawes and Curtis suit with dandruff on his collar will come by and tell us a few jokes in Latin. You all speak Latin, don't you?"

A minimum of mirth greeted his remark.

"No, gentlemen." MacPherson's feet had been propped on a filing cabinet in front of his chair. Now he dropped them to the floor with a thud. "The wife may want to think it was terrorists. I don't. This looks to me like a business deal gone wrong. Or something to do with a gambling debt. You know how those Iranians like to gamble."

"From the maid's statement, they must have known who he was. She said they asked for him by name when they rang the bell, right?" the young constable who was the Exhibits Officer observed.

"Might also mean they could read the telephone book," MacPherson noted. "But you make a good point. Otherwise, why the masks? They must have been worried he could have ID'd them. In which case he had to know who they were, right? Iranian terrorists he's not going to know from the Queen Mother, is he? And they had to have studied his movements very carefully in order to get in there at just the right time as they did. Looks right professional to me."

"One thing puzzles me, Guv," the Night CID said. "He's got all that funny money in those envelopes in the safe. What did we figure? Eight thousand pounds? Travel money the wife says. A lot of it in Cypriot pounds. Hungarian whatever the hell it is they use down there. But he's got no visas, no entry stamp in his passport for those places. How come?"

"Very good point," MacPherson growled in approval. "Maybe he's got a second passport squirrelled away in a safety deposit box somewhere. And don't forget, Hungary and Cyprus may be your run of the mill second world countries, but when it comes to money laundering they lead the league table, don't they?"

"So what about drugs?" one of the younger men asked.

"So what about them? The way the wife described that missing envelope, he could have had a couple of kilos of heroin in there. But then he also could have had a million pounds in bank drafts, couldn't he?"

MacPherson stood up. "Look," he warned with the sense of judicious moderation that characterized all his criminal investigations, "don't anybody go drawing any conclusions yet, but I say we start to work on the assumption that this is somehow related to the man's business aspect."

He had begun to pace the room. "We're going to find out everything we can about this guy's life. Bank records. Telephone logs, BT and mobile. Interview all of those people he was investing money for. Find out where he was investing it. Bring in a couple of constables from Financial Affairs to help you go over his records. His plastic. Where did he travel? Did he go alone? Did he go with his wife? Go through that house with a fine tooth comb. Check out his computers. The lot."

He raised himself up onto his toes to give a final stretch to his back. "We meet here for prayers every day after lunch. Remember all of you, this is a police investigation, not the telly. It's slow, laborious work. Take the time you need but just be sure you get it right."

———

A pair of Cherokee jeeps each containing four men armed with AK-47s rode fore and aft of the ancient U.S. Army surplus General Motors two-by-four. The lead jeep had twin sixty caliber machine guns mounted on its roll bar for additional firepower. Seated next to the driver of the GM was Ghulam Hamid, the veteran of the Shah of Iran's security service who had bought Ahmed Khan's 42 kilograms of raw opium after his long evening of haggling in a hut in Afghanistan's Helmand province.

Now Hamid had 2000 kilograms of raw opium packed into his GM two-by-four—slabs, loaves, mounds the size of basketballs swathed in leaves. They represented harvest of a week's work in Helmand province. They had cost him an average of $30 a kilo, a total of $60,000, all paid for on the spot, in cash, in Pakistani rupees. Not for nothing was opium known as a cash crop.

His well-armed little convoy passed out of the city of Kandahar, capital of the province, under the "Arch of Triumph" the Taleban had erected to mark the capture of their first important city in Afghanistan in 1995. Festooned to the sides of the arch were the remains of the trophies the Taleban's zealous warriors had seized from the townspeople in their drive to instill a sense of Islamic purity in the city. There were CDs, video and audio cassettes, their tapes ripped out, Walkmans, a few worn copies of *Playboy* and *Penthouse,* all symbols of the decadent, morally corrupted west the Taleban had been determined to eradicate in their new, Islamically pure state. No CD or audio cassette decorated that festive arch more frequently than the album which had been the favorite of Kandahar's young males before their elder brothers in the Taleban had arrived. It was Madonna's Christmas 1992 release "Sex."

Hamid settled back in his seat, drifting into a reverie inspired in part by the fumes coming from the load of raw opium behind him. It had been in a truck just like this one that his career had begun in Pakistan. With the Russian invasion of Afghanistan, Hamid had offered his services to Pakistan's security organization, the ISI, Inter Services Intelligence. His first assignment had been running the Soviet Bloc arms purchased by the CIA from the secret airfields on which they were regularly landed in Pakistan to the mooj camps on the Afghan side of the Khyber Pass.

It had only taken a couple of trips for Hamid to recognize the economic opportunity the job offered. His trucks were coming back down the Khyber empty, which was to his way of thinking stupid. He knew poppy was being grown in the fields around the mooj camps to which he was delivering his arms. And he also learned that a dozen heroin refining labs had sprung up along the Afghan-Pak border. Why not organize a little Federal Express service to help those labs out, Hamid reasoned. Instead of running his trucks back empty, he'd fill them with raw opium. Who was going to stop and inspect an ISI truck? Nobody. He would provide the lab owners with a failure proof delivery service—for a substantial charge for each kilo he delivered. Hamid was wise enough to cut his Pakistani ISI superiors in on his scheme. It took them at least thirty seconds to appreciate the beauty of its structural symmetry.

The volume of opium coming down the Khyber soared as the war expanded and so too, of course, did the earnings it poured into the coffers of the ISI. That cash flow enriched a number of the ISI's top officers. More important, it gave to the organization a source of funds for operations the central government in Islamabad didn't want to finance openly such as purchasing arms for the Muslim guerrillas revolting against Indian rule in Kashmir.

With time, the trafficking pattern changed. The focus of poppy production moved southwest into the Helmand where Hamid had just collected his 2000 kilos of raw opium. It became easier and more natural to move the bulk of the produce through the arid wastes of Baluchistan towards the city of Quetta in Pakistan instead of bringing it down through the Khyber. There the raw opium was converted into heroin in primitive labs, then moved to the Makran seacoast. From the shore, it was ferried out to freighters for onward movement to Europe and the U.S.

Three families in Quetta, the Issa, Rigi, and Notezai clans, had seized the opportunity to turn themselves into the patron saints of the heroin traffic. What the cartels of Medellin and Cali had been to the cocaine traffic of the nineteen-eighties, their so-called Quetta Alliance became for the heroin trade of the nineties. Within seven years there were an estimated 500 multi-millionaires, in dollars, living in the area, all enriched either directly or indirectly by the traffic. One was Ghulam Hamid. They built themselves walled compounds, cool and green oases in the midst of Quetta's desolate landscape, complete with pools, fountains, rose arbors, miniature hanging gardens of Babylon, luxuriant green lawns. Their garages were filled with the BMWs and Mercedes Benz's they collected the way kids in the west collected Tinker Toys. They married off their children in $50,000 extravaganzas, and with their leftover cash bought seats for their friends or themselves in Pakistan's regional assemblies. The result was a Pakistani government as totally corrupted by drug money as was Mexico's——and, because of Pakistan's strategic importance, equally secure from U.S. government pressures.

Hamid had allied himself with Mohammed Issa as the chief overseer of his activities. Issa never dirtied his fingers by touching the traffic himself. The deal for the 2000 kilos of raw opium Hamid carried in his truck had begun, as almost all deals in the traffic now did, with a telephone call from Istanbul. The caller was a fellow Iranian, a devout follower of the mullah's regime but that was of no consequence to Hamid. What was involved here was making money not practicing religion or politics. His caller was the financial intermediary for one of the dozen heroin refining labs operating in the Istanbul area. He wanted 200 kilos of morphine base and would pay $1250 a kilo for it delivered to his contact in Iran. The 2000 kilos of raw opium in Hamid's GM would produce approximately 210 kilos of morphine base in his primitive mountain lab. That would earn Hamid's boss Issa roughly $262,500.

Hamid's "lab" was set beside a creek filtering down from the high mountain crests on either side of the Khojak Pass, five kilometers (three miles) east of the Afghan frontier village of Spin Boldak. Converting raw opium into morphine base, required a regular source of water. What it then took above all else was time and patience. The opium had to be dissolved in boiling water, mixed with lime fertilizer, filtered, boiled again, mixed this time with concentrate of ammonia and filtered again. The final result, morphine base, was a granular substance somewhere between cane sugar and flour in consistency, milk chocolate in color.

There was no way that Hamid, responsible for all that raw opium, could leave the lab site during the process. He who was used to sleeping in satin sheets in the air conditioned splendor of his villa in Quetta would have to sleep on an Indian rope and wood charpoi in an underground cave with twenty of his snoring, farting, vermin-infested workers. He who enjoyed bathing himself in his marble walled and tiled bathroom with its gold plated appliances would have to defecate in a common trench beside his employees, splash himself into a semblance of cleanliness in the same mountain stream that they bathed in. Instead of enlivening his evenings with a drink or two of Chivas Regal Scotch whiskey, he would get a glass of tea and, for his dinner, a few strips of meat ripped off a roast sheep rolled up into a clump of soggy rice.

Worst of all, the man who could barely remember the words of the Shahada, the Moslem profession of faith, was going to have to kneel down and bow his head in prayer five times a day with his fellow workers. Democracy, thought the man who had once served in the Shah's secret police, stinks.

Still, his little ordeal was going to bring Hamid a very substantial reward. This particular load of dope, once it was handed over to its new owners in Iran, would earn him close to $70,000.

He had nothing but scorn for those apostles of a radical Islam who saw in the produce of the Helmand opium fields the source of wealth with which they might buy the weaponry, the means, to destroy the decadent civilization of the west they so despised. Hamid spat on their *fatwas,* their religious edicts, sanctioning the trade because it hurt the enemies of Islam.

He was in the traffic for one reason only, to make money as fast as he could. As for the morality of the drug traffic, his answer was simple:

"If those kids in the West were dumb enough to use his dope, that shit, then fuck 'em, they deserved the misery it was going to bring them."

———

As Ghulan Hamid reached his lab, a few hundred miles to the west, an incoming IranAir jumbo jet from Vienna taxied past the gleaming red marble of the passenger terminal at Tehran's Mehrabad Airport towards the air freight hangar well to the south of the airport's main structures. It had been a perfectly ordinary flight except for one anomaly. It was listed as a freight flight; yet sitting on bucket seats in the plane's half-filled cargo bay were five passengers, all young males. The team of hit men who had murdered Tari "Terry" Harmian at his home in London had come safely back to Tehran.

From the Iranian's airfield at Hartenholm north of Hamburg, the five had been flown to a private landing strip on a farm a hundred miles from Vienna. There they'd been handed over to representatives of Neptune Air Freight Services, the firm which handled IranAir's freight business at the Vienna airport. Fitted out with company coveralls, the five had helped load the aircraft, then simply remained on board when it was time to clear the plane for departure.

That was typical of the "unofficial" services the company provided the Iranians, for, of course, a substantial fee. Indeed, much of the hi-tech equipment and weaponry flown in from Hartenholm had ultimately been smuggled out of Europe via Vienna International Airport.

Sadegh Izzadine, the mullah in charge of the *Gouroohe Zarbat,* the Strike Force, to which the five young men belonged was waiting for his returning team with a pair of Mercedes Benz sedans. He extended his hand to the team leader. "You have done well, my brother. The trust we placed in you and your fellows has been wholly justified."

The young man nodded respectfully, then drew a fat manilla envelope from the interior of his coveralls.

"Your package, *Ghorbar,*" the youth announced.

Izaddine smiled and passed the envelope to an aide. "This goes down-town," he ordered. "To the Professor's office. For *Operation Khalid.*"

Then he waved at the waiting cars. "Come, my brothers. The rewards for a job well done await you."

————

Back in Europe, it was just a few polite minutes past nine when a black Mercedes Benz 300 SL drew up in front of a gleaming glass and steel panelled office building in the Swiss town of Chur, nestled at the base of the Swiss Alps and some of the world's most famous ski resorts. A company logo in red and white fixed to the front facade of the building just over the main entrance identified both the name of the firm it head-quartered and the nature of its commercial activities—CIPHERS AG.

Three Swiss executives shivering slightly in the crisp mountain air waited at the top of the steps of the entrance for the Mercedes's passenger to alight. Their presence was a mute if obsequious testimony to the impor-tance of the visitor and the potential dimensions of the sale he represented.

The three Swiss executives almost fell over themselves rushing down the steps to greet him.

"Professor Bollahi," their leader chortled, "welcome to CIPHERS AG. Did you have a pleasant trip?"

"Indeed," nodded the Kair Bollahi, the architect of Operation Khalid. In fact, his trip had not been pleasant at all. He had been too con-cerned with the need for obtaining an absolutely unbreakable coding system to protect the secrets of his cherished Operation Khalid from the electronic eavesdropping of the Americans and their damnable Israeli friends to enjoy it. CIPHERS AG had the equipment that could offer him the security he needed, he knew. But would they agree to sell it to him?

"Our *Geschaftsfuhrer*—President Director General—Thomas Zurni is waiting to receive you in his office, Herr Professor," the sen-ior Swiss executive announced. "May I lead the way?"

The *Geschaftsfuhrer's* office suite was panelled in dark mahogany, its walls hung with oil paintings of the Swiss Alps, and a dark blue carpet, pilings so thick an advancing shoe sunk into them up to the top of its soles, covered the floor. A long conference table was already set with pots of steaming coffee and plates of golden brown croissants.

"My dear Professor." Herr Zurni smiled, circling around from behind his desk. "It's a pleasure to have you here with us this morning."

For a few moments the two parties went through the ritual of exchanging names, taking their seats at the conference table, filling up their coffee cups and buttering their croissants. Then the head of CIPHERS AG got them down to business. "Perhaps, Herr Professor," Zurni said, "you might give us a brief description of your enciphering requirements, then my staff and I can suggest to you how we might be able to fulfill them."

"Of course," the Professor replied. He placed his hands palms down on the table and let his eyes quickly study each of his Swiss interlocutors. What was he looking for in those faces as determinedly bland as their nation's foreign policy was determinedly neutral? Some hint of disapproval? Animosity perhaps?

"As I believe you all know, I am the Managing Director of the London office of the National Iranian Oil Company. As such, I am primarily responsible for the export of our nation's oil, our principal source of hard currency earnings."

He paused just a second. "This is not, as I am sure you are aware, an easy task. There are unfriendly powers who seek to put obstacles in our way. I don't need to tell you who they are or what tactics they employ. In any event, this is an intensely competitive and highly volatile business. If my price is one tenth of a cent a barrel better than my competitors, I get the contract. If not, I risk losing it. Therefore, it's vital for me to have a rapid, absolutely secure channel with which to communicate with my subordinates, one on which no one, and I mean absolutely no one, can eavesdrop."

The Professor's gaze had been moving from one Swiss to another as he spoke, looking for any hint of skepticism, or disbelief in the story he'd just attempted to sell them. It now returned to Herr Zurni. "I understand by the way that your Swiss banks encrypt their wire transfers when they're sending funds abroad."

"Yes," Zurni agreed, "they do. Most of them, I might add, use our equipment. They know that America's NSA intercepts all of our satellite transmissions looking for laundered money."

The Professor nodded. He was hardly surprised by Zurni's statement.

"The heart of my communications network would, of course, be in Tehran. London would be our secondary base and I estimate that I would need about thirty outstations. We might, on occasion, have to transmit by shortwave radio but the ideal would be to have a way to transmit totally secure written communications over satellite links."

"Certainly," smiled Herr Zurni. "A basic set of specifications and one we are quite prepared to meet. Professor, let me say a few words about the international marketplace for enciphering equipment. The Americans, we must all agree, make wonderful systems, IBM, Datotek, E-Systems. The new systems they run on the Cray 3 computer at the NSA are a marvel. Incredibly strong."

That was not exactly music to the Professor's ears. "I am aware of the Americans' abilities," he noted, a touch of acidity entering his tone, "even though I am not in awe of their society as a whole."

"Indeed. Now it is forbidden in the United States to export equipment or software programs for enciphering without a proper license. Those licenses fall into the same category as hi-tech weaponry and nuclear applications. To get a license, an American firm must provide their NSA with the neccessary technical information to allow the agency to decrypt any of the coded messages the purchaser transmits on the equipment he's bought from them."

"That doesn't make that equipment very secure, does it?"

"I'm afraid not. The Americans want to keep their ability to eavesdrop on terrorists and criminal organizations. We fully appreciate that concern and we would not knowingly sell our equipment to such people." A smile as large as the check he anticipated this morning's work would earn his firm illuminated Zurni's face. "Fortunately, no such concerns exist here."

"And are you here in Switzerland required to report the identities of your customers to your government?"

"Absolutely not."

Knowing when to bait the hook is a successful salesman's first rule and Zurni, shrewd salesman that he was, felt the time had come to set out his hook.

"Herr Sprecher," he asked the executive beside him. "Perhaps you could demonstrate for our guest how our systems work."

Herr Sprecher pressed a button under the table which lowered a display screen from the conference room ceiling, stood up, made a respectful half bow to the Professor and began his spiel.

"Most people assume that because there are 26 letters in the alphabet, a code will have to contain 26 characters. "A" becomes "S," or the number "7", "B," "X," or "19," and so on. That was the principle on which most World War II codes worked, the Germans' Enigma or the Japanese "Purple" machine. Modern coding systems do not work that way at all. A modern code can employ 50, 100, 200 characters depending on the model you have chosen. Let's take as an example the name "Mahmoud," a fairly common name in your language. It contains seven letters or characters, right?"

The Iranian nodded in agreement.

"I will employ for our demonstration one of our particularly strong 200 character codes. The first time the word "Mahmoud" will appear in a message encrypted in this code, it will come out looking like this. He pressed a button and *Z653AE#+K>* appeared on his screen. "Ten characters, rather than the seven you were expecting, right?"

"Interesting," agreed the Professor.

"The second time 'Mahmoud' comes up in that same enciphered text, this is how it will look." Sprecher pressed his button again and *BYT51PZ{&MD%* flashed onto the screen. "Twelve characters this time." He gave his button another squeeze and this time *U@(9W* appeared. "And here it is later in the text, now with only five characters, two less than in the name itself."

The Professor was mesmerized.

"The only way to decrypt those texts is to have the key to the code." Three times, Sprecher tweaked his button and with each tweak one of the garbled series of characters became "Mahmoud."

"What does the equipment that performs this work look like?" Bollahi asked.

Sprecher opened a drawer in the conference table and took out a black box. "Like this. Very much like your standard telephone answering machine. You hook one outlet of this box to your computer, the other to your outgoing telephone line or to a modem. You type up the message you want to send on your computer. You hit your 'enter' key and send the clear text of the message into the black box. The black box then converts the clear text into the encoded or enciphered text."

"What's in that little black box?"

"A micro-processor or a micro-chip if you like. What that chip is in reality, however, is an algorithm."

"A what?"

"An algorithm which is fundamentally a mathematical formula or an equation. Two times two equals four is a primitive algorithm. What is in our little black box is a string of mathematical formulations 100 kilobytes long, or approximately 50 full pages of text woven into of a single, inter-locking mathematical formula."

The Professor smiled. "Ah yes, of course. I had briefly forgotten my advanced calculus. And the secret code that you propose to sell us is there in that black box?"

"Not at all. The black box or the algorithm, if you will, is just the mechanical device which will turn your clear text into an encrypted message choosing its characters absolutely at random in response to the secret coding key with which you yourself—and no one else—has programmed it."

He picked up a black computer disc. "What you will do is program a code key for each of your stations onto a disc like this. You yourself will program each disc, selecting its code key from an almost infinite variety of possible code combinations. Then you will program the black box for Amsterdam with Code Key Number One, for example, the box for Prague with Code Key Number Two and so on until you have assigned each of your outstations its own code key."

"Each outstation's telephone number will be linked to the code key for that particular station in your headquarters box. So after you typed up a message for, let's say Amsterdam on your computer, you hit the 'enter' key. The black box will automatically encrypt the message in Code Key Number One, then dial the Amsterdam phone number and send on the encrypted text. The black box in Amsterdam will be programmed to recognize a message coming from your phone number and to know that that message will be in Code Key Number One. Using that key, it will automatically decrypt your message and display it on Amsterdam's computer screen."

"How," asked the Professor, "can I be absolutely certain that no one else is going to have a copy of those discs which you will be providing me?"

"Because when you get the discs they will be absolutely blank, unformatted. You can even use your own discs if you want for 100% security. The only information the coding discs will contain will be the information you yourself have put there. As I said, this is a 200 character system, as strong as any in the world. Its characters can be employed in an almost infinite variety of combinations in which the letter 'A', for example, can appear in a hundred different ways, all in one message. You and you alone will have the coding keys because you and you alone will have selected it for each of your stations."

Now the professor was smiling. Maybe this really is the way to outfox those American bastards at the NSA, he thought.

"It's a beautiful system," the appreciative Swiss acknowledged. "There can be no stealing. No human betrayal is possible. If someone breaks into your London office and steals your black box, you simply replace it with a new box onto which you've programmed a new key. Prague can't read Amsterdam's messages and vice-versa."

"How can I be absolutely certain this code of mine can't be broken?" the Professor asked. "We all know the Americans at the NSA intercept all satellite communications and try to break those that are in code."

"Oh, indeed, we know that. They can and will intercept your communications," the Swiss engineer acknowledged. "We can't prevent them from doing that nor can you. Their problem will be that what they will get in their intercepts will be pure garbage."

"Even with those super-powerful computers they have that people say can crunch their way through millions of possible permutations to break a code?"

"They won't crack this code."

"Why not?"

"The code with which we are going to equip you will have ten to the power of 100 possible permutations. That means that in order to break every possible combination of your code, the NSA's computers would have to run one thousand billion operations."

The dimensions of such figures boggled even the Professor's alert mind.

"Now you are aware, are you not, that a computer cannot compute faster than the speed of light because electrons cannot flow faster than that."

The Professor was well aware of that.

"Therefore, even using their most powerful, brute force computers non-stop, the NSA can only bust one million possible combinations of our code a second. To run them all would require a thousand years. Codes must be broken in hours, days at the most if they're going to be of any value to anybody. No one, I can assure you Herr Professor, is going to be able to break your code. Not the Americans. Not the English. Not the Israelis. No one."

The Professor snorted with such evident delight he was forced to pull out his handkerchief and blow his nose. This was it, he realized. This was a way at last to guarantee the security of his communications from penetration by his American enemies. "You've convinced me," he declared. "How much will the installation I require cost?"

Herr Zurni, the boss, took over again. "Each outstation is 65,000 Swiss francs, so thirty stations would be 1.95 million francs. The more powerful headquarters station is 200,000 francs and the software half a million. The total would come to 2.65 million Swiss francs or, in dollars."

"Deutschmarks, please," the Professor insisted.

Zurni took out his pocket calculator and announced, "Three million, three hundred-twelve thousand, five hundred deutschmarks."

The professor nodded in agreement, straining as he did to keep the smile from his face. He would have paid five times that for a system that would keep the secrets of Operation Khalid secure. He took out a check book on the Iranian Bank Melli in Munich and wrote out a check, signed it and passed it to Zurni.

"How soon will our equipment be available?"

"In less than four weeks, I promise," Zurni said, rising and extending his hand. "It's a pleasure to do business with you, Herr Professor."

A few minutes later, Zurni and his associates watched from his office window as the Iranian's Mercedes pulled away from their headquarters.

"Thomas," asked the engineer who'd briefed the Iranians, "how the hell can you be so sure those guys don't want that stuff for those Hezbollah people or some of the other terrorists outfits they run? What makes you so damn certain they're really into oil?"

"Certain?" Zurni laughed. "I'm certain of nothing. Except this." With that he flicked a fingernail against the check worth close to two million dollars which he held in his hand.

———

The 2000 kilos of raw opium Ghulam Hamid had purchased in Afghanistan's Helmand Province had finally been converted into morphine base in his primitive "lab" on the Afghanistan-Pakistani border. Aired, dried and sealed into one-kilogram plastic packs, the morphine base was ready for its onward journey to Iran at nightfall.

The drug caravans moved almost exclusively at night to avoid detection by the CIA's overhead satellites. A few years back, most of the traffic had moved by camel caravan. The animals could cover 40 kilometers (25 miles) in a night and earned their drivers a thousand rupees for each hundred miles they covered. There were even animals known as "homing camels" who moved from northern Afghanistan to Iran. Those camels had been, quite literally, addicted to opium by their drivers. They learned to move to their ultimate destination without human guidance by plodding along a series of familiar stopping places at each of which they knew they would get a bite of opium.

Now, the ships of the desert had been replaced by Toyota 4 x 4's, armed with rocket launchers, anti-aircraft pieces and heavy machine-guns. Hamid's 210 kilos of morphine base were loaded into five such vehicles.

The caravan passed through Spin Boldak, then headed into the sands of the Rigestan Desert. Navigating by compass and the stars, the five vehicles headed up a wadi, a dried out river bed. It was potentially a very dangerous thing to do. Heavy storms out of sight well to the north could occasionally turn those wadis into raging torrents. It was one of the ironies of this desert that a camel driver was more likely to drown on its sun-scorched wastes than he was to die of thirst on them.

———

Boring, boring, boring, Jim Duffy thought. How many intercepts had he gone through already this morning? Two hundred, three hundred? And all these idiots on those tapes could talk about was God, the weather, making money, or their sick grandmothers. Don't they ever play around in the mullah's Iran, cheat on their wives or partners? Anything that would put a little spice into this boring job they'd given him? When George Bush had the CIA, they said he loved to listen to intercepts of Leonid Breshnev talking baby talk with his mistress. Wasn't there anybody in Iran, Duffy wondered, into something fun like that?

He shook his head to force his mind back to business and called up a new intercept on his screen. This one was blessedly short.

"Jaffar?"
"Yes."
"Your shipment of 210 crates of apples (cough) will leave the day after tomorrow."

"Thank you. I'll be waiting for the driver's call."
"The day after (cough) tomorrow, God willing."

Well that was easy enough, Duffy thought, flicking a switch to bring up the next intercept. As he did, a red light blinked on his screen. It meant that the NSA officer feeding the texts to the computer wanted a word with him.

He picked up his direct link phone. "Duffy," he announced.

"That voice you just heard say anything to you?"

Duffy ran the intercept tape a second time, listening intently, trying to find any hint, any sound that might have recalled Said Djailani's voice. He tried to see his Gucci Mooj sitting there in front of him again in an ISI safe house, his pistol on the table between them, nibbling on the cardamon cookies Duffy always offered him and sipping sweet Iranian style tea. Try as hard as he could, Duffy couldn't find any note that reminded him of Djailani's voice on the tape. Unless, he realized, it was the man's cough.

Like most of his mooj, Djailani was a chain smoker and forever hacking up the contents of his lungs. But hell, how many heavy smokers were there out there with a cough like his? "I'd really be hard-pressed to find anything in there. Maybe, just maybe, a familiar echo in the guys cough. Why?"

"The conversation strikes me as odd. Do you figure those guys out there are on to the fact we're picking them up, reading them?"

"Listen pal," Duffy said. "You know what those guys in the Hezbollah in Baalbeck in the Bekaa Valley do when they have a message they want to send to Beirut? They write it out by hand, then send it down with a messenger. The messenger holds it up in front of the guy it's meant for, he reads it, then they burn it. That's how Goddamned security conscious they are. So why do you think that guy's talking in code?"

"That place he's calling from, Zabol. It's out there in the northeastern corner of Iran, over by the Afghan border. It's nowhere'sville. All they've got there is camel shit. And they sure as fucking hell don't have any apple trees."

"Ah, that's interesting. Good thinking, pal. Do you know who the number's registered to? Got a name?"

"Zabol General Trading."

"Where was he calling?"

"A number in Istanbul. It's a mobile so we haven't got a fix on it."

Duffy reflected a moment on his NSA colleague's concern. Was the guy just trying to be an amateur detective? Or could he possibly have something here?

"Have you got any other intercepts"—he glanced at the number, 98.5421.637.405 on his screen—"from that phone?"

"Negative. Presumably they must call Tehran from time to time but if they do it would be over a land line so we wouldn't pick it up."

Yeah, Duffy thought, technology has its limits in the spy business.

"How far back do you guys keep the innocuous crap you sweep out of the air? The stuff you're not programmed to look out for?"

"Sixty days."

Encourage the young officer, Duffy thought. Good management practice. And who knows? Maybe the guy has something. "What do you recommend? Do you think it would be worth our while to take a shot at running a voice signature analysis on that voice? Then crunching the result through your computer backlog to see if anything interesting drops out?"

"Yeah, I think it might. It's going to take time. Not the signature analysis. Running it through the backlog."

"Never mind. Let's do it."

————

The journey of Ghulam Hamid and his harvest of the poppy fields of Afghanistan's Helmand Province was coming to an end in a filthy warehouse four hundred miles east of Tehran. A jeep load of Iranian Pasdaran convoyed him up to the warehouse entrance. Far down the southern horizon he could just make out the rooftops of the remote market town the warehouse had once served. It was called Zabol.

Inside the warehouse, stinking of oil and grease, Hamid watched as his men began to unload his 210 kilos of morphine base from his jeeps. Each plastic pack was carried to a trestle table where it was weighed by a pair of Iranians. Occasionally, one of the Iranians would unseal a pack chosen at random, inspect its contents and verify its purity.

The process had almost been completed when Hamid sensed a stir at the far end of the warehouse. Turning towards the commotion, he saw a man in an Afghan Chitral hat and flowing robes moving towards him through a jostling crowd of Iranian hangers-on. This, he guessed, had to be the famous mujahiddin chieftain Said Djailani. He was well over six feet tall, towering over the Iranians around him like some Biblical prophet rising above his soldiery.

That impression only heightened as Djailani drew closer. He was, in a crude, unformed way, a strikingly handsome man with a dark black beard, blue eyes, a sharply hooked nose and eyebrows so thick you could, Hamid thought, grow potatoes in them. A dark brown mole surmounted by tufts of black hair grew from the base of his cheek at the left of his mouth giving him a striking resemblance to the photos Hamid had once seen of Saudi Arabia's great warrior king Ibn Saud as a young man.

When he reached Hamid, he made a slight but stately half-bow, touching as he did his hand to his forehead and heart. "The blessings of Allah be upon you, my brother," he intoned.

Hamid imitated his ritual gesture and, as he did, his downward glance revealed a twist of gold braid trimming the man's slippers, a touch of color curiously out of keeping with the drabness of the rest of his dress.

Djailani glanced at the trestle table where the process of verifying Hamid's delivery of morphine base was being completed. "My men tell me everything is in order. Congratulations, my brother." He gave a sharp clap to his hands and indicated a round, low table barely a foot off the ground a dozen yards to their right. "Come. We shall have tea and finish our business."

They moved to the table where Djailani sat, tribal style, on the ground. Hamid, his knee joints creaking in protest, joined him. A servant poured them each a steaming glass of green tea, the beverage Iranians usually preferred to the Arab's coffee. From inside the folds of his ample robes, Djailani drew out a pack of Marlboro cigarettes and lit one. Then he called for a sheet of paper, a pen and a rubber stamp. In very deliberate, beautifully formed Farsi letters, he began to write.

He might have been an ex-mujahiddin warrior with a beard infested by fleas, Hamid knew, but Djailani was an educated man. He could kill you with his bare hands, but he could write poetry with them, too. Djailani was a graduate of the Kabul Technical University. In fact, there was a story which had been circulating for years in Afghanistan that he had sought to enforce Islamic custom on his female fellow students by tossing acid in the faces of those who dared walk the campus unveiled.

When Djailani had finished, he stamped and signed the document and handed it to Hamid. It was an attestation of the fact Hamid had delivered to him 210 kilos of morphine base of acceptable quality to be compensated at the agreed to price of $1250 a kilo. Back in Quetta, Hamid would deliver that document to his employer, Mohammed Issa. That simple paper exchange was a part of an eastern banking system called "Hawala"—reference—in Urdu, "Hundi"—trust—in Hindi. Millions of dollars moved every day in Asia by the system. That paper was as good, as negotiable as a U.S. Treasury bond.

Their business done, Djailani sat back to contemplate his newly acquired morphine base. It was, by the size of the shipments he was used to handling, relatively modest. Poor Hamid had no idea, of course, that the price already agreed upon for the final delivery of his base to a lab in Istanbul was $4000 a kilo, a figure which would represent for the Iranians with whom Djailani was working, a profit of $577,500, more than eight times what Hamid had just made for his work.

That figure represented in a sense, the "transit tax" the Pasdaran and, behind them Iran's hardline mullahs, were charging to allow the base to pass through Iran. It was to Djailani a beautiful operation. It kept the dope out of Iran, away from the Faithful. Iran had once had a population of opium addicts second only to turn of the century China's in terms of the percentage of its population affected by the scourge.

Now, Djailani thought, they were making sure they passed that curse of the dope on to the rotten, debased youth of the west. It was like being able to speed the virus of the bubonic plague safely through one's own lands and then depositing it on the doorsteps of one's worst enemy.

———

Like most good diplomats, Ambassador James Longman was trained to express his condolences to a citizen mourning the loss of a loved one abroad with an unctuous sincerity worthy of the President of the American Society of Undertakers. And in the case of the woman sitting before him in his office at the U.S. Embassy in London, the ambassador was administering his ritual stroke with some genuine interest.

The murder of the lady's husband had, of course, made the front pages of all the British tabloids so he was quite familiar with its more lurid details. Nancy Harmian was dressed in black widow's weeds, but she was stunning. And she made her points with the intensity of La Passionaria haranguing the citizenry of Madrid during the Spanish Civil War.

"The police just won't listen to me," she asserted for the third time since their conversation had begun. "I keep telling them it was the Iranians who killed my husband. And what do they do? They keep asking me for more bank accounts as though the poor man was some kind of financial crook."

"Do you have any evidence at all that your husband was involved in any anti-regime activities?" the ambassador prodded.

"No. But why else would they have killed him?"

"Why indeed."

"Do you think it's the government, the Foreign Office interfering because they're afraid of offending that loathsome regime in Tehran?" The tension, the stress animating this beautiful woman was as palpable as in other times the aura of her perfume might have been.

"A Scotland Yard murder investigation, Mrs. Harmian? Quite frankly, no I don't. That would be most unusual indeed."

"Well, isn't there something you here at the embassy can do to get them to wake up to what I'm trying to tell them?"

The ambassador fixed his two index fingers together in an inverted "V" and pressed them to his lips, a gesture meant to underscore the judicious superiority of the observation taking shape in his diplomat's mind.

"You understand that we here in this house cannot attempt to intrude in anyway into an investigation being conducted by the police in our host country. Particularly when there are no American citizens involved."

"There must be something you can do."

"Yes. What I can do with your permission is pass what you have told me on to those people here in the embassy who are concerned with this sort of thing." He would never, of course, have murmured those dread initials CIA, but he noted from the reaction in Mrs. Harmian's eyes that he didn't have to. "They have their back channel ways of looking into such things."

"Back channel, side channel, it makes no difference to me," Nancy Harmian vowed. "All I want is one thing—justice for my poor, murdered husband."

Within an hour after she'd left the embassy, a minute of the ambassador's meeting with her was on the desk of the CIA's London Station Chief, Bob Cowie. He, too, had seen the details of the murder of Tari Harmian in the tabloids and had conducted his own routine investigation.

On the strength of her words to the ambassador, he made three calls, one to each of the Iranian dissident organizations with which the agency maintained contacts: a group of royalists in London, a more broadly based organization in Paris, and the old leftists of Beni Sadr and the Tudeh Party in Germany. The answer was the same from each. None of them had ever had any dealings with Harmian. He did not contribute to their cause. He only appeared to have been interested in keeping his head down and making money. The ambassador's minute went into Cowie's inactive files.

Shortly after sunrise on the morning following Ghulam Hamid's delivery of 210 kilos of morphine base to Said Djailani's warehouse, a five-axled Fruehauf TIR (Transport Inter-Europeene) truck with German license plates rolled into the building. It was just another of those enormous vehicles servicing modern Europe, one of the millions flowing back and forth from Dover to Istanbul, Copenhagen to Rostok, every day of the year. They were the arteries through which the lifeblood of European commerce flowed. They were also a smugglers dream and a customs officer's nightmare come true.

Smugglers' traps could and frequently were built into almost every imaginable hiding place on those trucks: in fender wells, packed inside the rubber of their massive spare tires, into secret compartments built into their flooring panels, their roofing or their side walls. And, in addition to those hiding places, of course, contraband or drugs could also be stashed somewhere in the trucks' diversified cargos, most often going to a variety of destinations.

Two experienced customs officers required sixteen hours to search a TIR truck for contraband. The consequence? Virtually none of the TIR trucks circulating in Europe were ever searched unless the police had precise information that they might contain illegal cargos.

The history of the huge trailer grinding into the warehouse was indeed interesting. Painted on its side panels was the logo of its owner of record, TNZ Freight Forwarding Services of Frankfurt, Germany. It was one of five trucks the company had in service.

TNZ was, in fact, owned by a holding company on the island of Jersey in the English Channel which acted on behalf of its real owner, an Iranian living in London. One of his three sons managed the firm's day to day operations in Frankfurt. Problem was, the other two sons were in jail in Tehran.

From 1991 to 1994, the father who was affiliated with an anti-mullah group based in Germany, had allowed his trucks to be used to run P4 plastic explosives into Iran where they were placed in the hands of anti-regime Marxist guerrillas. Unfortunately, one of those guerrillas had been caught red-handed with his plastic by the Pasdaran, the Revolutionary Guard. Under torture, he'd revealed where he had gotten it.

As it had happened, the owner's two younger sons were in Tehran at the time overseeing some of the company's normal business operations. They were arrested and their father in London informed that henceforth the only contraband his trucks were going to carry would be placed in them by the Iranian secret service. If anything should happen to those clandestine cargos enroute to their final destination, the father was informed, he would become the grieving parent of two dead sons.

The truck had already been loaded with its normal cargo, a variety of Iranian foodstuffs destined for a wholesale grocer in Hamburg who serviced the city's enormous Iranian expatriate community. A metal panel fixed onto the rear of the truck's platform just below its doors was removed. It concealed a hollowed out trap built into the trucks flooring. The trap was six feet long and accessed by an opening two feet wide and six inches deep. Ghulam Hamid's 210 plastic packs of morphine base were packed onto a wooden tray which slid neatly into the trap. The panel was then slipped back into place and smeared with grime and grease to make its presence virtually impossible to detect. The rear doors were locked shut and an obliging Customs Officer fixed an Iranian customs seal onto the doors. The truck left early the following morning enroute to the border crossing into Turkey at Gurbalak.

Now, the product of the opium fields of Helmand was on its way to its ultimate consumers, anonymous and almost undetectable, on the boundless ocean of world commerce.

BOOK THREE

One Foot in
PARADISE

It was a dream coming true at last, a dream that had been years in the making for Colonel Dimitri Wulff. Seconds before, the captain of his Cyprus Airways Flight 847 from Moscow had pronounced the magic phrase: "Ladies and Gentlemen, we are starting our descent into Larnaca International Airport." Peering out of his cabin window, Wulff could see a string of lights lacing Cyprus's shore, blinking diamonds on the field of night's black velvet. Could they mark the coastline of Limassol? Limassol, where Richard the Lion Heart had crowned his queen? Where he would shortly crown his own new queen, Nina, the red-headed, green-eyed ex-model twenty years his junior whose hand he now clutched so firmly in his own?

Wulff sighed and leaned his head back against his headrest. It was over. This was the culmination, the climax towards which he'd been scheming and striving, for what? More than six years now. In the battered red leather suitcase fitted under the seat in front of him were the keys for his passage to a promised land. How hard he had had to work to keep them safely hidden all these years from the prying eyes of his colleagues, his superiors, his wife. Now at last both he and they were safe in port, their long and fearful voyage done.

In that case, too, was his well worn prospectus for the Les Sirenes Condominium apartments on the Mediterranean seashore in Limassol. They would be his second destination on Cyprus. He and Nina had already selected their condo, a two bedroom apartment on the fifth floor with a balcony overlooking the silvery blue waters of the Mediterranean. They would spend the long, lazy mid-mornings on the beach under cloudless skies, lunch by the condo's Olympic swimming pool, sipping white wine in an atmosphere perfumed by lemon blossoms and lilacs, then make love to the point of exhaustion in the fading sunlight of the magic island at the crossroads of three continents, appropriately enough, the legendary birthplace of Aphrodite, the Greek Goddess of love and beauty.

How far all that would be from Moscow with its horizons as bleak as its prospects, its intrigues and its corruption, its atmosphere rancid with the fetid stink of a once great society collapsing into crime and chaos. Wulff had been a distinguished member of that society before Gorbachev and Yeltsin and Putin and all the other scum had turned the great socialist dream into a mafia nightmare. In his immaculately tailored uniform as a senior colonel in the Red Army's Elite Artillery Forces, Wulff had felt the respect, the admiration of his fellow citizens wherever he walked the streets of the old Soviet Union, whether in Moscow, Smolensk or Almaty. He had been a Privileged Person in the days before those swine had tried to turn him into what? A pauper. And his beloved Red Army to which he'd devoted his life, the pride of a great people, the fear of its enemies? What had they done to the world's greatest military force? Turned it into a shambles, ill-trained, ill-equipped, ill-disciplined, ill-fed, and ill-housed, incapable of defeating a gangster rabble from Chechnya. And the final, unforgiveable insult—unpaid. Well he, at least, had managed to survive the havoc they had wrought.

As their plane finally taxied to a halt at its gate, Wulff ended his little reverie. He leaned over to kiss Ninotchka on her cheek. "So, little one, it is done." Then he tucked his red leather case securely under his arm and led the way off the plane.

Once they'd passed the brief Cypriot immigration formalities, he led her to the baggage claim area.

"Wait here, darling," he said. "I have one thing I must do."

One of the features of the Republic of Cyprus is a set of corporate and banking laws meant to turn the island into a major center for off-shore banking and business operations. They have been remarkably successful. The streets of Nicosia, the capital, were now lined with the offices of banks from every major financial center in the world. Over 700 established enterprises had full fledged business offices on the island and small, private firms, thousands more.

Among the regulations—some preferred to say non-regulations—governing the island's financial activities was one which stipulated that any individual arriving in Cyprus was entitled to bring with him any amount of cash in any currency he chose to, provided only that he declare it upon his arrival. He was then free to deposit his currency in any one of the islands dozens of foreign banks and wire transfer it to any destination in the world. That was a facility much appreciated by the money launderers and tax evaders of this world.

While Nina waited for their bags to appear, the Colonel strolled over to the Currency Declaration desk adjacent to the baggage area to make out his declaration. Nothing in it surprised the bored Cypriot clerk manning the booth. After all, a recent holiday season, less than 50 foreign visitors had declared over $20M in various currencies on their arrival, enough to finance a few fairly elaborate vacations.

Clutching his battered case under his arm, Wulff returned to gather up Nina and their bags and marched her out to the taxi ranks where they took a taxi for the 30 mile (50 kilometer) trip to the Holiday Inn in Nicosia. Ever the cautious man, a trait developed in his years in the Red Army, Wulff decreed that they would order up room service and have their dinner in their suite. Their celebration would wait until tomorrow evening. One aspect of that celebration, however, was not going to be postponed. Wulff went to sleep an exhausted man, his resources joyously depleted by the inexorable demands of his young companion. Sliding off into that rapture inspired by their coupling, he had time for just one thought: he already had one foot in paradise.

Wulff was at the doors of the Sovereign Guarantee Trust on Makarios Boulevard when they opened at nine the next morning. As soon as he had explained the reason for his visit to the pretty, dark haired young Cypriot receptionist, he was escorted to the office of the bank's Senior Vice President for New Accounts, John Iannides.

Iannides ordered two cups of the dark and strong liquid which is *never* referred to on the Greek side of Cyprus as Turkish coffee and began to explain for the colonel's benefit some of the facilities the bank could offer to prospective clients. For example, the colonel might like to take advantage of Cypriot corporate laws to form an offshore company of his own. He could then shift the headquarters of his company to, say, the bank's main headquarters on the Cayman Islands, thus avoiding Cypriot income tax on any business the corporation might conduct outside the island.

For all the contempt in which he held Russia's new capitalist masters, Wulff was by no means ignorant of the intricacies of the free enterprise system. He was perfectly aware of the benefits forming his own corporation could offer and indicated to the banker that that was what he wished to do.

Iannides gave an approving nod to acknowledge the wisdom the colonel had just displayed. New Cypriot corporations, he explained, could not issue blank or bearer shares as was the case in certain notorious money laundering centers such as Panama. An expression similar to that which might have bespoiled Iannides' features had he bitten into one of the island's famous lemons crossed his face. It was meant to provide the colonel some indication of the enormity of the gulf setting the Cypriot Republic apart from banking havens such as Panama.

However, he hastened to add, if the colonel did not wish the shares in his corporation to be issued in the names of his shareholders, there was still a way under Cyprus law to keep the ownership of his corporation secret. The new corporation's shares would be issued to a nominee shareholder named by the colonel. For example, he, John Iannides, could appear on the shares as their nominee holder. Equipped with a power of attorney, he could then engage in business transactions on behalf of the corporation if the colonel desired. The colonel's identity as the real owner of the corporation's shares would be be locked into a private vault at the Central Bank of Cyprus. The Central Bank was sworn never to disclose the identity of a corporation's owner except in the case of a major, well documented criminal investigation.

That, the colonel agreed, seemed the wise thing to do. "If I wanted to buy a condominium in Limassol, the corporation could do it for me?"

Most certainly, Iannides informed him. "I as your Cypriot nominee will vouch to the Council of Ministers that the corporation and its owner possess no other residential property in the republic. That is the only requirement you have to meet. You will be authorized to buy your condo and to live in it as much as you like. And, as a retired foreign resident, your income tax here will be limited to just 5% of whatever income you choose to bring into Cyprus."

An expression of almost perfect happiness illuminated the colonel usually dour Slavic features. "Da," he said. "Let's do corporation."

Iannides drew the paperwork he would need to form a new corporation and open its bank account from his desk drawer.

"Your opening deposit will be . . . ?"

"One million, six hundred thousand dollars."

"In . . ."

"Cash."

The answer did not surprise Iannides who had seen the red leather case clutched in the colonel's hand when he'd entered his office. It could, of course, have contained another financial instrument, bearer bonds or gold deposit certificates, but few Russians had yet achieved that level of financial sophistication. Cash, usually dollars or deutschmarks, were the instruments they preferred. Nor was the sum the colonel had mentioned out of line with Iannides's past experience.

The colonel had leaned over, unbuttoned his shirt, and was stretching out a key from a chain hung around his neck with which he now unlocked his case. His treasure was stacked in sixteen piles of one thousand one hundred dollar bills—$100,000 in each pile. They were wrapped in the now yellowed folds of Pravda for April 19, 1992, the day that he had carefully counted them out, wrapped them into stacks and finally hidden them in his case in a hollow behind a panel he'd pried open at the back of the clothes closet of his Moscow apartment.

For years, one thought had almost paralyzed him with fear—that fire might sweep through his apartment and consume his treasure. He had even invoked the horrors of cancer or a heart attack to force his wife to join him in giving up smoking. And now at last, it was all here on a banker's desk, ready to disappear into the great anonymous ocean of the world's banking system.

Iannides let the colonel unwrap his little bundles by himself. The man was deriving so much tactile pleasure from the act it seemed a pity to deprive him of that delight. He, in the meantime, had taken a Brandt money counter from his drawer. Given the number of cash deposits they received, a good money counter identified a modern Cypriot banker as surely as a tin star had once marked sheriffs in the American west.

While the colonel watched wide-eyed, Iannides fed his piles of one hundred dollar bills through his counter with a whirring noise not unlike that made by a flight of partridges rising before a line of beaters. Sure enough, the colonel's count had been right, sixteen thousand one hundred dollar bills, $1.6M in all.

Iannides then turned to the paperwork necessary to set up the colonel's corporation and open its new account with the bank. That chore performed, there remained one last task to be completed, he explained, and then they would be through for the day.

"We deliver the currency which you gave us to the Central Bank of Cyprus. Once they've checked and verified it, they'll credit us with $1.6M and we can then credit your corporation's new account with that sum."

"There is," Iannides continued, "one formality we have to go through. There are a number of counterfeit American one hundred dollar bills in circulation. Are you aware of that?"

The colonel gave a shrug of substantial indifference. "Da. In Moscow some people say that. These not from Moscow."

"Good. What we have to do for our and your protection is photograph each of these bills before we send them on to the Central Bank. That way, if the Central Bank discovers any counterfeits in our deposits, we can establish who was the owner of the false bills and debit his account accordingly. To photograph them, we use a special board that can handle 400 bills at a time. So, for your deposit, we'll need 40 photos. Since this is your money, I'm sure you'll want to be there with us when the photos are taken. That way there'll be no question it's your money we're photographing and not someone else's. For that reason, we'll ask you to sign each photo as it's snapped. Is that agreeable?"

"I like to have my lunch in Limassol."

"No problem at all. We'll have you out of here in plenty of time for that. In fact, I'll order up a bank car to run you down there when we're through."

Wulff smiled. These people were treating him with respect, the way he'd been treated in the old Soviet Union before those reforming bastards seized power.

Iannides led him into the photo room. A plywood board studded with niches the size of a hundred dollar bill lay on a flat topped table. The first four hundred of the colonel's bills were laid by one by one into each slot. At the center was a card bearing his name, passport number and the date he'd entered Cyprus. The camera was overhead. When the board was ready, the lights were dimmed, the picture snapped and the process then repeated with four hundred new bills.

They were finished well before noon. Iannides escorted the colonel down to the waiting bank car.

"Enjoy your lunch," he urged. "The corporate paperwork will be completed in 48 hours and then you can go ahead with the purchase of your new Cypriot home if you like. As Othello says in Shakespeare's great play, 'Welcome, sir, to Cyprus.'"

———

It was late afternoon in Nicosia when John Iannides returned to his bank from lunch. By then, the photo rolls of the colonel's one hundred dollar bills had been developed and printed. The bills themselves had already been wrapped into bundles and sent to the Central Bank in an armoured car. Partially out of prudence, partially out of curiousity,

Iannides decided to do a quick spotcheck for himself of one of the photo rolls to see if by any chance a few counterfeit bills had found their way into the colonel's collection. He asked his photographer to select one of the rolls at random and bring it up to him.

Iannides spread the roll on his desk and began to study it. He was no expert when it came to detecting the ultra-sophisticated counterfeits of the U.S. one hundred dollar bills baptised the "Superbill." Very few people were. The bill was the most realistic piece of counterfeit money ever made, a false note so good the U.S. government had finally been forced to begin circulating a new one hundred dollar note in February 1996. So as not to panic the world's currency markets, however, the U.S. Treasury did not recall the old bills and as a result, millions of dollars worth of fakes remained in circulation. Like most bankers around the world, Iannides had been provided with a set of guidelines by the U.S. Treasury to help him spot the counterfeit bills.

He relied on just one of them in making his spot checks. With a magnifying glass, he examined the 13 five-pointed stars ringing the seal of the U.S. Treasury on the right hand side of the face of each bill. On the good bills, the points of the stars were all precise and clearly defined. On the fakes, two of the stars lacked precision and sharp definition as though, perhaps, the instrument employed by the engraver who'd forged the plates from which they'd been printed had gone dull from use.

It wasn't an easy job. He had to peer and squint closely at each bill before deciding if it was real or a fake. By the time he got to the bottom of the first column of the colonel's bills, Iannides was horrified. Seven of the twenty bills were, by his calculation, counterfeits.

Taking up a red grease pencil to mark each bill he suspected of being false, Iannides set to work to check the remaining bills on his photo roll. The result was a disaster. He had marked almost half of the bills as potential fakes. If his calculations turned out to be correct when those bills had been run past the currency expert at the Central Bank, half of the colonel's little treasure trove was going to go into the incinerator. He was going to be a very unhappy camper, indeed, when they gave him that bit of news.

That also presented Iannides with a little practical dilemma. Under international banking practice, if a banker was presented with counterfeit notes by a client he felt was acting in perfectly good faith, the banker's only obligation was to see that the notes were destroyed. If on the other hand, he felt his client was attempting to force forgeries into the banking system, then he was supposed to call in the police.

Iannides reflected on his meeting with the colonel. To come into a bank and put a suitcase half full of counterfeit bills on a banker's table for deposit, a man had to be either crazy or acting in good faith. The colonel, he was convinced, was not crazy. Everyone knew there were hustlers in Russia pushing these fake notes. The colonel must have been screwed by one of them. Iannides did, however, feel that he was obligated to pick up his phone, call the Central Bank and advise them to go over the truckload of bills he'd just sent them very carefully.

They already had. Because of the enormous amount of currency being funnelled into Cyprus, the bank had an expert trained by the U.S. Treasury to detect the fake U.S. Superbills. His run at the colonels money pile had born out Iannides suspicions. Over half of the Colonel's bills were counterfeit.

The procedure he followed in such cases was straightforward. The U.S. Treasury had a Secret Service agent stationed in Cyprus. He was called in and given the fake bills, already stamped "Counterfeit" by the Central Bank, for destruction. The Secret Service Agent, of course, asked where the notes had come from. Since the banker who'd sent them to the Central Bank had said he felt he was dealing with a good faith transaction and not an attempted crime, the Secret Service Agent got a stony stare for a reply. The answer to his question involved bank secrecy and the Cypriots did not chose to lift the veil on such matters unless someone put the proof of a serious crime in their hands.

What the banker did do, however, as soon as the Secret Service agent had left, was call the officer in charge of the fraud squad of the Cypriot police and report the details of the matter to him for his records. The officer then entered that information into the Nicosia police computer data bank together with the name of the Russian colonel who'd submitted the fake bills to his banker, his passport number and the date he'd entered Cyprus.

———

"Mr. Duffy?"

"What do you want?" Jim Duffy looked up from yet another mesmerizingly interesting intercept, this one dealing with the failure of a mullah in Ahvaz to deliver sufficiently fiery Friday sermons in his mosque.

"Mr. Lohnes wonders if you could come up to see him on the seventh floor," his visitor asked.

"I'd walk up the stairs on my hands to get away from this crap." Duffy replied shutting down his computer.

The office suite of the DDO, Deputy Director for Operations, adjoined the director's with huge windows looking out across the agency's front entrance towards the Virginia countryside. Like the director's, it had its own kitchen and dining facilities and a dressing room. Mine by all rights, Duffy thought, his stomach souring with anger as he walked in. Stop, he told himself. Do like Shirley MacLaine says—forget about those negative emotions.

"Jimbo!" It was Jack Lohnes coming into the anteroom of his suite to greet him. "Any luck with those intercepts?"

"Fuck all."

"Never mind. I think we've got something that beats the hell out of intercepts for you." Lohnes took him into his inner office. They sat down in Jack's couch and easy chair corner next to a young officer Jim didn't know and Jack didn't bother to introduce. The coffee was already waiting.

"When you left, had we gotten into this business of the counterfeit one hundred dollar bill?" Lohnes asked. "The note the Treasury baptised the 'Superbill?'"

"Yeah. It was showing up in Beirut in volume. As I recall we couldn't make up our minds who was doing the counterfeiting, the Syrians or the Iranians."

"Well, we finally figured it out. It was the Iranians. They started pumping the bill into Lebanon to the Hezbollah so those guys could finance their social programs, rebuilding the houses of the faithful destroyed in Israeli raids, setting up new community centers, schools, stuff like that. Then, when they saw how good their funny money was, the ayatollahs started slipping it into the international currency markets."

"I suppose that's why we wound up putting out a new one hundred dollar bill."

"You bet your ass it was. That damn fake note of theirs was so good the Federal Reserve had to recalibrate its own counterfeit detection machines in order to pick it up. Can you imagine? The ayatollahs forced us to make the first major change in our currency in 75 years. Rubin and the suits over at the Treasury were scared shitless the thing would break into a big public scandal and start a run all around the world on the hundred dollar bill. You know, we've got 380 billion dollars in currency floating around out there, two thirds of it off-shore and a helluva a lot of it in one hundred dollar bills. A whopping big, interest free loan to Uncle Sam. Blow a hole in that when you're trying to cut your budget deficit and see how much good it does you."

"How the hell did the Iranians pull it off? Since when were they supposed to be master forgers?"

"You know when you pick up a new bill and rub it through your fingers, you think you can fell ridges in it, right?"

Duffy nodded.

"That's because of the way the money's printed. The Bureau of Engraving and Printing uses an Italian process, a thing they call Intaglio printing. To do it you need these huge, sixty ton presses that can exert enormous pressures per square inch. Only two companies in the world make those presses, the one here that supplies the Bureau of Engraving and Printing and one in Lausanne, Switzerland."

"You're not going to try to make me believe the Swiss set the ayatollahs up in the counterfeiting business?"

"Oh, hell no." Lohnes had started to clean his fingernails with a bent paperclip and for a second his concentration wandered. "It was the Shah. He bought two of those Swiss presses in the mid-seventies so he could start printing up his own currency like a big boy. The Bank of England was printing his rials for him in those days. The Swiss, the De La Rue Giori Company, installed the presses for him, one up in Shimran in the suburbs of Tehran near his summer palace and one in Karaj, about 25 miles northwest of there. But along came the revolution. The poor old Shah never got to use them. The presses just sat there for years collecting dust. Then sometime in the mid-eighties when the ayatollahs were running out of money because of the war with Iraq some bright guy said, 'Hey, why don't we use those presses the Shah bought and print up some dollars of our own? Solve our liquidity problem?'"

Lohnes flicked his bent paperclip into a spotlessly clean ashtray. "They got the East Germans, the Stasi, to find them a couple of expert engravers in Leipzig to make fake plates for them. We still don't know where they got the paper which is very, very close to what we use."

"How many of these damn things did they make?"

"Nobody knows. Treasury admits publicly to ten billion dollars worth. That's a joke. In the intelligence community they think it's well over twenty billion."

"And they got away with this, ripping off poor old Uncle Sam like no one in history ever has? And nobody let out a peep? Poor old John Q. Public in this country still hasn't got a clue about what happened to his precious U.S. dollar?"

"Counterfeiting is the responsibility of the Secret Service and they did a lousy job on this one. We turned up pretty hard evidence from the intercepts by the fall of 1994 that the Iranians were doing it but we couldn't get the Treasury to buy it."

"Why the hell not?"

"They were scared. How would the markets react? All that crap."

Duffy chuckled. Few things brought him greater pleasure than contemplating the discomfort of government bureaucrats.

"Anyway, then we stationed a satellite over Tehran and got some lovely photos of those bastards carting their nice new fake bills out to trucks to take them to market, so to speak. This time the administration had to believe us whether they wanted to or not."

"And they all sat down and cried, I suppose."

"No. For once, they showed some balls. We sent a little delegation out to Nicosia to meet secretly with the Iranians. Told them to knock it off or there were going to be an awful lot of stiff necks in Tehran from looking up at the cruise missiles whizzing by."

"They stopped?"

Lohnes shrugged. "We think they've at least slowed down. But Treasury keeps a sharp watch out for the fake bills which brings us to why you're here. Yesterday the Central Bank in Cyprus got almost a million bucks in fake bills delivered to them."

Duffy whistled softly.

"Of course we asked the Cypriots who'd deposited the money and, of course, they told us to fuck off, it was bank secrecy." Now Lohnes was smiling an expression of infinite satisfaction—an enemy might have said smugness. "They reported it to their police, however. It's the procedure they follow."

He turned to the young man he'd failed to introduce to Duffy at the beginning of their meeting. "What you're about to hear, Jimbo, is need to know on the most restricted basis. The program we're going to tell you about is as secret as anything in this building gets these days."

The young man blinked behind his thick horn rimmed glasses. "I'm the DDO's computer nerd, Mr. Duffy." Duffy still hadn't been given his name. "The Cyprus police use a special software program to organize their data base. They don't know it, but it's made across the river in Maryland. It gets marketed to police departments all around the world through a company in Hamburg, Germany as though it was German made. To disguise its U.S. origins."

Hey, Duffy thought, that's smart.

"What's great about this particular software program is that it's got a trap door, a kind of a Trojan Horse if you will, built into it. It allows us to gain secret access to the computers that are running the program. All we have to do is log onto the computer of a police department out there in the Third World that uses it via its modem, flash in what we call a secret super-user password, and we can download what they've got in their data base without leaving any record that we've been in their computer. It's a great way for us to get our hands on the files of terrorists from some of these people like the Greeks who are notoriously uncooperative when it comes to international terrorism."

"Now I understand why that program's Top Secret."

"Jim," said Lohnes, "when we got that Secret Service report about the fake bills turning up in Cyprus last night we went into the Nicosia police department's data base to see what they had on the report. The deposit was made by an ex-Red Army colonel named Dimitri Wulff. He arrived in Cyrus forty-eight hours ago."

Lohnes paused. "Now here's what's critical. We ran his name through the Moscow Station's files. He was in the elite rocket corps of the Red Artillery—their tactical nuke force. Stationed in Ulba in Kazakhstan in the spring of 1992 when they were cleaning out their nukes. You'll remember as the director told you last week, we got that report about the Iranians getting three nukes out of there—the report we were never able to either authenticate or knock down once and for all. Well, Colonel Wulff's assignment to Kazakhstan fits right into that time frame"

"Holy shit!" Duffy exclaimed. "Is that guy still on Cyprus?"

"As far as we know."

"How fast can I get there?"

———

"That's him."

With an almost imperceptible gesture of his head, the CIA's Nicosia Station Chief indicated a heavy-set man slumped over a barely touched plate of *moussaka* in a booth of their *taverna*. At his elbow was a bottle of vodka. He had made considerably more progress working his way through the vodka than he had attacking the food on his dinner plate.

"I guess he's gotten the good news that his pension fund is going to be about a million bucks short." Jim Duffy snorted.

"Oh, the bank didn't waste any time passing that on to him. I mean there are always wonderful folk out there anxious to bring you bad news." The Station Chief sipped tentatively at the beer he'd ordered to cover their presence in the *taverna*. "He arrived here with a redheaded bimbo half his age," he whispered. "She took off for Moscow yesterday. Probably figured he wasn't going to be quite the red hot lover she thought he would be now that he was a million bucks light at the bank."

Beyond the windows overlooking the colonel's booth, Duffy could see the stately outlines of old Nicosia's 16th century Venetian walls. Feigning a fascination with those ancient stones, he studied his target with a series of quick, surreptitious glances. The capacity of Red Army colonels to absorb alcohol was the stuff of legends. It looked to Duffy as though the Russian had gone through two-thirds of a bottle of vodka. He had to be pretty well pissed.

Watching him, however, he couldn't detect any tell tale signs of it. Occasionally, his shoulders would start to sway but the Russian checked their movement with the instinctive reflexes of an accomplished drinker. The man had a head of thick neatly groomed, silvery hair. His eyebrows, also silvery gray, seemed from the distance to cover half his forehead. His face was puffed and flushed. That would be the vodka not the great outdoors. The shoulders hunched over his dinner plate were thick and powerful as was the massive fist that enveloped the glass beside his vodka bottle.

What we have here, Duffy guessed, is your old Soviet man, sprung from the proletariat, brought up to defend the great Marxist Leninist Revolution. Probably joined the Red Army after watching one of those propaganda movies about the Great Patriotic War. He would still be a firm believer, despite—or because of—everything that had happened since 1989. Like the Irish Catholic kid the Jesuits caught when he was young. Might never see the inside of a church later in life, but you'd better believe the faith was still there, seared into his soul for all eternity.

How do I go after him, Duffy wondered? Sail straight into him? Duffy's Russian was fluent. He'd majored in the language at Oklahoma which was why the CIA had come to call on him in the first place. He was probably the first second-string All-American linebacker in a decade who spoke fluent Russian.

As he watched, he saw the colonel grab the bottle and pour an inch of vodka into his glass. His hand was rock steady. He swirled the liquor for a moment then gulped it down in one swallow, Red Army style.

You had to figure two things, Duffy thought. First, he's got to be feeling very sorry for himself. That was probably why he was pouring the vodka down his throat like there was no tomorrow. Vodka was, after all, the prime lubricant of Russian melancholy and here was a guy with very good reason to be melancholy. Second, suppose it really was the Iranians who'd passed him those fake bills? Did he know that they were the good folk who were making them? To stiff assholes like him? And if he didn't know that, just what would be his reaction if someone passed him those glad tidings? Disbelief? Would he be furious that he'd been had? Furious enough to tell Duffy what the agency wanted to know?

"Order us something to eat and a bottle of vodka," he instructed the Station Chief. "I'll let him get through the rest of his bottle while I'm lining my stomach."

Twenty minutes later, Duffy saw that the colonel was nearing the end of his bottle. He swept up his own and walked over to the colonel's booth. "*Mir y drushba*—peace and friendship," he said, holding his bottle out. "Let me share some of this with you." He laughed heartily. "In the spirit of our new world."

He poured an inch of vodka into the colonel's glass and slid, unbidden, into his booth. The Russians eyes were red-rimmed. Had he been weeping? For his lost million bucks? His red head? Duffy clinked his glass to the colonel's. "Good health, sir. Beautiful island, Cyprus, isn't it?"

The Russian tossed back his vodka with a gulp and a grunt. "I guess so."

"You here on vacation?"

The colonel looked puzzled as though for a moment he could no longer quite remember what he was doing on the island. What business was it of this brash American what he was doing here anyway? So like the Americans. Loud. Always poking their noses into other people's business. Still, the man did have a fresh bottle of vodka. "Da," he reluctantly acknowledged, eyeing the bottle. "Vacation."

"Gee," Duffy laced his reply with the proper mix of envy and admiration. "You're real lucky. Unfortunately, I'm here to work, not play."

Americans, the colonel knew, always seemed obsessed by two things, where they came from and their work. Their first words after "hello" were usually "where are you from?" or "what do you do?" Since he didn't give a damn where this man came from, it seemed the polite thing to do to ask him the second question. "What you do?"

"I'm in the money business."

"You make lots of it?"

"Wish I did. No, I go after people who do."

A flash of wisdom illuminated the vodka fogging the colonel's brain. "Ah. You tax man."

Duffy laughed, then leaned closer to the colonel as though he was about to impart to this perfect stranger a particularly weighty bit of truth. "I'm an expert on counterfeit money with the Chase Manhattan Bank. You see, we Americans have a terrible problem." As he was saying this, Duffy was slipping two one hundred dollar bills from his pocket.

A veil of suspicion, meanwhile, had flickered across the colonel's regard, precisely the emotion Duffy wanted to stir.

He spread his bills on their table. "This bill," he said picking up a new note, "is genuine. But this one"—he now had the Superbill in his hand—"is a fake." Swiftly he pointed out its few, almost invisible flaws. "Best counterfeit ever made. You know who makes it?"

By now the flicker of suspicion on the colonel's face had turned into a full-fledged storm cloud. Nonetheless, he shook his head in a way that indicated his ignorance of the answer to Duffy's question was real, not feigned. OK, pal, Duffy thought, I'll turn the lights on for you and see how you react.

"The Iranians."

"Iranians!" There was no mistaking this time just how genuine was the surprise, the shock in the colonel's voice. "Not possible!"

"One hundred percent certain, my friend. They make them in Tehran. Printed twenty billion dollars worth of the damn things. Passed them out right and left to a whole lot of poor suckers who had no idea they were being had."

"Those bastards!" The words shot out of the colonel's mouth in a growl so menacing it told Duffy everything he wanted to know. With a slow, very deliberate motion he leaned back against the cushion of their booth, slipped the good bill back into his pocket and held the fake up in his hand. For a second he stared at it.

"Yeah, they've hurt a lot of people with these things. Particularly in your country. Shattered a lot of dreams."

The colonel meanwhile, had poured himself a hefty shot of vodka from Duffy's bottle and tossed it down. "Bastards!" he growled again.

"They're bastards, alright." Duffy's face was illuminated by the artificial glow of a mirthless smile. Time to take the mask off. "Colonel Dimitri Wulff, let be up front with you."

"You know my name!"

"Of course, I know your name. I also know that you deposited close to a million dollars of these fakes at the Sovereign Trust on Monday morning. And that you were stationed in Ulba in Kazakhstan in 1992."

"So!" The force hissed out of the colonel's voice like the air escaping from a child's balloon that's just been punctured. "You're CIA. That's who you are."

Duffy shrugged. "If you wish. The important thing here is that we're friends now. We can work together. You help me, I help you."

"You get my million dollars back?"

"I'm afraid nobody can do that for you. They went up in smoke in an incinerator at the embassy a couple of days ago. But I think I can help keep some people off your back. If you tell me exactly what it was you sold the Iranians for that dough. How you did it."

"I tell you nothing."

Once again, Duffy made what was meant to be a shrug of monumental indifference. "You're an artillery officer. Ever heard of that Canadian guy, Bull?"

"Never."

"He was the guy who was developing a long range artillery piece for the Iraqis. Got shot very dead in Brussels one night."

"By who?"

"Your guess is as good as mine. But tell me, do you know how far we are from Tel Aviv here? A twenty minute ride on an airplane. Now if it was the Mossad who did Mr. Bull that night because they didn't take too kindly to a guy building the Iraqis a cannon that could dump artillery shells onto Tel Aviv, how do you think they'd react to the good news that a Russian Colonel who'd sold nukes to the Iranians was staying in Room 306 of the Holiday Inn in Nicosia? Fly in here to give him, say, a medal? I mean how do you figure on spending that $600,000 you've got left in the next two hours? Before they can get here?"

"You bastard, American."

"Oh, that I can be, my friend, that I can be. But you tell me about those nukes you sold the Iranians and I'll forget I ever met you. Otherwise I just might decide to tell some friends of mine in the Mossad where they can find you. It's all up to you." Duffy poured some more vodka into Wulff's glass. "Here. Have something to drink. It'll help you think straight."

"Why you say nuclear?"

"Because I don't see the ayatollahs paying one point six million for high grade TNT."

The colonel gulped down the vodka Duffy had poured for him. Once again his shoulders started into their gentle swaying motion. This time, however, his reflexes failed to check their movement. "They paid two million."

"So where did the Iranians make contact?" Duffy pressed. "In Ulba?"

"No. I was on leave in Almaty."

Despite the vodka fogging his brain, the colonel could see the scene as clearly as if he were reliving it again. He'd been at a reception at the newly opened embassy, in full uniform with all his decorations on, when the two Iranians came up to him. They immediately showed him a kind of respect, a deference Red Army colonels rarely encountered those days in Moscow. The senior of the two, the one the other referred to as "Professor" was an elegant, well-dressed man—even if he did have a three day growth of hair on his face. Like a good Moslem, he was drinking fruit juice.

Later, as they were leaving, the Professor came up to him. "Colonel," he said, "I would like to see you again. In more discreet surroundings, perhaps."

Wulff had said nothing in reply.

"Tomorrow," the Professor had continued, "I am going to visit the Zenkov Cathedral. Unusual for a Moslem, no? Afterwards, at two o'clock I will be on a bench at the gate to Panfilov Park opposite the entrance to the cathedral. I think you will find what I have to suggest to you very interesting."

Curious, Wulff had gone as the Professor had suggested.

"A work of matchless beauty," the Professor said gesturing to the pink and white facades on the cathedral. "The largest wooden church in the world. And built without the use of a single nail. A triumph I as an engineer can admire."

Wulff had not replied. He always preferred to let others talk.

"A pity if such a great edifice were to be destroyed—the way they are now destroying your once great nation." For ten minutes the Professor had lamented the collapse of the USSR, however unlikely such a sentiment might have seemed in a devout Moslem. "Your world is crumbling all around you, my dear colonel, the world you believed in, that you served so well. You and people like you are going to be discarded on the junk pile of history by those people in Moscow." On and on he went painting what turned out to be a dismayingly accurate picture of Russia and the colonel's future. Then he had proposed his solution, his way out of the misery awaiting the colonel.

"What was he after?" Duffy quietly asked. "Intermediate Range Ballistic Missile warheads?"

The colonel dismissed that with a toss of his head. "I had never even seen such things."

"How about nuclear artillery shells? You sure as hell had seen those."

Wulff turned a look that blended hate and hopelessness on Duffy. "Of course I had seen them. They were my speciality as I'm sure you know."

Duffy was indifferent to the colonel's hate. It was the hopelessness that was now spurring him on.

"So how many did you sell him?"

"Three."

"What caliber?"

"152 millimeters."

"Was it difficult? Smuggling them out?"

The colonel snorted and then poured himself more vodka. "Simple. Everything was so confused in those days. Our 152 millimeter nuclear shell is marked by two red steel bands around its barrel. To set them apart from high explosive shells. We took three shells from the high explosive vault, put bands around them and then we substituted them for three shells from the nuclear stockpile."

"You had help?"

"My duty sergeant."

"How did you get them out?"

"I was responsible for the security of the nuclear stockpile. I assigned my sergeant to guard duty one night, we loaded them into my official car and drove away."

"Listen, Dimitri, didn't it ever occur to you they might wind up using those things against you one of these days?"

"You are crazy. Never they would do such a mad thing. They wanted them so they could use them against the Jews."

The tone of voice in which the colonel uttered that phrase made it clear that, as it was the case with so many Russians, anti-Semitism was endemic to his soul. The use to which his benefactors might one day put his shells had not unduly disturbed him.

"And you drove off, met this Professor type and handed the shells over to him in the middle of the night?"

"Da. We met by the side of the road on the steppes and he and two of his people, they took the shells from the car. Then he gave me a suitcase that was supposed to have two million dollars in it. Four hundred thousand for my sergeant, the rest for me. Bastards! Almost all of them fake."

Duffy's answering laugh was notable for its lack of genuine merriment. "Hey, pal, what can I tell you? Life's a bitch."

———

The Deputies Closed Circuit Conference is a relatively recent innovation in Washington crisis management. Originally, it was designed as a way of keeping the White House press corps ignorant of the fact a crisis was brewing by avoiding a parade of chauffeur driven limos delivering the capitol's bigwigs to the White House. That spectacle always shrieked "crisis" to the watching reporters.

The conferences linked up the second-in-command in each of the agencies involved with the national security—State, Defense, the Joint Chiefs, the CIA, the FBI, Justice, Homeland Security, and the National Security Council—on a secure, closed-circuit TV channel. The conferences have proven to be such an easy and efficient way to conduct business that they are now an almost daily occurrence, crisis or no crisis.

The meetings are usually chaired by either the National Security Advisor or her deputy and run from the NSC conference room in the White House basement. On the afternoon of his return from Cyprus, Jim Duffy was summoned to Langley's seventh floor conference room to participate at the side of the agency's Deputy Director. In view of the importance of the business at hand, the President's National Security Advisor herself took the chair. "As if we didn't have enough to concern ourselves with already in this damnable Axis of Evil, what with the North Koreans and the after effects of our campaign in Iraq," she began. "We have before us today a new matter of grave national concern. As many of you are aware, we have been concerned for some time with a report that the Iranians managed to obtain three nuclear devices in Kazakhstan while the Russians were closing down the Soviet nuclear installations there. Despite all of our efforts employing our best human and scientific resources, we were unable to establish whether the report was true or not. I am sorry to say that we now have hard, incontrovertible, evidence that the report is indeed true. The Iranians possess three 152 millimeter nuclear artillery shells sold to them by a renegade Red Army colonel."

She turned to Duffy's image on her TV screen. "Jim," she said. "Tell the folk what you discovered."

There was a reflective silence on the audio system when Duffy had finished his report. Then the Deputy Secretary of State said, in an audible half-whisper, "The President's worst nightmare!"

"I've asked Dr. Leigh Stein, a senior nuclear weapons designer from Los Alamos on temporary duty at the Department of Energy to link up with us and brief us on the significance of this development," the National Security Advisor announced. "Leigh."

A balding man with thick horn-rimmed glasses and the intense air of a professor lecturing a particularly dim-witted group of pupils appeared on the Energy Department's camera. "From what I've been told, these shells clearly belong to the most recent generation of Soviet nuclear artillery. They employ Plutonium 239 as their core fissile material."

"How much explosive force would they generate?" the Deputy Secretary of State asked.

"As they're presently configured, not very much. These things were designed for use against massed armored formations. I mean, you wouldn't waste one on a platoon of infantry. Their yield would be in the low kiloton range."

Because of the nature of their closed circuit TV hook-up, Stein could not see all the members of his audience, but he could sense the enormity of their relief at his words. "Thank God," a voice off-camera somewhere said. "Baby nukes. What the hell can they do with them?"

"I said 'as presently configured' gentlemen," Stein warned. "I somehow don't see the Iranians stuffing these shells into a howitzer and firing them at somebody. Who would they fire them at? Fishermen on the Caspian Sea?"

"So then just what the hell can they do with them?" It was the National Security Advisor, an edge of uneasiness entering her voice. "Just how much of a threat do they represent?"

"No one can answer that question—except the Iranians themselves, of course. The best we can do is guess. But if I had to make a guess it is this: they will extract the plutonium cores from each of those shells, then try to reconfigure them to produce devices capable of giving them a much more powerful explosion."

"How much more powerful?"

"Potentially, if they're able to reconfigure those cores to get the maximum explosive efficiency out of them, they could get up to 30 kilotons—enough to devastate any city on the face of this earth."

Now the men in Dr. Stein's unseen audience reacted at his words. From some came a series of plainly audible gasps.

"Jesus Christ!" exclaimed the Deputy Secretary of State. "You're telling us the Iranians now have the means to destroy Israel?"

"In the circumstances, my friend," chuckled the National Security Advisor, "I think you'd be well advised to invoke the name of another prophet. The fact is, however, we have the potential for a ghastly problem on our hands. This is the President's nightmare come true—weapons of mass destruction in terrorist hands. It was the fear of that that was really behind the Iraq assault, wasn't it?"

"But could the Iranians do this?" someone finally asked. "Are they really capable of doing what you're suggesting? Are they scientifically sophisticated enough to reconfigure these things properly?"

An attractive woman suddenly appeared on the Department of Energy's camera, obviously prepared to answer the question. It belonged to Dr. Jean "Rocky" Robotham, a Ph.D. in nuclear physics from Michigan, the Deputy Secretary of Energy. At 42, she was one of the senior nuclear physicists in the country yet she radiated the charm and poise of an afternoon talk show hostess. "I hate to have to tell you this, but I think they are. There's a certain arrogance in the West that tends to ignore the fact the Third World is full of first-rate scientists entirely capable of producing their own super weapons. Intellectually, the Iranian scientific infrastructure is far superior to the Iraqis' and look how far down the road to nuclear weapons the Iraqis got."

She paused. Dr. Robotham's previous charge had been running the Department of Energy's NEST—Nuclear Explosive Search Teams. The nightmare being contemplated on these TV monitors had been her constant concern for five years. "The main barrier keeping nations like Iran or Iraq from getting nuclear weapons has always been the difficulty they faced in getting their hands on the fissile material needed to make a weapon. In this case with Iran, that barrier has apparently just come down. Now all they're going to need is money and the means to smuggle some hi-tech equipment out of the west. The brains they've got. Don't forget the Iranians' nuclear program goes back over twenty years to the Shah's days."

"Dr. Robotham, how would they do it? And what can we do to stop them succeeding?" the National Security Advisor pressed.

Two faces, Dr. Stein's and Dr. Robotham's, appeared on the screen. The admiration illuminating Dr. Stein's glance at his colleague was not exclusively scientific in nature. "Rocky," he noted, "why don't you give them the weapons design lecture? You're a much better teacher than I am."

His fellow scientist radiated the smile of an Oprah Winfrey welcoming a particularly felicitous question.

"Alright," she said. "I'll try not to get too technical for you as I take you through this, but if I do, just stop me. As Dr. Stein told you, what they're going to have to do to get the maximum explosive yield out of the plutonium 239 metal making up those shells is reconfigure them. Step one, they'll take the plutonium out of the shells. They'll be elliptical in shape so what they'll do is melt the metal down and recast it in a spherical form. That should give them about 5 kilograms of alpha phase plutonium metal with a density of 19.86 grams per cubic centimeter. That, gentlemen is about as good as plutonium metal gets. They will then have to predetermine with extraordinary precision the exact placement of an array of perhaps thirty detonation points to be placed around the perimeters of each of the spheres they made from their shells."

"And you really believe they can do that?" pressed the National Security Advisor who possessed far more than an amateur's knowledge of nuclear weapons design.

"They could. It won't be easy. It's a highly complex scientific process. They will have to run a large number of computer simulations to be sure they've got it right. But they have computers that can do it, we know that. The knowledge is out there in the open literature if you know where to look for it. They will have to shape their explosives into segments to produce a sphere, engineer those segments with great precision and be certain the explosive they're using is chemically pure and of a constant consistency. It will take time, but can they do it? Yes, I believe they can."

The National Security Advisor let out a pained sigh. "OK. What's next, Doctor?"

"The key to forcing a nuclear explosion from a core of plutonium is to fire off the high explosive detonators packed into that sphere which is wrapped around your plutonium simultaneously with absolutely perfect synchronization." She clasped her hands in front of her as though she was grasping a softball. "That way they will exert a perfectly symmetrical squeeze on the plutonium. Now each of those detonation points is going to require three things: First is the high explosive I just mentioned. HMX will do. That's the easy part. It's widely and openly available."

Good teacher that she was, the doctor reached into her desk drawer for the materials she was going to need to illustrate her lecture.

"They're also going to need two rather sophisticated hi-tech devices for each detonator."

She held up what looked like a tiny glass bubble with three wires attached to it. "This is called a krytron. Some of you gentlemen may be old enough to remember those Old Niagara flush toilets grandpa used to have. Pull a chain and an enormous burst of water got released to clear out the toilet bowl. In a sense, a krytron functions like those old fashioned toilets did. It's an electrical switch or valve if you prefer. Open it or turn it on, and it will allow a big electric charge to blast through it unimpeded in one huge, incredibly fast burst. It's that lightening fast speed that's the critical factor."

She placed the chip on her desk and waved what looked like a thick, stubby pencil at the camera. "Now this is called a capacitor. Its heart is a central core of copper wire woven into a coaxial cable. A capacitor has, fundamentally, the ability to store up that enormous electrical charge you're going to flush through the krytron at the moment of detonation."

She took a deep breath after laying her capacitor on her desk beside the krytron. "What they will have to do to achieve their nuclear explosion is marry up a krytron and a capacitor for each of their very carefully predetermined detonation points. They in turn will be wired to a central electrical power source which is primed to release an electric charge in response to say, a radio signal, a change in atmospheric pressure if it's a bomb, a timer, whatever they want to use. So what you've got at each of those detonators is a capacitor attached to a krytron attached to the high explosive, OK?"

A muttered series of grunts indicating her audience was following her lecture thus far responded to her query.

"Now when that central electric signal goes off, what it does is open up simultaneously the valve in each of your krytrons. When that happens, the charge that's been stored in the capacitors you've hooked up to those krytrons is released to whack into the high explosive at each of your detonation points with stunning force. The key is the speed, nano-seconds with which it happens. It's a time span so short, the human mind simply cannot even begin to comprehend it. But what it means is that all of the detonation points will fire at precisely the same instant, thus giving you that perfect synchronization you need to produce a nuclear explosion when plutonium is your fissile material."

A smile, a baleful smile perhaps, but a smile nonetheless crossed the doctor's face marking the end of her little lecture. "That's it. Nuclear explosion theory in a nutshell."

"Can they get their hands on these things, these krytrons and capacitors? Just how difficult is that going to be?" prodded a worried National Security Advisor.

"That's a very difficult question to answer." The smile had disappeared from Dr. Robotham's attractive features. "Obviously, it will be as difficult as we can possibly make it, but the problem is both capacitors and krytrons have other, non-nuclear uses. Capacitors are used in ultra-fast photography. Krytons to fire high energy lasers, for example. That makes controlling their sale and use very difficult."

"Who makes those damn things?"

"Here in the states, capacitors of the quality required for a nuclear application are made by Maxwell Technologies up in Massachusetts and CSI Industries out in San Diego. I don't think we need to be worried about them."

"And in Europe?"

"Germany, Switzerland, France, the U.K."

"The Germans lead the league in selling hi-tech equipment to people that shouldn't have it," growled the Deputy Secretary of Defense.

"Yeah," chimed in his counterpart at the CIA, "and the Swiss will sell anybody anything. After all, they're neutral, aren't they?"

Dr. Stein now moved to take the Energy Department's microphone back from Dr. Robotham. "I'm afraid that with a little effort and a lot of subterfuge, getting their hands on the capacitors they're going to need isn't going to be all that difficult. Fortunately, the krytrons won't be quite so easy."

"Why is that?" asked the National Security Advisor.

"For all practical purposes about the only people in the world who make things commercially that fire fast enough to trigger a nuclear bomb are at a company up in Salem, Mass. called EG&G. We figure they're about as secure as you can get."

"One hundred percent secure?"

"Nothing in life is one hundred percent secure. Except the fact that it's going to end."

"OK, Dr. Stein," the National Security Advisor continued. "How many of these things are they going to need? And what will they cost?"

"Using that fairly primitive design Dr. Robotham just outlined, at least 90 krytrons, 90 capacitors. Plus say another 30 of each at a minimum to experiment with to be sure they've got things right. So say 200, 250. They'll cost a couple of thousand dollars apiece. Plus whatever'll they have to pay in bribes to get their hands on them. Money isn't going to be the factor holding them back here. It's the availability or non-availability of the stuff they're after."

"Is there any way they can shortcut that? Set up their bombs without having to obtain all that stuff?"

"Well"—it was Dr. Robotham again measuring her words very carefully—"it is just possible to set up a firing circuit less cumbersome than the one I've described, but the knowledge, the tricks you need to employ to do it are not available in the open literature. It would require an experienced bomb designer and also what is called a neutron gun, a very, very sophisticated device which is extremely difficult to use properly in detonating a nuclear device." She paused. "So my answer to you is no. There's no doubt in my mind that the route they'd take is the one I've just described for you."

"And how do they deliver such a device to a target, assuming they're been able to put it together?"

There was nothing reassuring in Dr. Stein's reply. "However the hell they want. It would fit into one of those Shihab 3 missiles they're working on right now. An airplane's bomb bay. Even the trunk of a car."

"They really could stuff this damn thing into the trunk of a car if they wanted to. Smuggle it into Tel Aviv. Or New York. Or even into Washington, God forbid."

"Sure they could. Park it somewhere and set it off with a remote radio signal."

The National Security Advisor took a handkerchief from her hip pocket and dabbed at the beads of perspiration beginning to sparkle on her forehead. "Mr. Duffy, congratulations. You did well to get us this news, however unwelcome it may be. I know the ancient Greeks liked to drive a spear through the foot of the bearers of bad news, but in this case I think I'll just ask you for your thoughts on the consequences of what you learned."

Duffy bit his inner lip, a reflexive gesture designed to both speed up his thought process and slow down his tendency to employ language too brutally direct for gatherings such as this.

"It seems to me we haven't even begun to address the most important question this raises yet."

"Oh, really?" snapped the advisor. "Just what do you mean by that?"

"I mean how the hell can we find out where they've hidden these damn things? We can't just sit around and wait while they go through these complex scientific processes our experts just described. We've got to find out where the hell they've hidden them and take them out before we wake up one fine morning and find they've planted them on somebody's doorstep in Tel Aviv. Or over on Pennsylvania Avenue."

"Send in a Special Forces team to take them out you mean?" the Deputy Secretary of Defense asked.

"Why bother?" rejoined the Deputy Secretary of State. "Find out where they are and we'll just whisper the address in the Israelis' ears and let them deal with the problem. The way they handled that Iraqi nuclear reactor in Baghdad a few years ago."

"OK, Mr. Duffy," pressed the National Security Advisor. "Just exactly how do you figure we're going to go about finding these damn devices? Iran's a helluva a big country. There are lots of places over there where they could hide them."

"Yeah," sighed Duffy, "there sure as hell are."

"So what do we do?"

"Well, I'm afraid the first thing we don't do is count on our reconnaissance satellites to bail us out of this one." Duffy was still pondering the problem, trying to answer his own question. "We could park everyone we've got in a fixed orbit over Iran and I don't think they'll pick up any trace of those three nukes."

"How about NSA intercepts?"

Duffy couldn't help smiling at that question. "Oh, they're a barrel of laughs. Believe me, I know. But, yeah they are a possibility alright. Although I think the Iranians will be smart enough to either communicate by some other means than telecommunications or employ a code so crazy we won't understand what the hell they're saying."

He rubbed his forehead. "I know how unpopular the notion is in this town these days but I think this is one problem we're going to have to solve with human intelligence."

"Are you suggesting the agency has people on the ground in Iran we're not aware of?"

"I wish I were but as you all know the agency's budget has been chopped to hell and our human resources in Operations were the first to get whacked."

The National Security Advisor gave Duffy her "we'd expect that from Genghis Khan" look. "So just what do you suggest we do then?"

"It seems to me from what Dr. Stein told us that these krytrons are the eye of the needle through which the Iranians are going to have to pass on their way to a workable bomb. And they'll have to come west to do it."

"Why wouldn't they go to China?" someone asked.

"Have you seen the trouble the Chinese are having with their own Moslem population?" Duffy replied. "You think they're going to help a bunch of Islamic whackos in Tehran make themselves nuclear arms? No, I think they've got to find a way to come sneaking around in the west looking for them. What I'd like to do if my boss agrees"—he glanced at the agency's Deputy Director—"is go up to Salem, Massachusetts and have a chat with the good folk who make these krytron things."

———

Some 72 hours after Jim Duffy's departure from Cyprus, an early morning jogger discovered the body of Colonel Dimitri Wulff lying face down in a ditch not far from Nicosia's old city walls. The police investigation determined that he had been killed by a single round fired at close range into his right temple by a Makarov .38, the standard sidearm of the Red Army. The weapon itself was found not quite six feet from the colonel's body. Had it been dropped there by his killer? Or had the colonel tossed it away in a final, dying gesture after shooting himself? That was a question the Cypriot police were never able to resolve.

BOOK FOUR

The Turkish
CONNECTION

J im Duffy circled out of Boston's Logan Airport Rent-a-Car area and headed north up Route 1A towards New Hampshire. Was he off on a wild goose chase coming up here, playing a long shot in the hope this trip would give him some clue to locating those three Iranian nukes before the mullahs could find a way to arm and use them? How often, he asked himself, does your average long shot come in?

Driving past the cut off for the Ted Williams Tunnel, he saw a signboard indicating the ports of call lying ahead on his drive up Boston's North Shore: Revere Beach, Lynn, Salem, Marblehead, Newburyport. A faint, sad smile made a brief attempt to lighten the scowl on his face. Marblehead. Newburyport. He recognized those names as the summer playgrounds of the agency's Founding Fathers—guys like Tracy Barnes, Dick Bissell, C.D. Jackson, Des Fitzgerald, all gone now just like the style of the agency they'd founded was gone. They'd been the Brahmins, inspired by the notion of service to the nation, graduates of Groton and Saint Paul's, Yale and Harvard, those to whom much had been given and who had been prepared to give much in return.

Of course, a lot of them could well afford to be unselfish servants of the nation. Their daddies had accumulated trusts, gilt-edged investments, prime real estate, not overdue mortgages, unpaid debts and surly bill collectors like his daddy had. Still, you had to hand it to them. They had made the rules, set the tone and tradition of their little brotherhood: service, sacrifice, duty. And, of course, silence. Above all silence. Not like today when you couldn't pick up a newspaper without seeing the initials CIA in the headlines somewhere.

He and guys like Frank Williams were from the agency's second generation, products not of the old Ivy League schools, but of Notre Dame and Texas A&M, Michigan and Tulane. The blood in their veins was red not blue. But he and the others in his generation had been inspired by the Founding Fathers, embraced their values and emulated their example.

Now? His own generation was on the way out in its turn, and so, too, perhaps was the agency the Dulleses and the Barnes and the Bissells had sired. The CIA was barely fifty years old yet already you could sense the dread decay of approaching death about the place. Nobody was sure just what the agency was supposed to do anymore. "Mission" had once been a word pronounced in Langley's corridors with a reverence similar to that of a priest passing out the Eucharist with the words "Body of Christ." Hear it now and it was probably a reference to a Baptist preacher running a revival meeting down by the Washington Monument. The younger officers seemed more concerned with the state of their pension than the state of the nation. And the leadership? The Director of Central Intelligence was as disposable as a Kleenex tissue these days. Clinton alone had gone through four of them.

Yet, if you really looked at the world's problems seriously, the planet was as dangerous a place as it had been in the old Cold War days. The Soviets, the KGB, the Communist Parties of the satellite countries had at least responded to a logic, reacted with a reasoned pattern of behavior. OK, it was their logic, their behavioral patterns but they were still value systems you could count on them following.

Today? The world was non-symmetrical and materially the West and the U.S. in particular, were by far its strongest side. But these fanatics on the other side of that non-symmetrical world had managed to convince themselves that spiritually they represented the stronger side. That spiritual strength, they believed, gave them a power we westerners with our idealization of unbridled individualism and materialism didn't possess.

Look at those Hamas guys the FBI had caught in Brooklyn. They had wanted to walk into a crowded subway station with a bomb wrapped around their waists and blow themselves up. To kill a bunch of innocent strangers. Why? Was the sheer insanity, the total irrational nature of their act supposed to demonstrate their spiritual superiority to us and our society? Or was theirs the blind despair of a people who felt helpless in the face of wrongs an uncaring world had inflicted on them?

Duffy shook his head and lowered his window to send a wake up blast of icy air onto his face. A gray sky's oppressive shroud dulled the edges of the passing landscape. Far off to his right he glimpsed the waters of the Atlantic, its surface as dull, as gray, as sullen appearing as the sky overhead.

The White House, the Congress, the press, that part of the public that thought about these things, were all screaming for the agency's blood these days. It was too big, cost too much money. The military had had to deal with Saddam Hussein, not our famed covert ops. The agency no longer had a *raison d'etre,* its critics said, it was rudderless on a sea of indecision.

Well, Duffy thought grimly, just let those mad mullahs find a way to detonate their nuclear artillery shells, and the world would learn in hell of a hurry what the agency's mission was supposed to have been. Except, of course, if that happened and the Agency had failed to thwart the mullahs, it would be too late. The ghosts of the Founding Fathers who'd learned to sail their dinghies up here so long ago could kiss their agency goodbye.

———

As Jim Duffy pondered the fate of his agency, some 4000 miles to the east, a five-axled Fruehauf TIR truck with the markings of the TNZ Freight Forwarding Services crept along the road circling up into the Zaki mountains from the Iranian town of Maku to the Turkish border crossing. It took the driver almost an hour to cover the twenty kilometers separating the town from the whitewashed, flag-bedecked buildings marking the border.

Despite the late evening hour, five other TIRs were already wait-ing to clear customs at the border when his truck joined the line. Gur-bulak was Turkey's busiest eastern land crossing. An average of almost 800 trucks passed every 24 hours through the half a dozen over-worked and underpaid Customs officers manning the post. To the left of the TNZ truck as it waited its turn to clear was a huge inspection shed equipped with modern cranes, hoists, jacks and an assortment of other power tools. The shed had been built and paid for by the United Nations Drug Control Program in Vienna for the express purpose of helping the Turkish Customs stem the westward flow of the produce of Afghanistan's poppy fields. Tonight, as it had been almost from the moment of its official inauguration, it was deserted.

The driver half dozed, half kept an ear cocked to the Turkish bal-lads on his radio as he inched his trailer towards the Customs Post. There was no question of bribing anyone to get across the border. There was no need for that because, for all practical purposes, there was no customs inspection. A Turkish Customs Officer tore out the first page of the driver's International TIR carnet, circled around to the back of his truck to glance up at its doors making sure an Iranian Cus-toms seal was in place, then waved him on his way.

———

EG&G Electro-Optics, the firm Jim Duffy had come to visit, was a division of a company which had been intimately associated with the U.S. nuclear weapons program since the days of the Manhattan Pro-ject. Its three founders were all high speed event physicists, a trio of MIT educated geniuses whose contribution to the development and sophistication of U.S. nuclear weaponry was almost beyond reckon-ing. Today, the firm they'd started was engaged in a wide range of non-defense related activities from x-rays to medical diagnostics to sealing devices. Nonetheless, here in this huge warehouse on the edge of Salem Harbor, EG&G continued to make the ultra-secret devices which would ultimately be responsible for firing the U.S. nuclear arsenal in the now unlikely event that the need for that should ever arise.

A secretary showed him into the office of Dr. Harry Aspen, the division chief who oversaw their manufacture. The man's wide bay windows gave onto the harbor and half a dozen sailboats cocooned in canvas for the winter. The guy could pop out of his office at lunchtime in the summer and take a sail. Even a farm boy from Oklahoma like Duffy could appreciate that. Dr. Jean Robotham, the Department of Energy's nuclear weapons expert who'd briefed the deputies closed circuit conference on Duffy's return from Nicosia had set up his meeting with Aspen. While she had almost certainly not labelled him as CIA, Aspen, Duffy assumed, was certainly smart enough to figure out which part of the National Security establishment he was coming from.

"So!" a voice boomed out behind him. "A man who wants an education in krytrons."

Duffy turned to greet his host, a lanky man with a gray crew cut and the slightly turned in shoulders of someone who had spent a lot of his life hunched over a computer screen.

"How about a little coffee to make the knowledge go down easier?"

For a few minutes, the two men went through the ritual chitchat that always preceded such meetings: the lousy weather, Duffy's drive up from Logan, and the ineptitude of the Boston Celtics. Then they got down to the business at hand.

"OK," Aspen asked. "What is it I can tell you about krytrons."

Duffy, of course, was not about to reveal to his host the classified information concerning Iran's three nuclear devices even though he was in no doubt that Aspen possessed a Top Secret clearance. "Let me put it in a nutshell. How hard would it be for the Iranians to get their hands on 200 of them?"

The EG&G scientist smiled. "The kind, I presume, that are suitable for setting off a nuclear bomb."

"Of course."

"The kind we make here. I would rate it as extremely difficult, if not impossible."

For the first time since he'd woken up that morning a sense of relief began to ease through Duffy. "That certainly sounds reassuring. But what makes you say that?"

Aspen opened his desk drawer and took out a glass bulb trailing a set of wires. Duffy immediately recognized it as the device Dr. Robotham had shown them at their closed circuit deputies conference.

"This is our model KN22 krytron. It is the only krytron commercially available anywhere in the world today with the characteristics required to fire a nuclear bomb."

"You mean the English, the French, the Israelis don't make them?"

"Of course they do. In small, state-run labs whose production is reserved strictly for their military. The devices we make here in this building for the Pentagon to fire our nuclear and thermo-nuclear warheads don't look anything like this. They aren't even called krytrons anymore. Nobody, absolutely nobody except the U.S. military, ever gets near them."

"And yet that little thing you've got there you call a KN22 can fire a nuclear bomb?"

Aspen picked up the krytron, twisted it almost playfully in his fingers then passed it to Duffy. "You'd better believe it can. What this does is zap on command a huge amount of stored up electrical energy onto a target with what we call a rise time that makes a blink of your eye seem like an eternity."

The scientist pointed to the glass bulb. "In there you've got an ionized gas in a vacuum and a radioactive source, Nickel 63."

"Fine, but why the hell is it the Iranians can't get their hands on 200 of those damn things?"

"As I told you, Mr. Duffy . . ."

"Jim."

"We're the only people in the world who sell these things in the marketplace. But nobody buys one from us without our first having gotten an export license from the Department of Commerce. There are places in the world that are black listed for this product and you can bet your ass Iran is foremost among them."

"Sure, Doc, and the world is also filled with people who spend their days and nights thinking of how to find ways around our export licensing requirements."

"Oh, there are always people out there trying to get their hands on krytrons. We've even had damn fools with big wads of cash in their hands come right into this building and try to buy a few off the shelf."

"But how can you be sure when some guy comes to you to buy these things, fills out all the forms, that he's not lying?"

"Well, you can't. What we have here is a chain and as in all chains, there are weak links. When someone asks us to sell them krytrons, they have to tell us exactly what they want the device for, what instrument they're going to use it in and where, exactly, they intend to use it."

"So a guy makes up some bull shit story for you."

"Yeah, the system does rely to a degree on our customer's honesty. But it's a small world out there. There aren't many uses for a KN22. High energy lasers for cutting and abrading metals. We know most of the players. We're suspicious. Sure our reps are programmed to sell, but they know the name of the game. They're clued into what's going on. But here's the real point, Jim. You said how can the Iranians get 200 of these, right?"

"Correct."

"Well, I only manufacture a hundred of them in a year. We never sell more than a dozen at a time. Four or five is the usual order. Ask us for 200 of them and you'll set off alarm bells that will shake this building." Aspen offered Duffy a knowing smile. "And a few buildings in Washington, too, I should think."

Duffy ran the math through his head. A dozen or so a year. It would take the mullahs a fair bit of time to get to 200 at that rate. "You reassure me, Doc. You make the Iranians' job seem a lot tougher than I thought it was going to be."

"Do I? Well, I didn't intend to."

Duffy's stomach suddenly tightened up a notch or two. "Now what the hell is that supposed to mean?"

"Look, we make and sell these things even though they're capable of detonating a nuclear device because they have other, perfectly legitimate uses. If we made it impossible for people to get them for legitimate purposes, then somebody else outside our control would come along and make them for people who needed them for those legitimate uses. And they might not be as zealous as we are in keeping them away from people who shouldn't have them."

"OK, but you said nobody else is out there selling them so that still leaves our Iranians out in the cold, doesn't it?"

Aspen's face suddenly took on the professional doubters cast, the regard of an art expert appraising a work of dubious provenance. "Maybe not. I have my private nightmare in this regard. I don't think they have to get their 200 krytrons from us. I think they can make them themselves."

"Make these things? In Iran? Really?" A solid American conviction in the superiority of the nation's scientific skills underpinned Duffy's astonishment.

"Really. Like all things that look difficult, it's not quite as difficult as you might think. Fortunately, the world doesn't know that. But if some halfway smart engineers got hold of a dozen of these things, I'm afraid they could break them down and figure out how to replicate them. The Japanese have been re-engineering things for years."

Duffy slumped in his chair, his heavy frame sagging under the impact of that choice bit of news. "So they don't need 200 of your damn krytrons. They only need a dozen."

"To go this route, yes."

"Where would they get them?"

"Well, probably eighty percent of the world's high energy lasers which could legitimately use these things are made and used in Germany. Unfortunately, the Germans will deal with just about anybody. I guess that's where I'd look first."

A cloud of discontent enveloped Duffy. "A few minutes ago, Doc, I was about to tell you you'd made my day. I think you've just unmade it."

"Sorry, but I think it's always best to be candid about these things."

Duffy stood up and looked out at the gray waters of Salem Harbor. "Doc, I know how vigilant you guys are about keeping an eye on people who want to buy these things. But we've got a little problem on our hands right now. I'd like to ask you to turn that vigilance up a few notches. If you see anything, and I mean anything, that looks unusual on this krytron business coming across your desk, could you please get hold of Dr. Stein as quickly as possible? He'll know how to find me."

"Glad to," Aspen replied rising in turn from his chair.

———

Istanbul's Kapali Carsi, Covered Market or Grand Bazaar, is an attraction to rival the city's other historic tourist sites, the Blue Mosque and Santa Sophia. It is a city within a city—half museum, half marketplace, a warren of twisting alleyways, streets, paths, and walkways, containing over 4000 shops, hundreds of warehouses, a mosque, 19 fountains and a dozen working wells, all assembled under the arches of a roof parts of which date to Byzantine times.

The shopper can find virtually anything in the bazaar's dusty, somber corridors: worthless junk selling for a dollar or two and Ottoman emerald and diamond bracelets worth millions, brass and copper-ware, whirling dervish dolls, hookahs, water pipes, boxes of cedarwood inlaid with pearls, Yildiz porcelain, opaline vases, gold coins a thousand years old, and Rolex wristwatches fresh off the plane from Geneva; blue and white ceramic designs to protect their wearer against the evil eye, and magic elixirs to make the barren fertile.

The bazaar is also a massive money machine through which over eight billion dollars in cash passes every year, most of it in U.S. dollars or German deutschmarks. A man connected to the right *Doviz,* money changer, can get rid of a million dollars without leaving a trace of where it's gone as easily and as quickly as a tourist can lose his way in the bazaar's alleyways.

As he did every working day of the week, Jaffar Bayhani unlocked the door to his modest looking money changer's stall on the Fesciler

Sokagi, the street of the ancient guild of fez makers, at precisely eight o'clock in the morning. A diminutive, white haired figure who looked far older than his 52 years, Bayhani's appearance may not have inspired much confidence in his physical prowess, but when it came to moving money, that frail man was a force to be reckoned with. From that stall of his he could and did shift millions of dollars to destinations all over the globe.

Bayhani was an Iranian, one of a million of his countrymen living in Istanbul, giving the Turkish city the largest Iranian expatriate colony in the world. Descended from a family of *sarraf,* Farsi for money changer, he had gravitated to the Grand Bazaar on his arrival in Istanbul in 1972 as a refugee from the Shah's regime and set up his money changing business. He worked at a desk in the stall's front room where any bazaar passerby could see him, but his real office was in the back room to which his steps now took him. It contained an enormous walk-in safe, three fax machines, two computers, one of them linked to the Internet, a bank of half a dozen mobile phones, three ordinary phones, and a teleprinter delivering him Reuters Financial News Service. Just behind his second computer was a portrait of the leader who remained his model and inspiration, the Ayatollah Khomeini.

That scruffy, unkempt little money changer with three days of white stubble glazing his face like a partially melted frost on a wheat field was the liaison between several of the city's most important heroin traffickers and the Iranian Pasdaran—Revolutionary Guard— which insured, for a price, the free flow across Iran of the raw material, morphine base, the Turks' heroin labs needed to function. The beauty of the operation was that only this untidy little money changer knew who all the players in the game were: the Turk who was buying the base, the Pakistanis who were supplying it, the Iranians who were making sure it got safely to Istanbul.

Bayhani immediately noticed that the red light linking his answering machine to his bank of mobile phones was flashing. The message had arrived as expected. After listening to it, Bayhani consulted his "files," a sheaf of handwritten notes covered by figures and markings known only to the little money changer, an assortment of information about as easy to decipher as the hieroglyphics in a Pharaonic tomb.

The order for the morphine base now snaking its way down the Trans-European Highway from the Turkish – Iranian border had been placed in his shop six weeks earlier by Selim Osman, the eldest of five Kurdish brothers who ran one of Istanbul's most important heroin smuggling operations. Some time tonight, Selim Osman's men would unload their 210 kilos of morphine base from the TNZ TIR truck. At that moment the dope would become the Osman family's property and they would be responsible for payment in full of the $4000 per kilo price they'd agreed to no matter what happened to the base once it was out of the TIR truck. Selim Osman had already "fronted" $200,000 for the load to the little money changer's Cayman Island bank account. He could be counted on, Bayhani knew, to wire the balance to the same account within 24 hours. Bayhani would then wire transfer the full amount minus his $40,000 commission to another account in the trust department of a different Cayman Islands bank. He did not know who was the man or the men in Tehran who controlled the account but he was sure they were senior members of the Pasdaran, Iran's Revolutionary Guard. They would use it, he knew, to further the great task of bringing the message of a renewed, a reinvigorated, a proud and unforgiving Islam to the world.

He was proud to be a part of that movement. He could measure its advance all around him in Istanbul. In the working class suburb in which he lived, the vast majority of the voters supported the Islamic Freedom and Development Party. Today there were two dozen mosques with Iranian trained mullahs preaching the doctrine of the new, militant Islam at every Friday service. Any woman visiting the Islamic run municipality of Istanbul had better present herself in the modest dress of the faith if she hoped to get anything done.

Bayhani had played a vital if clandestine role in effecting those changes in the secular nation of Kemal Ataturk. Some of the Turkish drug dealers with whom he dealt paid for their dope in cash. On Tehran's orders, he kept the money locked in his walk in safe.

Occasionally, a passerby would drift into his stall, give him a password Tehran had furnished and ask him for a sum of money.

He, of course, had no idea who his visitor was or what he was going to use the money for. Those callers never returned for a second visit. The money changer had no doubt, however, that the money was being used to support the cause, whether to fund the activities of the banned Islamist Welfare Party or to help the Iranian brothers to slip carefully chosen Turkish young men into Iran to receive training in the use of arms and explosives against the day they might need to employ such weapons to defend the faith against Turkey's secular generals. None of that concerned him at the moment, however. It was now urgent to get this good news into the hands of his buyer, Selim Osman. On one of his local phones, he dialed the Barcelona Gran Hotel, half a mile away in Aksaray.

"Dear friend," he announced in a voice as vibrantly alive as that of a maternity nurse announcing the arrival of his first born to a new father, "your goods are on their way. They will reach your delivery site tonight."

———

Selim Osman took the money changer's call gazing out his office window at the Barcelona Grand onto the crowds thronging the Pasazade Sokak. Russians, Ukrainians, Beylo-Russians, Rumanians, Bulgarians, they swarmed from shop to shop, gawking at the merchandise, holding it up for inspection, fingering it, haggling over prices with arms waving as wildly as an Italian extolling the merits of his sister or arguing with a policeman about a parking ticket. The Japanese had brought Bangkok the dubious blessings of "Sexual Tourism" in the eighties. What was luring the crowds to the narrow streets of Istanbul's Aksaray was a new kind of tourism, "Textile Tourism."

Russia, once Turkey's most feared potential foe, had become her principal trading partner thanks in large part to those hordes moving below Osman's window. Each of them had come to Turkey as a tourist.

Each was allowed to take home $1000 in duty free goods. They took back two or three times that, concealing the reality of their purchases with understated invoices which the shop keepers of the Pasazade Sokak were only too happy to furnish them.

Selim Osman and his brothers had delighted in that booming textile business. Its dramatic rise had paralleled the equally dramatic rise in their business, smuggling heroin into Western Europe and had inspired them to set up as an ideal cover for their activities a family textile business of their own called Texas Country Jeans.

Selim turned away from the window and marched back to the desk of his elaborately furnished office. It had been decorated for him at considerable cost by Gul Oztark, a lady to be reckoned with in Istanbul society. The handwoven silk and wool carpet on his floor had originally been designed, or so she had assured him, for one of the 285 rooms of Sultan Abdul Mecit's Dolmabahce Palace, and his desk top made from the planking of one of the Ottoman Emperor's ships lost in the Battle of Lepanto. Osman had never heard of the Battle of Lepanto when Madame Oztark had sold him the desk. That didn't matter. What mattered was the social standing such badges of distinction conferred on him.

Osman was, in fact, barely literate. He had not even finished primary school in his native Lice Province in southeastern Turkey. He never read a book because he couldn't. He rarely went to the movies, never to the theater and didn't know what the opera was. The high point of his intellectual accomplishments was his ability to work out the profit margins of a business deal on his pocket calculator.

That, however, he did extremely well. All four of his younger brothers were involved in the heroin traffic beside him, each with his own clearly defined responsibilities. Hassan, the next in line, was responsible for the operation of the laboratory where the 210 kilos of morphine base now on its way to Istanbul would be converted into pure heroin. Refat, the third brother, was the family enforcer, the hard man indispensable to any efficient criminal enterprise. His job was "killing and carrying." He hired the "dogs," the bodyguards, organized the killings or the threat of a killing when that was needed, worked with the owners and drivers of the TIR trucking firms or the tourist buses who moved the family's heroin to Europe. Abdullah, the fourth son, was stationed in Amsterdam. The family used Holland with its lax drug policies, as the warehousing site for its dope, the place where heroin could be stored in large quantities before it was broken up into smaller, more easily concealed loads for shipment to France, Spain, Germany and the U.K. The youngest brother, Behcet, lived in Stoke Newington in London where he'd been given the job of expanding the family business in England.

All were multi-millionaires with most of their millions concealed in overseas bank accounts far from the curious gaze of the Turkish government. Some had been laundered in properties such as Selim's Barcelona Gran Hotel. Every penny of the $22 million dollars he had invested in it had been furnished to him, ultimately, by the heroin users of Europe and the United States. This office which he'd built into the building was as close to an anonymous headquarters from which to run his affairs as it was possible to find. And, on the top floor were four large double rooms Osman set aside for Russian tourists of a different sort from the textile grubbers clogging the streets of Aksaray. "Natashas," they were jokingly referred to, young Russian ladies who were financing their stay in Turkey with the sale of merchandise considerably more pleasurable—and costly—than blue jeans.

The success of the Osman's family's drug trafficking enterprise, however, was not due solely to Selim's business acumen. The Osmans were Kurds, the quasi-feudal rulers of a large tribe-like clan based in the Kurdish village of Tepe, 40 kilometers (25 miles) east of Diyarbakir. As the eldest son, Selim had become the owner of 50 tiny villages clustered in the hills around Tepe on the death of his father. He was, as his father and his grandfather before him had been, in a very real sense, the ruler of those villagers.

The Osman brothers' loyalties, and through them those of their villagers, had always been with the Turkish central government in Ankara. Selim despised the Kurdish Workers Party, the PKK and its

Marxist doctrines. He had no intention of letting them force him out of his Mercedes 600 and into a packed bus along with everyone else.

The closeness of the family's ties to Ankara had been immeasurably strengthened in 1990-91. At the time, the morphine base flowing into Turkey from Iran was controlled by other Kurds allied to the PKK. The drug dollars that traffic earned were coming back to plague Turkey in arms, assassinations and terrorist bombings. Despairing of the ability of the Turkish Army to employ tactics brutal enough to break the PKK insurgency, the government of Tansu Ciller decided to turn the tactics of the terrorists against the terrorists themselves, to hunt down their leaders and particularly the drug barons who were financing them and murder them with hired gunmen.

The Ministry of the Interior formed a special organization, the *Ozel Harekat* to do just that. They turned to people like the Osmans to provide them with the guns for hire they needed. In return, the suppliers of those guns for hire could expect to take over the heroin traffic of the PKK drug barons they murdered.

The Osmans second source of strength was an all-pervading sense of the family that was reflected in everything they did. Effective drug law enforcement anywhere in the world depended on penetrating the trafficker's organizations and no drug trafficking organizations were more difficult to penetrate than the Turks. The Italian mafia liked to use the word "family" to label their criminal groupings but it was a misnomer. They were bound together by their vows of *omerta,* silence, and a sense of clan, not by ties of the blood. The Chinese Triads relied on the uniqueness of their Chinese culture and language, their regional origins and the brutality of their Red Pole enforcers to protect the integrity of their clans from law enforcement.

With the Turks, or more often, the Turkish Kurds, it was simpler and more effective. If you weren't a brother, a cousin, an uncle, a nephew, you didn't get past the front door. That presented law enforcement's efforts to penetrate their organizations with a Herculean challenge.

The five brothers only rarely handled the drug themselves. The individuals who worked in their secret lab, the truck or bus drivers

whose vehicles carried the heroin, were never members of their immediate family but loyal villagers from around Tepe. They knew that if
they were caught with the drug, the Osman brothers would take care
of them as long as they kept their mouths shut.

If Her Majesty's Customs, for example, made a lucky hit on a TIR
truck carrying the Osman's dope into the U.K., the driver could be
counted on to react with wide-eyed wonder. "Heroin? In my truck?
However did it get there?"

He would serve his time knowing his family in Istanbul was being
taken care of, his salary banked for him. When he returned, the grateful Osman brothers would reward him for his good behavior with a
new TIR truck of his own. On the very rare occasions when someone
threatened to step out of line, Refat in his black Mercedes 600 with its
"34" Istanbul plates would pay a visit to the defector's family in whatever remote village they happened to be living. His appearance was
usually enough to persuade the family to convince their wavering son
that silence was the only wise and honorable course.

If it didn't, the Osman brothers way of dealing out punishment
reflected their strong sense of family values. Nothing was more important to a Turk than his eldest son. That child's life meant more to him
than his own or his wife's. So when someone stepped out of line, it was
the oldest son who got hammered.

All five brothers lived very comfortable but discreet lives. Not for
them the flash, the flamboyance of the Colombians, like the late Pablo
Escobar with his private zoo or the Ochoa brothers with their vast
estates filled with brave bulls and show horses. Selim and Refat, the
enforcer, lived side by side in identical duplex villas in Florya, Istanbul's newest and most expensive housing development. Hassan, who
oversaw the family's secret laboratory, lived outside Istanbul, across
the Sea of Marmara on the arm of land stretching along the Izmit inlet.

Selim, as the eldest, set the tone for the style that was supposed to
characterize Osman family life. He observed most of the outward
manifestations of his Islamic faith. He fasted during Ramadan—it
helped him keep his weight down and offered him a yearly chance to

curb his drinking. He went to Friday prayers at the mosque at least once a month, more often when he felt it was important to be seen at the service. Yet rare was the evening when he didn't enjoy a vodka or two and a generous portion of Turkey's robust red wine. He would no more turn down a good pork sausage then he would an invitation to bed the sexiest belly dancer in Istanbul.

He was genuinely devoted to his wife and children, particularly to his two sons. Divorce was unheard of among his circle of friends and the notion an anathema to Selim himself. That, however, had nothing whatsoever to do with his prerogative as a Turkish male, to take his sexual pleasures wherever and with whomsoever he chose.

The notion that his drug, which was bringing its flashes of heaven and its descent into hell to so many young Europeans and Americans, might one day affect his own beloved children had quite simply never occurred to Osman. Why should it? Turkey's drug traffickers, many of whom were Osman's friends, never touched the poison they sold and heroin addiction was still relatively unknown in Turkey.

Osman picked up one of the three telephones on his desk and called his brother Hassan's mobile.

"Our textiles are arriving tomorrow tonight. There will be 210 packs." The fact there would be ten extra kilos was of no concern. The vagaries of the conversion process meant that these things rarely came out exactly to the kilo.

"At the usual depot?"

"Yes. Will you make the arrangements to pick them up?"

"Of course. I have the Falcon standing by to take the delivery."

The "Falcon" was so named because as a young man in Lice Province his hobby had been raising and training falcons for hunting. He was a cousin of the Osmans', close enough to be trusted but distant enough so that if anything went wrong, linking him to the five brothers would take both a considerable leap of imagination and some very substantial evidence from the police.

"I think it would be a good idea if all of us had dinner together tonight. Perhaps at Beyti." Beyti, located in Florya, specialized in meat dishes and was widely regarded as the best restaurant of its kind in Istanbul, indeed in all of Turkey. "Bring everybody. The wife and children."

Selim Osman's invitation was an order. In the unlikely event that anything went wrong with the delivery, who could point the finger of suspicion at the Osman brothers who'd been enjoying a festive family gathering in front of dozens of witnesses?

It was now time to start thinking about how and where to unload his delivery of morphine base once the family lab had converted it to heroin. Selim thought best in the tranquillity of the hamam, the Turkish bath. Besides, a glance at his watch told him it was time to begin the pleasures of mid-day. He ordered up his bodyguards and car.

————

On the other side of the Atlantic, a reluctant Jim Duffy was settling back into his cubby hole of an office, his "vacation day" in Salem, Massachusetts behind him. He stripped off his coat, undid his tie, and clamped on his earphones, ready to focus on the computer screen linking him to NSA Headquarters. As he turned the power on, a red light blinked on his screen. The NSA officer feeding the texts to the computer wanted a word with him.

"Mr. Duffy?"

"Hey, don't tell me you've been able to get that voice signature analysis we were after and you're ready to crunch it through your computers?" Duffy replied. "Or have you got some real good news for me? Like you're running out of intercepts."

"Don't worry, I still have plenty of those. But," he continued, "I've come up with something else while you were away I thought you might find interesting."

"Shoot."

"You remember I told you that the guy we listened to talking from that hick town out in Eastern Iran was calling a mobile phone in Istanbul?"

"Right."

"Do you know anything about cloning mobile telephones?"

This guy, Duffy told himself, is probably one of those techno-wizards they like to recruit at the NSA, Ph.D.'s in Advanced State Calculus whose idea of a fun evening is staying up all night trying to beat the IBM Chess Master program. "Cloning sheep like Dolly I've heard about. But mobile phones? No, I'm not up to speed on that."

"Well, cloned mobile phones are something a few very clever bad guys like to use. They get their hands on a stolen mobile. To make a clone from it, all they need is an ordinary laptop computer and the right software program and another mobile. They hook up the stolen mobile to the computer running that software and pull its ESN, its Electronic Serial Number, and its phone number off the chip it's got in there, follow me?"

"Sure."

"Then they plug the new mobile into the computer, pull off its Electronic Serial Number and its phone number and replace them with the ESN and the phone number they took off the stolen phone. Now they can toss the stolen mobile into the junk pile, OK?"

"Sure. But what's the point of the exercise? The guy whose phone was snatched cuts off his access service. The phone is useless."

"To make calls, yes. But the phone number of the stolen mobile is programmed now onto the chip you've put into your clone. OK, the access service takes the number out of circulation. But still, if some-body dials that number, the clone is going to ring. You've got a way of receiving calls that are pretty much untraceable."

"OK, so what are you telling me?"

"I got hold of our NSA representative at the embassy in Ankara and asked him to get me a list of all the mobile phones taken out of service in Turkey in the last six months because they were registered as stolen. Guess what?"

"Our mobile was on that list?"

"Right. Belonged to a real estate agent in Izmir. He reported it stolen seven weeks ago. And the call we picked up to his phone was made three weeks ago. You have to figure the guy using that mobile is some smartass who wants to receive untraceable calls over a clone."

"Good work, my friend, damn good work. Suppose we run that stolen mobile phone number through your NSA backlogs and see if anything interesting falls out."

————

"Give us a bomb to strap around our waists," the young men in the street below chanted. "We will die with a smile because it is the shortest road to paradise."

From his office window in suburban Tehran, Ali Mohatarian bestowed the blessings of a smile on the little group. The sight of their dark, glistening eyes reassured him in moments of concern and self doubt such as those through which he was passing now. They were the hope for the future, the vanguards of a new, better society inspired by the great Iranian Islamic revolution, ready to become the agents of divine will, martyrs, members of a select brotherhood of the elite.

The Western press in its infinite ignorance would talk again of young men outside this building begging to become "suicide bombers." How stupid! Islam forbade suicide. They clamored to become martyrs, not suicides. Martyrdom was an act that could only be accomplished with the sanction of a religious official—and then only when its purpose was to disrupt the works of the infidel enemy.

Disrupting the works of the infidel enemy was weighing heavily on Mohatarian's mind this afternoon as he strode back to his massive eighteenth century desk, a souvenir left behind by the building's previous occupants, the Shah's security service, the SAVAK. In a few minutes he would convene one of the rare meetings of the organization he commanded, the *Komitet-ye Amaliat-e Makhfi,* the Committee for Secret Operations, the most important and most secretive organ of Iran's Revolutionary Government. Its task was eliminating the enemies of the mullah's regime at home and abroad.

Now, however, he was convinced that the real challenges facing the regime were here in Iran, not abroad. Discontent with the righteous rule of the mullahs was on the rise everywhere. The enormous majority won by President Khatemi in the recent presidential elections had been a stunning shock to men like Mohatarian, a devasting revelation of just how unpopular their Islamic regime had become.

"The Revolution is dying," was the watchword being whispered on the street corners of Tehran. Black market western consumer goods were flooding the country in defiance of the mullahs' edicts. In the capital's middle class neighborhoods, people drank Scotch whiskey and French wines inside their homes, women threw aside their veils, danced, gambled, watched western films on their cassette players. When the once feared *Pasdaran,* Revolutionary Guards, knocked at their door now, it was usually to collect a bribe, not to round up more victims for the mullahs' jails.

The regime had banned TV satellites to keep the evil and morally decadent images of Western television from bespoiling the minds and morals of the people. What happened? The smugglers began to bring in smaller, more easily concealable dishes and now Pamela Anderson had become a sex goddess in the land of the all enveloping black chador.

Much more worrying, however, the very foundations of the Mullah's rule, the authority of men like Mohatarian, were now being challenged by the so-called "moderates" around President Khatemi. How could anyone be "moderate" in the fight against the enemies of Islam? If Iran's glorious experiment in Islamic rule were undone, it would proclaim to a cynical world that Islam was not a suitable framework for the governance of peoples—that the Sharia, Islamic law, was not a proper framework for administering a modern society.

What was needed was something to save the revolution, some powerful reaffirmation of its vitality, a triumphant public demonstration that it was not dying but vibrantly alive, that it represented the key to the future of Islam and hence to the world.

Mohatarian twisted the tip of his black mustache into a tight little curl, the reflexive gesture he habitually made when he was deeply concerned. He was just a few months short of fifty, with the intense, emaciated look of the true ascetic, a man to whom the physical pleasures of life were meaningless.

How to save the Great Islamic revolution, he asked himself? How to triumph over the Satanic evil of the Americans and their accursed Israeli friends, to succeed where Osama bin Laden and Saddam Hussein had failed? One day of course they would have in their hands the nuclear arms they were going to produce thanks to their reactor in Bushwehr and the enriched uranium they would get from the centrifuges they were installing in Natanz. But that day was still three, four years away. They needed something now, today, to save the revolution. The Professor with his Operation Khalid and the three nuclear devices he had bought from the Russians in Kazakhstan thought he had the answer. But did he? Well, they might soon find out.

He gathered up his papers, cast a last, fond glance at the young men in the street outside and set off for his conference room.

There was Rafiq Dost, the mullah's financial wizard; the Professor, Kair Bollahi, ready to give them his critical status report on Operation Khalid; Sadegh Izzaddine, the commander of the *Gouroohe Zarbat,* the Strike Force, whose commando had just returned from their mission in London; Imad Mugniyeh, the man responsible for the destruction of the U.S. Marine barracks in Beirut, now a senior leader of the Hezbollah and the operative the CIA regarded as its enemy Number One; Said Djailani, the old Afghan warrior who now was responsible for collecting the drug revenues that financed so much of their work, and Ahmed Vahidi, the head of the El Kuds—Jerusalem— force who provided Mohatarian's organization with infrastructure support in the form of small arms, safe houses, false or real papers, passports and visas.

"Never forget the words of our great leader Ayatollah Khomeini, may peace be upon him," Montazi urged shaking his amber prayer beads to indicate his invocation was drawing to a close, ". . . I do not care if we are understood. I only want us to be feared."

Mohatarian nodded his thanks to the aged cleric and turned to Sadegh Izzaddine to open the meeting. "We must congratulate you, my Brother, and the members of your organization for yet another job well done."

Izzaddine acknowledged his compliment with a movement of his head so slight as to be almost imperceptible. From a worn leather briefcase he held pressed to his ample stomach as a mother might clutch a newborn, he took a thick manilla envelope and passed it across the table to the Professor.

"I hope you will find everything you need is in there. My men did not have time to check it to see if anything was missing before leaving the traitor's house."

The Professor glanced approvingly at the handwritten scrawl in Farsi on the envelope—*Khalid*—as his eager fingers started to tear it open. One by one he lined up the documents it contained on the table with the fussy precision of a grandmother lining up the ingredients of her favorite dish on her kitchen counter.

Some of the documents were plain but most were handsomely engraved in dazzling colors of which gold was the hue most frequently employed, and covered with eagles, stars, flags, or the portraits of stern-faced men, the founding fathers of nations and island republics so small few of the men at the conference table even knew they existed. They were stock certificates representing the ownership of eight different corporations. All were bearer shares which meant that whoever held those shares in his or her hands controlled the company they represented. From Panama, the Turks and Caicos, the Grand Caymans, and Singapore, the sites in which those companies had been incorporated represented a Who's Who of the world's offshore banking and money laundering centers.

Attached to each clump of stock certificates was a Power of Attorney appointing an individual to act with full powers on behalf of the company the shares represented. There was only one name on each of those power of attorneys, that of Tari Harmian. In addition, each clump had a sheet of paper on which was marked the address of the trust department of one of five Cayman Island banks in which that company's assets were deposited. A sleepy sandbar 500 miles south of Miami, in 1975 the Caymans were little more than a spit of sand buffeted by the Atlantic winds. Now in 2004, the Caymans was the world's fifth largest banking center, home to over 500 banks through which close to a trillion dollars passed each year, unseen and unsupervised by any credible banking authority. As a result, the secrecy of those banks made their Swiss counterparts seem virtually transparent by comparison.

The Professor studied each of the piles before him in some detail and then bestowed his warmest smile on Izzaddine. "Congratulations, my Brother. Everything is here. The traitor did not have time to carry out his threat."

Said Djailani beamed at his words. He knew that the millions of dollars held in the accounts of those eight companies were the harvest of the "transit tax" he had been collecting on each kilo of morphine base passing through his controls enroute to the heroin labs of Istanbul. How marvelous! The idiotic youth of the west were rotting their brains away with their drugs while the money he was deriving from their habit was helping to finance the programs they were here to discuss this morning.

Mohatarian set his hands palms down on the conference table indicating it was time to address the main reason for their gathering. "Our nuclear program, my Brothers," he declared. "As you all know our great Islamic scientists have assured us that our nuclear reactor at Bushehr will be ready to begin operations no later than the middle of 2005. I spoke with them this morning and they assured me their work was on schedule. However, we have a problem caused by those American devils. That damn instrument of the devil Bush has been pressuring the Russians to promise him they will station permanent inspections teams at Bushehr to oversee the changing of the fuel rods and their shipment to Russia for reprocessing. He has even hinted that if they refuse to do so, the Israelis may attack our installation as they did the Iraqi reactor in Baghdad. The United Nations, again pressured by the Americans, are also insisting we bring our installation for enriching uranium under the control of the International Atomic Energy Agency in Vienna. So, as you see, the Americans with their obsession with what they like to refer to as the Axis of Evil, are determined to prevent us from acquiring the nuclear arms we need and deserve."

He leaned back to allow his words to register with his audience. Then he continued. "However, my Brothers, we have other means to fulfill our goals, means those damnable Americans ignore." He looked across the table at Bollahi. "Operation Khalid, Professor."

Bollahi rose and circled the table so that he could address the gathering from the proper professional position at the head of the table. "Brothers, as you will remember from my last report to you, we successfully extracted the fissile cores from the three Soviet nuclear artillery shells we bought from the Russians in Kazakhstan. As we suspected it would be, it was Plutonium 239 in its metallic form. Each weighs 5.7 kilograms and was configured in an oval shape so it could be used as an artillery shell. My team succeeded in reconfiguring those ovals into spheres which was critical for our next step."

He paused to be sure his next words would receive the attention he felt they merited. "Since our last meeting my weapons designers have worked night and day on their computers to produce a design which will allow us to obtain the maximum explosive yield possible from each of those three spheres."

"How powerful an explosion?" asked Imad Mugniyeh whose bomb at the Marine Corps barracks in Beirut had been the largest, single non-nuclear blast since the Second World War.

"Close to 25-30 kilotons a sphere."

"But what does that mean? In terms of what they can do to a big city?"

"It means that any one of those bombs, properly placed, could come close to wiping Tel Aviv off the face of the earth."

A reverential silence, altogether appropriate to the enormity of what he had just said, greeted his words.

"So!" exulted Mohatarian. "Who cares what the Americans do?! We will have our bomb in spite of them—and in secret!"

"Yes," the Professor agreed, "that day is coming, but it is not here yet. A very difficult task still lies ahead of us."

"What task?" demanded Mohatarian.

"We need two high technology items which we must have if we are going to be able to make our designers' plans work, and getting our hands on them may be even more difficult than getting our three artillery shells was."

"What are they? What's the problem?" Mohatarian pressed.

"They are called capacitors and krytrons," the Professor replied to an audience that had evidently never heard of either item.

"Don't tell me money is a problem," Mugniyeh laughed. "Not after what we just heard." The man was a cold-blooded killer but he was not without a sense of humor.

"No, money is not the problem. It's that the Americans have them and they won't sell them to us because we are the hated, evil Iranians."

"Can't you find a way around them?" Mohatarian asked.

"Perhaps. With subterfuge, and using a third party the Americans will never suspect of working with us. I have an idea but I do not wish for the moment to elaborate on it."

If there was anyone in the room who could talk with authority about buying hi-tech items the U.S. didn't want the Iranians to have, it was the Professor. From 1980 to 1995, he had supervised the purchase of 80 billion dollars worth of goods, most of them German, but some Austrian, Italian and French. His favorite tactic was to buy up small-sized firms in financial difficulty, dealing in defense-related industries. He would buy them, of course, in the name of offshore companies like those registered on the stock certificates he'd just recovered as a way of disguising the real identity of the firm's new owners.

He could then order products forbidden to Iran to be shipped to his new firm. Since the firms were inside the European Common Market, they could be shipped directly to his firm without an export license or any other troublesome piece of paper. Once they'd arrived at his new plant, he'd discreetly ship them to his airport north of Hamburg then illegally fly them off to Iran, frequently via Austria.

"I don't want to appear overconfident, my Brothers," he smiled. "But I am convinced that with my plan and a little time, we will have what we need."

Mohatarian plucked at the flesh of his neck, seeming to tug his head downward to give his blessing to the prediction the Professor had just uttered. He did not smile. Smiles came about as easily to Iran's chief terrorist as they did to a woman who had just had her fifth facelift. "You shall have the time you need my brother. You have never failed in your devotion to our cause. One day soon, I am sure, you will place in our hands that ultimate power the Americans are so determined to prevent us from having."

He turned to Mugniyeh. "I want you to start now to select the best, the most courageous fighters to deliver these bombs for us right into the heart of the Israelis' lands. Begin to prepare a plan, a plan that cannot fail," Mohatarian continued.

"Before we close our meeting," the Professor interjected, "I wish to make one vital point. Nothing will be more important to us than keeping Operation Khalid a total secret. No one must know of our project except my engineers working on it and those of us here in this room. We must not communicate among ourselves anything concerning our project by writing or by telephone, by cell phone or radio. Not even in a call from one room of this building to another. The Americans are diabolical in their ability to intercept communications. Fortunately, we now have a way to thwart them."

The Professor then outlined in detail the top secret coding equipment which he'd purchased in Switzerland and exactly how it worked. "Nothing, absolutely nothing concerning Operation Khalid must be transmitted except over this new system."

"It will be done as you have advised," Mohatarian declared. "Even more important, no one is to mention our project to anyone in the camp of Mohammed Khatemi and these so-called moderates with which he's surrounded himself."

He turned to the Professor. "When do you return to Europe?"

"I leave for Germany tomorrow."

"May God bless your noble work."

Night had long since fallen on the Eastern Mediterranean when the Dodge pickup truck eased off the E80 auto-route and onto the access road to the Gebze *Alani* lay-by, fifty kilometers (thirty miles) east of Istanbul. The driver advanced so slowly it was almost as though he was trying to slip his pick-up onto the enormous esplanade unseen.

It was hardly worth the trouble. The lay-by, the size of a couple of football fields, was nearly deserted. Half a dozen trucks, four of them TIR tractor-trailers were scattered around the huge esplanade, their dark forms resembling elephants grazing in a jungle clearing in the middle of the night. At the outer edge of the parking area, close to its center, a faint yellow light glowed from the shack that offered drivers a toilet or a cup of coffee. It was empty as far as the Falcon could see as he rolled past in his Dodge pickup. None of the trucks in the lay-by had their cab lights on. Their drivers were probably all sleeping on the bunks behind their seats. There was not a single private car in sight.

The Falcon spotted the TNZ Freight Forwarding Services truck he was looking for near the exit, set apart from the other TIR's in the lot like a rogue elephant shunned by his herd. He circled around the truck and parked so that the rear end of his pickup was parallel to the rear of the TIR.

Then, the Osman brothers' trusted cousin lit a cigarette, got out of the pickup, and strolled around the fringes of the parking area, looking for any hint of a police trap. The police rarely patrolled these lay-bys but when you worked for the Osman brothers, you went by the book. The only thing he saw, however, was the distant glimmer of moonlight on the Sea of Marmara.

Satisfied, he walked nonchalantly back to the TNZ truck, climbed up to the door of the cab and rapped gently on the window. A sleep-sodden face appeared, eyes blinking uncertainly, then an unseen hand lowered the window a couple of inches.

"Oranges," the Falcon said. "I've come for the oranges."

"*Efendim,* sir," the driver replied in what the Falcon thought probably represented the outer limits of the dumb Iranian bastard's knowledge of Turkish. Two thousand years we've lived side by side and we still can't communicate with each other. The driver knew, of course, that he was carrying dope but he had no idea where it was hidden. Had he been stopped by suspicious customs officers, there was no way he was going to be able to help them find it. The Falcon, on the other hand knew exactly where the "oranges" were and started off for their hiding place at the rear of the truck. The driver went back to sleep on his bunk bed. Tossing dope around was not something he was paid to do.

At the back of the TIR, the Falcon located the support bar of the rear light cluster and slowly ran his fingertips along its inner surface until they found what they were looking for, a button not much larger than a teenager's pimple. He pressed it.

The panel concealing the two-foot-wide entry port of the hollow trap built into the bedding of the truck dropped open. The Falcon had now only to grasp the edges of the wooden tray bearing the morphine base and start sliding it out of the trap.

He worked as fast and as hard as he could. These were the critical moments. If a police car drove in now because some cop needed to have a pee or take a nap, he was dead. Unloading the morphine base took just over twenty minutes. When he'd finished, the Falcon pushed the tray back into its place in the trap, closed the panel and drove off. He did not bother to wake up the driver. Why? he thought. Let the bastard sleep.

He had only a few kilometers to go before he turned off the auto-route towards a destination marked by a roadside sign *"Feribot"*—fer-ryboat. He timed his arrival to make sure his was the last vehicle onto the roll-on, roll-off ferry. That way he could be sure no tail had picked up his Dodge. He also made sure his was the last vehicle off the Yalova ferry, allowing him once again to be certain no one followed him as he drove along the coastal road stretching down the finger of land thrust-ing out into the Sea of Marmara from Izmit to the village of Taskopru where he turned left up a dirt road.

The lab was barely a kilometer out of the village of Kabakli Kogu, a collection of a dozen primitive homes clustered around a mosque. Next to the mosque was a community hall built in 1933 to herald for the mullah's flock the arrival of the new secular Turkey of Mustafa Kemal Ataturk. The lab itself was perched on a hilltop overlooking 13 hectares (28 acres) of basically worthless land. A dozen neglected apple trees, imaginatively described by a real estate agent as an "orchard," straggled down the hillside to the ravine cutting along the base of the land.

It was there in that ravine, however, that was located the priceless and vital asset that had prompted the Osmans to buy the property: a vastly productive well.

Water, and lots of it, was critical to the operation of a heroin lab. From that well, their workers could draw off all the water they needed for their lab without arousing a water company's curiosity about just what it was they were watering on 28 acres of uncultivated land. Once used, they could flush the water back out onto the hillside where no one would come across traces of the chemicals left over from the refining process.

The lab was not much bigger than a two-car garage. The eaves running along the roof were hinged so they could be propped open when the conversion process was underway to evacuate the noxious fumes it produced. The finished result deserved to be called a laboratory about as much as a hay wain deserves to be called a Rolls-Royce. It was ramshackle, primitive and rundown and it blended in perfectly with the surroundings. Since the lab had processed its first morphine base in 1992, it had been turning out close to 2500 kilograms of heroin a year, two-and-a-half metric tons, a very impressive contribution to Turkey's annual heroin exports.

The lab did contain one innovation designed by Hassan Osman himself. It was an underground cellar built into the hillside and entered by a trap door covered with dirt when the lab wasn't working. In that cellar, the lab's workmen stored their sixty-gallon drums of acetic anhydride and ether, their hotel-style electric mixer, their plastic pots three feet in diameter, all the equipment they needed for their work. Burst into the lab when it wasn't actually turning out heroin and it looked like any poor peasants tool house.

The Falcon pulled up in front of the gate and blinked his headlights. The entrance was sealed off by a white iron grill, one half of it sagging like a flag at half mast from a broken hinge. A pair of shadows emerged from the cottage adjoining the lab and ran to open the gate. The Falcon drove his pick-up along the side of the cottage right up to the door of the lab.

He then tramped back to the cottage leaving the two workers to carry the 210 sacks of morphine base from his truck to the trestle table waiting for them in the shed. Two more men were in the living room of the cottage watching a German pornographic video-cassette, all its grunts and groans thoughtfully sub-titled in Turkish. One of the two was the key man in the operation, the chemist or the "cooker."

Like the others, he was a Kurd, a man in his late forties, a gaunt figure well over six feet tall with a stubble of gray hair cut close to his scalp, sunken cheeks and a distant, melancholy glaze to his face. Like all of the cookers in Turkey's clandestine labs, he was referred to respectfully as "doktor" and like almost all of them, he was hopelessly addicted to the toxic substance he produced. The fumes given off by the conversion process were strong enough to drug an elephant. The other workers could escape into the fresh air periodically but not the doktor. He had to remain in the shed overseeing operations, limiting his intake of the drug's fumes as best he could with a surgical mask. He and the other addicted cookers like him were walking refutations of the absurd notion that smoked heroin was somehow not addictive.

Because of his addiction, the doktor, like most of his colleagues was paid partly in cash, partly in heroin, a tactic designed by their employers to keep those cookers docile and malleable in between the arrival of loads of base at the labs they serviced.

To even suggest that the label "doktor" implied in the gentleman's case some degree of academic accomplishment was a grotesque joke. He had barely managed to finish primary school. Like most of Turkey's good cookers, he'd learned his trade as a kid in Lice Province in the late sixties watching an older cooker, in this case his uncle, at work. To that basic practical knowledge of the steps required to convert morphine base to heroin, he brought, as all good cookers did, an instinctive flair for the job. Just as there are chefs who seem constitutionally unable to make a bad sauce, there are doktors who possess an innate genius for converting morphine base into heroin.

In a sense, this barely literate Turkish Kurd was the lineal descendant of the godfather of modern heroin chemists, an illiterate French merchant seaman named Joseph Cesari, the patron saint of the famous French Connection. In the kitchen of a country farmhouse in Provence, 50 kilometers (30 miles) from Marseilles, Cesari could turn out heroin at an astonishing 98 percent purity, a feat few cookers could duplicate 45 years later.

Seeing the Falcon walk in the door, the doktor snapped off his pornographic video in mid-orgasm and stood up. "So we are ready to begin?"

"When you are."

The doktor picked up an alarm clock and set it against his watch, then led the way out the door down to the shed. The process upon which he was about to embark required seventeen separate steps over 24 hours and once it was started it couldn't be stopped without losing the entire batch of heroin being cooked up.

The doktor's first act was to weigh out forty of the one kilo sacks of Ghulam Hamid's base on his scale to be sure their weight was exact. Then he dumped the contents into the first of the three huge pots in the shed. He could process forty kilos (88 pounds) of base a day, a marked improvement over Joseph Cesari's output, but otherwise, the procedure he was starting had changed little since the days when the French merchant seaman had been the Brillat Savarin of heroin cooks.

Next he weighed out a kilo of acetic anhydride, a colorless, highly flammable liquid, one kilo for each of his 40 kilos of base. The barrels from which he poured them out still bore the name of their manufacturer, Hoechst GmbH of Frankfurt, Germany's largest manufacturer of chemical products. Turkey, in fact, did not produce so much as a barrel of that chemical used, among other things, in insecticides, medicines and film processing.

Since acetic anhydride was such a vital element in the conversion of morphine base to heroin, the nations of Europe had signed a convention in Vienna in 1988 that was supposed to control the chemical's export when there was reason to believe it might be used to produce heroin. In a blatant gesture of indifference to those legal constraints, Hoechst had agreed in 1993 to ship a staggering 200 tons of the chemical over the period of a year to a Syrian company operating out of the free port of Abu Dhabi. With one order, Hoechst was agreeing to ship out enough acetic anhydride to process potentially all of Turkey's heroin exports for the next two and a half years.

When the executive who authorized the sale went through the motions required by the treaty of asking what the chemical was going to be used for, he was informed it would be employed to make camel shampoo. The quantity of chemical in question could have shampooed every camel on the globe several times over. Nonetheless, the Hoechst executive went right ahead and approved the sale.

The chemical, of course, never lathered the hump of a single camel. The Turkish police seized two huge consignments of it as traffickers were attempting to smuggle it into Turkey. The barrels ranged in the doktor's shed were some of the hundreds of others that hadn't been intercepted on their illegal journeys to labs like his.

Carefully, slowly, the doktor poured those 40 kilos of chemical onto the brownish granules of the morphine base in his huge pot. In minutes, it began its bubbling transformation from morphine base into heroin.

BOOK FIVE

Rien Ne Va **PLUS**

Jim Duffy had just begun to work his way through his daily load of intercepts when the red alert light on his computer blinked informing him that his liaison officer at the NSA wanted a word with him.

"Mr. Duffy, I think we've got something!" The young NSA officer made no attempt to conceal his exuberance. The guy is about to prove to me why that agency he works for is worth the four billion bucks of taxpayers' money they get every year, Duffy thought.

"As you instructed, I've started to crunch the phone number of that cloned mobile out in Istanbul through our computer back logs. Two calls dropped out," he reported. "Both from London. From the same telephone number."

"Have you got a location on the London phone?"

"Yeah. It's one of those red British public pay phones. On Eccleston Street just outside the Belgian Consulate in Belgravia. A very up-market area."

"Shit!" Duffy growled. "A pay phone. Wouldn't you know? Is the Iranian Embassy anywhere near there?"

"No. It's way over by Hyde Park."

"Were the calls in English?"

"No, both of them were in Farsi. I ran both intercepts by our linguistic experts. They say there's no doubt—both parties were native Farsi speakers."

"When were they made?"

"Just over three weeks ago. Three days apart. Each of them was made around mid-day."

"So, either the guy who was making those calls was afraid his home or his office phone was tapped or he didn't want anybody tracing those calls back to him."

"Or both."

"Right. He probably lives or works not too far away, say half a mile from that phone booth, wouldn't you think?"

"Yessir, I think that's probably right. Like to listen to the calls? We've translated them. Sounds like they're making an effort to be very discreet."

"Put 'em on." Duffy switched on his computer link to the NSA at Fort Meade, Maryland and the text of the first call came blinking up on his screen.

"Jaffar?"

"Yes."

"Tari here. Are you well?"

"Thanks be to God."

"I met with the Professor in Budapest recently. We are going to make some changes in our operations."

"I am at your service."

"Do you have many *[speaker's pause]* shipments coming in from Said?"

"Four."

"What is their value?"

"It will be close to a million and a half."

"Hold them in your account in the islands. You will receive new instructions from me for transferring them."

"Understood."

"Said does well."

"Everything is working fine since he has been in charge."

" Does he still trim his sandals in gold?"

" I don't know, my friend. I have never met him. We only speak."

"Good. We will talk soon."

"God willing."

"That's the first one," the NSA officer reported.

Gold sandals? Duffy was ready to whoop in delight. Could that guy in Istanbul be referring to his Gucci Mooj? Clearly, this guy Tari was talking about money with his friend in Istanbul. Was this the money Djailani was supposed to be skimming off the drug traffic? Finally, these damn intercepts were getting him somewhere. "OK. Pop the second one through," he ordered.

"Jaffar?"

"Yes."

"Tari here. You are well?"

"Thanks be to God."

"Have you received my new instructions?"

"This morning."

"In addition to the deliveries you mentioned, is there anything else due soon?"

"Said told me yesterday three more are coming."

"Good. Move everything according to the new instructions."

"At your orders. Shall I inform our brothers in Tehran?"

"I've already handled that. We shall talk soon."

"God willing."

Duffy studied his screen a second. "Get everything you can off that number we intercepted in Iran for the day following that call. This thing is finally getting interesting. Let me make a couple calls and I'll be back to you."

Duffy glanced at his watch. It was four-thirty, nine-thirty in the evening in London. The station chief was an old pal of Duffy's but he had certainly left his office for the day. Would he have a secure phone link to Langley from his home? Almost certainly. But was he home? Or was he out drinking camel curds at the embassy of Inner Mongolia to help celebrate their National Day, the kind of heavy duty assignment CIA station chiefs were pulling down these days. Should he beep him, pass him an order to get back to the embassy and a secure phone for what might turn out to be a particularly nebulous mission?

He was ready to let him enjoy his evening in peace when he remembered all the times Washington had pulled him out of bed in the middle of the night for something as urgent as learning the middle name of the Foreign Minister of the Sudan. Screw it, he thought and ordered up an urgent night action message to London.

An hour later as he was getting ready to close up his office for the night, his phone rang.

"You're on a secure line to London," an operator's voice informed him as he picked it up.

"Jimbo!" his caller exclaimed. "Welcome back. I heard they'd made you start working for a living again. Whatever have they got you doing?"

"Making trouble for nice guys like you." Duffy had recognized the voice immediately. He and Bob Cowie, the London Station Chief, had served together briefly in the seventies at the CIA's Manhattan station.

"I hope my call didn't pull you away from any event critical to our national security," Duffy asked. "Like dinner at Annabel's?"

"Not at all. I was at a little dinner for eight at the Baron Bentinck's. Your summons only served to enhance the air of mystery in which I seek to shroud myself."

"That ain't easy these days when they're trying to turn us into a bunch of filing clerks," Duffy observed.

"Indeed! How sad to be a keeper of the secrets when there seem to be no secrets left to keep. What pray, can I do for you? For old times sake."

Cowie laughed when Duffy had finished outlining his request. "So I'm to find you an Iranian named Tari or, more likely, Tariq, who is into money and hopefully dope and frequents Belgravia which, quite frankly, is the last place you're likely to find admirers of the Iranian Revolution. Of the late, lamented Shahinshah, perhaps. But certainly not the mullahs."

"Well, however bizarre this one may seem, it's front burner," Duffy assured him. "It's even got the director's eye, bless him."

A bell suddenly went off in Cowie's brain. "Hey," he said, "I just might have something for you. You in your office?"

"Of course."

"Don't go away. I'll be back to you in a couple of minutes."

"What's up?" Duffy asked when his phone rang minutes later.

"Well, I have some rather good news for you assorted, as is so often the case, with a sprinkling of bad news."

"Give me the good news first."

"I've found your Iranian, I think. First name Tari just as you'd wanted. Last name Harmian. Residence barely a seven minute stroll from that public pay phone you gave us."

"That's great! What bad news can you possibly have for me after that?"

"He's dead."

"Oh shit!"

"Murdered in a particularly grisly fashion about a month ago. In his home. Virtually in front of his wife. He made the front pages of both the *Daily Mail* and the *Daily Express,* which is a most impressive way to go. The *Mail* speculated that he'd been involved in drugs. The *Express* was rather more inclined to put it down to the arms traffic."

"How about the cops?"

"It appears that it was a highly professional killing. No clues left behind. Apparently, Scotland Yard at the moment doesn't have a clear handle on who did it. But now here's what's very interesting from our point of view."

"I'm all ears."

"The wife. She's American. California girl. She came in here a few days after the murder to see the ambassador. She claims her husband was killed by the Iranian secret service."

"Why does she think that? Was he active politically?"

"She says he talked to the killers in Farsi. Ergo they had to be Iranian. The Yard, she claims, refuses to listen to her. They want to put the death down to some kind of financial wheeling and dealing that went wrong. Or maybe an unpaid gambling debit."

"What do you have on him?"

"Not much. To all extents and purposes he seemed to have been just another member of London's rather large and generally well to do Iranian expatriate colony. Refugees from the mullahs. He had a stateless person's passport. Oxbridge type, I gather. After the wife came into see the ambassador, I checked him out with the dissidents we're in contact with. He'd never been involved with any of them."

"Well, Robert, I think I might just come over to have a chat with the Yard and his grieving widow. Can I bring you anything? A couple of porn magazines perhaps?"

————

"Jim, you've been away too long." Jack Lohnes, the agency's Director of Operations chuckled to his first visitor of the morning. "You're not clued in to how sensitive the Brits are these days. We just can't go in there and start walking on their grass without first liaisoning with our counterparts at Six."

"Well, this would just be a kind of preliminary canvass, wouldn't it? Check out the implications of what we gleaned from those intercepts. I mean, after all, the wife's one of ours. Surely, we've got the right to have a private conversation with her, assuming she's willing. Which, after what she told the ambassador, she certainly is."

"Jim, she can be helpful. But face it, the people you really want to get on to are at Scotland Yard. They will have gone in there, taken over the guy's files, his computer discs, run his phone bills, bank records. If there is any clue lying around as to how this guy Harmian was working with Djailani, that's where it will be. In the Yard's investigation files. How do you think we ask them to show all that to us without telling them where you're coming from?"

Duffy made his best effort to adorn his face with a winning smile. Timidity, he was discovering, was the hallmark of the CIA these days. "Hell, Jack, why don't we just tell the friends at Six what I learned in Cyprus about those three Iranian nukes? Let them on to what it is we're really after here. Then they'll pry open that murder investigation for us themselves."

"Nobody around here is going to be eager to do that, Jimbo, believe me. After Iraq, our brave European allies, even the Brits, get quite uptight when we hint at the wisdom of putting a couple of cruise missiles on Tehran. It'll be 'here come those nasty Americans beating up on the poor Iranians again.' You should have heard the screams of righteous horror we got out of Paris and Bonn when we hinted we might pop a couple of cruise missiles onto Tehran for their killing those 19 kids in the Air Force barracks in Saudi. We start saying 'hey, the Iranians have nukes' and Paris and Bonn and our Labor friends in London will leak it. Whisper to their press that we're getting ready to obliterate Iran on the strength of some unproven rumor. We'll have Tony Benn on Channel Four screaming about how the Americans are trying to further their evil, imperialist Post Cold War schemes."

Duffy hiked his feet onto his friend's coffee table and leaned back into his U.S. Government issue sofa, model 14B, designed for the offices of officials with the equivalent rank of Brigadier General or higher. Lohnes, he understood, was not being timid; he was being realistic.

"OK," he said after a moment's thought. "Suppose we come at it from another angle. We play the drug card. We're the DEA. We suspect this guy might have been into narcotics which in fact he was, at least tangentially. We want to sit down with our English cousins, show them what we've got, see what they've got, all in the interests of advancing our common aims in the war on drugs."

Lohnes laughed. "You mean instead of trying to tiptoe past them when they're not looking, we resort to dissimulation, falsehoods and duplicity?"

"Yeah, all kinds of good stuff like that."

"Might just work," Lohnes acknowledged.

"You know, we take them out to lunch, informal like, belt down a few pints of Guinness, rub shoulders, compare notes. The CIA? Who the hell are those guys? Never heard of them."

Lohnes was silent for a moment thinking "Do I run this one past the director to cover our asses in case something goes wrong?" There were guys at the agency now who went around with chapped fingers because they were always sticking them up in the air to see which way the wind was blowing. Lohnes, however, was not one of them.

"OK, I think your idea just might play. But then you'll have to take that DEA guy Flynn downstairs along with you. He'll know how to talk the talk and walk the walk with the Limeys. You just sit there and listen and learn."

———

"Rien ne va plus." Whether in Istanbul or Monte Carlo, Las Vegas or London, that croupier's cry always contained the same note of finality, the sound that marked the little ball's dying passage through the grooves of a roulette wheel.

"Dix-Sept, Noir, Impair—Seventeen, Black, Odd," the croupier sang out as the ball dropped into a slot.

As the croupier began to rake in the wheel's losing bets, Refat Osman, the third of the five Osman brothers approached the table preceded by the kind of entourage that might have accompanied the chief of state of a minor African nation on an official visit to Paris.

First came three of his "dogs," bodyguards, stocky, scowling men, their eyes systematically scanning the table for an unfriendly face or an unwelcome gesture. Next came a pair of "Natashas," the Russian ladies of Istanbul's night, both blondes, one wearing her hair in a disorderly beehive, the other letting hers fall straight to her shoulders. Both wore dresses that clung to distinctly post-modern Russian figures, figures as far removed from those of the dumpy babushkas shovelling snow in their mothers' Stalinist days as Beverly Hills was from Smolensk. Finally, advancing with the dignified pace of a general inspecting his honor guard, came the Osman brother in charge of "killing and carrying."

Ten years younger than his brother Selim, the family patriarch, he was taller and, because he spent more time in a gym than in the *hamam,* considerably more athletic. He would have been considerably better looking as well were it not for the fact his features seemed cold and composed, frozen into the expressionless mask of a man to whom both humor and compassion were alien emotions.

As the Barcelona Gran Hotel was his brother's office, this private club was Refat's preferred locale for carrying out his business and this late evening hour the height of his working day. Nothing except the funeral of a friend or a foe could get Refat out of the bedroom of his Florya duplex before noon. Turkey's Islamist government had closed the nation's gambling casinos in one of its last official acts, but gaming tables still existed in a few restricted private clubs like this one in Istanbul's Taksim area.

Refat usually spent the late afternoon drifting through the third class bars and hotels of Laleli, a run-down neighborhood inhabited by Third World citizens, Pakistanis, Nigerians, Lebanese, and Iranians. They were people Refat some times had to call on to accomplish his more sordid tasks, but it was here that he scheduled his major meetings. For Refat it was the ideal venue in which to make discreet contact with politicians and policemen on the take.

He pressed a $500 chip into the hand of each of his "Natashas," urging them to enjoy themselves while he wandered off to meet a few friends. With a nod, he designated one of his "dogs" to watch over them while he was gone. They were after all, his personal property and trespassers were not welcome on the premises. Then he drifted through the crowd on his way to his first business meeting of the night.

Refat's meeting was with the owner of a TIR trucking firm, the Interstate Rapid Serviz Shipping Company, one of the 425 such firms in Turkey. Those firms ranged in size from one-man, one-truck operations to transportation giants running over a thousand rigs into Europe, the republics of the old Soviet Union, Syria and Lebanon. They comprised the largest fleet of TIR trucks in Europe, vital, the Turks maintained to move their foodstuffs to market in Europe and bring back the manufactured goods the country didn't produce. Horse shit, remarked cynical police and customs agents in Western Europe. What the Turks needed all those trucks for was to move dope.

Refat's contact ran a medium-sized firm running fifty trucks, principally to Germany, Holland, and France. For almost a year he had been the prime carrier of the Osman's heroin. Refat had developed a considerable degree of confidence in the man. Still, once he'd placed the dope in the trucker's hands, he had no idea in which of his trucks it would be heading west, what route the truck would take or who the driver would be. Those were secrets the trucker chose to keep to himself.

"So," the trucker said, taking a taste of the whiskey Refat had ordered for him. "You've got 180 pairs of jeans ready for delivery?" A pair of jeans was the code they employed to refer to a kilo of heroin.

"Yeah. I'm told we'll be ready to consign them to you Monday night."

"Where are they going?"

"Amsterdam. The usual place."

The trucker was a corpulent man in his late fifties, a former driver who'd fought his way up to his current entrepreneurial status. His hair, at least what was left of it, was white, his complexion florid. His teeth were like the stars, they came out at night and Refat could hear them clicking now as the trucker used a gulp of whiskey and soda as a mouthwash before swallowing it off. "Good," he declared. "No problem there."

Indeed, for the past year he'd been running heroin into Amsterdam with no more difficulty than Federal Express has running overnight parcels across the Atlantic.

"We meet at the bank at ten then?" he suggested.

Refat nodded his agreement. The meeting would reflect a little confidence boosting measure Refat had devised as an insurance policy for his family's heroin while it was in transit. Once he'd placed the heroin in the trucker's hands, it was the man's responsibility to see that every gram of it reached its destination. There was just one exception to that. If the police or customs somehow managed to seize the dope, the loss would be the Osmans'.

Tuesday, the two men would open a jointly held, double-keyed safety deposit box at the Turk Merchant Bank in Bebek. Refat would put $180,000 in cash into it, the truckers transportation fee for 180 kilos of heroin. The trucker would place a sealed envelope beside it. It would contain the name of the driver he had assigned to take the dope and the registration number of his truck. That way, in the unlikely event police or customs somewhere along the line should seize the load, he would be able to prove to Refat by matching the information in the envelope with the newspaper reports of the seizure that it was indeed, the Osmans' dope the authorities had confiscated.

Refat tapped the driver on the thigh, drawing away as he did from the man's face. His breath was so vile it could have curdled milk at six paces. "I'll confirm the delivery time to you Monday."

With that he glanced across the room. His Natashas were still huddled intently over their roulette wheel. *Rien ne va plus,* girls, he thought, getting up and shaking hands with the trucker.

———

United Airlines Flight 918 from Washington's Dulles airport to London Heathrow lifted off into the winter night thirty minutes behind schedule. As it reached its cruising altitude, Jim Duffy unsnapped his seat belt and sank into the comfort of his club class seat.

By U.S. government procedures, federal employees are supposed to fly the Atlantic in economy class along with the majority of their fellow countrymen. Washington does, however, allow exceptions to the practice for employees of ambassadorial rank or higher or those who have a physical disability which would make a long flight in an economy class seat an uncomfortable experience.

Jim Duffy's left knee had been generously sprinkled with shrapnel from a Soviet rocket launcher as he was leaping for cover in a ditch during a dust-up in the Parrot's Beak in 1985. He shouldn't have been there in the first place, of course. Casey had laid down strict orders that no CIA officer was to stray north of the Afghanistan-Pakistan border. What would have been more satisfying to Moscow than to be able to parade before the world's television cameras a CIA officer taken prisoner in Afghanistan while fighting with the mujahiddin?

On the other hand Duffy knew his mooj warriors had no respect for men who were not willing to expose themselves to the dangers of enemy fire. What could Duffy do? How could you send men out to die if they had no respect for you or what, by extension, you represented? He had elected to ignore Casey's orders and, wrapped in the robes of an Afghan fighter, gone north across the border with his commandos.

The mooj had gotten him back to one of their training camps just inside Pakistan where his wounds were put down to the accidental explosion of a hand grenade. For a couple of years, Duffy had been left with a stiff and occasionally sore left knee and the agency's doctors had given him a travel waiver entitling him to an upgrade to club class air travel.

Now his knee was as limber as a ballerina's but when he'd returned to duty, a friendly doctor had winked and extended his waiver. On the grounds that they would have to work together during their flight, Duffy had gotten the DEA's Mike Flynn upgraded as well.

"Gentlemen," the stewardess said, placing two tins of macadamia nuts on the armrest between them, "can I get you a drink before dinner?"

"Why not?" Duffy grinned. "How about a scotch and soda. Lots of ice. In fact, why not make it a double. Save yourself a trip later on."

"Sure. And you, sir?" she asked the DEA agent.

Flynn reflected a moment. "Maybe a Diet Coke."

Duffy glanced at him, barely able to conceal his disdain. I get you moved up here where the drinks are free and you order, he thought, a Diet Coke?

"Where you from, Flynn?"

"Worcester, Mass."

Duffy tried to remember what, if anything, he knew about the place. "Oh yeah," he said. "Holy Cross. You go to Holy Cross?"

"Yes. I've always admired the intellectual rigor of the Jesuits."

My God, Duffy thought. A Diet Coke? The intellectual rigor of the Jesuits? This guy is going to be a barrel of laughs on this little trip. "So how do you like working with the agency's Counter Narcotic Section? Must be quite different from the stuff you're used to doing for the DEA." Duffy accompanied his query with his best approximation of a "just between us brothers" smile.

"Oh, it's different alright. But I'm finally getting used to the way you guys do business."

"Yeah. We move in somewhat more mysterious ways than law enforcement does." Even Duffy was a little troubled by just how smug those words sounded as they escaped his mouth.

"Mysterious?" Flynn laughed. "Devious would be a better word. But it is a political education, I'll admit that."

"How so?" Duffy asked.

"Well, at the DEA we tend to think in black and white terms. Is it against the law or not? At your place I've been getting an education in some of the other realities that govern—some people might say limit—our ability to fight the drug traffic."

Duffy glanced down the airplane's aisle. "Where the hell's my scotch?" he grumbled. He was going to have to work with this guy so better ignore his choirboy's outlook on life.

The stewardess had, in the meantime, arrived to help them extract their trays from their armrests and was now setting them up for dinner. Duffy took a long swallow of the scotch the stewardess had set before him and a handful of macadamia nuts. "Anyway, what's your take on those intercepts I showed you?"

"Hard to escape the conclusion that the late Mr. Harmian was getting ready to rip off his pals in Tehran, isn't it? That last line there where he tells the guy he's talking to in Istanbul, not to worry, he'll handle Tehran is the tip-off."

"I agree," Duffy said. "You have to ask yourself 'did that guy in Istanbul call Tehran anyway, just to make sure everything was OK?' That would have sent up a few warning signals, wouldn't it?"

"For sure. You know one of the things we might want to ask the Yard to do for us is run through the phone logs of that red pay phone Harmian used. Maybe he was using it for other calls he didn't want picked up."

"Good thinking. By the way, do you think our English friends are likely to pick up on the fact I'm not really DEA?"

"Probably. The Brits aren't fools. It isn't going to do wonders for our relations with them when they do."

Flynn, course, had not been briefed on the Iranians' possession of three nuclear devices.

"Well, the time will come when we'll bring them into the picture. There are some other national security concerns at stake here that will reassure them, I think."

———

"Genial chaos." That was perhaps the best way to describe the atmosphere all around Refat Osman on his afternoon stroll down the steep alley running from just below the luxurious high rises of Istanbul's Taksim Square towards the waters of the Golden Horn. The alley was so narrow two cars couldn't pass each other on its paving stones and when they tried to, the consequence was a cacophonous chorus of horns and angry voices. Laundry lines covered with everything from diapers to bed-sheets hung from the windows along the alley, snapping in the chill wind off the Bosphorous like the sails of an armada of small craft changing tacks in the midst of a regatta.

It was a neighborhood of gypsies, gangsters, and garages, and Refat's destination was one of the score of small garages along the alley, the Opel Oto Mecanik. It, in fact, belonged to the Osman family. As he entered, the garagist rushed up to grasp his hand. "I've got one!" he smiled.

"At this time of year?" Refat replied. "Really?"

"Yeah. Over in Beykoz"—Beykoz was a community on the Asian side of the Bosphorous—"a 1996 Vega. The guy lives in Hamburg. He's here with his wife for his father's funeral. They're going to be driving back to Germany in about a week. And she's German, not Turkish."

What had triggered the garagist's excitement was the prospect of putting into play a highly innovative scheme designed by Refat for smuggling heroin into Western Europe. It was why he owned this garage. He had never driven an Opel in his life nor did he ever intend to do so.

That innocent Turk over in Beykoz for his father's funeral would go out shopping one day soon. Stopping for a red light in Istanbul's chaotic traffic, he would suddenly hear a loud crash as the car behind him smashed into the rear of his Opel.

The driver of the other car, usually the Falcon, would leap out and come rushing up to him. Instead of being angry, however, he would be, for a Turkish driver, remarkably contrite. It was all his fault, he'd say.

He'd let his attention wander. A pretty girl passing by. Or his worries about his mother's health. And the terrible thing was his insurance had run out. Fortunately, however, he had a brother, cousin, friend who ran an Opel garage. A real mechanical genius. He'd get him to fix up his car like new, throw in a new paint job for his troubles. He, the guilty party, would, of course, settle the bill directly with his friend.

And indeed, Refat's Opel Oto Mecanik would do a first class repair job on the man's car—with a couple of imaginative innovations thrown in. The owner's address in Hamburg would be duly noted down from his registration papers. A duplicate set of his keys would be made. And the garagist would build a trap large enough to hold ten to fifteen kilos of heroin behind the felt lining of the trunk at the base of the rear seat.

Off the unwitting Turk and his German wife would go in their freshly painted car, driving home to Hamburg with fifteen kilos of heroin tucked into Refat's secret trap.

In Hamburg, one of the Osman's men would shadow the car, observing the Turk's driving patterns. He parked over night in the street in front of his house? One night around two a.m., using the duplicate set of keys that had been made in Istanbul, Osman's men would come by, take the car to some quiet street nearby, unload the heroin and return the car to its parking place.

The ploy worked best in the fall and summer when thousands of Turks, resident in Germany or elsewhere in Europe, drove home on vacation. In the one in a thousand chance that the unsuspecting Turk was caught in a Customs check, what could he do? He had no piece of paper, no bill, no estimate to prove that his car had ever been in the Opel Oto Mecanik. There were dozens of garages just like it up and down the Dolpadere. Well, what the hell, Refat thought. This was too good an opportunity to miss. That Turk out in Beykoz was going to go back to Hamburg with a gleaming new coat of paint on his Opel Vega.

"DCS MacPherson?"

"Aye," replied Detective Chief Superintendent Fraser MacPherson, the man in charge of the investigation into Tari Harmian's murder, "himself speaking."

"Hold just a moment please for the Commander of Special Operations."

MacPherson's bushy eyebrows peaked in concern. The CSO, he thought. What the hell does this bloke want from me? He doesn't speak to me from one year to the next.

"Ah, MacPherson," the CSO said coming onto the line, his voice lubricated with feigned cordiality. "How's business then? Everything alright?"

"Right as the rain we haven't been getting, Commander. How can I help you?"

"Re that murder investigation you're running . . ."

"Which one, Commander? I'm running six of them."

"The one with that Iranian guy."

"Ah, that one."

"Making any headway?"

Someone at the Home Office is pushing his button, MacPherson thought. For some reason the case was generating political heat which was not reassuring. "Not much, I'm afraid to say. A right tough one it is. Why?"

"I've just had a call from a friend over at the American Embassy. The DEA man, their drugs officer. It seems he's got a couple of big shots from Washington passing through town. Apparently they're aware of the case. They'd like to meet you." Oh would they now, MacPherson thought. This is about as coincidental as the chimes of Big Ben ringing out at midnight. It means the Americans have got something on Harmian. Question was, would they be sharing it with him? Not bloody likely knowing how the Americans worked. Still professional courtesy dictated that he accept their invitation—particularly since it was being conveyed by the Commander of Special Operations.

"Certainly, Commander. What would you suggest?"

"Lunch tomorrow? Say at the Bunch of Grapes Pub on the Brompton Road just past Harrod's? Those visitors might want to go shopping after lunch. One o'clock suit you?"

"I'll be there with pleasure."

———

Barely one week after the Falcon had unloaded his 210 kilos of morphine base from the TNZ TIR truck at the lay-by outside Istanbul, its conversion into heroin was complete. He had picked up the drug, 240 kilos vacuum-packed into one kilo sacks, and delivered it to the family's Texas Country Jeans factory-warehouse in the village of Enseler on the road to Istanbul's Ataturk Airport.

The Osman brothers had built a closet with a steel fire door into one corner of their Country Jeans office, ostensibly as a storage place for their valuables, in reality as a hiding place for their most valued possession, refined heroin awaiting onward shipment to Europe. No one was in the warehouse except Refat when the Falcon arrived. Refat checked the sacks in one by one.

Two hours later a second truck, bearing the markings of InterState Rapid Serviz Shipping arrived at the warehouse. It was driven by one of the trusted drivers of the trucker Refat had met the evening before in his "office." Refat watched in silence as the driver loaded 180 of his newly arrived sacks into his trucks and drove off—a million and a half dollars worth of "merchandise" disappearing into the night. None of the Osman brothers would have any idea where their dope was, or what was happening to it until it showed up in their warehouse in Amsterdam one, two, three weeks later.

———

We're staring at each other from across the two sides of this luncheon table like a couple of college teams, Duffy thought, kids about to square off in one of those riveting local TV quiz shows with names like

"Campus Challenge"—the kind of program no one watches except the contestant's mothers.

On the U.K. side you had the Commander of Special Operations of Scotland Yard and the detective running the investigation into the murder of Tari Harmian. On the American side, he was flanked by the DEA's London Country Attache and Mike Flynn. To let the Englishmen know what a good sport he was, Duffy had ordered a pint of draught Guinness from which he now took a tentative sip. It was almost as warm as the chicken broth his mother used to serve him when he was sick as a kid.

"Jim and Mike here," the Country Attache was saying, "are members of a Washington Task Force studying current developments in drug money laundering. They have some very solid reasons to suspect that the late Mr. Harmian was involved in it."

"Why would they be thinking that now?" MacPherson asked.

Flynn, who'd been told to handle the DEA's end of their little chat, answered. "First, his occupation which your press gave as a 'private investment counsellor.' We're finding more and more in our work in the states that that's just an acronym for money launderer." He glanced towards the Commander. "Perhaps you've been encountering the same phenomenon."

"Moving money he was, alright," MacPherson agreed, "but are you suggesting a drug connection here? If there is, I haven't found it." He was determined to see what cards the Americans were going to play before he played his. They had something. They hadn't come all the way from Washington just to drink warm beer. "We are convinced the Iranians are now major players in the international heroin traffic, and particularly in the heroin that's coming into your country. Your victim was, after all, an Iranian."

"Maybe. But all the evidence I have indicates he was clean of any ties to the regime in Tehran. We checked out his background. He came out as a solid supporter of the old Shah."

"Sometimes these people deliberately take on a false political coloration to disguise their real functions."

MacPherson shrugged. "Maybe. You can surmise this and you can surmise that if you want. I have to go where the evidence takes me at the end of the day. And so far I've found nothing to tie Mr. Harmian to either drugs or the mullahs. Now if, on the other hand, you have something that can further my investigation . . ."

As he was finishing his sentence, the Scot's alert eyes saw Flynn glance towards the heavier guy drinking the Guinness. That's it, he thought. They've got something they think ties Harmian to drugs and those people in Tehran and they're here to see if I can confirm it for them.

Duffy took a swallow of his lukewarm Guinness with a minimum of enthusiasm. It was time to cough up the jewels. He took a copy of the two NSA intercepts from his pocket and slid them across the table to MacPherson.

"I don't think I have to spell out the source on these for you, Chief, and we'd much appreciate your discretion here. One of the two speakers in these intercepts is the late Mr. Harmian. The other is a guy in Istanbul. We don't have a handle on him yet but we do suspect he's moving Iranian drug money."

MacPherson studied the two intercepts with great care, then slumped back in his chair. The information they contained put a whole new spin on his investigation. Finally, he emitted a heavy sigh, a sound so deep and painful, it was almost a groan. What he was about to say wasn't going to make him look good in front of the commander.

"Look," he told the table, "when I started out on this investigation, I was convinced this man's murder was somehow related to his business aspect. Or maybe a gambling debt. The wife was screaming 'terrorists' at me just because her husband had said something to the killers in Iranian. Quite frankly, I didn't see it. The crooked business deal seemed much more likely so we proceeded on that assumption. Based on what you've just shown me, I now fear we were wrong. We should have listened to what his wife was telling us from that first morning."

"Mykonos," Duffy said.

"What?"

"That case in Berlin where the Iranians sent in a hit squad to gun down a couple of Kurdish dissidents in a Greek restaurant. It's the way the Iranians operate. I think we're looking at a copycat case here."

MacPherson was almost gray. "If that's the case, we might as well close the case file right now. We'll never get an arrest. They're gone, vanished."

"Chief," Duffy said, his tone as understanding as he could make it, "don't hold that against yourself. If these were Tehran's gunmen, and it sure looks that way, you can bet they were off this island before you'd even had a chance to speak to Harmian's widow."

"Chief," the Commander said, "why don't you summarize for our friends here just what you've got to date."

"Certainly, sir." The American had clearly been up-front with him, MacPherson thought, so he'd lay it all out for him. Carefully, methodically he led them through his investigation to date, the missing envelope, the calls Harmian had made to his wife, ostensibly from Paris but in reality from Budapest and the Caymans, his loaded Visa card, the fact his standard of living outstripped his evident means to support it.

"What the hell could have been in that damn envelope?" Duffy groaned.

"Answer that for me, laddie, and I'll tell you who killed him and why. But based on what you've given us, we'll be closing this one. You and your associate are certainly welcome to come by and go through the material we have before it goes into storage."

"How was the wife, by the way? Was she helpful?"

"Deeply and genuinely bereaved we all felt. And, yes, very cooperative."

"I trust you won't mind if I called on her? Pay her our respects?" Duffy asked.

"Certainly not."

When the check came, the Yard officer moved to pick it up.

"Come on," said Duffy, "we can't let Elizabeth Windsor pay for our lunch, can we?"

"Why the hell not?" growled MacPherson. "She can bloody well afford it."

———

Later that afternoon, a red and yellow van of the Interstate Rapid Serviz Shipping Company joined the line of TIR trucks waiting for Turkish Customs clearance at the Halkali Customs station just past Istanbul International airport. It carried a typically mixed cargo, raisins for a grocery wholesaler in Dusseldorf, tomatoes for a cannery in Frankfurt, used tires for a second hand car dealer in Antwerp, and textiles for clothing wholesalers in Aachen, Rotterdam, the Hague and Amsterdam.

Like all the other vans in the line, the driver had to pass through thirteen different checkpoints to get his final Customs clearance. For each item in his load, he was required to produce a delivery note specifying the weight, contents and value of the packages he was carrying.

At the eighth check point, the Turkish Customs seal was officially fixed to the van's rear doors. Unless the van was carrying certain categories of textiles which would earn their exporter a customs rebate, the likelihood of a customs inspector actually inspecting the van's cargo was almost nonexistent. A quick glance into the cargo was usually deemed enough. The driver then shut and locked the van's doors and the inspector put his seal on them so that the cargo couldn't be accessed without breaking the seal. Each seal bore the number of the inspector who'd placed it there as did the official stamps he now placed on each page of the driver's International TIR Carnet, a page for each frontier the truck was going to cross enroute to its final destination. Because all of his deliveries were going to be inside the Common Market, the driver himself would break the seal when he made his first delivery in Germany.

The system was complex, bureaucratic—and virtually worthless. As angry Customs officers in nations like the U.K. liked to remark, "a Turkish Customs seal isn't worth shit and anyone who thinks otherwise is a perfect asshole."

As soon as he'd received his final clearance, the driver pointed his van up the Trans-European Highway towards the Turkish-Bulgarian border crossing at Kapitan Andrevo, 180 kilos of the Osman family's heroin carefully secreted into a set of false side panels in his truck's van.

A thorough, eight-hour, rip-the-truck-apart customs inspection would have revealed the hiding place. The chances of that happening, however, were infinitesimal. During the year over 800,000 TIR trucks entered or departed Turkey *alone*. Yet in that same year, of the millions of TIR trucks running along the highways of Europe, only 20 were intercepted carrying heroin. Almost without exception they had been checked as a consequence of inside information rather than a customs officer's zeal. Those figures were a measure of how totally unlikely it was that this particular Interstate Rapid Serviz van was going to be caught smuggling dope.

At the frontier, the Turkish border guard checked to see that the truck's customs seal was properly fixed to the van's doors. The Bulgarian did the same thing, pulled the Bulgarian entry page from the driver's TIR carnet, its international travel document, and sent him on his way. From that moment on, the driver could count on virtually clear sailing until he reached his first delivery point in Germany.

The product of the *jeribs* of Ahmed Khan, the cupidity of Ghulan Hamid and the ambitions of the Osman family was now gliding towards its final destination, the lungs, nostrils and veins of an anonymous regiment of young Westerners. Some would mix it with tobacco and smoke it. Some would "chase the dragon," sprinkle it on a piece of silver foil, heat it up with a cigarette lighter and gasp up the fumes it gave off as it melted. Others would sniff it. A few would employ it with lactose or baking soda in a hypodermic needle either by main-lining it into a vein or popping it under their skin. However they employed it, it would give each user a brief glimpse of heaven and a subtle invitation to hell.

BOOK SIX

They Who Shall
TRIUMPH

*E*very time Nancy Harmian glanced into the mirror on her Pierre Phillipe Thomire dressing table, the horror of her husband's murder overwhelmed her once again. Seeing herself this February morning, her face taut, her eye sockets still dark from mourning, her eyes filled with tears.

Over a month since Terry's death and what had those famous Scotland Yard detectives done? Nothing. They'd managed to convince themselves Terry was killed in revenge for some crooked financial dealings—Terry, the most honorable of men. Or, even more outlandish, that he who never gambled had welshed on some kind of a gambling debt. The way they were carrying on, you would have thought it was her poor Terry who was the criminal, not the men who had murdered him. And the American ambassador? What had he done to help? Not a damn thing besides offering her that obligatory stroke they were all taught to give grieving widows.

She looked at the Patek Phillipe watch Terry had given her for her birthday and blinked back yet another tear. It was twenty past ten. Mary was due in ten minutes—if she was on time which she rarely was—for their joint outing to the Alfie's Antique Market, her first since Terry's murder. Maybe there in those cluttered shops and stalls, trolling for unremarked treasures, an under-appraised painting, a statue whose real value a dealer ignored, she could get her mind off Terry's murder for at least an hour or two.

"Madame." It was Rebecca, still at her side despite her own harrowing memories of that night. "There are two men here to see you."

"Men?" Nancy asked. "To see me? Who are they? The police?"

"No, ma'am. They said they were from the embassy."

"Ah! Take them into the living room and offer them a cup of coffee, Rebecca. I'll be down as soon as I finish putting on my makeup."

The living room in the Harmian's Belgravia townhouse was on the first, the grand floor. As Jim Duffy moved towards the sofa to which the maid was pointing, his eyes did a quick inventory of the room. It's decoration was a masterpiece of understated elegance. He recognized a Pharoanic mask, the kind you might expect to see at the Smithsonian, half a dozen ivory Moghul miniatures on one wall, a glass topped round table containing what looked like a collection of Bronze Age implements. Whoever had decorated this room had exquisite taste and the bank account to indulge it.

"Gentlemen."

The ambassador had told Duffy Nancy Harmian was attractive but his words hadn't adequately prepared him for his first glimpse of the young woman striding towards him. She was tall, probably five ten and she bore herself with almost martial solemnity, her shoulders back, her head and chin held high, stretching her long fine neck up from the throat of her black silk blouse in an imperious white line. It was, he thought, as though that rigorously imposed posture was her way of mastering the painful burden she was carrying. Her blonde hair was immaculately combed, her face drawn, a trifle gaunt even, suggesting that sorrow had deprived her of a pound or two in the weeks since her husband's murder. Above all, Duffy thought, she radiated a sense of composure and self-awareness. This, an inner voice warned him, was not a lady to be trifled with.

"Mrs. Harmian," he said. "My name is Jim Duffy. This is my colleague Mike Flynn. The ambassador suggested we call but first let me express to you our deepest condolences on your husband's shocking murder."

"Thank you," Nancy replied, thinking 'more of the usual pablum' as she did. "Do sit down."

She settled into an armchair facing the sofa on which Rebecca had seated her visitors offering her a position from which to scrutinize them as the maid poured her coffee. Duffy, the man who'd introduced them, was probably closing on fifty. He had a pair of massive hands and shoulders with which to knock down doors—or perhaps, people too quick to get in his way. His jacket was unbuttoned and a glance revealed not even a finger-sized roll of fat spilling over his belt. Somehow, she thought, I don't think this Mr. Duffy has spent his diplomatic career stamping U.S. visas into other peoples' passports. His smile was warm but there was a distant, almost a sad cast hovering about his eyes. Did they hide something, some glimmering of knowledge too harrowing to be revealed, some personal sadness to painful to be shared?

The younger man with him was just past thirty, wiry where Duffy was solid, clearly tense in his upright position as though somehow playing the subordinate to Mr. Duffy was not a role he much enjoyed. "How can I help you gentlemen?" she asked, swallowing the first sip of her coffee.

"Mrs. Harmian," Duffy began. "The ambassador gave us the minute he made after his meeting with you following your husband's murder and we'd like to discuss it if it's not too painful for you."

"Of course. Anything to be of help."

"I was particularly struck by your conviction that your husband was murdered by men representing the regime in Tehran."

"I'm sure of it. Even if the police never wanted to listen to me."

"Let me assure you, Mrs. Harmian, I do."

"Nancy, please. You're an officer at the embassy?"

Duffy dredged up the hint of a cough, designed, Nancy was convinced, to afford him a fleeting second in which to ponder the question "to lie or not to lie."

"No," Duffy said. "We're in from Washington."

Give the man a point for honesty, Nancy smiled to herself. He may even admit he's CIA one of these days.

"Your conviction is based as I understand it, Nancy, on the fact your husband spoke to his killers in Farsi?"

"Exactly."

"Even though you yourself don't speak the language."

"I know my husband, though." Nancy stifled an erupting sob. "Excuse me. It's been barely a month. I can't get the tenses straight. I knew my husband. He was doing that deliberately, I'm sure of it. It was his way of telling me the killers were Iranian. And that they weren't his London Iranian exile friends, either."

"Frankly, Nancy, I think you're right. Your husband's murder has all the earmarks of the way the Iranian Secret Service, what they call the VEVAK, works. They never send out a lone hit man. They work in teams of four or five as they did here, to make sure nothing goes wrong, to cover all the contingencies. They're well trained, highly professional killers. They don't leave prints or traces or clues for the police to follow up on."

"Yes, I've heard of them."

"To our knowledge, they've carried out over ninety of these execution-style murders in the U.S. and Western Europe. And been caught only half a dozen times. That's a pretty good track record."

Our knowledge? Nancy thought. That's it. The man is CIA. What else would he be?

"The thing, Nancy, is this. We've studied these murders very closely. There's a pattern to them. Tehran doesn't order them on a haphazard basis. They use them to eliminate people they think are actively trying to overthrow their regime. Or to punish people they feel have betrayed them or their trust. They even stage a trial in front of what they call a Revolutionary Tribunal in Tehran before they order the killing."

Duffy hesitated an instant before continuing. "So if it was, in fact, the Iranian secret services people who murdered your husband, the first question we have to ask ourselves is 'why?'"

For the first time since she'd entered the room, Duffy felt Nancy Harmian's composure shaken. She seemed to shrink into the cushions of her easy chair, her almost haughty poise somehow diminished by the impact of his question.

"I know. I lay awake at night asking myself that same question—why?"

"Did you ever have any indication, any hint, even the faintest reason to suspect that your husband might have been working with some organization trying to overthrow the mullahs?" Duffy, of course, knew what the answer to that was. He'd heard those NSA tapes.

"Absolutely none at all, Mr. . . ."

"Jim."

"Jim. Now remember, I only knew my husband for two years. I can't give you chapter and verse on his life during the years before we were married. But we almost never talked politics. Between ourselves. Or with other people, at least when I was around. Some people might put that down to Middle Eastern male chauvinism, you know, don't talk politics with women, but I don't. I think Terry just wasn't that interested in politics."

"What were his feelings about the regime in Tehran?"

"The mullahs? As far as I could tell he didn't have much use for them. Thought they were trying to take Iran into the twenty-first century with values made for the seventh century. He just didn't seem to give much of a damn about them one way or another. His mind was always on the financial markets."

"Was he religious?"

"Not at all. He never prayed as far as I could see. Didn't observe Ramadan. Drank. Not a lot, but whatever he wanted, whenever he wanted."

"But you did insist on giving him a Moslem burial."

"Of course. He always said he was a Moslem even if he didn't practice his faith. It's like me. Ask me what I am and I'll tell you I'm a Catholic even if I haven't been to Mass in months. That's why I felt he should have a Moslem burial. It's what he would have wanted if only he'd gotten the chance to ask for it."

Duffy leaned back into the sofa. Learning to assess people's character was as important to a CIA operative as learning how to pick locks was to a burglar. This woman in front of him, he thought, was telling the truth. Her ignorance of her husband's relationship to the mullahs, whatever the hell it had been, was real, not feigned. It was now time to nudge things forward a bit, to nail down the fact that the speaker on their NSA tapes and the late Mr. Harmian were, indeed, the same person.

"Nancy, I know you don't speak Farsi, but let me ask you this: if you heard your husband speaking the language, do you think you'd recognize his voice?"

Nancy shrugged her shoulders, her gesture rustling the black silk of her blouse. "I should think so, yes. Why?"

Duffy nodded to Flynn who took a micro-cassette tape player from his pocket. "I know this could be a painful exercise for you Nancy, and if it is I apologize, but it might help us advance the search for your husband's killers. Could you just listen to this tape for me and tell me if you recognize any of the voices on it as your husband's?"

To make sure their little exercise was going to be as foolproof as possible, Duffy had inserted a conversation between two agency Farsi speakers at the top of the tape and eliminated the word "Tari" from both of the conversations in which Harmian was involved. Nancy sat expressionless through the first conversation. But as soon as she heard the words "I met with the Professor in Budapest recently" she sat bolt upright and gave a barely stifled cry. "That's him!" she sobbed. "That's my Terry!"

She sat in horrified but fascinated silence as the two taped phone conversations played on, signalling with a nod of her head each time her murdered husband was speaking. Her identification of his voice left no doubt for Duffy and Flynn. The man whose calls the NSA had intercepted was her husband, Tari Harmian.

"Who was he talking to, Jim?" she asked when the tape stopped. "Where did the tape come from?"

"I wish we knew who that other guy was. All we know is that it was another Iranian living somewhere in Istanbul. The tape, well, I'm sure you know we have services that handle this sort of thing."

"What were they talking about?"

"Again, we can't be certain. They were using some kind of code. We suspect it involved moving money. But we do have some very solid indications that the guy he was talking to is tied to the regime in Iran." For the moment, Duffy thought, he'd keep drugs out of their conversation. There was always the risk mentioning that subject might diminish her eagerness to help.

"So that means you must think Terry was somehow involved with them, too?"

Nancy sensed a genuine sadness in the look Duffy gave her. "I'm afraid it does, Nancy." His tone of voice had softened down to that of a doctor giving the next of kin some bad news. "We haven't figured out how yet or what he was supposed to be doing for them, but it's got to be connected to his murder. And whatever the hell it was he had in that envelope. It must have been awfully important to get them to butcher him the way they did."

Nancy rested the nape of her neck onto the top of her easy chair and closed her eyes. Her lips moved slowly as though she was articulating a silent prayer for her murdered husband. "I suppose all this means we'll never find Terry's killers, doesn't it?"

"Not necessarily, but it's not going to be easy. He worked here at home, didn't he?"

"Yes. His office was downstairs in the room where they killed him."

"What would be really helpful, Nancy, is if you could try and think back to any people who came here to call on your husband who seemed suspicious to you, anybody at all, any telephone conversations you overheard that somehow had a strange ring to them, any packages or mail you saw lying around that you found curious?"

"Most of the people who came here were English. City people. Or his clients. I knew them, of course. If I happened to walk by the office and they were there, I'd go in and say 'hi.'"

"Do you suppose we could have a look at the office?"

Nancy sighed and uncoiled her lean figure from her chair. "Why not? I've got to warn you though I haven't been in there since that night. After the police finished their work, I had some cleaners come into to put it in order, then locked it up."

"Nancy, if it's going to be too painful for you . . ."

"Never mind, Jim. I've got to go back in there sometime, don't I? I guess this is as good a moment as any." With those words, she took his hand as a daughter might grasp her father's in a scary moment in front of the TV and led the way downstairs.

The odor of Lysol mixed with lemon oil rolled from the study in a cloud as she unlocked its door. Harmian's desk was clean, the blood and gore scrubbed from the walls behind it. The safe door was open on its hinges, its interior empty. Obviously, the Yard still had all his papers. A large leather wing-chair was positioned in front of Harmian's desk.

"That's where his visitors sat," Nancy whispered. As she did, she suddenly pulled her hand from Duffy's. "Wait a minute!" she went on. "You asked about strange visitors. I remember one day about three weeks before Terry was killed. I was coming back from the market, around, oh, five o'clock in the afternoon. As I unlocked the front door to let myself in, I heard Terry and a man in here shouting at each other in Farsi. It sounded like they were fighting but when I walked in to say 'hello' they were all smiles, as though they'd somehow put those smiles on just for my sake."

"Did you know the man?"

"No. I'd never seen him before. Terry introduced us but I can't for the life of me remember his name."

"What did he look like?"

"Tall. Taller than Terry. Maybe fifty years old. A very erect, martial bearing, the kind of thing you'd expect from an old army officer. He was very well dressed. A Savile Row blue suit, I'll bet." She paused trying to re-create the memory of the moment in her mind. "There was one funny thing about him that stuck in my mind. He didn't exactly have a beard but it looked like he hadn't shaved for four or five days. I thought he must have been bothered by some kind of a skin rash."

"Or perhaps," Duffy suggested, "he was growing back the Beard of the Prophet that he'd had to shave off for some reason or other. Do you think you'd recognize his face if I could find a picture of him?"

"Perhaps. Hard to tell without seeing the photo."

"Look, Nancy, I'd like to check in at the embassy. See if I can get some photos to show you. Will you be around this afternoon?"

"After five."

"If it's OK with you, I'll call back in again about then."

"Of course." Nancy opened the front door for them. After Flynn had started out Duffy turned back to her. This time it was he who took her hand in his. "Nancy," he said, "I think I have some idea of the pain you're suffering. I lost my wife a little while ago to a murderer of a different kind. Cancer."

Ah, Nancy thought, that explains the sadness in those eyes of his.

"It's hard, very hard," Duffy whispered. "Time does make it better, it's true. But no matter what they say, it doesn't cure the pain, it only eases it. I'm sorry for your hurt."

Impulsively, Nancy leaned forward and kissed him, French style on both cheeks. "Thanks," she whispered.

———

The CIA Station at the American Embassy in London's Grosvernor Square is sealed off from the rest of the building by it's own biometric security system. Jim Duffy punched his personal code into the number pad beside the entrance to the station's offices, then inserted his hand into the mouth of the scanning device just below the pad. The scanner ran a quick image of his hand, compared it to the scan of Duffy's hand on file in the computer's data bank and finding that their biological parameters matched, automatically unlocked the door.

The station chief's Executive Assistant was waiting to escort him to Bob Cowie's office. The term "secretary" had been erased from the agency's lexicon long before it had become a politically incorrect phrase in other employers' manuals.

"So," Cowie smiled, "how'd the meeting go?" He was dressed in a single-breasted dark blue pinstripe suit with double vents in the back and just the right nip in at the waist. Cowie, Duffy thought, always dressed as though he was on his way to a wedding or a funeral. The London station and Cowie were that rarity in the working marriages arranged by the agency's personnel office, the perfect fit. He went to Hawes and Curtis, his tailor, as regularly as Mother Teresa once went to Mass, liked his beer warm, and even knew what an "over" was in cricket. Probably whistled the Eton Boating Song in his morning shower as well.

"Good. She's really trying to be as helpful as she can. Listen, what kind of a photo gallery do we have on these Iranian secret service types?"

"Limited, I'm afraid. Of the men who killed her husband, certainly nothing. They would have been sent here by Tehran on a one-off basis. You can be sure they're safely back home now. They won't be coming back West again, ever."

"How do they smuggle these guys into Europe and move them around so easily?"

"To begin with, they have a chain of safe-houses all around Europe, a lot of them in Germany. We and our brave European allies have busted some on those rare occasions when the Europeans get the wind up. We know two things for certain: these guys have money and lots of it, usually in cash. And they have a first class fake I.D. factory out there in Tehran grinding out counterfeit documents for them."

"Well, if they could counterfeit the one hundred dollar bill to near perfection, that's hardly surprising. Still, how do they get in and out of this sceptered isle? That's not supposed to be easy, is it?"

"It's easier than you might think. The Eurostar Train under the channel tunnel is a favorite vehicle. As I said, they have first class fake documents. They'll have a return ticket, a prepaid reservation at the Holiday Inn for five days. All they want is an in and out tourist visa so they can do like Christopher Robin and go watch the changing of the guard at Buckingham Palace. The big shots will come in via Heathrow, maybe with a fake French carte de sejour if they can speak some French, or an Iranian diplomatic passport issued in some name Immigration hasn't got in their data base."

Cowie switched on his computer, entered his secret access code and twisted the screen so Duffy could see it. He punched a few keys and an image appeared on the screen of a burly man in a flowing black robe entering a Mercedes 600. "This is Sadegh Izzadine. He runs their Strike Force, the outfit that undoubtedly was responsible for the murder of your Mr. Harmian."

"Nice car."

"Ah, dear boy, the mullahs gave up hair shirts as soon as they took power."

Duffy smiled. Cowie was from North Dakota. *I wonder how that phrase 'dear boy' would play out there?* "Where was that picture taken?"

"In Tehran. A dissident shot it for us from across the street as Izzadine was leaving his office. With one of those sub-miniature cameras of ours that looks like a button on his overcoat. Has a roll of microfilm sealed inside."

"Hey, well done. Have we got many guys like that on the payroll?"

Cowie hesitated a second then decided Duffy's 'need to know' was certainly sufficient to let him answer the question. "A fair number. Basically, you've got four Iranian dissident organizations in Europe that we work with. There's one here in London. Royalist in inspiration. They want to put the Shah's son back on the Peacock Throne as a democratic monarch, a kind of Iranian Juan Carlos. Personally, I think the idea's a non-starter, but they're very well wired inside Iran. First class penetration. Then you've got two groups over in Paris. One calls itself the Flag of Freedom. Liberal democrats. They've got a lot of clandestine support inside the country, particularly in the big cities. They can put a propaganda leaflet under the windshield wipers of thousands of cars in Tehran in a single night if they want to."

"Impressive."

"Indeed. The third group is the National Council of Resistance. They're the biggest and the toughest. Split between Paris and Baghdad. They've got 30,000 people under arms. Trouble is, they were in love with Saddam Hussein. They had to be if they wanted to stay alive.

A lot of them are ex-Marxists although since they've come tiptoeing around to us for money, they've seen the light of political reason."

Cowie paused as though he was running a mental inventory of Iran's dissidents through his mind. "Finally, you've got Beni Sadr's people. He, as you'll recall, was the first President of their Islamic Republic. They're strong in Germany."

"And the agency is supporting all these outfits?"

"To an extent. Only with money, mind you. Not bombs and bullets. Of course, if they use some of the money we pay them for information to buy bombs and bullets, there's not much we can do about that. But Iran is not Iraq. One Axis of Evil war is enough. We figure they're three to four years away from getting nukes. The idea here is to foment a soft revolution, not a hard one."

"Oh Bob, please. Spare me. I didn't know we had forty-year-old serving officers in this agency who still believed in Santa Claus."

Cowie laughed. "Listen, Jim, remember our training days, all those indoctrination courses we had to go through at Camp Peary? You know how they kept drumming into us the idea that the greatest thing the CIA ever did was to pull off our famous coup d'etat in Iran in 1953? Weren't we smart, paying off all those bazaar merchants and the Greco-Roman wrestlers to riot against Mossadegh and bring the Shah back from exile in Rome? Wow, the activist CIA doing what it was designed to do, making the world safe for democracy and Big Oil? Well, I say, bullshit, rubbish. The anti-Mossadegh coup was the dumbest thing the agency ever did."

"Heresy, Bobby, heresy in its purest form."

"Listen, what would have happened if we hadn't staged that coup? The Shah would have lived out his life as an exiled playboy king, bouncing around from St Moritz to Paris to Marbella. He would have been a helluva lot happier doing that than trying to be a Middle Eastern despot. And better at it, too. Iran would have drifted into some kind of semi-democracy and as a result, we wouldn't have these damn mullahs driving us nuts today."

"Oh, horseshit, Bob. Mossadegh was a rascal."

"So what? So were a lot of the people we lovingly embraced over the years. We demonized him as a crypto-communist because he wanted to nationalize Anglo-Iranian oil. Did we stage a coup d'etat to overthrow King Faisal in Saudi Arabia when he took over ARAMCO? Hell, no. Mossadegh's sin was that he was a few years ahead of his time, that's all."

Cowie tapped his computer keyboard. "Anyway, we're not here to re-live the past. I'll call up what we've got on our locals in here for you."

"Where do our VEVAK friends hang out when they're not cutting people's throats?"

"For the most part they hole up in their embassy and slip out in the middle of the night when they think no one is looking. And they have three safe houses on the other side of the Thames that belonged to the Shah's regime which they use on occasion. Although needless to say our friends at MI5 have fitted them out with a full wardrobe of electronic bugs. Right down to their electric toothbrushes, one suspects."

"Do they pick up anything interesting?"

"Nothing. Just because some of these mullah types bang their heads on the floor five times a day saying their prayers doesn't mean they're soft upstairs. They know the score. The only things they'll say in those houses are things they want Five to hear. Now . . ." He indicated his computer screen on which had appeared a photo of a group of Iranian women demonstrating outside the London embassy. A man, his face circled, looked down on them from the embassy balcony. Cowie scrolled his computer so that the man's face filled its screen. "This is the head of the VEVAK here in London. Used to run an anti-Shah student's organization in the good old days."

He clicked his way through a series of other photos, accompanying each with a brief description of the man in the picture and his functions. He paused when he came to a man in a dark blue overcoat striding down a crowded street with a black attache case in his hand.

"Ah! Now here's an interesting chap. Used to run the London office of the Iranian National Oil Company. His real job, however, was buying hi-tech stuff for their arms industry. A very smart man, indeed. Name's Bollahi but they call him the Professor."

"The Professor!" Duffy sat up. The Professor was the term the late Mr. Harmian had used to refer to the man he'd met in Budapest, wasn't it? The man who'd approached Colonel Wulff in Almaty had also been identified as the Professor. Was it possible this was the guy Harmian was arguing with in his study three weeks before he died?

"Did he ever grow a beard?"

"Jim, these people are always in and out of their beards. They shave them off when they don't want be tagged as Islamic. Usually when they're moving around on their fake ID."

"Hey, hit the index and see what we have in there on this guy."

Cowie tapped the Professor's name, Bollahi, onto his keyboard and the access code for the agency's central computer data bank for Iran. Five single spaced pages of text came up on the screen. Duffy leaned over and began reading.

"An engineer!" he exclaimed. "With a doctorate in mechanical engineering! What the hell is a heavy hitter like that doing with the mullahs?"

"Jim, they need people like that if they're going to get anything done in the international marketplace. Praying is one thing; buying arms is quite another."

Duffy was fascinated now. "He was reported in the old DDR twice before the wall came down. One of our sources claimed he was looking around for nuclear related materials."

"Why not? They've looked for nukes every place else, haven't they?"

Duffy continued to stare at the computer screen as Cowie slowly scrolled it down.

"Holy shit, Bobby!" he suddenly shouted, pointing to the screen. "Look at this!"

DD\AFF\N\232\report dated 12.10.97. (The code indicated that the source was a German national involved in finance.)

Subject is sole registered holder of account #00314572 at the Bank Melli Munich. Source saw account statement one week prior to reporting date with positive balance in excess of dollars U.S. 50M.

"Those Iranians are going broke, half of their people living on peanuts and this guy has fifty million bucks in his bank account? This man has to be a major, major player."

"Arms cost money, my boy. Particularly the kind the Professor likes to buy."

Duffy continued to study the computer text line by line until he got to the latest update on Bollahi.

Subject left UK for Tehran 10.9.00 when he was reported wanted for questioning by German authorities in connection with the Iranians purchase of a private airfield at Hartenholm, north of Hamburg, Germany. To London station's knowledge he has not returned to his executive duties with NIOC London although it is believed (agent sighting 1.17.01) that he has slipped back into the U.K. on an Iranian diplomatic passport issued in an other identity. Subject has also been reported by second hand informant reports as working in the Cologne-Dusseldorf and Schelswig Holstein areas of Germany. Telephone records seized by German customs in raid on Dusseldorf headquarters of Iranian DIO—Defense Industries Organization - revealed six calls placed from the DIO office to the office number in Tehran employed by subject. Subject has also been reliably reported working in Milan, Italy using as his cover the office of The Foundation of the Oppressed located on Via Padona on the first floor of the building housing the Larino Bank. Source BM/I/34 reported 7.12.01 that he had access to room in Iranian Consulate Milan containing nuclear related documents to which only one other individual last name Yazdi, First Name Unknown is reported to have access.

Yeah, Duffy growled, the *Bunyod -e Mustazafin*—The Foundation of the Oppressed. It was one of the richest and most thoroughly corrupted of the mullah's institutions. It siphoned off the earnings of enterprises like the Hilton Hotel in Tehran that the mullahs had seized. Ostensibly, they were supposed to aid the poor, the downtrodden. What they aided were the big wig mullahs, their secret defense and intelligence projects, the Iranian drive to get nuclear and biological weapons, Islamic terrorists throughout the world. This son of a bitch, the Professor, was into their nuclear program up to his ears, alright. He's the guy who bought the damn things from our late friend, that Russian colonel. If he's studying secret documents in Milan, the chances are he's trying to figure out how to make them work.

"Look, Bob, would you print me up a dozen photos of these people? Including one of the Professor. I want to see if Nancy can ID any of them."

"Nancy?"

"Mrs. Harmian."

————

Across the English Channel, the red and yellow van of the Turkish Interstate Rapid Serviz Shipping Company rumbled along Amsterdam's A10 circular motorway towards its final destination. The truck was empty now—empty, that is, except for the 180 kilos of heroin concealed in the trap built into its side panel.

For the driver it had been a singularly uneventful journey. Like most TIR drivers, he had slept in the bunk bed behind his cab, left his truck and his cargo only to eat, shower and use the toilets of the lay-bys along his route. Once across the Turkish Bulgarian border, he'd barely had to nod to a customs inspector. At his first stop, a grocery wholesaler in Dusseldorf, he had broken the customs seal on his van's rear doors himself before delivering the wholesaler 200 kilos of raisins.

It was well after six o'clock when he dipped into the Goen Tunnel under the North Sea Canal and turned west towards the highway's Volendam exit. The countryside was already wrapped in the black mantle of the northern winter night and the highway ahead of him clogged with other lumbering trucks. Three of the world's four largest seaports, Rotterdam, Antwerp and Amsterdam, were all located within a circle 100 miles in diameter. Each disgorged a steady stream of container trucks onto the highways to join the thousands of TIR trucks already moving there. As a result there was more heavy commercial traffic pounding along the highways of Holland, Belgium, western Germany and northern France than there was on any comparably sized piece of real estate on the globe—more, even, than in the Boston to Baltimore corridor on the north Atlantic seacoast of the United States.

The driver knew that caught up in that massive flow of traffic he was virtually immune from any chance of a random Customs inspection. Besides, in the unlikely event that there were any Dutch customs officers assigned to wander the highways, he was safe now. Everyone knew Dutch customs stopped work at five sharp. There was the famous story of the container in which Dutch Customs at Rotterdam, acting on a tip provided by the U.S. DEA, had discovered 14,000 kilos of hashish bound, ostensibly, for Poland. It was a few minutes to five, time for everyone to go home, so the container with its hashish still packed inside was parked for the night in a secure customs garage. When the morning shift showed up for work the next day, the enormous container and its 14,000 kilos of hash had disappeared, never to be seen again.

Whistling softly to himself, the driver turned off the A10 onto the Nieuwe Leeuwarderweg running down to the Het Ji canal and the maze of little waterways, inlets, and mooring slips cut into the canal's dark and uninviting waters. There, he turned onto the Papaverweg, a finger of landfill stretching parallel to the canal's waters. The strip was devoted almost exclusively to warehousing depots where goods were unloaded, either to await delivery inside Holland, a pick-up for export elsewhere or simply held in transit pending a decision on their final destination. Some were glistening glass and steel buildings three and four stories high, others like the one to which he was headed at 36A, plain one or two story wooden structures.

Abdullah, the fourth of the five Osman brothers involved in the heroin traffic, was waiting in his office at the back of the building when the driver backed his van into the parking bay beside the office. The front of the building housed a furniture warehouse whose owners, all home by the hearth now, had no idea of what their neighbors' real activities were. In any event, a TIR truck backing into a bay along the Papaverweg was about as likely to be remarked on as the sight of a Dutchman on a bike pedalling his way through Amsterdam's streets.

Abdullah Osman came out and the two men opened the rear of the van and unlocked its secret panel. The heroin packed into one kilo plastic sacks tied together into a chain like sausage links had been difficult to load, but could be extracted from its hiding place with ease and speed. The unloading operation took less than five minutes and the driver was gone, on his way back to Turkey.

Abdullah Osman's half of the building had been leased in the name of a Dutch company, Turktex BV, of which 36A Papaverweg was the registered address. The brothers did, indeed, use it as a depot for their textiles, bluejeans and leather jackets, which served as a cover for their heroin operation. A shed like structure behind the office provided a storage space for their goods as well as an underground hiding place into which Abdullah now carefully packed this latest consignment of Osman family heroin.

That task finished, Abdullah walked back upstairs to his office. His first gesture was to place a call to the youngest of the five Osmans, Behcet, at his home in the London suburb of Stoke Newington.

"Listen, Babe," he said, employing the nickname the family used for their youngest, "the stuff's arrived. I'll forward you your share in a couple of days."

The heroin traffic in Holland was controlled principally by nine Turkish families, six in Amsterdam and one each in Rotterdam, Arnhem and Apeldoorn. Of the nine, the Osmans were perhaps the most important. They were all careful not to war with each other in Holland. Disputes were settled back home in Turkey. The Turks had been able to seize control of the heroin traffic into Holland in 1976 because the Hong Kong Chinese triads which then ran the business had gotten into a bloody tong war. That enraged the usually tolerant Dutch who rounded up the principal traffickers and threw them out of the country. Theirs had been a mistake Turks like the Osmans were not about to make.

At thirty-two, Abdullah typified the new breed of heroin trafficker running the Dutch business. Unlike his elder brothers, he was slim, frail almost. With his spectacles, his thinning blonde hair, the air of almost infinite goodness he tried to radiate in public, he resembled a cleric of the Dutch Reformed Church propounding his message of infinite tolerance as the supreme reflection of Christian goodness. He lived an impeccably respectable family life with his wife and two children, didn't know what the inside of an ecstasy popping Dutch disco looked like, rode around in a distinctly unflashy French made Peugeot. Nevertheless, he was an infinitely shrewd operator working under the motto: "do nothing to draw attention or piss the Dutch authorities off."

That was understandable. Probably less than 20% of the heroin he'd just received would wind up in Dutch lungs or noses. As the other eight Turkish families did, he used Holland principally as a storage facility, a place to warehouse his product until he could pass it on to clients in the U.K., Belgium, France, Germany and Spain. That was not a situation he was going to jeopardize by aggravating the tolerant Dutch police. It was also reflected in the fact that Interpol in Lyons, France, the French OCTRIS, Her Majesty's Customs, and the U.S. DEA estimated that a *minimum* of 14,000 kilograms of heroin was smuggled into Holland a year, more than five times the needs of the Dutch addict community. That had turned Holland into Europe's heroin warehouse. The German, French, English and Belgian narcotics authorities estimated that 70-80% of the heroin seized in their countries had either transitted or been stored in Holland

"Holland," embittered U.K. Customs officers lamented, "is England's Mexico."

———

One by one, Jim Duffy placed the ten photos the London Embassy had furnished him in front of Nancy Harmian. She scrutinized each with an intensity indicative of her burning desire to advance the hunt for her husband's killers. With a sad shake of her head, she rejected the first five as meaning nothing to her, turning each photo face down on the table beside her.

The Professor's picture was the sixth in Duffy's pile. Setting it in front of Nancy, he made a conscious effort to convert his face into an expressionless mask so he wouldn't give Nancy any hint of the importance he attached to it. She studied the man in his dark blue suit with the same intensity she'd given to the other photos, then placed it, too, face down on her growing pile of rejects.

A disappointed Duffy was placing the next photo before her when her hand shot out and grabbed back the Professor's picture.

"Let me look at that one again," she said.

She sighed as she pondered the Professor for a second time. "I'm trying to imagine what this one would look like with a beard."

"Don't forget, Nancy, any male can grow a beard. And shave it off when he wants to."

She set the Professor's picture aside then finished studying the last photos in Duffy's pile. None of them stirred any reaction in her memory cells. When she'd finished, she picked up the Professor's picture yet again, studied it closely, then shut her eyes tight.

"Yes," she announced finally. "I think that's him. Even if he's not wearing a beard. What's his name? Do you know?"

"Bollahi."

"Yes!" Her cry rang out like the triumphant yelp of a tennis player who's just won match point. "That's the name. I remember it now. Professor Bollahi, Terry called him when he introduced us."

Duffy smiled and gathered up his pictures. "That was the man I was hoping you'd pick. I trust I didn't send out any extra-sensory messages to trigger your choice."

"Jim! Surely an officer of the CIA which I now assume you are doesn't believe in that sort of rubbish. What does this man do?"

No sense in pretending to false innocence, Duffy thought. This woman was too smart for that. He'd let the CIA crack pass with his best wan smile. "Bollahi used to run the Iranian oil operations here but his real job was procuring hi-tech weapons for the Tehran government."

"Do you think he was involved in Terry's murder?"

"Directly? I doubt it. Indirectly, I think it's very possible, yes. He could have requested the people in Tehran who order these things to arrange the murder."

"But why, for God's sake?"

"That I wish I knew, Nancy."

"You're not suggesting my Terry was involved in the arms traffic? For the mullahs? I just don't buy it, Jim."

"Perhaps, Nancy, he got into it during the Iran-Iraq war before you met him. It was hard, I think for any Iranian, no matter what he thought about the mullahs, not to feel the tug of patriotism in those days."

Nancy shook her head in bewildered disbelief but Duffy pressed on. "The arms traffic is like that sticky paper they used to have to catch flies when we were kids. It's easy to get into it but once you're there it's almost impossible to get out."

"Terry must have been working for someone like you people. Or some anti-regime group. Reporting to them on what the mullahs were doing."

"If he had been in contact with us or any of the anti-regime people we work with, I'd know it. The reason your husband was murdered was because someone in Tehran wanted whatever the hell was in that envelope badly enough to kill him."

"What could it possibly have been, Jim? What, for God's sake?"

"A lot of things. A few million dollars of the mullahs' money in bearer bonds. Or gold deposit certificates. More likely, I think he might have had access to a breakdown of where the mullahs' money is hidden offshore. The banks and the account numbers they use, what banking havens they're hiding their dough in. They've got more money squirreled away outside Iran than the poor old Shah ever had."

A look of incomprehension and despair almost swept across Nancy's handsome features. "How is it possible to share your life, your bed, your body, your mind, your hopes, with a man for two full years and still not be able to find the combination to whatever safe he's got in his soul where he's hidden his real secrets? How can that happen?"

"More easily than you think, Nancy." Duffy was not yet ready to get into drugs. He'd save that information for another conversation. She'd suffered enough today already. "Eleanor Philby, the last wife of Kim Philby, the Russians master spy, never dreamt he was working for the KGB. Richard Sorge's mistress in Tokyo during the Second World War had no idea his real allegiance was to Stalin, not Hitler. Some people are born to deceive, I think. They take to it as naturally as a Labrador takes to water. I suspect that's the reality that explains your husband—and what happened to him."

Nancy rose. "I need a drink to handle all this. Can I get you something?"

Duffy glanced at his watch. It was half past seven. "I guess I can claim I'm off duty now. I'd love a scotch on the rocks."

Nancy poured him one and a vodka for herself.

Duffy raised his glass to hers. "To solace. To time's comforting balm. May it help to make both of us whole again."

Nancy felt a tear sting the surface of her eye. "Thanks, Jim," she whispered.

"I promised my associate Mr. Flynn, I'd give over my evening to him," Duffy explained sipping his drink, "so I'll have to be on my way pretty soon. I don't know what the hell he's got in store for me except that I doubt it's going to be a barrel of laughs, but you and I must talk again soon. Perhaps, if you'd like, over dinner some night."

In a strange way, Duffy couldn't believe he'd just said that. He hadn't considered extending a woman an invitation to so much as a glass of water since his wife's death. And here he was asking a woman whose own husband was not yet five weeks in the grave out to dinner.

Nancy hesitated, obviously somewhat taken aback by his gesture. She took a long sip of her vodka, and fixed her gaze firmly on his. "Yes, Jim," she said, "I think that would be nice."

In the great German seaport of Hamburg, the man whose photograph had so fascinated Jim Duffy and Nancy Harmian was at that moment pacing slowly across the Kennedybrucke spanning the city's Lake Alster. This evening, the Professor was clean shaven, just as he had been in the photo in which Nancy had recognized him as the man she'd seen in Terry's office barely three weeks before his murder.

As he had told his colleagues in Iran he would, he'd flown from Tehran to Vienna following the meeting of the Committee for Secret Operations, ready to put into operation his plan to obtain for Operation Khalid a supply of the hi-tech devices critical to detonating their three nuclear arms. From Austria he had slipped into his private airfield at Hartenholm aboard one of his German-registered Cessnas. The measured pace with which he was now crossing the bridge was deliberate. The Professor had been given a course in detecting and avoiding surveillance. His teacher, once a member of the Shah's secret service, had passed on to him the tricks he'd learned from his instructors in the CIA and Israel's Mossad.

The bridge was an ideal place to pick up surveillance. There were no parked cars or vans from which he could be spotted. There were no other pedestrians in sight. The traffic had to flow by quickly so he had only to be alert for a car—or more likely two or three cars—circling around and passing him repeatedly as he sauntered towards his destination.

Convinced he was clean, Bollahi headed towards the red "A" for Apotheke of a pharmacy on the Warburgstrasse once he'd left the bridge. He went inside and after a few judicious moments of studying the store's cold remedies to see if anyone had followed him in, bought a pack of aspirin and left. No one was loitering on the sidewalk outside the store and, he saw, the car was waiting across the street.

He moved quickly towards it. "So," he said to the driver, opening the door and getting in, "we meet again."

"How are you, old friend?" the driver replied, shaking his hand. "You look wonderful. Two years younger than you did the last time I

saw you. Must be that Moslem ban on the booze that keeps you looking so fit."

Fit was not an adjective anyone would have used in referring to the
driver. Josef "Joe" Mischer had a full, fleshy face. Wattle-like rolls of
skin hung from his jawbone, an aberration to which he inadvertently
called attention with a handlebar mustache. He was notably over-
weight, the kind of man who can never keep his shirt tucked properly
into his pants. The Professor had always looked on him as a well educated boor, helpful—he was, after all, a first class engineer—yet
someone who was occasionally inclined to behave like a half drunken
docker rollicking through the Reeperbahn.

He smiled as Mischer accelerated away from the curb. "Don't
worry, old friend. I won't waste your time—or mine—giving you a
sermon on the values of Islam's ascetic lifestyle. We have better things
to talk about, you and I."

"Great!" Mischer exulted. "I figured you didn't come up here to
look at the girls in the windows. It would be wonderful to work with you
again." And profitable, too, he knew. Those well-tailored blue suits the
Professor liked to wear had deep pockets and engineering was not Joe
Mischer's primary interest in life. Making money was, and he wasn't particular about how he did it or who he did it for. He had once tried to help
the Professor get access to nuclear technology in the old East Germany.
Right now he was a one-man clearinghouse for the production of three
Dutchmen manufacturing Ecstasy tablets in their garage in Hilversum.

"So what's up?" he asked. "You've got old Mike working himself
silly up there in Pinneberg and he won't whisper me a word about what
you've got him doing."

Mike Mashad was the Professor's key aide, the Marbella-based
Iranian exile he'd dispatched to Hamburg after summoning him to his
London office.

"Good for Mike. He appreciates, as I am sure you do, the value I
attach to extreme discretion in my working associates. Do you remember those two trips you and I took to the DDR before the Berlin Wall
came down?"

"Shopping for high energy lasers that could be used in isotope separation." Joe laughed. "Like maybe separating uranium isotopes?"

"Humor is perhaps not your greatest strength, my dear Joe," the Professor cautioned. "But yes, indeed. Too bad the East Germans weren't ready to deal with us. They could use the money now and we could use their technology. You were, as I recall, very knowledgeable on the whole question of high energy lasers."

"Yeah, I spent time studying the subject."

"Good. We may have a way of putting your knowledge to work. Where exactly is Mike?"

"He's living in a small hotel up there in Pinneberg. It's a twenty minute drive from here."

Mike was waiting in the sitting room of his suite when they arrived. To the Professor, he looked like an eager schoolboy bursting with the desire to be called on by his teacher so he could show off how much he knew. He almost begrudgingly ordered up coffee for them all and managed to keep silent until the room service waiter had left.

"Alright, Mike," the Professor said finally. "Let's hear your report. You can speak freely in front of Joe. He may have a role to play in the next stage of our operation."

Mike bounced to his feet. "Well, first of all, the good Herr Steiner, just as you suspected, is in the shit. Up to his earlobes in it."

"Poor man," the Professor commiserated.

"Poor he's going to be alright, and very soon," Mike went on. "He worked for Haas, the big German laser specialists for about twelve years. He was involved in developing new products for them, OK?"

The Professor gave what could have been a wave of either understanding or indifference with his elegant white hand.

"In 1998, he got this brilliant idea, or at least he thought it was brilliant, for building a better laser. Everyone's dream is to build a laser that can do things faster, deliver more cutting power than the next guy's laser. So he quit Haas and went into business for himself to build the world a better laser."

"Conveniently forgetting, of course, the fact that he'd acquired the knowledge he was going to use to build his new toy while he was working for someone else."

Mike snorted to indicate just how untroubled he was by the moral implications of Steiner's act.

"Nonetheless, it does reveal something about what kind of man Herr Steiner is, doesn't it, Mike?"

"If you say so, Professor. Anyway, I went down to the townhall and checked LASERTECHNIK GmbH, his company in the registry of firms incorporated here in Pinneberg. It was incorporated on October 16th, 1996 with a capital of 50,000 deutschmarks. Steiner was listed in the incorporation papers as the sole shareholder and CEO. The firm's place of business was listed as the building on Kaiser Wilhem-strasse where Steiner had rented office and factory space. The purpose of the business was given as developing and manufacturing high-energy lasers. That's all the information you're required to put down on your initial registration form."

"Fifty thousand deutschmarks aren't going to build you a lot of lasers, Mike."

"Oh, hell no. What happened was that ten days later Steiner advanced the company a loan of three million deutschmarks which apparently represented his entire life savings in order to give his company some working capital."

"Our friend Herr Steiner appears to have believed in what he was doing."

"Too much so, if you ask me. Anyway, by April 1997, the money's run out so he goes to the Commerzbank and floats a loan for five million deutschmarks. Apparently, he wanted to secure it with shares in LASERTECHNIK, but the bank wasn't buying. Too risky, they told him. They wanted his house as security. So he gave them a lien on it without telling his wife."

"You certainly make Herr Steiner sound like a real gentleman, Mike. Clearly the kind of man we can do business with. But tell me, how did you learn all this?"

"There's a bierstube across from his factory where his employees go. I started to hang out there and got on very friendly terms with the bartender, who it turns out is a close friend of Herr Steiner."

Wonderful, the Professor mused. The Islamic Republic of Iran has to rely on bartenders for its intelligence information.

"I also checked his credit rating out with one of these firms here who will sell you information on a company's financial reliability. Told them I wanted to know if I could run the risk of giving him ninety days credit for a million deutschmarks on some raw materials I was going to sell him. They told me no. He was sinking in debt and his credit is worthless. Furthermore, I understand the bank's about to call in their five-million-mark loan and they're not interested in grabbing LASERTECHNIK shares. They're worthless. They're going to take his house and let Herr Steiner and his family go down and wander around the Reeperbahn with all those Poles and gypsies."

"Does his wife know this?"

"Apparently not. My friend the bartender think's he's desperate. He's afraid he might even try to kill himself."

"We certainly don't want him doing that. Not until we can come to his rescue. What I want to do is buy up a substantial share of LASERTECHNIK. Perhaps fifty percent," the Professor announced.

"But Professor," Joe Mischer protested, "according to Mike those shares are worthless."

"Not to me they're not. What do you think he'd take for 50% of his company, Mike?"

Mike shrugged. "Who's to say? If you cleared up his debts, got the bank off his back, and gave him enough working capital to go on with his research, I think he'd kneel down and kiss your hand."

"That will hardly be necessary." The Professor now turned his attention back to Mischer. "Joe, I'd like you to go see Herr Steiner as soon as you can. Impress him with your knowledge of lasers, tell him how admiring you are of what he's trying to accomplish, what an opportunity you think it represents. Tell him you want to become asso-ciated with his enterprise. That you're prepared to offer him a substantial injection of capital for 50% of the company. Enough to clear his debts, make a partial payment of his bank loan and leave him with a million or so deutschmarks to go on with his research. Say a package of three million deutschmarks." The Professor glanced at Mike for his blessing on the figure he'd named.

For Mike, this was a routine deal, the kind of thing he and the Professor had done in buying up over a dozen European firms. "Something around there should do it."

"I suppose," the Professor continued, "we'll have to register the name of the new shareholder in the books at the townhall."

"Of course."

"In that case, Joe, you'll buy the fifty percent share in the name of TW Holdings. It's a Vaduz company and its registered address is 19 Albrechtstrasse, Liechtenstein. It's got an account at the Liechtensteinische Landesbank. Once you've set the terms of the deal, TW Holdings will place the sum you agreed to in an escrow account with the notary public who will have to record the transfer of the shares. Have the notary issue you a certificate for 50% of the shares in LASERTECH-NIK made over to TW Holdings when you and Steiner have appeared before the notary to make the sale. Then send the certificate to the company address in Liechtenstein. The notary will go through the required legal motions to register the change in share holdings at the townhall."

Joe eagerly indicated his agreement. He would negotiate the deal for something just under three million deutschmarks, charge the Professor four and split the difference with his new business partner Herr Steiner. That was exactly what the Professor expected. Such was the cost of doing business in secret, on the margins of legality and with people like Joe Mischer. What was important, however, was not the money involved but scrubbing the purchase clean of any possible suggestion of Iranian involvement.

The Professor's was a classic ploy. Go look up TW Holdings in Liechtenstein and all you would find would be a brass plaque on some lawyer's door. Behind it would be a dour lawyer as talkative as a stone statue on Easter Island. Among the many things he would not tell you would be the fact that TW Holdings was a wholly owned subsidiary of Trade World, Inc., a Panamanian company whose finances were run out of the trust department of a Cayman Islands bank. It was one of those firms whose bearer share certificates had been in the envelope for which Tari Harmian had been murdered. Harmian had invested the "tax" receipts skimmed off the passing drug traffic by Said Djailani in the shares and bonds held in those firm's portfolios. Now, of course, they and the company they represented belonged to the Professor and behind him the mullahs in Tehran.

"What I'd like to ask you to do, Joe, once the deal's set, is to install yourself in the company as Herr Steiner's right hand. As discreetly as possible. There is really no reason to advertise your presence or the change in the company's ownership. You and I will work out a private compensation package to cover your work and I'll tell you what I want you to do once the operation's running smoothly."

"No problem," Joe smiled. He knew how generous the Professor's compensation packages could be.

For the first time since he'd entered Joe's car in downtown Hamburg, the Professor felt able to sit back and relax. He was reasonably certain at last that his plan to obtain the hi-tech devices critical to Operation Khalid could be made to work. It would cost a few million deutschmarks. But if those deutschmarks bought him a supply of the devices Mike had once referred to as "tadpoles with a glass head," it would be worth every pfenning he'd spent. Once they had them, his young scientists had promised him they could replicate them by the dozens. That would win Iran access to the most powerful force on God's earth. No price was too great for that.

———

"How about a nice cup of English tea?" Detective Superintendent Fraser MacPherson asked Jim Duffy and Mike Flynn as he showed them into his office early the next morning. "Or is it only harsh black coffee that you Yanks take to start the day off on the right foot?"

"Tea would be just fine," Duffy replied. "When in Rome . . ."

"Aye, Rome. Sure this was a Rome once upon a time, heart of empire and all that rot. Built on the blood of brave young Scottish soldiers, their empire was. Ah well," MacPherson declared hoisting his heavy frame from his desk chair to pour out mugs of tea for them all.

"So," he announced when he'd returned to his desk, "I passed on what you chaps told me over lunch at the Commander of Operations' morning prayers today. Without sourcing where the information came from, of course."

"Morning prayers" was the label given to the daily meeting of the senior officers of MacPherson's district of the Met, the London police force, an area in the center of the capital embracing almost 30 police stations. "Bit of an awkward moment that." MacPherson's chagrin was writ across his face for both Americans to see. "Having to stand up there and tell everybody the thing had gone pear-shaped.."

"Gone what?" Duffy sputtered.

"Police slang. The wheels fell off. The investigation wasn't going anywhere. For all practical purposes we'll be closing the investigation into Mr. Harmian's murder down. Sticking it into the Unsolved Homicides File."

"Well," Duffy consoled him, "don't be too harsh on yourself, Chief. Unless you'd grabbed those guys in the act of butchering Harmian, I think your chances of making an arrest in that case were pretty close to zero."

"Bloody business it was, too. We don't see many like that here, thank God. Funny thing is, he came up such a good guy in our investigation. Foreign Office allowed him to live here, gave him a right proper Resident's Permit. They don't do that for everyone, you know. And he certainly came to this country with more than his buttons."

"His what?" This time it was Flynn who was perplexed.

"More than the buttons on his shirt. He was a man of means. How does someone like that get mixed up with the people who killed him?"

"If only we knew," Duffy sighed. "You were kind enough to suggest at lunch the other day, Chief, that we might take a look at the material you gathered in your investigation before you store it away."

"I did indeed. Hands across the sea. The Special Relation and all that. Let me just give you the ground rules here. If I have to run this by the toffs down at the Home Office as I'm supposed to, you'll be celebrating your sixtieth birthday here before I get an answer out of them. So this is just between us. It never happened, right? Go through the material, make notes if you want to but just remember: you never saw it here."

"Thanks, Chief," Duffy answered. "You can count on our discretion. And we really appreciate your help."

"OK, lads, let me take you down to the evidence room."

For the next six hours, Duffy and Flynn worked their way through the mounds of bank records, bills, correspondence, telephone logs, credit card invoices, sworn testimonies and all the other material Scotland Yard had accumulated during their investigation into Harmian's murder.

"I'll tell you one thing," Flynn declared as they reached the halfway point in their labors, "I've seen a lot of police investigations in my life but I've rarely seen one as thorough as this."

"And with so little in it that's going to take us anywhere," Duffy groaned. "This guy Harmian must have been living two lives, the one we have here in all these records and another one somewhere else where he didn't leave any traces for anyone to follow."

"Yeah. You noticed, Jim, the logs of the calls he was making from his trips abroad back to his wife on her mobile?"

"Right."

"Then you go through the payment records of his plastic and you never find a charge in there for any of those places he was supposed to be. How come?"

"Maybe he was using cash. But you've got a good point, Mike. He didn't want to leave a paper trail, did he?"

It was half past three when Flynn suddenly said, "Hey, look at this. Boy, these guys are really thorough." He waved a paper in his hand at Duffy. "It's the telephone log of that red public payphone he used on those two calls we intercepted. They figured he might have been making calls he didn't want traced from there because it was the closest payphone to his house."

"Jesus, that is good thinking. Let's have a look."

The two men worked their way slowly through the list of the numbers called from the payphone in the month before Harmian's murder. After each was a pencilled identification of where the number called was. Duffy quickly spotted the two calls to the Istanbul mobile which the NSA had intercepted.

Suddenly, he stopped at a call made at 1502 Thursday January 8th. Next to the number called was the notation "NIOC"—the National Iranian Oil Company, where according to the London CIA station the Professor maintained his clandestine residence. Harmian had been murdered on January 30th. Nancy, his wife, thought the angry meeting between her husband and Professor Bollahi had occurred about three weeks before his death—right in this time framework. Could this call have been related somehow to that meeting?

It would have been made over a landline so there was no way the NSA could have intercepted it. On the other hand, Duffy mused, there was MI5. Were they by any chance tapping in on this line? If they weren't, they should be. There goes my day tomorrow, he thought.

A few minutes later, their work finished, their thanks duly expressed to MacPherson, the two men flagged down a cab in front of the headquarters of New Scotland Yard. "You know, Mike," Duffy said, settling back for the ride to the embassy, "there are some pieces to this story we are working on here that I've got to brief you on when we get back to the embassy. We've been keeping you at arm's length on some of them, but fuck it, I'm not going to do it anymore."

————

The headquarters of MI6, British Intelligence, and MI5, its sister service, domestic counter-intelligence, were in a gleaming new glass and steel building not far from the Vauxhall Station. The location was so closely guarded a secret only about three-quarters of London's taxi drivers were aware of the address. The headquarters did, however, have all the appurtenances of modern security systems: thick, grenade-proof windows screening the entrance which was at the head of a well exposed flight of steps, and underground employee parking accessed only through guard operated steel gates.

Like many of his contemporaries, Duffy had listened to the legends of the old wartime SIS—Secret Intelligence Service—headquarters in the Broadway Buildings where, it was said, the essence of security was the aging Scot who ran the elevator because he knew personally everybody who had any business in the building.

Duffy was given a rigorous security screening, passed through a metal detector and given a thorough pat-down before an armed guard took him to a small sitting room to wait for his escort.

Someone back at Langley had had to set all kinds of bells ringing to get him this meeting on such short notice. As soon as he and Flynn had gotten back to the embassy from their visit to Detective Chief Superintendent MacPherson's office, Duffy had gotten on to his friend Jack Lohnes at CIA headquarters with his request. God knows how far up the line Lohnes had had to go with it. To the director, certainly. To the National Security Advisor? To the President? Maybe.

And, of course, the whole thing could turn out to be an exercise in futility. Maybe the Brits weren't tapping the National Iranian Oil Company lines. Or maybe if they were, they weren't going to be prepared to share the harvest of their tap with the agency.

"Mr. Duffy?" A lean young man glowing with the air of extreme physical fitness Duffy knew was associated with Her Majesty's Boy Scouts, the SAS, had entered the room. "My name's Jason. I'll be your escort this morning." The tone with which he said that, Duffy thought must have been based on an imitation of a waiter in one of those trendy southern California restaurants: 'Hi. I'm Harry. I'll be taking care of you this evening.' "The Deputy Director is ready for you."

Jason led him to what appeared to be a private elevator that took them to the top floor where it opened directly into a suite of offices.

Once again, there were a pair of security guards behind whom was a sitting area, then two large desks. At each desk was a somewhat severe looking secretary. Both were dressed with that restrained elegance which had made English girls such prized secretaries in New York advertising agencies back in the days before the computer had turned secretaries into an endangered species.

"This way," Jason said, leading him past one of the secretaries into a spacious office overlooking the Thames. The Deputy Director stepped from behind his desk, hand extended in greeting. "Welcome, Mr. Duffy, your reputation precedes you. My people in Islamabad were full of praise for your operations in Afghanistan."

"Thanks," Duffy smiled. By tradition, he knew, the head of British secret intelligence was always referred to as "C." What, he wondered, do they call his deputy—"C-minus"?

The deputy was waving him to a comfortable armchair and proposing the standard "tea or coffee" option. When they'd been served and had waltzed through the London weather number, the deputy declared, "I've been told to listen very sympathetically to what you have to say. Just what is it I can do for you?"

That put Duffy in a delicate position. How much had Langley had to tell the British cousins to fix this meeting for him on such short notice?

"Well, as you know, sir, the Iranian government's efforts to acquire weapons of mass destruction, and particularly nuclear weapons, are at the forefront of our national security concerns."

"Indeed, as they are for us as well."

"Right. Well, we are very worried at the moment about a particular aspect of that Iranian threat. My query is very precise and very simple and goes to the heart of that concern. On January 8th at 1502, a telephone call was made from a red public payphone number 235.7728 in Belgravia to the offices of the National Iranian Oil Company. We have reason to believe that that call may have been related to this threat which concerns us. Because the call was made on a landline, the NSA was not able to access it. So my question is this: are your people running a tap on that NIOC number and if so, would you have a record of the call I'm interested in?"

The deputy director slumped back in his easy chair. "You understand that that material, assuming we have it, would be very highly classified."

"Of course."

"Perhaps you could elaborate just a bit for me on this particular 'concern' you're referring to."

Well, there it was, Duffy realized. Either he laid it on the table now or he was never going to see that intercept—provided, of course, it existed. "It's a matter of which your agency is aware. It's that report we all attempted to check out in the nineties according to which the Iranians had obtained three nuclear devices of an unknown nature in Kazakhstan as the Russians were dismantling their arsenal there."

"Yes, I remember. If memory serves me correctly we were unable to pin down whether that report was true or false. Since I think it had originated with the Israelis, there was, as I recall, some scepticism about just how genuine it was."

"Right. Well, we now know it's true."

The deputy sat up as though he'd just been braced by a drill sergeant. "*We* do? I assume your 'we' refers to Langley. Have we been made aware of this? Officially, I mean?"

"Officially, sir, I don't know. Liaison is not my responsibility. Unofficially, you have been as of this moment." And now, Duffy thought, get me that fucking intercept.

"Well, you understand, we here at Six don't run our domestic wiretapping program. That's the responsibility of Five and the GCHQ—Governmental Communications Headquarters. We can and do make requests where international security concerns are involved, but Five and the GCHQ process them. To be perfectly honest with you, I have no idea whether or not they are tapping the NIOC's communications."

"Well, I'm sure you are aware of the role the NIOC plays as a front for Iran's armament procurement program."

"Just as I am aware of the brouhaha we'd have on our hands if the liberal press came out with the news we were tapping what is supposed to be, at least, a commercial enterprise. The *Guardian* would probably accuse us of using the tap to speculate on oil futures."

"Yeah," Duffy chuckled, "we all have our problems in that regard, don't we? But I can assure you, sir, that my request enjoys the support of the highest possible authority."

Duffy was winging it there. His phrase "highest possible authority" was a euphemism in official-speak for the President. Would he have supported this request? Who the hell's to say, Duffy thought, but timidity had never resolved any of the problems he'd encountered in his career.

The ploy worked. The deputy rose, went to his desk and pushed a button. Seconds later, an attractive young woman in her early thirties entered the office. Her arrival was so swift she must have been standing by for the deputy's ring. She was dressed in that same sort of understated elegance employed by the secretaries outside.

"This is Victoria Parker, my liaison with Five and GCHQ," the deputy said, introducing her. He passed her the NIOC and pay phone numbers and the details of Duffy's request.

"Victoria, be a dear and get on to GCHQ and see if they're reading this number and if so, ask them to make us a transcript of the call our American friend here is interested in."

Dear? Duffy thought. Use that phrase talking to a female officer at Langley and you'd be drawn and quartered in front of the Political Correctness Board.

"This may take a little time," the deputy suggested passing Duffy a copy of the *Daily Telegraph*. "Perhaps you'd like to glance through this while you're waiting."

In fact, it didn't take much time at all. The attractive Miss Parker was back in barely five minutes with a sheaf of paper in her hand which she passed to the deputy. He read it carefully, then passed it across his desk to Duffy.

"I'm not sure how much help this is going to be, but feel free to study it to your heart's content. However, no copies please. If you need one you'll have to route the request through the usual channels, the NSA to GCHQ."

GCHQ - MOST SECRET

0108981502Z
VOICE ONE:0171.235.7728
PUBLIC PHONE ECCLESTON PLACE LONDONSW1
VOICE TWO:0171.371.2067
NATIONAL IRANIAN OIL COMPANY HEADQUARTERS LONDON
AUTHORIZATION REF: HO1997/23471
TRANSLATED FROM THE ORIGINAL FARSI BY H T MOTZARFFIN
GCHQ 345692

VOICE ONE: Professor, this is Tari.They just told me about your Khalid program. It's madness. Utter, damn madness.

VOICE TWO: Tari, please. This is not the place to discuss these things.

VOICE ONE: It's OK. I'm in a payphone. Listen, don't you know what the reprisals for something like that would be? We'd be wiped off the face of the earth. It will be the end of our nation, our people.

VOICE TWO: Tari, control yourself. If God is giving us this weapon it is to fight the enemies of Islam. Our leaders . . .

VOICE ONE: Our leaders have gone mad. I came to work for you to help save my country not to help destroy it. I quit. I am shutting down my transfers to your Falcon. Right now.

VOICE TWO: Tari. Can you be at your home in one hour? I will come and see you so we can discuss this in a reasonable manner.

VOICE ONE: (Inaudible)

END OF CONVERSATION

"Is that helpful?" asked the deputy.

"Helpful? I don't know," Duffy replied. "Confusing? You bet."

He got up and paced for a few seconds in front of the deputy's desk. "Listen," he said when he'd come to rest, "I told you unofficially a couple of moments ago that we now have hard proof that the Iranians possess at least three nuclear devices. What I'm afraid this intercept may be telling us is that those damn fools want to use them."

————

This has got to be every bit as awkward for her as it is for me, Jim Duffy thought, gazing at Nancy Harmian studying the menu in the little French bistro to which he'd invited her for dinner and a chat. Christ, he felt like a high school kid out on his first date.

"Looks wonderful," Nancy smiled, and set aside her menu. "However did you find it? Or"—the suggestion of a malicious twinkle lit up her eyes—"do our national security organs furnish their travelling agents with a list of the chic restaurants in each of the cities they're going to be visiting?"

"The address of the nearest Burger King would be more my employer's style."

The waiter arrived and set their drinks down on the table between them. Nancy picked up her vodka. For a second or two she swirled the liquor around the ice cubes in the glass, the twinkle in her eyes dimmed by a sudden flash of melancholy. She shook her head as though her gesture might throw off the heavy hand of the past plucking at the skirts of her spirit. She raised her eyes to Duffy.

"To time, Jim. I guess we both need that more than anything else, don't we?"

Smiling, Duffy raised his glass in turn. "Yeah. Time that knits up the ravelled sleeve of care." The words were barely out of his mouth when he made a little choking sound. "Christ! I got it wrong, didn't I? It's sleep not time. That's what happens when you try to impress a lady."

Nancy laughed. "It's the effort that counts. I didn't know our intelligence officers were given to quoting Shakespeare. I would have thought Longfellow was more your style. *The Midnight Ride of Paul Revere* or something."

"That's the FBI."

Nancy had picked a crust of the sliced-up French baguette from the basket on their table. She tore off a piece and began to chew it with the deliberate gestures of someone sampling a great delicacy for the first time. Duffy watched fascinated. There were some women, and Nancy was one of them, who could endow the most mundane of gestures with a special air of elegance. "So," she smiled at him, "I suppose your remark confirms by elimination my conviction that you're CIA."

Life, Duffy knew, was a lot easier if you occasionally bent the rules to your own convenience and this, he suspected, wouldn't be the only rule he'd be bending tonight. "You said it, I didn't."

"A long time?"

"All my working life."

"Whatever got you into it?"

"I was dumb. I was a patriot." Duffy waved his drink. "No. Put that on hold. Sounds patronizing. First of all, because the agency came after me. I majored in Russian in college. That was flattering. And what they were offering sounded like a helluva life, which it was. And finally, that boring notion of service to one's country did keep rearing its ugly head so I cut it off by signing up."

"Well, that's one way of dealing with it, I guess. Still, I like a man whose life isn't weighed down by regrets."

Duffy took a long swallow of his drink. "Oh, I've had my share of those."

"Professional?"

"That I really can't get into, Nancy."

"Not personal, I hope for your sake. If I had to make a guess, it would be that you were probably a pretty good husband for your late wife."

Duffy put on his impish kid's grin. "Is there such a thing as a good husband? I don't know. Sometimes, I think it sounds like an oxymoron for our times. Put it this way. I don't think I was a bad husband."

"No," Nancy said, "I'm sure you weren't. Just as I think I was a pretty good wife to my poor Terry in those two years God gave us together. Are you making any progress in your work by the way?"

"Some." Duffy smiled.

Nancy sipped her vodka. "You're holding out on me, Jim. You're dying to tell me something and you don't quite dare. I can read it on your face. Why don't they send you agency types to acting class?"

Duffy took a long drink of his own to order his thoughts. Just how much could he tell this woman? He recalled the pages of her statement to the police, of the hell she had put herself through to try save her husband's life. She deserved something. Like knowing maybe that her husband wasn't quite the bad guy he now seemed to be.

"Tell me, Nancy. Did your husband ever talk to you about something called a Plan Khalid?"

Nancy looked puzzled. "No, never. And Khalid isn't a Persian name. It's Arabic. Why?"

"I shouldn't tell you this but I think you've got a right to know it so I'm going to tell you anyway. You remember that guy Bollahi whose photo you picked out of the pile I brought you? The guy called 'The Professor?'"

"Sure."

"Well, we know now that your husband had been working with him for some time. Bollahi, as I think I may have told you the last time we talked, is a heavy hitter in the Iranian government's arms procurement program."

"Tari? Buying arms? I can't believe that. He barely knew the difference between a shotgun and a twenty-two. His English friends were always inviting him out on their shoots but he never went."

"I don't think he was involved in actually buying the arms. I think he was handling some of their finances. Probably investing their money for them until they needed it. Anyway, he broke with the Professor over this Khalid business, whatever the hell it is. He told Bollahi he was afraid Iran would be destroyed in reprisal for it. My guess is he refused to hand over the money they needed to finance it and that's why they killed him."

"Khalid," Nancy mused. "You know Jim, after Terry and I married, I spent some time studying the Koran, then the history of Islam. Khalid was one of their first great warrior heros during the days of the

Caliphate after the Prophet's death." She sat back and moved her long, well manicured fingers to the throat of her black silk blouse. "He marched six, seven hundred men across the Syrian desert in a couple of weeks which was a prodigious feat in those days, then attacked the Byzantine army. He threw the Christians out of Palestine. Drove them up to what's now the Turkish-Syrian border. In a sense, he was a liberator of Palestine. You don't suppose that's what this Khalid is all about, do you? Some kind of a modern plan to duplicate his feat? Those mullahs may be crazy but surely they're not crazy enough to try to attack Israel. What would they do it with?"

"Don't bet on it, Nancy. Where madmen or fanatics are concerned, it isn't the reasoning that leads to an act that matters. It's only the action itself that counts."

The waiter had glided up to take their order. So, Duffy thought, his eyes moving between the rack of lamb and the magret of duck. What Nancy just said could very well explain what this Plan Khalid was about. Confirmed what he'd read at MI6, didn't it? The mullahs wanted to find some way to employ their three nukes on Israel. Use those damn things to give us a second Holocaust.

———

These were the moments in the day, or to be more precise, the night, the Professor cherished above all others. He was relaxed, his prayers accomplished, his mind at ease. He was stretched out on his hotel room bed wrapped in the body-length white djellabah in which he liked to sleep, his hand still resting on his precious Koran inscribed to him by the Ayatollah. It was open to the Surat he had just finished reading, Surat al Mai'idah 55, "Lo the Party of God, for surely they are they that shall triumph."

The Party of God—Hezbollah. He knew the party's manifesto by heart and its words drifted through his mind now. "Freedom is not freely given but is to be won through the exertions of souls and blood." Like the blood of those brave young men who had carried their bombs into the heart of the occupiers' lands. They had been adherents of Hamas, a Sunni Moslem organization, but now, under Tehran's leadership, they were all, Sunni and Shiite, Hamas and Hezbollah, brothers united in the same sacred struggle to return the earth of Palestine to *Dar el Islam,* the Land of Islam, to totally eliminate the alien Israeli nation from Islamic soil. When the time came there would be, he knew, brave young men ready to die for that holy mission, and it would be his task to place in their courageous hands the terrible weapon they needed to achieve their victory.

Tonight they were well on their way to that sacred goal. Just as he had expected, Herr Steiner had grabbed at Joe Mischer's offer to buy 50% of LASERTECHNIK as eagerly as a drowning man grasps for a life preserver. The price they had settled on was 4.2 million marks. Steiner had not posed a single question about the ultimate owners of TW Holdings in Liechtenstein. He had assumed it belonged to Mischer who was using it as part of a tax avoidance scheme like almost everyone else who operated behind the screen of a Vaduz company. There was absolutely nothing that could suggest, even remotely, an Iranian involvement in the purchase of half of LASERTECHNIK.

Joe was already operating from an office near Steiner's in his factory, ingratiating himself with his new associate, quietly studying LASERTECHNIK's operations. It was about time to make their next move. First, though, the Professor had to make the neccessary financial arrangements and bring Tehran up to date on the situation.

He opened up his laptop computer and tapped in the access code for his financial records. The code had been programmed into his computer by a special software program he'd purchased in Dusseldorf. If someone attempted to access his records using the wrong key twice, the program would automatically erase them.

Now the menu for all his financial holdings was laid out before him: the record of his account at the Bank Melli in Munich, the accounts of the Foundation for the Oppressed in Liechtenstein, Switzerland and the Caymans, none of them places he thought, looking at the screen, which one would associate with the oppressed of this world. Next, he punched up the Acquisition account into which Said Djailani funnelled the receipts of the transit tax he was collecting on the morphine base passing through his hands on its way to Turkey. The figures that now came up on his screen were a satisfying sight, one that more than justified their decision to put the former Mooj commander in his tax collector's job. In the nine months since Djailani had been working for them, 31.7 million dollars had been deposited into the Acquisition account. Its current balance, he noted, was 9.2 million dollars.

Normally, the bulk of that sum would have been moved automatically into the Cayman account of the traitor Harmian who would have invested it on behalf of the dummy companies he controlled in the short term money market where it would be available for movement to the Professor's accounts as soon as it was needed.

Harmian, however, had yet to be replaced by a trusted new money manager so cash was piling up. The Professor now called up Salvation, the account he employed as the ultimate control for most of his surreptitious arms purchases. It showed a balance of 2.6 million dollars. Falcon owned Trade World which in turn owned TW Holdings, the firm he'd used to finance the purchase of fifty percent of LASERTECHNIK. The Professor loved to pyramid his purchases that way. It made it impossible for any financial analyst, however, shrewd, to trace a firm's ownership back to him and on to Tehran. It was time, he decided to shift some of those accumulating drug profits to Salvation and start them on their way to Liechtenstein.

He shut down his financial program and hooked his laptop up to the black encoding box of the new, high security coding system he'd purchased from CIPHER AG in Switzerland. He had brought the black box with him on his trip from Tehran after programming it just as he had been instructed to do by the Swiss. He had formatted one of his blank discs by making his own random selection from the coding keys CIPHER AG had furnished him, thus in a sense devising a code to which only he had the key. Now, he was ready to employ the Swiss system for the first time.

Then as an additional measure of security, he had installed a special telephone to receive his messages in his office in Tehran. The phone was listed in the name of a philosophy professor at the University of Tehran who had just died of pancreatic cancer. Tomorrow he would check out of this hotel and hide himself in the furnished apartment Mischer had rented for them both in his name. He opened up his laptop computer and connected it with a cable to his black encoding box. He then disconnected the hotel phone and inserted the lead from the black box into the phone jack. That done, he set to work.

In the name of Allah, the Merciful, the Compassionate, may His blessings be upon you my brother and upon our great enterprise. I am now able to tell you that the German has accepted our offer and we have installed our representative in his office. I shall undertake the next critical step in the realization of Khalid shortly. In the meantime, I would ask you to ask our brother Djailani to transfer 1.75 million dollars from the Acquisition account to my Falcon account so that I can arrange to send the balance of TW Holdings purchase price to the German's account.

The Professor concluded his brief message with the usual flow of Persian courtesies and hit the "enter" key on his laptop. He heard his text pass into the coding box with the kind of "clack" he associated with copying a text from his hard disc to a soft disc. Then he heard the coding box dialing the telephone number which had belonged to the dead professor. After two rings, he heard a whine like that of a fax machine indicating the decoding box hooked up to the phone in his Tehran office was on line, ready to receive his text. Another swift clack and the text was transmitted. With that his coding box terminated the call. A miracle, the Professor mused. Worth every franc he'd paid the Swiss for it.

BOOK SEVEN

The Trojan Horse of
MENWITH HILL

The United States Government possesses no facility more secret than the Menwith Hill Station of the U.S. Army's Intelligence and Security Command nestled in the rolling green knolls of the Yorkshire Dales, just outside Harrogate off the A59, 170 miles from Central London. It is, for an ultra-secret site, remarkably easy to identify from a passing car. Half a mile away, a driver can already spot the station's 23 radomes rising on the horizon like enormous white golfballs awaiting the stroke of some giant's putter. Then closer in, 100 "polar masts," aerials and antennas, ring the base like porcupine quills in three concentric circles.

Menwith Hill represents the absolute summit of the U.S.'s technological ability to wrap the globe in an American electronic embrace. Those radomes and polar masts suck an electronic bouillabaisse from the skies, the soup of cyberspace, every form of communication from satellite transmissions of phone calls and faxes, to cellular phone calls, pornography on the Internet, the encrypted wire transfers of billions of dollars, the electronic fingerprint of an Iraqi tank firing a missile or a Russian fighter launching an air to ground strike on a target in Chechnya. Indeed, virtually any form of electronic communication other than those passed on an untapped fiber optic cable could lie within Menwith Hill's hungry grasp.

So restricted is the installation, no member of the British Parliament has ever been allowed to enter its premises. The land on which the base is built is U.S. property, purchased in 1951 and governed by a still secret protocol signed by Harry Truman and Winston Churchill. Its 2,000 employees, civilian and military, embrace an astonishing spectrum of skills from the ability to speak Tibetan to running the most sophisticated computer programs Man or Bill Gates have yet devised.

On this chill February morning, Jack Galen, the 42-year-old base Chief of Operations, walked down the footpath from his residence in Apartment Block 42 on the Top of the Hill towards the low-lying, windowless buildings of his Operations Block. Galen was a civilian, a senior officer of the NSA—not surprising since while technically Menwith Hill had been placed under military command out of a concern for British sensibilities, it was, for all practical purposes, run by the NSA.

It was 0630 and Galen was, as always, half an hour early for the day's first shift change at seven a.m. Ahead of him, the quarter mile long Ops Block was bathed in intensive high security lighting. He walked between the parking lot and the chain-link security fence with its barbed wire overhang to the double glass doors of the building labelled Steeplebush II, the only outside entry into the Ops Block. The MP on duty inspected his security pass with his color ID photo and a separate tag listing the security areas he was entitled to enter—in Galen's case an alphabet soup of code names.

He went into the base canteen and bought himself a large cup of coffee to jumpstart his day, then took the elevator up to the OPS floor where a second set of security guards checked his ID.

"Mr. Galen," one of them announced, "there's something waiting for you in the SCIF."

The SCIF—Sensitive Compartmented Information Facility—was the Holy of Holies of this ultra-secret installation—a windowless, sound-proofed room entered by a cypher-locked door to which only twelve of the Hill's 2000 employees had the combination.

"So what's up?" he asked the Duty Officer inside.

The officer gestured to a gray file folder on one of the three desks in the room. "That came in last night. It's a new BRAINWAVE transmission."

Galen picked up the folder. It was stamped "T.S. (Top Secret). Eyes Only C\OPS - F830." The folder, he saw, contained a magnetic tape and a transcription of the material on the tape, a hopeless jumble of letters, numbers, and symbols like *%$#@.*

The NSA officer groaned and took a long swallow of his hot black coffee. He was going to need all the stimulation he could get in the next hour or so. He threaded the tape into a machine rigged to one of the two computer screens on his desk. One by one, the machine projected the characters on the tape onto the computer screen, enhancing its size as it did. Galen studied the first character, the letter "W," then called up the second, the symbol "&." At the fifth, the letter "A," he stopped. Tucked into the very top of the letter, just under the point where the two sides of the letter joined was a microdot. He copied the letter onto his second screen, then continued his work.

It took Galen well over an hour to work his way through the hundreds of characters in the encrypted text which had been intercepted by the NSA's eavesdropping equipment. Every so often, he would find a microdot tucked into some obscure corner of one of those characters. When he did, he would add it to the chain of characters building up on his second screen.

That first phase of his work completed, Galen left the SCIF for yet another secure workplace, the SBI—Sensitive Background Information storage depot. There he logged out the computer disc for BRAIN-WAVE with the Duty Officer and returned to the SCIF. He inserted the BRAINWAVE disc into his second computer. The disc contained a schematic diagram of the algorithm which had encoded the text intercepted by the NSA's listening devices. The diagram now picked out each of the microdots which had been secretly embedded into the message as it was being put into code. It compared them to the data base on the BRAINWAVE disc and then cast a series of letters and numbers onto the screen. That mysterious stream of letters was the key of the code which had been employed to encode the original clear text.

Galen entered that key into his first computer and started the magnetic tape through the machine. The jumbled chain of characters on the tape now suddenly came up on the computer screen in the clear, in the sender's original text: "In the name of Allah, the Merciful, the Compassionate," it began. The NSA officer watched fascinated as it unfolded before his eyes.

"Venal Swiss bastards," he chortled reading it. "We got 'em again."

BRAINWAVE was one of the NSA's greatest and most secret triumphs. Knowing full well that Swiss companies like CIPHER AG would sell anything to anybody provided the price was right, the NSA had managed to infiltrate a Swedish mathematican into the elite team of scientists that had constructed the immensely complex algorithm which powered CIPHER AG's coding machines. The algorithm, of course, had to be able to recognize the coding key the sender had selected in order to put his text into code. Acting in collaboration with the NSA, the Swede had doctored the algorithm so that it would embed into the jumble of the coded text a secret chain of microdots. Properly read by someone who knew those microdots were there and could isolate them, they would reveal the coding key the sender had employed. "A Top Secret Trojan Horse" was how the handful of NSA officers aware of the trick had labelled it.

The Swiss, like Herr Zurni at CIPHER AG, had no idea that their marvellous encoding equipment had been compromised. They happily sold dozens of their machines to all comers, the Vatican, the Syrians, the Iraqis, the Radical Islamic Sudanese government of Hassan el Turabi, money launderers, and Libya's Muammar Khadafy.

It was thanks to a BRAINWAVE intercept that the U.S. had the proof the Libyan was behind the bombing of the La Belle disco in Berlin. The Reagan adminstration had not been prepared to yield up the secret of how it had gotten that proof, however, when it solicited Allied support for its air strike on Tripoli. Margaret Thatcher was prepared to take the American president on faith. Ever sceptical of U.S. intentions, François Mitterand was not, and refused U.S. aircraft permission to overfly French soil on their way to Tripoli.

The text of this intercept meant nothing, of course, to Galen. He noted that it did contain names like "Falcon" and "Djailani" and that it had been sent from a number in Hamburg, Germany to a number in Tehran. His standing orders were to get BRAINWAVE intercepts back to NSA headquarters at Fort Meade, MD immediately.

He drafted a full report to go along with text of the intercept on the N.S.T.S.—National Secure Telephone System—and had it on its way from the number two "Golfball" outside his office long before the men and women at his U.S. headquarters who would have to deal with it were out of bed.

———

"Djailani!" Jack Lohnes, the CIA's Deputy Director of Operations almost rose out of his seat reading the text of the NSA's BRAINWAVE intercept. "Isn't that the guy Jim Duffy's trying to run down? His old pal the Gucci Mooj who's supposed to be collecting the Iranian VAT on all the dope that's going by out there?"

"Yessir," his aide replied.

"Duffy's still over in London, isn't he? Have the Hill get everything they've got on this intercept to their liaison office at the embassy for him." He paused a second, thinking. "And something else. Ask Fincen to run these three names, 'Falcon' and 'Acquisition' and 'TW Holdings,' through their data bases and see if they come up with anything. If they do, get it over to Duffy ASAP."

"I'll get on to them right away," Lohnes' aide assured him and headed for his phones.

———

Getting into Room 4210 of the Menwith Hill Senior Liaison Office at the U.S. Embassy in London was, Jim Duffy reflected, even more difficult than getting into the CIA's suite of offices. When his identity had been verified for the third time, his person electronically swept for hidden microphones or tape recorders, he was finally ushered into the office of the NSA civilian running the place.

"Mr. Duffy, Fort Meade has asked us to show you a Top Secret intercept our station picked up and decoded last night." The mention of the words *Fort Meade* and *intercept* almost made Duffy gag on the memories of those, long tedious hours he had spent listening to intercepts in the basements of the CIA. Dear God, don't get me started on that again, he thought, picking up the gray envelope the NSA official proffered him.

It contained a single sheet of paper stamped:

TOP SECRET BRAINWAVE
AUTHORIZED EYES ONLY

Oh my God! Duffy gasped, reading the words *the next critical step in the realization of Khalid shortly*. This has to be from the Professor. "Where the hell did this come from?" he asked the NSA official.

"It was sent from Hamburg, Germany. The Forum Hotel."

"Where was it going?"

"To a private residence in Tehran on which, quite frankly, we have absolutely nothing."

"There's no signature. And no name for the guy it was sent to."

"The text was sent in code, a very restricted private cipher to which probably only a very few people have access."

"So how the hell were you able to read it?"

The Menwith Hill Liaison Officer smiled. "That's NSA need to know, Mr. Duffy." In other words, it was none of his business. "However, I have a second message I've been instructed to give you concerning FINCEN's search of their data base for anything to do with those three company names cited in the intercept. This is what they came up with." He passed Duffy a second gray file folder similar to the first.

Duffy tore it open and exclaimed, "Bingo!"

Falcon, the first of the three companies that had been mentioned in the intercept, had just rung the bell. That was the company into whose Cayman Island bank account that guy Harmian, who the Iranians had murdered in London, was transferring the dough he'd skimmed off the heroin traffic. The guy who wrote the intercept—who had to be the Professor—called it "my Falcon account."

So there it was, just as the director had suspected at that first meeting he had attended after being summoned back to Langley. The Iranians were using the heroin traffic to finance their terrorism program and worse, their efforts to convert those three nukes of theirs into workable bombs.

"The Fincen Data Bases," Lohnes message continued, "contain no record of any transactions registered on behalf of either Acquisition or TW Holdings. Falcon, however, was the company of record in an effort organized in March 1992 to purchase and export from the United States rocket lamps for use in missile guidance systems in violation of U.S. Export Control Law from Aerospace Systems, Inc. of Houston, Texas."

Duffy thanked the NSA officer running the room and headed downstairs to find Mike Flynn.

"Had to be our friend Professor Bollahi who sent that coded message, doesn't it," Flynn observed as soon as Duffy had filled him on the intercept. "Who else would it be? Question is, is he still in that hotel? And if he is, can we find him?"

"I doubt it," Duffy replied. "I think he's too slippery a fox for that."

"Still, why don't you get onto your people in Langley and see if they can find him. Put him under discreet 24-hour surveillance if they do—discreet enough to keep him from spotting it and getting spooked."

"There's a major problem there, Mike."

"What's that?"

"There's no way the CIA can run an operation on a scale like the one we'd need here without employing the resources of German counter-intelligence, the BfV, *Bundesamt fur Verfassungsschutz,* what they call their Office for the Protection of the Constitution in Cologne. We'd have to come clean with the Germans on what's going on."

"So?"

"Langley's not going to be very anxious to do that. Our relations with our German cousins are at an all-time low since Iraq. They have a whole different attitude towards the dangers the mullahs pose to the world from ours. Their idea is 'do business with them then maybe they won't make bombs.' I think Langley would worry that somebody from the BfV would whisper a word of warning to the Professor. Tell him to get the hell out of Germany."

"Suppose we take it from a DEA angle? Tell the krauts our Professor is into dope? Which in a certain way he is."

"Yeah. That might fly. Let me mull over it, Mike. What really has me worried is that phrase 'I shall undertake the next critical step in the realization of Khalid shortly.' What the hell does he mean by that?"

———

The wind, the mournful wind from the West was sighing off the Atlantic, stirring the waters of the River Shannon into wavelets as it swept its way inland to dump its drizzle on Ennis, Limerick and the expanse of Ireland's Shannon International Airport. From his office in Bay T53 of the airport's free zone, Jimmy Shea stared morosely at the driblets of the ocean's froth slithering down the building's floor to ceiling windows. Boggy it'll be for a month now, he thought.

Sure it was an afternoon to spend by the hearth or better yet in the convivial warmth of a pub, a couple of pints of stout to hasten away so dreary a day. Shea was lost in his moody reflections and didn't hear his secretary the first time she called out, "Phone for you, Jimmy. A Mr. Steiner from Germany."

On her second effort, she finally got his attention. Steiner, he thought, flipping through the Rolodex in his mind, just who was he now? He was moving the phone to his ear to take the call when the answer came: he was that Haas engineer over in Hamburg who'd gone off to build the world a better laser. LASERTECHNIK he'd called his company. Rumor had it that like so many of those who set out on that path, what Steiner was building was a mountain of debts, not better lasers.

"Herr Steiner," he boomed into his phone with all the practiced bonhomie of the expert salesman, "how've you been keeping these past months?"

"Well," Steiner replied, "you remember we spoke a year or so ago about my ideas on how to build an improved high-energy laser."

"Indeed I do."

"The project went on ice for awhile but things are much better now. I've got some new financial backing and we're up and running again."

"Ah, that's grand, Herr Steiner. I hope EG&G will fit into your future plans."

"I'm sure you will and, in fact, that's the reason for my call. The first thing I'd like to do is to place an order with you now for 75 thry-trons, your model HY53."

Shea sat up straight. At $3,000 each, an order for 75 HY53's was good business, indeed. Until he'd heard that figure, he'd been playing the oblig-atory politeness game with Steiner. Now, the German had his full attention.

"We'll be happy to fill that order for you, Herr Steiner. If you'll just fax me a confirmation, I'll have it off to Salem before the close of business tonight."

"Wonderful. Now I'm also working with some people from the medical faculty at the university here on a related project. We're exper-imenting with an idea we have to develop a very high powered laser for use in skin surgery. Particularly for removing facial blemishes. If we can make this work, I think we'll be able to revolutionize the whole field of facial surgery."

"Sure the world will be a better place if you succeed in that, Herr Steiner."

"I think we can. It's going to take some work and as I said a lot of experimenting. My idea is to put a sodium crystal into a crystal cavity that can take 6 to 7 kilovolts and hold the plane of polarization in such a way that it stops that laser light from exiting the cavity until we can get a maximum electron build-up in there. Then we'll use a Pockcell to shoot out that concentrated energy in a laser pulse that only lasts a couple of nano-seconds. Not your usual microseconds."

Shea had a doctorate in electrical engineering so he possessed more than a passing familiarity with laser technology. "Yes," he said, "that just might be effective."

"I hope so. Now to trigger that Pockcell's action we'll need your KN22B krytron, so what I'd like to do is flesh out that order for 75 thrytrons with an order for a dozen KN22B's."

"No problem, Herr Steiner. You know, of course, that because of their possible use in nuclear technology, we have to get a U.S. Department of Commerce export license for all our krytron sales."

"Certainly. I understand that."

"What we'll need from you is a completed export license declaration form and a statement telling us where and how the krytrons are to be used."

"No problem at all, I'm sure, since they're going to be for use here in Germany. If you'd like to fax me now a set of the documents you require, I'll fill them out and Fedex them back to you tomorrow morning along with the confirmation of the order and a check for your down payment. Will twenty-five percent be agreeable?"

"That will be grand, Herr Steiner. I'll get these off to you now and we'll be looking for your order."

"Fine. How long will it take to fill it do you suppose?"

"Not long. Three to five weeks."

———

By midafternoon of the day following his call to Jimmy Shea, Herr Steiner had a Fedex package on the EG&G salesman's desk at the Shannon International Airport Free Trade Zone. Shea eagerly ripped it open. Everything was there: a confirmation of Steiner's order for 75 HY53 Thrytrons and 12 KN22B Krytrons, a certified check for $62,500 and the two forms required to obtain a U.S. Export license for the krytrons signed by Steiner and stamped with the LASERTECHNIK company seal.

Shea picked up the first of the two declarations. It was in the form of a standard letter which EG&G addressed to any prospective purchasers of krytrons. It read:

As you may be aware, the international trading of krytrons is subject to regulations governing the non-proliferation of nuclear weapons. We are therefore obliged to obtain a declaration of end use from all our customers for these items.

Krytrons may be shipped freely under general license to the nations on the attached list of signatories to the nuclear safeguards convention. However, please note that the export to countries outside those nations is subject to your obtaining approval from the U.S. Department of Commerce and the relevant authority in Germany.

Steiner had signed the document acknowledging that he had understood and accepted those conditions.

The second document was a letter from Steiner to EG&G on LASERTECHNIK stationery.

We certify that the end use of the krytrons will be in a sodium crystal NYDAG laser for the purpose of developing a high energy, short burst laser for use in facial surgery procedures.

We further certify that the ultimate destination of these krytrons will be for use in Germany.

Nothing wrong with either of those declarations, Shea thought, after giving each a careful reading. Still, he was puzzled by this krytron thing. In his years at the Shannon office of EG&G, he'd never sold more than five krytrons at a time and then to U.S. companies working in Europe which used them as "explosive sets" in the detonation of non-nuclear charges.

He took the package over to his colleague Greg Hickey. The two had already discussed Steiner's order. Hickey studied the forms. "Yeah," he sighed, "a quarter of million dollars. Sure that's real business now. These papers are all in order, aren't they? And what he's proposing to do with those krytrons he wants strikes me as being a perfectly legitimate end use for them. Still . . ."

He frowned. "You know, let's call Johannes." Johannes Schmidt was one of the organizers of the bi-annual Munich Laser Fair. The laser industry was a tight little world. Most of its players knew something about most of their fellow players. Schmidt on the other hand was widely believed to know everything about everybody.

Fifteen minutes later, Hickey walked up to Shea's desk. "Steiner's story checks out," he informed him. "Johannes says he's got a new angel, some German guy who walked in the door carrying a bag of money."

"So, we forward the order to Salem then?"

"Yeah. Not much else to do, I guess," Hickey agreed. "Except maybe slug it for Paul Aspen's attention. He ought to have a look at it before it goes into the pipeline."

———

Thank God it's Friday? Paul Aspen angrily asked himself settling down before the mound of paperwork waiting for him on his desk at EG&G's Salem, Massachusetts manufacturing facility. What's to be thankful for? The meteorologists at Boston's Logan Airport were predicting six inches of snow for the weekend, his youngest child Jennie had just come down with the mumps and the Boston Celtics had managed to bring themselves to within one loss of losing any hopes of making the NBA playoffs.

With a sigh, he pulled the mass of paperwork towards him, calling out to Angela his secretary for his morning coffee as he did. "Better make it a double this morning, please."

The first of the memos on the pile waiting for his comments or action came from Shannon. Why, he wondered, were they communicating with him instead of going through their normal sales channels?

It took him a three minute speed read to get his answer.

"Angela!" he yelled. "Forget the coffee. Get me Dr. Stein down at the Department of Energy right away. Tell him it's urgent."

Even Aspen was surprised by the rapidity with which the government reacted to the warning he passed to Stein. Something major was up for sure, because less than ten minutes after he'd hung up with Stein, he had that guy Duffy who'd been in to see him about krytrons ringing him from London.

"I want to thank you very much for passing that material on to Dr. Stein," Duffy told him. "This is not a secure line so I don't want to get into any specifics here but I did want to double check one thing with you. The company that placed that order. It was called LASERTECH-NIK. In Hamburg, Germany, right?"

Aspen checked the pile of papers in front of him. "The company's name is right but it's in Pinneberg. That's just north of Hamburg, I think."

"Terrific. Can you do me a favor and just hold that order in your in-box until I can get back to you?"

———

On the other side of the Atlantic, Jim Duffy rang through to the CIA's Bonn station on a secure line. This situation, at least, posed no delicate protocol problems which would force him to coordinate his actions with German intelligence.

"Listen," he asked the station chief, "have we got anybody on duty in Hamburg?"

"Are you kidding? You know how Congress has been slicing up our budget."

"Never mind. Get onto the consulate. I want one of their officers to go down to the commercial registry of the town of Pinneberg and get me all the details they have in there on the ownership of a firm called LASERTECHNIK."

"How quickly do you need this?"

"Half an hour ago."

"Jesus, Jim, the counsel's going to go ape-shit when I tell him that."

"Let him. You tell him to get his ass down there himself if he has and to do it right now. He can forget about whatever critical meetings he has with those Hanseatic beer baron pals of his. Unless he wants to be opening up a new consulate in Ulan Bator."

Duffy's tone had clearly conveyed the sense of urgency he was seeking because the station chief was back on the line in barely an hour's time.

"Fifty percent of that company LASERTECHNIK belongs to the guy who founded it, a German named Steiner," he reported. "He just sold the other fifty percent to one of those Vaduz shell companies in Liechtenstein. It's called TW Holdings."

"Bingo!" Duffy shouted. TW Holdings. That was the name of the firm in the text the NSA had decoded, the one that belonged to that Iranian nemesis, the Professor. "Thanks, pal. Get you a medal for that."

In seconds he was out the door heading down to the embassy travel office. Today, he chuckled, Uncle Sugar is going to be happy to fly Flynn and me home on the Concorde.

———

Friday night, and another weekend was starting. In Paris's Strasbourg Saint Denis, Madrid's gypsy suburbs, Frankfurt's railroad station, and at Hamburg's Saint Paoli U Bahn stop, the dealers were ready to move—ready to push the marvels of their wares, much of it Osman family heroin, with a hiss and a murmur as they slipped through the milling crowds in search of a big weekend score.

In London, Eddie Foulkes—"Eddie the Rastafarian" to his clients, for the floppy black leather hat favored by the sect's followers which he liked to wear—was getting ready for the night's action. Eddie was not going to be caught short of product, not tonight. He had re-supplied himself with half a kilo of dope from his favorite wholesaler, Paul "The Irishman" Glynn. Glynn always had the good shit, fresh in from some family he worked with out there in Turkey.

Eddie had just discovered how good this latest batch of Glynn's smack was with a little chemical test. He'd sprinkled some of his new powder on a piece of silver foil, heated it with a cigarette lighter until it dissolved, and scrutinized the resulting liquid. The clearer it was, the purer the smack. This stuff had come out looking almost like Evian water, the sign he had some truly good shit here.

He could have taken this stuff around the block a couple of times—diluted it in dealer's slang—but Eddie the Rastafarian prided himself on the quality of his product. Shoot up with this smack, he thought, and his clients were going to be riding the heavens for hours—and remembering when they came down who they'd gotten their stuff from.

Of course, very few of his clients shot the stuff up these days. Or skin-popped it. The new kids he was seeing out there were all snorters or smokers. The scene had really changed in the last five years or so. Time was when he worked with a hard core of clients, junkies all, feeding a regular habit. He could count on selling almost the same number of one gram baggies at 100 pounds a bag to basically the same group of people day in and day out. Not anymore. It was like the super-market business these days, Sainsbury's and Safeways, big shopping days Fridays and Saturdays, dead days in the middle of the week.

Carefully, almost lovingly, Eddie measured out his heroin gram by gram on his scale then poured it into little glassine bags which he sealed tightly shut with a strip of tape. There were some assholes out there selling their dope for 45, 50 pounds. This stuff was so good though, he was going to try to clip 60, 70 pounds a bag for it.

Well, Eddie thought bundling up his last baggie, here comes old Eddie the Rastafarian, folks with some real good shit to make your Saturday night.

———

Twenty minutes later he was sauntering out of the Earl's Court tube station, ready to begin his evening patrol through the streets of his parish, the priest of a new and decidedly secular faith. Eddie first deposited most of the thirty baggies he hoped to sell during the course of the evening in a locked kitchen cupboard of the room he rented in the basement of a bed and breakfast on Earl's Court Square.

Then he started his rounds through the neighborhood, along the lines of the bed and breakfast pensions, their denizens getting the night air or a smoke on their front stairs, up to the Exhibition Hall, back down Earl's Court Road, checking out the fast food joints, the coffee shops, the pubs, even the Waterstone's Bookstore. After all, smart people used smack, too. He was coming out of Waterstone's and heading towards the tube station, when he saw a familiar silhouette a few steps ahead. Man, he thought, that's that blonde American bitch, the American broad who'd been dropping her knickers to pay for her habit. And some habit, she'd had. Two, three baggies, almost 200 pounds into old Eddie's pockets every day. Then, bam, she was gone, out of sight. Been tossed into the nick for soliciting, Eddie had figured.

He moved up almost stealthily until he was walking in step beside her. "Hey, lovely lady," he murmured, "how you be? Where you been lately?"

Belinda, that was her name although he didn't know it, looked at him startled. "I got my shit together, Eddie," she told him. "I cleaned up my act."

"Hey, girl, that's great. That's cool, real cool. How long you been clean?"

"Three months."

"Right on." Eddie showed her his ivories in what was meant to be an affectionate smile but came across more like a lascivious leer. "Three months. Now you come back, you be going up to heaven all over again."

"I'm not coming back, Eddie."

Sure, the dealer thought. That's what they all say. Until they gave in and took another hit. She was wearing a tan cashmere overcoat with slash pockets belted tightly at the waist so that pockets flared open. Eddie took a baggie and almost surreptiously dropped it into her open pocket. "Some real good shit around here these days, girl," he whispered, "real good. This be a little present from your old friend, Eddie, ever you need a pick me up."

"I told you I'm clean, Eddie," Belinda snapped.

"Sure, lovely lady. You ever need old Eddie, he be around for you," the dealer purred as he slid off into the crowds pouring out of the mouth of the tube station.

Belinda watched him go, her fingers closing around the little plastic bag he'd slipped into her pocket. Throw that thing away before it's too late, a voice inside her said.

Across the English Channel, in the French capital, an entirely differ-ent heroin scene was in preparation. At 26, Celine Nemours was the den mother of a regular little Friday night gathering. Its purpose: to unite a few friends ranging in age from 18 to 25 in the enjoyment of the laid back delights of sniffed heroin.

They'd all come to it through the same path, hash, then popping ecstasy pills at raves, and now to this cooler, mellower way of tripping. Celine was responsible for getting the weekly supply of dope. It was so easy, *superfacile,* now. All she had to do was pick up her mobile phone and call her dealer's pager. As soon as it answered she tapped in the personal code number he'd assigned her, 32, then hung up. A few minutes later he'd call her back from a phone booth and they'd arrange a place to meet where he'd swap his dope for her cash.

How different from the scene when she'd started doing dope in 1992. Then she and her Portuguese boyfriend had had to go to the Rue Mercadet in the 18th arrondissement for their stuff. It was a seedy dis-trict, crawling with junkies and whores. They bought their dope in a run-down apartment house. The maid's rooms lining the top floor had been taken over by Senegalese and Guinean dealers, a different one to each room, a dozen in all. It was like going into a bazaar in Central Africa. Now it was all done through the wonders of modern electronic communications!

The party began as they always did at 10:00. They drank, chatted and laughed their way through a little snack. When they'd finished, the girls cleared away the plates, Celine put a new techno CD onto her tape deck and opened up the first of her one gram sacks of heroin.

The whole scene was so different from the one she'd known when she started doing dope. People were still shooting then. They'd take their hit, and go nod off by themselves in a corner somewhere, locked into a drug-induced torpor into which only they had access.

This scene was mellow, super-cool. They'd lie or sit there, listen to the banging beat of the music, chat, giggle, fondle each other. And they didn't have that sour smell of people who hadn't taken a bath in a month the way so many of the older junkies did.

What the hell, she assured herself, lying back and letting the drug's warmth invade her, nobody ever got addicted on one *rail* a week. Or even two. Lay back and enjoy, she told herself.

———

Midnight on Hamburg's Reeperbahn. The working girls were out lining the street from the Saint Pauli police station up to the Herbertstrasse. Huddling from the bone-chilling cold in lime green, azure, mauve, apricot, off-gold one-piece ski suits, they looked like the competitors in a woman's downhill waiting for the race to start. Hungarians, Czechs, Poles, East Germans, they were the flotsam of socialism's collapse, cast up on these streets to practice capitalism in its most ancient and basic guise.

Ludwig von Benz sauntered up the street looking for the two Hungarian girls out there working for him. Like most of the girls on the street, his pair, Eva and Magda, were hooked on heroin. Ever the solicitous employer, Ludwig was bringing them a little treat to help them through this cold and busy evening.

He saw Magda first, leaning up against the windows of the Burger King, smoking a cigarette, her face drawn taut, an unfocused stare in her eyes. She did not look, it occured to Ludwig, like your average happy hooker. He kissed her on the cheeks.

"How's it going, doll?" he asked solicitously.

Magda gave a shrug of measured indifference. "The usual shit. A couple of Englishmen with so much beer in them they had dicks as limp as overcooked spaghetti."

Ludwig plucked the cigarette from her mouth. "Here, I brought you a little replacement," he said, offering another cigarette.

It was a joint known in Hamburg as "skunk," a mixture of hashish, heroin, and ordinary cigarette tobacco. He didn't have to tell Magda what it was. She grabbed it from his fingers, lit it and took a deep puff which she held in her lungs as long as she could.

"Ah, that's good!" she sighed blowing out the smoke.

"Get you through the night, it will." Ludwig smiled, kissing her again on both cheeks. Then, ever the Good Shepherd looking after his flock, he set off to find Eva and hand her a similar reward for a hard night's work.

———

Everything that could go wrong in my life has gone wrong, Belinda thought. Here I am sitting in this depressing room, in a strange city, in a foreign country, as totally alone as it was possible to be. The job she'd been promised, doing ad layouts for Laura Ashley, had fallen through at the very last moment, at three o'clock this afternoon when she'd checked in to begin work. They'd given the job to another girl. No explanation. No words of sympathy. Nothing.

All her hopes had gone crashing down with that setback. She was broke, dead broke, exactly forty three pounds and sixty pence in her bank account, not even enough to buy a ticket home. She was so down, so depressed, she couldn't drag herself out of her chair to try to sell her body—even assuming she wanted to which she didn't.

Despairing, she looked at the little baggie Eddie the Rastafarian had dropped in her pocket at Earl's Court. What sub-conscious evil force had pushed her to go walking into that danger zone? Why hadn't she thrown the dope away? Was that bag destiny, fate, sitting there, calling to her?

She grabbed the telephone to ring up her three closest supporters in Narcotics Anonymous for help. Please, please, she begged the jangling phone, somebody be home to give me strength, to give me hope, to keep me away from that little bag.

No one was.

She collapsed into sobs. Then, as though drawn by some compelling, unreasoning force, her eyes went back to the bag on the table. Mechanically, she went to her medicine closet and got out a hypodermic needle. From the drawer in her kitchenette, she took a tablespoon and bent its handle down, then filled it with powder from the bag. Taking her cigarette lighter, she heated the dope until it had dissolved into a clear liquid she could pour into the head of her syringe.

She went to her bed and lay down. With a practiced gesture, she slipped the needle into the vein of her forearm just below the bicep and pushed the plunger. Slowly, the product of the poppies grown on the jeribs of Ahmed Khan in a country Belinda couldn't even find on a map began to slip into her bloodstream.

She lay back. An immense warmth wrapped her from head to toe, its heat coursing like molten lead through her veins. She felt her pupils contracting. Nothing can harm me now, she thought. She was flying, feeling perfectly glorious as, with unrelenting fury, the finest product of the Osman family's cooker, its 70% purity level undiluted by any of the traffickers through whose hands it had passed on its way to her forearm, began its assault on her system. It was now, thanks to her painful efforts at Narcotics Anonymous, a system as unprepared to deal with heroin's effects as that of someone who had never touched the drug.

Her bloodstream rushed the heroin to her liver where her enzymes broke it back down into morphine which was rushed in turn to her brain's limbic system. There, the brain's nerve endings had begun to pour into her bloodstream the chemicals that were giving her such an intense rush of pleasure.

At the same time, the drug was dulling the reactions of her medulla which controlled the rhythmic pattern of her breathing. Her breaths began to come slower, and slower, and slower. As they did, unexhaled carbon dioxide built up in her brain's respiratory center, reinforcing the process until it became self-perpetuating. Totally unaware of what was happening to her, she was in the fatal embrace of an overdose.

There were no convulsions, no frantic gasping for breath as had been so wrongly depicted in *Pulp Fiction*. Her life ebbed away slowly, painlessly, almost peacefully. In seven minutes the respiratory center of her brain had shut down completely. Belinda's long battle was over. The heroin had won.

Well, Jim Duffy thought, you know you've got the government's attention when you see the Vice President coming into the office on a Saturday morning in blue jeans and a wind breaker. There he was, sitting right next to the National Security Advisor in the National Security Council Conference room in the basement of the West Wing of the White House waiting to hear Duffy's report.

Indeed, all around Washington other senior members of the government were sitting down in front of the TV monitors employed for the deputies' closed circuit conferences, ready for his words. With the exception of the Deputy Chairman of the Joint Chiefs, impeccable in his navy blues, there wasn't a necktie in sight. At Langley, Duffy had been given the seat of honor directly opposite the TV camera in the director's office, between the director himself and the DDO, Jack Lohnes. It was enough to give a man a swelled head, Duffy mused.

The National Security Advisor herself was in the chair this morning. "Gentlemen," she began. "You'll remember some three weeks ago the agency's Jim Duffy brought us the hard confirmation of that report that the Iranians have managed to get their hands on three nuclear devices from the Soviets as they were withdrawing their nuclear stockpile from Kazakhstan. He is here this morning to bring us up to date on how the Iranians propose to convert those shells into viable high yield weapons and what they propose to do with them. Mr. Duffy."

Duffy cleared his throat and leaned into the TV camera. First, he reviewed very briefly the circumstances of Tari Harmian's murder. "We know the Iranians are skimming off a transit tax on the morphine base that is passing through Iran on its way to the heroin labs of Turkey. Harmian's job was to invest the money they were taking in until this man"—Duffy activated a button on his control panel and flashed the agency's photo of the Professor onto their closed circuit screens—"needed it. He is Professor Kair Bollahi and his principal task is procuring weaponry for the mullah's regime and in particular high technology materials associated with weapons of mass destruction. I think that we can assume that he is the man in charge of their nuclear program."

Duffy flicked his panel button again and this time brought up the text of the telephone call between the Professor and Harmian intercepted by MI5 shortly before Harmian's murder. "First, we see in this, I think, the explanation of Mr. Harmian's murder. More important, it seems to me we can infer from that text that the code name for the Iranian's nuclear program is Khalid. Most important of all, that text infers, I think, that it is their intention to somehow employ these weapons once they are ready against Israel."

"They try a stunt like that," the Deputy Chairman of the Joint Chiefs growled, "and they'll become former members of the nuclear club. They'll become former, period."

"Gentlemen, let Mr. Duffy finish his report," the National Security Advisor cautioned.

"Approximately two weeks ago, TW Holdings, a Panamanian Corporation we know from NSA intercepts is controlled by our friend the Professor whose picture I've just screened for you, purchased a 50% interest in a laser manufacturing firm outside Hamburg, Germany called LASERTECHNIK."

"With their drug money?" the Assistant Secretary of State asked.

Duffy shrugged. "Probably. In any event, yesterday EG&G up in Salem, Massachusetts received an order from this firm LASERTECH-NIK for a dozen krytrons, those electrical switching devices which you will recall we were told the Iranians would need in order to detonate successfully the plutonium cores of their nuclear shells."

"Good work!" exclaimed the head of the FBI, not a man usually generous in his praise of the CIA. "Those are twelve krytrons those bastards will never see."

"As I recall," the Assistant Secretary of State said, "at our last briefing we were told that the Iranians would need 200 of those things to reconfigure their artillery shells, not a dozen."

"Right," Duffy acknowledged. "Since then, however, I've talked to the experts up at EG&G and it's their fear that if the Iranians could get their hands on a dozen or so of those things, they could, with their engineering skills, replicate them and produce the 200 they need in a very brief period of time."

That bit of unwelcome news produced a moment of shocked silence among the conferees. "Thank God you managed to uncover their efforts to get their hands on those damn things," the admiral from the Joint Chiefs declared.

"Let me ask this," said the Deputy Secretary of Defense. "Why don't we just ask the Germans to arrest this man you call the Professor and we'll ask for his extradition?"

"Because there is a substantial risk they won't do it," the Director of the CIA replied. "They're notoriously uncooperative with us on matters such as this. They just might whisper into his ear 'the Americans are after you' and get him on the first plane out of Germany."

"I have a much better idea," chuckled the National Security Advisor. "Why don't we give the guy's photo and a copy of his C.V. to the Mossad. Suggest to them that if they look hard enough, they may just find him around Hamburg somewhere. Then they can take care of him the way they took care of that Canadian Bull who was building a long range cannon for Saddam Hussein."

"Or that Hamas leader in Jordan?" smiled the man from State.

Christ, Duffy thought, this damn conference has gone around in circles long enough. He leaned into his microphone. "Gentlemen," he announced. "I think all of us are missing an opportunity which this situation might offer us."

"What's that, Mr. Duffy?" the NSA advisor asked.

Duffy fought hard to keep the Irish twinkle out of his eyes knowing how stunned some of the conferees would be at the idea he was about to throw on the table. "I am convinced our smartest tactic would be to allow the sale of those twelve krytrons to that German firm to go ahead absolutely normally, on schedule, with a minimum of fuss and attention paid to it."

"The guy's gone off his fucking rocker!" the FBI man mumbled, no suggestion of admiration for the CIA in his tone of voice now.

Duffy pretended not to have heard him. "What we know for a fact, gentlemen, is simply that the Iranians possess three nuclear devices that they got out of Kazakhstan. What we do not know is where those devices are hidden or what, if anything, they're planning to do with them. Until we can get the answer to those two questions, we are, quite frankly, incapable of undertaking any action that might neutralize the threat they pose to either us or the Israelis."

"And you think that somehow giving them the krytrons they need to activate those plutonium cores is going to help us get those answers?" the National Security Advisor asked in a tone that was barely civil.

"Yeah," Duffy said with what came undiplomatically close to a laugh, "I do." He had, in the meantime, pulled a krytron Paul Aspen had given him on his visit to Salem from his pocket and waved it in front of his TV monitor. "Some of you may recognize this little thing from our earlier meeting with the lady from the Energy Department. It's one of those krytrons the Iranians are after, presumably to allow them to detonate their devices."

He flicked the glass bulb smaller than a man's little fingernail with his thumb. "Now if that's what they want them for and they're desperate enough to go out and buy up a German firm to get them, then you can bet your ass these little devices are going to wind up right alongside the plutonium cores we presume they've extracted by now from those three nuclear artillery shells, right? I mean, those of you who remember the good doctor's lecture understand that these krytron things are supposed to become an integral part of the bombs' assembly. They have to be fitted right into the heart of the bombs themselves. So wherever they wind up has got to be precisely where those three plutonium cores are as well. The logic of that, is, I think, beyond question."

The National Security Advisor acknowledged Duffy's thought with a muted but nonetheless approving grunt.

"Now what I propose we do is bug each of these krytrons with a tiny transmitter-receiver. One that we can interrogate from a SIGINT satellite out in space. The transmitter beeps out an answering signal that says for all practical purposes 'hey, here I am.' We take a fix by triangulation on the location from which it sent its signal. Then we call in one of our new GPS photo satellites and zero its cameras in on the spot on the earth's surface from which the signal was sent and start to film that spot."

"How good will the film that aerial survey satellite gives us really be?" someone asked.

"Good enough to fix that beep at the center of a circle ten feet in diameter. In other words, we can follow a car, a truck, a guy walking down a street carrying the krytrons in a suitcase right up to the front door of the Iranian's nuclear storehouse wherever the hell it is. Once we've been able to do that, once we know exactly where they're keeping those damn things, then we can decide what to do about them."

"And you're sure we can fit a radio into that little tiny glass bulb? One that can do all that for us?" the man from State asked.

"I think so from some of my previous work but I know people who are really experienced in this sort of thing. What I'd like to do is lay the problem in front of them and see what their answer is."

For the first time, the Vice President reacted to the proceedings. "I think Mr. Duffy has one helluva of a good idea," he told the conferees. "I suggest we let him go talk to those people he wants to see and get back to us as soon as possible."

BOOK EIGHT

The Cave of the
MARTYRS

Two hours later, Duffy and a communications expert from the Directorate of Science and Technology were sitting in a conference room in one of those new glass-walled high-rise office buildings just behind the Tyson's Corner shopping mall. Ranged opposite them were three young men and a young woman, the principal officers of a firm called Eagle Eye Technologies. Your nineties whiz kids barely out of their thirties, Duffy thought, scions of Bill Gates all. Their average I.Q. was probably 185 and you could be sure they all had Ph.D.'s in some arcane scientific discipline. I'll bet half of them come to work on roller blades to cut down on carbon emissions, he mused. Probably carry their lunch with them in a rucksack, tofu or sushi with herbal tea to drink.

"So, Mr. Duffy," their leader Mitch Storrs asked, "just what is it Eagle Eye Technologies can do for you?"

When Duffy had finished filling them in on his project, he took out the krytron Paul Aspen had given him. "This tiny little thing is a krytron. Somehow, we've got to find a way with your help to put a bug into it."

Storrs plucked the device out of his hands. "Sure. I know what a krytron looks like. I did my doctorate at MIT in nuclear physics." Oh dear, Duffy thought, just like I suspected, I've got a line of child geniuses sitting in front of me.

Storrs studied the device to refresh his memory of its structure then passed it down the table so his colleagues could inspect it.

"Let me just give you a rough idea of what it is we do here," he told Duffy, picking up a metal belt buckle as he did. "Most of our work has been, historically, in the national security area. However, we're now expanding into commercial applications of our technology. We call our transmitter-receivers Eagle Eye Tags. We can put a tag, for example into a belt buckle like this. Or we can even implant a tag under the surface of your skin if it comes to that. Suppose, for whatever reason, you're afraid you might become the victim of a kidnapping. You wear your belt with our tag in its buckle everywhere you go. One day, you go missing. We bounce a signal to the Eagle Eye Tag we've put in the belt. 'Hey, we ask, where are you?' We pick up the response on a Global Star satellite. There are 48 of them up there, primarily voice communication birds but we have a trick of our own devising which allows us to use them to track somebody. Let me show you how it works."

Storrs turned on the computer built into the conference table. "We have a client down in Baton Rouge, Louisiana who's wearing one of our buckles right now." He tapped his computer. "I've just sent his buckle a message through our ground station here in Washington, D.C. The buckle's answer will come back to our station via the same satellite we sent the query on. We factor in a whole bunch of stuff, the time it takes to get the message back and forth, things like the Doppler Shift because, of course, that satellite's moving and with that, we're able to calculate the exact position on the earth's surface from which the buckle sent us its answering message. We get this."

A set of numbers appeared on his computer screen. "That's the latitude and longitude from which the buckle sent its signal." He played with his computer again and scrolled up a map of the Louisiana Bayou country on which a pair of red lines intersected. "That's where he is, right where those two red lines cross. We can tell where our man wearing that belt buckle is down to about three feet so we call it three-point accuracy."

"Did the guy feel anything when you interrogated his belt buckle?"

"Not a thing. Now let's take a look at your problem." Once again, Storrs picked up Duffy's krytron and waved it in the air. "There's a vacuum inside that little glass bulb which contains a slightly radioactive gas, Nickel 63. That's the good news. It means it's throwing off a little radioactivity all the time so that's going to make it extremely difficult for your Iranian friends to pick up our radio signal when it beeps."

"OK." Duffy smiled. "So what's the bad news?"

"There's not enough room in the bulb of your krytron to fit a transmitter and a receiver. A transmitter, yes. But not the two."

"How big is the transmitter you're going to use?"

"Tiny. It's just a speck of metal. We can put the whole thing, battery and all, inside that little glass bulb. We use gallium arsenide which is, for all intents and purposes, a high performance silicon computer chip. Looks like this."

Storrs picked up a tiny gold square. "The whole thing's in here. The power pack and the chip that does the transmission."

"Jesus!" Duffy gasped. "It's that small?" Even he had had no idea of how miniaturized these things had become. "That's nothing at all!"

Storrs beamed like the father of a Little Leaguer who's just hit a game-winning home run. "Transmits on a pre-set frequency, beep, beep, beep. You pick up the transmission then locate the precise spot on the earth's surface from which it came with the technique I just showed you."

"What's your power source?"

"Lithium."

"And you can program that to beep once a day?"

"We can program it to do what you want it to do. Do you want to locate the krytrons once a day? Or every hour on the hour?"

Duffy pondered that one for a minute. "Boy, to get a reading every hour would be a dream. You've got to figure that from the time EG&G hands these things over to the Germans who are fronting for the Iranians until the Iranians have gotten them to where they're going, we need to allow about a month to be on the safe side."

Storrs made a few quick calculations on his computer. "OK, say we give you a beep every hour on the hour. A battery would last five plus days. You say you've got twelve of these things going to the Iranians. We bug them all, with the transmitters set to relay each other. Krytron One covers you from Day One to Day Five, Krytron Two, from Day Six to Day Ten, and so on. That'll give you twenty-four beeps a day over a sixty-day period."

Duffy reviewed silently everything he'd learned thus far. These techniques were far more sophisticated than anything he'd imagined. "So what kind of a frequency would you want to use?"

"We prefer to operate on the 'L' band. It's a microwave frequency. I'd say something around 1.5 gigahertz would be appropriate."

"Look, Mr. Storrs, I'm not an electrical engineer but I understand the airwaves are cluttered up these days with a lot of electronic junk coming off radios, TV, cellular phones, radar, God knows what. How can you be sure your signal is going to get through all that to the satellite on the frequency you've selected?"

"Mr. Duffy," Storrs said bestowing on his visitors the condescending smile the masters of high technology reserve for the uninitiated. "There is no such thing as a transmitter that is going to transmit 100%, precisely bang on the frequency you've plotted for it. First of all, there are always echoes, what radio engineers call side lobes, off to the side of the main transmission. The main transmission you've plotted for 1.5 gigahertz may go out at say 1.501 or 1.5016, but you will also have these side lobe transmissions dropping off all the way from say 1.1 to 1.9 gigahertz. The thing is those side lobe transmissions can't be received and acted on because there's no power behind them. I mean, unless you have a receiver within say 12 to 18 inches from the emitting source, then you're not going to be receiving those side lobe signals and responding to them, OK?"

Duffy nodded.

"Now your satellite up there will be programmed to look for your transmitter's beep over a spectrum say from 1.4950 to 1.5050 and it's going to pick it up alright because of the power with which our little transmitter in your bugged krytron has thrown it out."

Duffy turned to his advisor from the agency's Directorate of Science and Technology. Time to get a little backup here.

"You in agreement on everything you've heard so far?"

"Absolutely. For this exercise, of course, we'll be able to use our national security satellites, SIGINT birds like Vortex or Mentor to follow the signals. They can triangulate where that signal's coming from with even greater precision than the Global Star they're using. These guys call what they do 'street corner accuracy.' Our birds can locate the transmitter right in the middle of this table."

"And getting a photo-fix on it?"

"Suppose this table is out there in the yard. A picnic table maybe. And your transmitter is sitting on it. Our new KH Jumpseat series birds will give you a picture of the table with the transmitter at the center of a circle with a five foot radius. You couldn't read the *Washington Post* from it but you could sure as hell pick up the logo on the front page."

"OK, let's try to figure out what could go wrong here. How about Iranian Signals Intelligence picking up the beeps and doing a fix of their own on them?"

Storrs answered. "There's a technique that allows you to spread your emissions over a wide spectrum of frequencies so if the Iranians are fooling around checking individual frequencies, they won't be able to pick you up without the correct spreading codes."

"Great. Now where are the places these things might be beeping from where we couldn't pick them up? An airplane?"

"Easy."

"A truck, a car, a train?"

"No problem."

"In a tall office building?"

"Depends on how tall and where the transmitters are in it. If they're five, six stories from the top, we'll get them."

"In an underground cave?"

"Negative. But when they come out of that hole in the ground in a car or a truck, we'll pick them up again."

"How long do you figure it would take you to bug these twelve krytrons?"

The young scientist smiled. "Not long. I think the best thing to do would be to do it up there in Massachusetts with the people on EG&G's production line. Maybe two days."

"Mr. Storrs." His words should have had the solemn ring of a preacher intoning a couple's marriage vows but as always with Duffy they were more ironic than solemn. "I think your country is going to need you. Would you please stand by for an urgent call in the next couple of days."

———

No matter how skeptical, how cynical a man or a woman becomes about the political process, Jim Duffy thought, there is still something awe-inspiring about taking a meeting with the President of the United States in the Oval Office. He'd been in such meetings before, of course, in the eighties when he was Casey's darling and he'd been brought here to brief Ronald Reagan on the progress of the Afghan war.

They said Reagan used to nod off during long meetings, but Duffy had never seen any indication of that. When the topic was killing commies, the Great Communicator had always been one hundred percent alert, one hundred percent focused. Back in this storied room again, admiring the Stuart oil of George Washington, the view out onto the White House lawn, a familiar thrill ran through Duffy. He'd been right after all that morning up in Maine to agree to come back to work.

Suddenly, the door opened and a marine stepped in, barking, "The President of the United States!" There he was, trailed by his National Security Advisor. He was bigger physically than he appeared to be on television.

The President circled the room shaking hands with the advisors he'd summoned to this meeting: the secretaries of State and Defense, the Director of the CIA, the Deputy Chairman of the Joint Chiefs, Dr. Stein, the weapons designer from the Department of Energy. When he got to Duffy, he paused, then took Duffy's extended hand in both of his, giving the CIA officer a look of laser-like intensity as he did.

Politicians, Duffy knew from experience, have a well honed ability to make the person to whom they're talking feel as though for one brief moment they're the most important person in the world. Even so, Duffy was surprised by the intensity with which the Chief Executive focused his attention on him.

His eyes narrowed to a half-squint and the voice came out with only a hint of the Texas Panhandle in his accent as he said, "You've done a great job, Mr. Duffy. We were lucky to get you back on board. When all this is behind us and we're no longer under such tight wraps security-wise, I'll see that the government makes proper amends to you for the circumstances under which you had to leave the agency."

Duffy was so astonished, he was barely able to mumble, "Thank you, sir." The President continued through the circle then took his place behind his desk.

"Please, gentlemen," he requested, "do sit down. George here"— he nodded to the head of the CIA—"has given me a full briefing on the problem posed by these three Iranian nuclear artillery shells. He's also filled me in on what Mr. Duffy learned about that German firm that's providing the Iranians with a facade to justify their purchase of high quality krytrons, and told me about his proposal to bug those krytrons with hidden transmitters. So I think our first order of business should be to listen to Mr. Duffy's report on the scientific feasibility of his idea."

There is nothing quite as intimidating as briefing the President of the United States. Duffy had seen a Deputy Secretary of State actually lose his voice and go hoarse briefing Ronald Reagan on Afghanistan, so he had carefully marshalled his thoughts. He was clearing his throat to start when the President spoke up again, this time directly to him. "Let me say this, Mr. Duffy. We don't stand on rank in this office. I want input, the best input I can get and quite frankly I don't give a damn who gives it to me."

"Yes sir," Duffy smiled. He was, much to his surprise, beginning to like this guy. He laid his points out one by one, glancing as he did at the President and his advisors to see if he was carrying the room. When he had finished and eased back into his armchair, the President's eyes swept the room, looking for a reaction to Duffy's words.

"Frankly, gentlemen," he said, "that sounds to my unscientific ears like a perfectly sound proposal. Does anyone have any reservations about what Mr. Duffy has told us?"

Nobody did.

"OK," continued the President. "Now before we get down to the mechanics of Mr. Duffy's idea, I want to look at what other options might be available to us. Let's look at the obvious one first: Our Department of Commerce just tells that German firm 'no dice.' No krytrons for you, friends."

"That will slow down the Iranians' efforts to convert their plutonium cores into high yield weapons, Mr. President," the Secretary of Defense said. "But will it stop them? I doubt it. The Pakistanis managed somehow to get their hands on an abundant supply of krytrons without coming to us, didn't they?"

A chorus of mumbled agreement acknowledged his words. "Alright," the President continued. "Assuming they do find a way to reconfigure those nuclear artillery shells, what do we calculate they plan to do with them?"

"Mr. President," Duffy said, "since I have firsthand knowledge of the intercepts we're relying on here, perhaps I should attempt to answer that. I think two points are critical. First, is that phrase from the man who's clearly in charge of their nuclear program in which he declares that the nukes are for use 'against the enemies of Islam.' As you know Mr. President for these extremists, Islam has two principal enemies, Israel and United States. I think their selection of the name 'Khalid' as the codeword for their operation makes it clear which of those two perceived enemies they've picked for their target." He silently blessed the wisdom of Nancy Harmian as he explained the significance of the word 'Khalid.' "It's someplace in Israel they're after, Mr. President, not Long Island."

"Right," the President agreed, "but let me play the devil's advocate for a minute. That's my role in these situations. What is really the Iranian agenda here? Do they want these weapons for intimidation? An offensive strike? Deterrence? Is it possible they really want these things as purely defensive weapons? Something they can deploy in some secret location and say, 'Hey, we have these things to defend our Islamic Revolution from outside attack. We have no intention of using them aggressively against anybody.'"

"Mr. President," the Secretary of State responded. "As a corollary to what you just said, sure, maybe their goal is to convert these warheads into workable bombs and marry them up to one of those long range missiles they're working on so desperately. Then, once they've done that, they stand up and announce to the Islamic world 'brothers, we now have an Islamic weapon that can strike anywhere in Israel.' Can you imagine the halo of leadership, of prestige, of power that would confer on them? Even if they had no intention of ever using them?"

"Could we live with that? More to the point, could the Israelis? Will they just sit around and allow such a thing to happen?" the National Security Advisor asked.

"Deterrence works fine, Mr. President, when your enemy is or are shrewd, rational people. For all his faults that bastard Saddam had brains in his heads. Some of the mullahs running Iran, not all of them anymore, but some of their top clerics, are blind fanatics. An ability to reason rationally just isn't a part of their makeup. Deterrence is meaningless with them."

The President made what sounded to Duffy like a despairing sigh. "Suppose then for the purpose of this meeting, they really do want them for offensive purposes. How are they going to deliver them?"

"Mr. President," the Deputy Chairman of the Joint Chiefs answered, "all they've got right now is a short-range, liquid-fueled SCUD. It's a crap missile. It's got a 600 kilometer range which will hardly get it to Tel Aviv, and certainly rules out any use of one of those weapons against us. Furthermore, I don't think there's anyway they could fit the bulky nuclear warhead they're going to wind up with here into a SCUD."

"How about that Shehab Three missile the agency says they're closing in on? Why wouldn't they use that?"

"Our intelligence indicates they aren't quite there yet. And they're still having trouble with its guidance systems. It stinks. Pinpoint accuracy they haven't achieved yet."

"Jack," the National Security Advisor cut in, "if you want to deliver a thirty kiloton weapon on Israel, you don't have to put it through the mayor's bedroom window in Tel Aviv, you know. Anywhere in the neighborhood will do just fine."

"How about employing a bomb as a terrorist device? Smuggling it into Tel Aviv or some such thing?"

"Mr. President," the Deputy Chairman of the Joint Chiefs responded again, his voice firm with conviction, "I think you can rule that out as a non-starter. Historically, once a nation state has managed to get its hands on nuclear weapons, they inevitably want to keep them under the tight control of their own organizations. They're not going to pass them out to some suicidal crackpots who may detonate them by mistake before they've gotten out of town."

"Where are the Israelis on this one? How much do they know?"

"They're aware of the three nukes situation," the CIA Director said. "We haven't brought them up to speed on our NSA intercepts and Duffy's work although they may have found out about that on their own. They're paranoid about the Iranian situation. It's the agency's feeling that for the moment it would be an error to pass them intelligence which is only going to increase their worries while doing nothing to further their knowledge of the problem or how to deal with it."

"Well, in view of what I've been hearing in this room, they have damn good reason to be worried," the President rejoined. "Mr. Duffy, you've been listening to all this. Change your mind on your idea at all?"

"No sir. We live in a world in which information is the ultimate form of power. And ignorance is the one unpardonable sin. Until we have found out exactly where those three nukes are, any debate on what the Iranians might or might not do with them or what we could do to stop them is fundamentally meaningless."

"Well said," the President observed.

"Of course," Duffy continued, "if we do manage to find out where they are, that's when our troubles will really begin. You know what the Bible says—he who gathers knowledge gathers pain."

"Ecclesiastes," the President, always happy to display his knowledge of the Book, rejoined. "You're certainly right there."

"Mr. President," the Director of the CIA declared, "we have got to keep every aspect of this situation top secret. We must not let the Iranians become aware of the fact that we know that they have these three nuclear devices. And second, we've got to keep this away from our Allies—the Russians, the Chinese, and, above all, the UN. If it ever gets out we'll have the whole world shrieking at us, 'Stop! Sit on your hands! Do nothing!' just the way they did before our showdown with Saddam Hussein. Your ability to take meaningful action if the day comes when you feel you have to take it will be fatally compromised."

"What kind of a time frame are we looking at here, Mr. Duffy?"

"Sir, as I understand it, twenty days would be the normal time you'd need to clear the export license through Commerce and move the goods to Germany. I think you can assume the Iranians will get them to wherever they're going in Iran as fast as they can. I'd guess we have a lead time here of about three weeks."

"Three weeks," the President sighed. "And then we may have to start wrestling with one of the worst decisions anyone's ever had to take in this room."

"Gentlemen, put Mr. Duffy's plan into operation," he ordered. Then he turned to the Deputy Chairman of the Joint Chiefs. "Admiral," he said, "I want the Pentagon tasked right now, this morning, to start looking at plans for the worst case option. That would be our deciding that we have to go in there and get those three nukes out of the Iranians' hands once we've learned where they are. Give me some force options for doing that."

"With conventional forces, sir?"

"Conventional. Or Special Operations. Have your Joint Special Operations Command study all the possibilities. That's what it was set up to do, wasn't it?" He now looked at the Director of the CIA. "I want you to study a covert operation led by the agency although Lord knows those haven't enjoyed much of a success rate lately. But I want people looking right now at ways to go in there and grab those damn nukes if we have to do it. A mission that will work. Not like the last one we ran into Iran."

———

Half an hour after the meeting broke up, the Presidential Press Secretary went down to the press room to brief the White House Press Corps.

"Hey, is there a crisis brewing?" the ABC correspondent asked. "How come all the top boys in school were here this morning?"

"Oh, there's a crisis alright," the Press Secretary laughed. "They were here to review the intelligence budget for the next fiscal year before it goes to the hill. You know the kind of arguments that always stirs up."

———

The cave, carved into a hillside of the Anti-Lebanon mountain range 15 miles (23 kilometers) southeast of Baalbeck in Lebanon's Bekaa Valley, was a shrine as sacred in its way to its limited number of followers as the Grotto of Lourdes was to the faithful of the Catholic Church. It was a monument to the memory of the martyrs of the Hezbollah who had voluntarily given their lives in the struggle against Israel.

Beside the entrance to the cave was a black pennant, a symbolic representation of the black battle banner of the Prophet. Suspended from the ceiling was a cloth bearing the words of the Ayatollah Khomeini: "The martyr is the essence of history." Inside the cave itself, illuminated by candles and a series of dangling electric light bulbs, were the photographs of each of the long parade of Hezbollah martyrs who'd blown themselves apart while delivering their bombs, beginning with the two Lebanese Shiites who'd driven their explosive-filled trucks into the barracks of the U.S. Marines and French paras in

Beirut in the fall of 1983. Below each martyr's photograph was recorded his name, the date and the location of his fatal mission and, where available, some phrase, some thought, recorded by the martyr himself just before he'd set off on his final journey.

Typical of them were the phrases inscribed under the photo of one young man who'd blown himself and his vehicle to bits in front of an Israeli checkpoint in southern Lebanon in 1987. "I am filled with joy," he had written, "knowing that I am about to die in such an operation. It is something to be proud of. Thus do we show the Israeli enemy that the faithful can strike them whenever and wherever we want."

The first score or so of the martyrs honored on the cave's walls were all Shiite Moslems, most of them Lebanese. The Shiite Moslem's vocation for martyrdom was the consequence of fourteen centuries of contemplating the historic injustice done to the house of Ali, the Prophet's cousin and son in law, when, on the Prophet's death, Ali's claim to the leader's mantle was rejected by the Prophet's followers who passed it instead to his father in law and chief disciple, Abu Bakr. On his death the title of *Khalifat rasul Allah* went to Omar, a leading member of an aristocratic clan in the Holy City of Mecca. From his line issued the conquering Ommayad caliphs who came to represent the Sunni majority of the Islamic faith.

That historic choice had left the Shiite community with a strong sense of injustice, of oppression. For the most extreme among them, that had led to the principle that established authority, established rulers, be they kings, shahs or democratically elected parliaments, were by their very nature illegitimate because only God could confer legitimacy on a human authority.

Those beliefs had given rise to the notion that a small, righteous party struggling against the overwhelming force of evil can triumph where a less focused majority cannot. The most extreme followers of the Ayatollah Khomeini and their fellows in the Party of God, the Hezbollah, were only the latest manifestation of that tradition. What to a frightened and perplexed world were acts of terrorism, were to them and other radical Islamists, the ultimate acts of devotion. Martyrs like the men pic-

tured on the walls of the cave were the standard bearers of a sacramen-
tal cult, a little band of brothers devoted to the principle that the warrior—the West would say the terrorist—must not survive his violent act
but must perish himself in the final redeeming act of his sacrifice.

To the Shiites on the cave's walls had recently been added a growing line of Sunni martyrs, the young men who had gone to their deaths
on buses in Tel Aviv, high explosives wrapped around their waists, or
walked into the fruit and vegetable markets of Jerusalem disguised as
rabbinical students carrying the attache cases which would destroy
them and anyone around them at the moment they were detonated.

Just how complex was the challenge such fanatics posed was being
illustrated this windy March morning in the Cave of the Martyrs.
Three young men, all dressed in white, were being shown the shrine by
the sheikh who maintained it. All three were Lebanese Shiites. All had
clamored for the chance to become martyr bombers at the Hezbollah's
nearby Janta camp reserved for its most promising volunteers. All
three had been carefully screened and studied by the sheikhs and
instructors overseeing the camp for the depth of their zealotry and
their ability to maintain their poise under pressure.

However, all three had two other things in common: they spoke
good French, a throwback to grandparents and parents raised in the old
French Lebanese mandate, and all looked distinctly un-Arabic. They
were, in short, ideal candidates from which to select a volunteer to
deliver the Professor's bombs to the heart of Tel Aviv in the climax of
Operation Khalid.

None of the three, of course, had any idea of what their mission
was going to be. They had simply been called away from their fellow
camp members and cloaked in their white garments—white because
on the eve of the mission, the youth finally selected to carry it out,
would be "married"—with death as his bride.

Now their guide waved to the photos of all the martyrs who had
preceded them. "Self sacrifice in the pursuit of a just cause is man's
noblest action. Who can understand the depths of belief that led these
great martyrs whose photos you see to their end?"

He scoffed. "The West says these brave men died because they were poor, they were desperate, they were stupid. Or because they were promised Paradise by the mullahs who convinced them to become martyrs. Are any of you desperate? Or poor? Or stupid?"

All three vehemently shook their heads.

The sheikh waved them to a place on the carpets covering the floor of the shrine. "Our leader, the man who will be in charge of the mission for which one of you will be chosen is here."

A gasp from the three went up at the sight of the figure entering the shrine. They had, of course, instantly recognized Imad Mugniyeh as the living legend he was for youths like themselves.

The man who had overseen the destruction of the marine barracks in Beirut warmly embraced each of the three, then joined them sitting cross-legged on the carpet.

"What an honor!" gasped one of the trio.

"No, it is I who am honored to be in the presence of such brave young men," Mugniyeh replied. "Each of you has been chosen as being worthy of carrying out a mission so important it will shake the Israeli"—he pronounced the word *Is-rah-eely* as many Arabs did— "enemy to his very foundations. The one among you selected for this great task will earn by his deed the place of honor here on this wall. For generations to come, his memory will be venerated, his name cited as *mara al taqlich*—a man to be imitated." All this was, of course, a psychological tactic to incite the trio to an intense competition to win the honor of being chosen for martyrdom.

"May we know what the mission is to be?" one of three asked.

"Yes. It will be to drive a car that has been carefully prepared into the center of Tel Aviv, the very heart of the enemy, and, once there, to detonate your charge as so many brave martyrs before you have done." The three assumed, of course, that Mugniyeh was referring to a vehicle packed with high explosives, the instrument of choice preferred by the Hezbollah in its actions against the Israelis.

Mugniyeh had no intention of disabusing them of that notion. He had been working non-stop since being asked at the meeting of the

Committee for Secret Operations to devise a plan to deliver one of the Professor's nuclear bombs to Tel Aviv. The key to the plan he was preparing was total secrecy. No one, absolutely no one outside the members of the committee, was to know the real nature of the bomb the Professor was preparing.

Step one in his plan was to get the bomb, once it had been prepared, from its hiding place in Iran to the Bekaa Valley here in Lebanon. That was the easiest part of the task. Iranian supplies for the Hezbollah arrived by road through Syria or via Damascus airport. In either case, there was never any Syrian control over their movement. That was the consequence of a tacit agreement between the late Hafez al Assad and the mullahs in Tehran. The Syrian leader's son was to be told nothing of Operation Khalid until the Professor's bomb had exploded in Tel Aviv. No one involved in the project in Tehran regarded him as a man who could be trusted with such awesome knowledge.

Step two was almost as easy. Once at Janta, the bomb would be placed in the car of a Jordanian supporter of the movement who travelled regularly between his home in Irbid in northern Jordan and the Bekaa Valley. He was so well known to both the Syrian and Jordanian border police at the Al Mufraq border crossing that his car was rarely given any security check more serious than a casual glance.

Step three was the most difficult and dangerous. The Jordanian would hand the bomb over to a cell of radical Hamas supporters who worked out of the Palestinian city of Nablus. It would be their responsibility to get the bomb across the Jordan River and into a secure hiding place outside Nablus. The security police of the Palestinian Authority and the Israelis patrolled the western bank of the river, the Jordanian Army the eastern bank. All three services monitored the traffic flowing across the Allenby Bridge. Getting past them and their infra-red night sighting devices was difficult. Nonetheless, Hamas had developed techniques which allowed them to smuggle their arms, explosives and men past them on a fairly regular basis.

By then, one of the three men in the Cave of the Martyrs would have been selected to carry out Step Four, actually delivering the Professor's armed nuclear bomb to downtown Tel Aviv. That, curiously enough, would be a good deal easier than Step Three. Mugniyeh spread out a large map of Israel and the Occupied Territories on his carpet. He had applied to the planning of this final phase of Operation Khalid all the meticulousness, all the attention to detail which had characterized his bombings of the U.S. Embassy in Beirut and the marine barracks, and had made him such a feared foe of the Americans.

He knew something the public did not. The security belt separating Israel from the Occupied Territories and the Palestinian areas was by no means as watertight as people assumed it was. His pudgy finger pointed to the Dead Sea.

"Many, many foreign tourists come here everyday to visit the sea, splash in its waters, even to swim in it. Some of them put its mud on their bodies. They think it makes them young." Mugniyeh laughed to indicate how crazy that idea was. Then he scrutinized the three young men hanging on his every word. "Many of them drive to the Dead Sea from Tel Aviv. How? In rented cars, of course. Those cars have license plates which identify them as having been rented in Israel and the name of the company that owns them, Hertz, Avis, on their rear windows. A very reassuring sight to any Israeli policemen who sees them passing by."

He jabbed at the map. "Getting from the Dead Sea to Tel Aviv is not difficult. You go by way of El Kuds, Jerusalem. There are checkponts on the Jerusalem Tel Aviv road but they rarely control cars with Yellow, Israeli license plates. Green Palestinian plates, yes. Any questions so far?"

His three candidates for martyrdom shook their heads.

Mugniyeh reached into his overcoat and drew out a pair of French passports which he laid on the carpet, specimens of the high class work turned out by the master forgers of the Iranian security service. He picked up the first one. It was blank.

"This passport will be given to whoever is chosen to drive the car to Tel Aviv with, of course, the driver's photo fitted into it."

"And the second one?"

Mugniyeh smiled, picked it up and opened it for their inspection. The trio regarded it, startled. This false passport had already been filled out and completed with a picture. The picture was of a young woman.

"Who is she?" one of the three stunned young men asked.

"She is one of your sisters. Her name is Latifa. On the day of the mission, the chosen driver will be accompanied by this brave young Palestinian girl. They will look just like a young French couple in a rented car and will therefore attract far less attention from the Israeli police than a single man would. Furthermore, Latifa knows the road from the Dead Sea to Tel Aviv extremely well."

"But she won't be with us when the bomb is exploded, will she?"

"No. She will leave the car once Jerusalem is behind you and you are well on the way to Tel Aviv."

"What car?"

"Before the mission, the driver chosen for the task will be sheltered outside Jericho by one of our commandos. Early on the morning of the attack, the bomb will be placed in the trunk of the commando's car and the commando, Latifa and the chosen driver will go to the Dead Sea."

"How big will the bomb be?"

Mugniyeh thought back on the Professor's lecture at the last meeting of the Committee for Secret Operations. "It will fit easily into the trunk of a car. Now you will drive to a relatively isolated spot by the Dead Sea shore which the commando knows well. You will wait there until a rented tourist car arrives. It will then be the commando's job to detain the tourists so that you can borrow their car."

By "detain" Mugniyeh meant murder, of course. "You will have no part in that operation. The commando will place the bomb in the trunk of the tourist's car and our chosen driver and Latifa will leave for Tel Aviv immediately."

The three candidates for martyrdom looked at each other proudly. "And where is the driver supposed to detonate the bomb?" one asked.

"Wherever he chooses once he is inside downtown Tel Aviv. At a red light for example."

"And how is it to be done?"

Mugniyeh took what looked like a cigarette lighter from his pocket. "The detonator will look like this. All you will have to do is push this button and you will have accomplished your great and heroic act. You will have earned your eternal reward, you will have won an honored place in our memory as a martyr among the martyrs."

Carefully, he set the lighter-detonator on the carpet for their inspection. Unbelievable, he thought. If the Professor and his scientists did their work properly, it was going to be easier to wipe Tel Aviv off the face of the earth with a nuclear blast than it had been to destroy the marine barracks outside Beirut.

———

"Where the River Shannon flows . . ." Jimmy Shea, laughing softly, hummed the tune to himself as he strode across the parking lot of Ireland's Shannon International Airport Free Zone, his coat collar turned up against the April drizzle pouring in from the Atlantic approaches. Sure we Irish are an incurable lot of romantics if we can write songs about a smelly old stream like that one he chuckled, opening the door to EG&G's European sales offices in the zone's Bay T53.

He shed his dripping raincoat, got himself a mug of black coffee, and settled down to look at the overnight faxes piled up on his desk.

"Greg!" he called to his associate Greg Hickey as he read the second one. "Will you look at this now? The American Commerce Department has given us an export license to sell Herr Steiner up there in Hamburg those krytrons he wanted."

"For that laser he's going to build to make people beautiful? The one where he puts a sodium crystal into a crystal cavity and gets himself a big electron build-up?"

"Aye. Salem says everything seems to be O.K. We're running with it. They'll be shipping his order to us in 72 hours."

"Truth to tell, Jimmy, I'm surprised," Hickey growled. "But I guess the Americans have to know what they're doing. Hell, we're here to sell aren't we? It's a nice order and we went through the hoops. Still, be damn sure we have our copy of Steiner's End User Certificate in our files."

"Oh, that I will. Guess I'll fax Herr Steiner we'll have his order up to him by FedEx on Friday."

Shea knew Steiner's krytrons would now proceed to Hamburg with no further problems. When they arrived at Shannon by air freight, they would be clearly labelled. Irish Customs, fully aware that their American counterparts would not let banned hi-tech items out of the U.S., would release them to Shea against EG&G's payment of the duty due on the order. With that, they would be inside the European Community free to move to Germany with no further customs clearances required anywhere along the line.

"Sure, you do that now." Hickey laughed. "And while you're at it why don't you ask Herr Steiner if he can do something about that ugly face of yours with that new laser he's making."

———

It was the Professor's latest hi-tech toy, an INMARSAT—International Maritime Satellite—M-type telephone, the kind roving reporters often used to flash their scoops back to their headquarters. The phone allowed its user to bounce its signal directly to one of four orbiting commercial communications satellites, thus avoiding the uncertainties of Third World communications or the scrutiny of over-zealous censors.

In the professor's case, his phone was equipped for both voice communications and for flashing out text messages encrypted by his Swiss-purchased coding system. He had to keep his messages short so that the watching U.S. satellite systems couldn't pin down the location from which he was transmitting by D.F.—direction finding. There were, he knew, more sophisticated machines used by the CIA which could fire burst transmissions so fast no listening device had sufficient time to get a geographical fix on their sending position. He, however, had not yet been able to obtain one.

He typed into the encoding machine he'd bought in Switzerland his message announcing to the Committee on Secret Operations the good news that his order for America's Top Secret krytrons had been cleared and that he would be able to start them on their way to Iran Friday, then transferred it to his INMARSAT. That done, he went to the window of the small house his associate had rented for him.

The INMARSAT looked a bit like a laptop computer. He opened the window and unfolded the machine's dish which resembled the laptop's screen. He pointed it southwest in the general direction of the Atlantic satellite to which he wanted to pass his message. His machine picked up a series of audible clicks. He twisted it until they reached their maximum strength which told him he had a lock on the satellite. Then he simply pushed a button and sent his message flying off to Tehran.

———

Two hours later Jim Duffy marched into the office of the CIA's Director of Operations punching his fist into the air like a golfer who's just sunk a twenty five foot putt. "They're biting!" he announced in triumph to his friend Jack Lohnes.

"How do we know, genius?" Lohnes asked.

"From this," Duffy chortled, handing him an NSA intercept. "Menwith Hill just decoded it. It's another one of those BRAINWAVE messages the Iranians are sending out on what they think is that supersecret enciphering equipment they bought from the Swiss."

The American devices we require will arrive at the factory Friday morning. I will personally pick them up and travel with them myself to Iran.

"Who sent this? Your friend the Professor?"

"Oh, I think so, yeah."

"Where was it sent from?"

"Well, that we don't know. The transmission time was too short. Both Menwith Hill and the Big Ear in Bad Aibling, Germany picked it up so you can assume it was from somewhere between them."

"Probably close to that LASERTECHNIK factory if he's going to pick them up himself. Do you suppose he plans to fly those things back to Tehran on a commercial flight?"

"He could. Why not? The package isn't going to be all that big."

"Jim, are you 100% sure the transmitters you've hidden in those krytrons are going to get their message back to us? You know what's at stake here. If this goes wrong, some Congressional committee will announce to the world that the CIA made it possible for the Iranians to arm nuclear charges. This agency is in enough trouble these days as it is. That, we'd never survive."

"Jack, we spent a whole day up in Salem checking them out. Our Sigint birds picked up every single peep they emitted loud and clear."

"OK, let's mumble a little prayer that your idea works. If the krytrons are going to be arriving in Germany Friday morning, I suppose we should set the first beep for 1200 GMT Friday morning."

"Right."

"We've got to get our best birds in place right now to follow those signals and do our overhead photography. The Central Imagery Office has to sked the satellites. The President will sign off on their program as soon as they've drawn it up. But the real work is going to be done by the National Reconnaissance Office over on Route 28 in Chantilly. They're the people who are going to have to pull down the Sigint satellite signals when they come in and blow up the photo overheads so we can follow those damn things to wherever the hell they're going. You and I have a date over there at noon to see Keith Small, the guy that runs the place and make sure everything is lined up the way you want it. But remember. You're carrying the hod on this one. Anything goes wrong and you'll wind up thinking the last guy who canned you from this place was your guardian angel."

———

"Gentlemen," Keith Small, the director of the National Reconnaissance Office, the NRO, declared greeting Jim Duffy and Jack Lohnes, "I've been ordered by the White House to place the full resources of this facility at your disposal."

Duffy detected in the tone Small employed to make his announcement the hint that the White House's instructions were as rare as they were unwelcome. Why? Had he erred in going to those guys at Eagle Tag instead of coming to Small? No one had toes more sensitive than a senior bureaucrat in the U.S. Government. Let an angel caress them and they'd say "ouch."

"The Central Imagery Office has sent me the schedule of your platform requirements," Small was continuing. "We're in the process of putting the birds you're going to need into place right now. What I suggest we do is go down to our operations floor where you can see for yourself what's going on and also get an idea of just what it is we can do for you."

Since the director of the NRO hadn't bothered to wave Duffy and Lohnes to chairs when they arrived, he had now only to lead them to his private elevator linking him to the operations floor.

The very existence of the organization over which Small presided hadn't even been officially acknowledged by the U.S. Government until 1992. Prior to that time, it had been based at the Los Angeles Air Force Base adjacent to the city's international airport, and Small's predecessors had been listed in the Pentagon telephone directory under the Air Force as the Directors of Space and Technology. The veil of secrecy behind which the organization operated had been pierced when the decision was made to relocate it in its new glass and steel headquarters near Dulles Airport. Initially, the idea had been to pretend the building was meant to house the offices of one of the NRO's major contractors, Rockwell International.

That charade lasted until the day the tax collectors of Fairfax County came by to levy their property tax on the new structure. Their quest stretched the patriotic devotion of Rockwell's accountants beyond the breaking point.

Small ushered Duffy and Lohnes into the anteroom of his Ops Center. Its centerpiece was an enormous globe turning slowly on its axis. It filled the high-ceilinged room. Around it whirled a swarm of bulbs the size of Christmas tree ornaments, each one representing one of the NRO's satellites in its orbit. The speed at which they were spinning around the slower moving globe had been calibrated to provide an accurate representation of the relative speed of the earth and those satellites whizzing around it. Assembling the display had been a challenging and costly engineering feat but it provided a wonderfully graphic illustration of the NRO's resources for the benefit of any budget conscious Congressman who came to call.

Duffy couldn't help laughing.

"What's funny?" Small asked.

"It makes me think of a horde of horseflies buzzing a brand new horse turd."

"A two-million-dollar horse turd," Small growled, moving closer to his prize display and picking up as he did a pointer to illustrate the lecture he was about to give his visitors.

"Working on your premise that the first signal the transmitter hidden in your krytrons will send out is going to come from somewhere near that laser factory north of Hamburg, what we've done is to triangulate the area with three of our Sigint Vortex birds. One is here"—he pointed with his stick to a red bulb—"over the North Sea about a hundred nautical miles west of the port of Hamburg. The second is over the center of the Jutland Peninsula, a hundred miles north of the city, and the third a hundred miles east out over the entrance of the Baltic."

He again indicated each satellite with his pointer. "Now the NSA will continue to read their communications as usual but we here at the NRO will pick up your transmitter's beep from each of the three birds. We will then triangulate the signals and fix the precise spot on the earth's surface from which the signal was sent. We can place that spot within a circle ten feet in diameter."

The two CIA officers smiled in appreciative wonder of what modern satellite technology could accomplish.

"Now we have also stationed one of our best photo reconnaissance satellites, a KH13 Advanced Jumpseat over the area." His pointer this time picked a dark blue bulb from the satellites whizzing over the heads of three men. It seemed relatively motionless. "It's orbital speed has been calibrated with the speed at which the earth is revolving so that it will remain in a fixed position relative to the earth's surface. Right now, we've positioned it over Hamburg. The beauty of the KH13, however, is that it's a steerable bird. If we have to move it in a hurry, we can speed it up, whirl it through space, and then park it over a new location, say Tehran, if that's where we want it to go."

"And that's the bird that will be taking pictures for us?" Duffy asked.

"Right. We furnish it with the longitude and latitude we come up with when we triangulate your krytron's signal. The KH13 will then zoom its cameras right in on that tiny small area, from which your beep was coming."

"And how long will it take to do that?"

"One to two minutes from the time your transmitter sent out its beep. We call that satellite accession time."

Small paused as though he wanted special weight given to what he was about to say. "Now," he declared in the dry austere voice of a certified public accountant revealing just how a firm's books had been cooked, "that time lag could be a problem for you. I'm sorry to have to tell you this but I think you gentlemen may have oversold the President and the National Security Council on just how infallible this scheme of yours really is."

Duffy could feel the intensity of Lohnes's glare boring into him. "Why do you say that?"

"I'll show you in a few minutes on some real time imagery we'll bring in from a satellite. Shall we move on?"

Have I been had, Duffy wondered, or did I really rain on this guy's parade by not taking him along with me to see the people at Eagle Eye Tag?

Small, in the meantime, had opened the door onto the Operations Floor. It was a huge room, half the size of a football field. For each of the NRO's photo satellites whirling around in outer space, there was a recovery team of four scientists grouped around a block of computer consoles and communication links binding them by a series of electronic umbilical cords to the birds they were monitoring. It was a scene, it occurred to Duffy, rather similar to those the world had grown used to watching when the NASA command center was monitoring the Apollo manned space flights on television.

"What each of these teams does here in this room is tell our satellites where to go, what to photograph. We then pull down the images ourselves or bring them in via one of our out-stations like Alice Springs in Australia and feed them in here. We store them, check that they are what we want and then we feed them to the national intelligence agencies, the CIA and the Defense Intelligence Agency. Or to Menwith Hill over in England. We're a provider facility, OK? We don't analyze the stuff that comes in. That's up to guys like you at the CIA."

Small then led them to the NRO's display auditorium. It contained five back-lighted flat panel display projection screens, all controlled by one technician seated at a computer console under the main screen. *Dr. Strangelove*'s Big Board was what it looked like to Duffy.

The director waved them to seats. "Now," he declared, "I want to just illustrate for you the kind of problem we could have with this idea of yours. I'm not saying your scheme won't work. It could. But it could fail, too."

Duffy remained silent, feeling a drip of sweat beading his forehead.

"Jack," Small ordered the technician, "bring up on the main screen the images we took an hour ago from that KH13 over Hamburg."

The technician fiddled with his computer and before long an image filled the screen. It was remarkably crisp and clear.

"What you're looking at is a circle ten feet in diameter of the street dividing the Hamburg railroad station and the entry to a shopping arcade running off it across from the station."

Both Duffy and Lohnes were amazed. Five pedestrians three of them carrying shopping bags were clearly visible on the sidewalk. If one of them had been looking up, you could probably recognize him or her if you knew the person. Two cars plus the rear end of a third were moving along the street heading south.

"Let's assume for demonstration purposes that this is the scene at the exact instant your transmitter beeped out its signal. So it had to have come from somewhere inside that circle. Maybe it's in the shopping bag of one of those five people. Or in one of the cars. But which one? If we take a leap of faith in technology and put it right at the center of the circle, it's probably in the trunk of the first car."

Small nodded to his technicians. "OK, Jack give us the next one."

Another remarkably detailed image appeared on the screen. "We took this shot exactly two minutes after the first shot. In other words after a time frame equal to what would be our maximum satellite accession time. Those cars, those people have all been moving during those two minutes as you can see from looking at this shot. Where are our five pedestrians now? Gone. Replaced by other people. How about the cars? Gone."

"Can't you expand the area you're covering in the shot? Widen it by a distance that would take into account the time elapsed between the transmission of the signal and your camera zeroing in on the spot?" Duffy asked.

"We can, Jack." Small's technician played with his computer again and the image widened to a circle that was perhaps a hundred feet in diameter. "There are your pedestrians and the two cars we caught in that first frame. But now there are ten cars in our frame. And a dozen more pedestrians. So there's your problem, gentlemen. Now we are going to be getting a beep every hour and we can certainly hope that one of those beeps will come from a spot sufficiently isolated so that when our bird sends back its first image we'll be able to see clearly where or from what object the signal was coming. With a bit of luck, then maybe we can keep the object or whatever the hell it was in the bird's eye until it gets to wherever it's going. But suppose we never get that shot? What happens then?"

Small gestured to his technician to turn off the image on the screen. "Look," he said, "we've run programs like this before. Sometimes they work. Sometimes they don't. I don't know what it is you're after here, but you'd better be aware of this. Your system is a long way from being 100% foolproof."

———

Entombed in a common vault of silent concern, Duffy and Lohnes strode across the NRO parking lot towards their waiting agency car.

"Well," Lohnes said finally, "that was a rather sobering little lecture, wasn't it?"

"Yeah."

"So what do we do about it?"

Duffy angrily kicked at a piece of loose gravel with his foot. "Jack, I don't think we do a damn thing about it. I think we let the operation go ahead just as we'd planned and hope to hell it works."

"And if it doesn't?"

"Well, then we're right back to where we are now. The Iranians have three nukes and we have no idea where the hell they are."

"Except we've given the Iranians a dozen krytrons they can copy so they can turn those three globs of plutonium we keep calling nukes into real, live workable bombs."

"Jack, it's going to work. It has to. We've got two months of beeps coming out of those damn things, for Christ's sakes."

"I wished I shared your optimism. Listen, I think you should get on a plane tonight and follow the operation from Menwith Hill. That way if we run into a glitch, at least you're going to be closer to where the trouble is."

"Good thinking, pal," Duffy laughed. "And also that way if it goes sour, I'll be able to take off for Tehran and ask for political asylum."

———

As soon as he'd been officially checked into London's CIA station, Jim Duffy headed for the first free phone he saw and dialed Nancy Harmian's number.

"Why, Jim," she said answering his call, "this is a pleasant surprise!" To Duffy's delight, the tone with which she pronounced those words seemed to reflect a genuine rather than a manufactured pleasure. "How is your work going? Or am I not allowed to ask?"

"OK and no." Duffy laughed.

"Are you going to be in London long?"

"Unfortunately not. I've got to go up north this afternoon."

"Oh!" Was there Duffy hoped just the suggestion of regret in her expression?

"Would you like to come by for lunch?" Nancy asked. "I can't promise you a gourmet meal on such short notice but it will probably beat what they're serving in the embassy cafeteria."

"I'd love to."

"One o'clock then?"

——————

Nancy opened the door of her Chester Square townhouse herself. The suggestion of gauntness mourning had etched onto her finely featured face was gone now, her appearance was less drawn, less sharply defined than it had been the last time Duffy had seen her. She was wearing faded blue jeans and a pale blue cashmere cardigan over her white silk blouse. Those clothes were quite a contrast to the measured formality with which she'd dressed in the weeks immediately following her husband's murder. Did her more relaxed outer style indicate some inward softening of the grief that had embraced her?

"I hope you're feeling as well as you look." Duffy smiled.

"Better, perhaps, than I was the last time you saw me." She led him up the stairs towards the drawing room. "It's been three months now. Some of my friends tell me the first three months are the worst. I don't know. What do you think?"

As she said that she gestured towards the bar. "Do help yourself."

"How about you?"

"I'll have a glass of the Sancerre," she said indicating a bottle in an ice bucket on the bar.

Duffy poured a glass for her and one for himself. "Three months? I don't know," he said taking the place she'd indicated on her sofa. "The worst phase went on a bit longer than that for me. I mean the so-called healing process isn't some kind of a spiritual antibiotic you rub into an injured soul."

Duffy took a sip of his wine, his mind drifting back to his long months in the Maine woods. "In my case, I had a strange reaction to my wife's death. I kind of wrapped myself into a cocoon of my own making. I didn't want to share my grief with anyone else. It was my private domain and I didn't want anybody, no matter how close they were to me, intruding on it. It was my way, I suppose, of clinging to my memories of her."

"You must have loved her very much."

"I did. Mourning is like so many things in life. There's no right way, no ideal way to deal with death, with loss. This notion of 'closure' the trendy folk like to throw around bears about as much relation to reality as soap operas do to life. I didn't really begin to come out of my shell until this agency I work for forced me back into harness, back into the real world."

Nancy gave just the suggestion of a shudder. "Yes," she whispered gesturing with her glass around her elegant drawing room whose appointments Duffy had so admired on his first visit. "I keep asking myself if I shouldn't change my life. Completely. I find it so hard to go on living in this house without him. It's not my memories of the murder that haunt me so much as those of the other times, the good times. I can't turn around or touch something without thinking about him, feeling him almost."

"Yeah," Duffy sighed, "the mortmain of the past. How hard it is to escape its clutch. What did you do before you were married?"

Nancy brightened at the question. "Oh, I was an odd duck. I was an ethnologue. I specialized in the civilizations along the Islamic flank of the old Soviet Empire, the Turcomans, the Uzbeks, the Kazakhs."

"Teaching?"

"Yes. I was on the faculty at Berkeley. I was granted a research fellowship at Magdalene College, Cambridge so I spent lots of time in London. That's how Terry and I met."

"With a background like that, I'm surprised my employers didn't try to sign you up."

"Oh, but they did!" she laughed. "I told the man who came to see me I was much too liberal for you people. Smoked pot, burned my bra, marched against the Vietnamese war when I was still a teenager."

It was Duffy's turn to laugh. "Sounds to me like you would have been the ideal recruit. The CIA is a nest of closet liberals. I'm moderately conservative and they think I'm Neanderthal man." Since this conversational vein seemed more promising than styles of mourning had been, Duffy asked, "Did you have your doctorate?"

"Almost. I was working on my thesis when Terry and I married. I was always going to go back to it, but . . ."

"You could now."

"I know. I've been thinking about it a lot. It would be a way to break with all this, wouldn't it?"

"If you found that work challenging and stimulating once, I'm sure you'll find it challenging if you go back to it."

"Probably." She drank off some of her wine. "Speaking of challenges, how is your work on Plan Khalid coming? Or am I not entitled to ask?"

"You're entitled to ask." Duffy grinned. "I'm just not entitled to answer. We're heading towards a denouement of some sort but what it's going to be, God only knows."

Duffy sat back, a thought, or rather a scheme, congealing into an idea in his brain, an idea he could slide towards Nancy as a poker player unsure of how far his hand can take him tests the water with a modest bet.

"Tell me, Nancy, how attached are you to life in London?"

"I love it here. But I'm not wed to it, you know what I mean? Sometimes I think a change of venue is what I need. But I couldn't go back to Berkeley after living here. Out there in that academic world they think they're center of the universe. I've realized now how wrong they are. In fact, they live in a singularly insular world of their own."

"It seems such a shame to waste a background like yours. There's such a desperate shortage of people with the kind of specialized knowledge you have."

"Where?"

"In Washington, for example."

"Washington?"

"Sure. And not just the government. Think tanks. Consulting firms doing business in the Islamic world. You can't imagine the opportunities available there for someone like you."

"But would I like living in Washington? I really haven't been there since I did the high school senior spring week thing. You know, the cherry blossoms, Mount Vernon, getting a civics lecture from your congressman, hearing the guide at the Bureau of Engraving and Printing announce for the ten millionth time 'we don't give away free samples.'"

"It's a wonderful city. Really. The best place to live in America as far as I'm concerned." Or at least it was for me once upon a time, Duffy thought.

"They say they have ten women for every man in Washington."

Duffy chuckled, unable to prevent himself from giving a swift and gentle stroke to her hand. "Nancy, I don't think I'd worry about that too much if I were you."

Rebecca, the maid had appeared at the door. "Lunch is ready, mum," she announced.

"Well, here's to change." Nancy smiled, finishing her wine. "Will you be returning to London when you finish you're work up north?"

"I hope so."

"Good. Then you can tell me more about life in Washington."

———

How long am I going to have to call this place home, Jim Duffy wondered looking around the Menwith Hill Satellite Accession Display

Center. It was strikingly similar to the NRO Center he'd visited 48 hours earlier with Jack Lohnes and Keith Small: the same array of back lighted flat panel display projection screens waiting to receive the images sent from space by their KH13 Advanced Jumpseat satellite. Beside him, one of the Hill's top technicians sat at his computer console ready to focus in those images when the time came.

They were linked by secure voice channels over the National Secure Telephone System to the two other display centers that would be receiving the images coming down from the satellite, the NRO's and the CIA's Satellite Display Auditorium, the most sophisticated of the three sites.

Duffy looked at the clock on the wall overhead. It registered 11:22 GMT\ZULU, Greenwich mean time, the time registered by England's Greenwich Observatory, referred to in the U.S. military as ZULU. It was just 38 minutes until one of their krytrons squawked out its first beep. Back at Langley, Jack Lohnes, he knew, was waiting in the agency with his Iranian and German desk officers beside him. They would be guzzling black coffee as they checked and rechecked their computer links to the agency data bases on Iran and Germany.

Coffee's the last thing I need, Duffy thought. A handful of tranquilizers would do me better. He could hear his stomach's nervous rumblings as he waited for that first beep. Would it get out? If it did, would their satellites pick it up? What kind of ground image was going to come up on that screen before him?

"Jim?"

He recognized Lohnes's voice.

"Do you read me?"

"Loud and clear."

"We just got word from EG&G. Fedex Germany reported to Shannon that their package was delivered and signed for at 11:17 GMT, 13:17 German time."

"At least that means we won't be getting a pretty picture of a FedEx truck for our first image. Tell me something. How far is that factory from the Hamburg airport?"

"About an hour's drive." Duffy didn't recognize the voice answering his question. Must be the German desk officer, he thought. If the Professor wanted to get his krytrons to Iran as quickly as possible, would he make a run for the airport? Fly out to Tehran commercial? "Why don't you guys run a check on what flights are going out of there in the next couple of hours?" Duffy proposed. "See if there's anything direct for Iran or with a good connection to Tehran?"

"We already have," Langley answered. "The only thing that will do him any good is a Lufthansa flight at 14:15 for Istanbul via Frankfurt. They could get an onward flight to Tehran from there."

"Jim." It was Lohnes. "We don't see your guys wanting to spend a few hours sitting around Istanbul airport with those things waiting for a flight to Tehran. Why would they risk that? Nobody dislikes the mullahs more than the Turkish Army generals do. They know that."

"Listen up, people."

It was a strange voice. Must be the guy manning the NRO desk, Duffy told himself. He was right. "We're just seven minutes away from our accession time. Let's keep our lines as clear as we can."

Seven more minutes, Duffy thought. Beside him, the Menwith Hill technician poured him out a cup of coffee from a thermos someone had thoughtfully set beside their console. Despite his earlier thought, he sipped it, trying to glaze his face with a patina of self assurance he most certainly did not feel. Nor did he speak. Better not to risk his voice coming out in a nervous squeak.

The time dragged by at a pace so agonizingly slow it made Duffy think of those torture-filled minutes when he was on his exercise bike pedalling flat out.

"Bird Two has accessed," the NRO technician suddenly announced, his tone of voice as devoid of emotion as that of the speaker announcing what time it was on a speaking clock. Two was the satellite over Jutland. "Bird Three has accessed. Bird One has accessed. We are triangulating," the NRO man continued in that same lifeless voice.

Duffy leaned back partially reassured. At least their signal had worked. Two minutes max and they should have an image up on the screen.

"Emission point was LAT 53:54, 9 North LONG 010:02, 4 East." The numbers flowed across the screen over their head as the NRO officer read them out. "We have tasked our bird to access the site."

"Do we know where that emission point is located?" Duffy asked Langley.

"We're scrolling it up on our computer mapping system now," Lohnes replied.

"Holy shit," his German desk man shouted. "It's seventy meters north of National Highway 206 on the fringe of the Segeberg State Forest just inside the grounds of a small private airfield at a place called Hartenholm."

"A private airfield!" Duffy exclaimed.

"But this isn't just any private airfield," the German desk man exclaimed. "It belongs to the Iranian government."

"You've got to be kidding me. The Iranians own an airfield in Germany?"

"Under cover, of course. They bought it in 1993. Your friend Professor Bollahi was the guy behind the sale although he used another Iranian who lives in Marbella as his straw man. Paid for it with a check on that account of his at the Bank Melli in Munich. The one the Iranian government keeps topping up for him."

"And the Germans let them get away with that? I can't believe it."

"Believe it, pal. Every time we try to lean on that government up there in Schleswig Holstein and get them to do something about the place, they tell us to get lost. A perfectly normal commercial transaction is what they say it was. Nothing wrong ever happens up there."

"Well, it sure as hell is happening now!"

"Down link image from Jumpseat coming in," the NRO announced.

The images they were about to see had been entered into the NRO's system mainframe and were now to be delivered to the screens at the CIA and Menwith Hill in more sharply defined digitalized imagery. Duffy watched fascinated as the image took shape on their screen. It was all there in glorious technicolor, the blue-greens and yellows, bright and clear. To the left of the image on the screen was what looked like the corner of a building of some sort. Parked beside it was a black car. To the right and encircling the front of the building was an expanse of lawn, a few burgeoning pinpricks of green beginning to thrust through its yellowish expanse. There was not a human being in sight.

"Can we open that up, please?" the technician sitting beside Duffy asked the NRO. "Go to a ten-by?"

"The NRO will expand the surface the camera's covering by a factor of ten," he explained to Duffy. "That'll give us a circle a hundred feet in diameter. We cover much more ground although, of course, we'll lose a lot of definition."

The image on the screen expanded, making it very clear that they were, indeed, focused on an airstrip. In the upper right-hand corner was what appeared to be a small control tower. Beside it, a wind stocking hung limp from its pole. To the left, a single-engined plane was parked.

"Can we get a closer look at that plane?" Duffy asked. "Does anybody know what it is?"

"Looks to me like a Cessna. Probably a 210," the German desk officer said from Langley. "Those two letters 'OE' on its registration numbers mean it's registered in Austria."

"There are people emerging from that building bottom left," the NRO informed them. "Do we want to go back in tight on them?"

"Affirmative," Lohnes answered.

As the satellite's cameras tightened down their area of focus once again, Duffy could see three men walking across the grass towards the plane. The man in the middle was wearing a dark overcoat and carrying what looked like a suitcase or a large package in his right arm. Was he at long last getting his first look at his nemesis, the Professor?

"Anybody recognize any of those people?" Lohnes asked.

"See that guy on the left? The one who looks like he's wearing a black leather jacket and some kind of baseball cap?" asked his German desk man. "I'll bet he's a guy named Said Ali. He's a Pasdaran, a Revolutionary Guard. The Iranian secret service sent him out from Tehran to run the airport for them. They've got a figurehead boss, an Iranian who's married to a German woman, but this Said Ali is really in charge."

The three men had reached the waiting airplane. The man tentatively identified as Said Ali helped the figure in the black overcoat into the plane, then passed him his suitcase. The third individual had in the meantime circled the plane and was getting in on the other side. Clearly, he was the pilot.

The NRO went back to the ten-by image so that they could follow the plane as it moved to a takeoff position at the western end of the runway. At all three watching sites, the NRO, the CIA and Menwith Hill, a dozen pair of American eyes watched as the Cessna, slowly building up speed, fled along the runway.

"No winds so he's using the Zero Five runway," the German desk man observed. "He'll probably head due east towards Lubeck once he's airborne."

Duffy watched transfixed. There they go. My krytrons are on their way to Iran.

Five minutes into the Cessna's flight, the NRO controller announced, "Our target has leveled off at just over five thousand feet. He's flying east-southeast on a heading of 135 degrees. If he sticks to that course, he will leave German airspace in approximately sixty-five minutes and cross into Poland."

"Are we going to be able to keep that plane in our satellite picture?" Duffy asked. "Wherever he goes?"

"Affirmative unless he starts to fly under some extremely heavy cloud cover."

"Well, he can certainly run into that up there at this time of year. Jack, shouldn't we ask Rhine Main Air Force Base to scramble an AWACS to fix that Cessna on their radar? Give us two fixes on him instead of one?"

"Roger that, Jim. We'll get in an urgent request to the Pentagon right away. I've also asked one of our aviation experts to come up here to the display center to help us monitor the Cessna's flight."

It was now 1247 GMT, just thirteen minutes from their second beep which would give them the final confirmation that their krytrons were indeed in that little plane whose progress they'd now followed as it passed out to sea at Traumunde near the old Nazi rocket testing range.

Seconds after the wall clock at Menwith Hill registered 1300 GMT, the NRO was on the line. "Our three Sigint birds have all accessed your signal. We are triangulating." There was a brief pause, then "triangulation places the signal at 5132 feet altitude, 14.6 meters aft of the target's current position. Your emitting source is aboard that aircraft."

Duffy felt like leaping from his chair and yelping out a triumphant shout but he limited the manifestation of his delight to a crooked grin.

"Listen, Jack," he asked his colleague on the other side of the Atlantic, "what are the possibilities of that little plane making it all the way to Tehran without stopping? Could they do it? Can they carry enough fuel for a trip like that?"

"I'll ask our aviation expert here to answer you."

"Mr. Duffy." The voice was unfamiliar so Duffy figured it had to be the expert. "You're right. Fuel is the key. Assuming he flies his best route which right now it looks like he might be doing, he'll fly across Poland on a southeasterly heading, cross into the Ukraine probably somewhere east of Lublin, skirt his way around Kiev then, staying well north of Turkish airspace, overfly Armenia and Azerbaijan until he reaches the Caspian Sea, where he'd head south into Iran. That's a distance of about 2000 miles."

"So, can he do it?"

"Providing he has bladder tanks in there to carry extra fuel, he might just be able to make it. It would be dangerously close though. He'd be better off stopping somewhere to take on fuel."

"Well, it's not like driving down a superhighway. You just don't pull a plane up to a gas pump and say 'fill 'er up.' People where he lands are going to ask the pilot where he's coming from, where he's going. Ask him for a flight plan, I.D., no?"

"Don't count on it. You go into a small airfield in Poland and ask for a load of aviation fuel, are they going to ask you for your flight plan? I doubt it. I think they'll be happy to make the sale."

"But surely, fuel or no fuel, he can't fly all that way without being picked up on somebody's radar? Forced to land and explain what the hell's he's doing and where he's going?"

"OK, normally, he's supposed to file a flight plan for a trip like that before taking off with the German AIS, Aeronautical Information Service. But suppose he's trying to make this flight illegally without letting anybody catch on to what he's up to. The first thing he sure as hell is not going to do is file a flight plan with the AIS or anybody else. He knows that in Germany, he can take off and land without a plan as long as he doesn't intend to leave German airspace."

The expert paused. "He pulls his transponder so he's not squawking out a signal to air traffic control radar and takes off. Flying at four, five thousand feet which is his best altitude for fuel consumption, the chances are nine out of ten the German civil radar isn't going to pick him up. Once he crosses into Poland he's gone as far as the Germans are concerned."

"By the way," Duffy asked, "will that AWACS plane be able to tell us if he's pulled his transponder?"

"Affirmative. Anyway, he crosses into Poland, circles around the Warsaw Air Traffic Control Radar. Ditto Lublin. If he stays down there at four, five thousand feet, chances are no one's going to pick him up. Or if they do, they'll figure he's a flock of geese."

"And the Ukraine?"

"They're hopelessly fucked up these days. Their radar's down half the time and when it's up, it's usually not working properly. Their people are poorly trained. As for Armenia and Azerbaijan, they don't even have radar cover."

"You make it sound awfully easy."

"It is easy. A lot easier than the non-flying public realizes. It all comes down to how much extra fuel he's managed to cram into that plane. I presume the NRO is making a tape of these images we're getting off the satellite."

"Affirmative," the NRO answered.

"Can you run the Cessna's takeoff sequence for me on one of my agency monitors?" the expert asked.

"Roger that. Your sequence is coming up," the NRO replied.

A few minutes later, the aviation expert was back on the line. "For a no-wind situation, the pilot sure ate up a lot of runway on that take-off," he reported. "He's got one helluva a load on there. As far as we know he's only got two people on board, his passenger and himself. And one suitcase. So if we assume the rest of his load is fuel, well, maybe he can just make it all the way."

"Jim," Lohnes cut in. "The AWACs has him on their screen now. His transponder isn't squawking. He's trying to sneak his way through alright."

"Your target aircraft has cleared German airspace," the NRO announced. "He's now crossing into Poland north of Szczecin on a heading of 115 degrees east southeast."

The NRO had funnelled onto one of the screens in each of the three monitoring sites a NAVTAC—Navigational Tactical Display Map—of the territory over which the Cessna was flying, the aircraft itself represented on the map in the form of a little red plane. Some might call it cute, but as far as Duffy was concerned it was a hell of a lot more interesting than watching the real thing plodding through the skies on the satellite's camera.

"NRO," the aviation expert at Langley asked, "can you give us an airspeed for our target aircraft please?"

"One-hundred-fifty plus miles per hour," was the answer.

"Figures," the expert observed. "You gotta reckon that bubba's trying to hold on to his fuel."

Bubba? Duffy mused. Must be a Texan talking. Or maybe a fellow Sooner.

"At that speed we can give him a rough ETA in Tehran of 2400 GMT, 0300 local. Or maybe a bit later depending on the route he flies."

So, Duffy realized, we're going to be condemned to sit here for hours watching that little red plane creep across Poland and the Ukraine. Leaving Menwith Hill while the operation was on was out of the question. So, too, was getting up and going for a stroll around the premises. Even senior officers of the CIA didn't go wandering around Menwith Hill without an escort. All I can do is sit here and think, he told himself, about the next step if the operation worked.

Where would the Iranians have hidden those three nukes of theirs? Somewhere down around their half-finished nuclear power facility at Bushehr near the mouth of the Persian Gulf? No, the mullahs were too smart to do that. They knew that if the day ever came when the Israelis wanted to take out their nuclear capabilities the way they'd taken out the Iraqis' Osirak reactor in Baghdad, that was the first place they'd come looking.

It was much more likely that they'd hidden them somewhere around northern Tehran where the Shah's old National Atomic Energy Department had been, right next to the Iranian Telecommunications Center in the heart of a densely populated residential area. Any strike in a neighborhood like that was going to involve a horrendous number of civilian casualties, Iranians who were probably already bitterly anti-regime. How was that going to go down with all those Iranians whose support we were hoping was beginning to shift away from the mullahs? And how would it play out with Moslem sentiment around the world?

After all, what we would be saying in effect to the Moslems of the globe is, "Hey, we're not going to tolerate you Moslems having access to nuclear weapons. The Israelis, they're OK, but you Moslems, nah, we don't trust you with these things."

Sometimes it seemed like every time we tried to make a move to check the spread of radical Islam, we wound up strengthening their movement instead by increasing Islamic hostility towards the west. If this damn idea of his was a success, one thing was sure. Its harvest was going to be one hell of a nightmare for the U.S. Government.

Ten hours later, Duffy was still there, staring up at the satellite display screen, watching the little red symbol representing their Cessna crawl down the center of the Caspian Sea heading almost dead south now for a landfall in Iran. The AWACs aircraft from Rhine Main Air

Force Base had been replaced by a similar craft operating from Incirlik Air Force Base in Turkey.

The pilot now had just 160 miles, another hour's flying time over the Elburz Mountains, to Tehran. He was running late, so that would put him on the ground in Tehran at about 0100 GMT, 0400 local. He would be coming down right in the middle of the night. The satellite was sending back infrared nighttime images but you couldn't begin to compare the definition they gave you to the sharpness of the images you got in the daylight hours. Tracking the Professor—by now Duffy had no doubt that he was the man in the dark overcoat— and his suitcase into whatever vehicle met him, then following that car to his krytrons' final destination was going to be the toughest part of this whole operation. How ironic! The scheme had gone off like clockwork up until now yet here on the very last lap, it could all come apart.

"Attention, people!" the NRO controller called out. "Our target aircraft has just come left sixty degrees. He is now flying south southeast on a heading of 240 degrees."

"What the hell do you suppose that means?" Duffy asked the Menwith Hill technician beside him.

"Maybe he's not going to Tehran after all."

The NRO had meanwhile traced the path the Cessna's current course would take on the map on which it was plotting the plane's flight. It pointed towards the spot where the frontiers of Iran, Pakistan and Afghanistan met, running well north of the major cities of Qom, Isfahan and Yazd.

"Attention, people!" the NRO desk officer called out again. "Target aircraft has just broken radio silence to inform Tehran tower that he has enough fuel to reach his final destination. He estimated his ETA at 0530 local, which is 0230 GMT."

"Both the NSA and those AWACs have been monitoring him for radio communications," the Menwith Hill technician informed Duffy.

"Did he say what his final destination was?" someone at the CIA asked the NRO.

"Negative, but given his current speed it will be about eight to nine hundred miles from his present position."

"Hot damn!" Duffy exclaimed. "He'll be coming down in something close to daylight."

"That boy they got in there is one hell of a fine pilot," the CIA's aviation expert acknowledged. "I reckon by this time they shoulda been peeing in those gas tanks to stay airborne."

Despite the long sleepless hours he'd endured, Duffy was wide awake now, the adrenalin pumping through his system as he waited the final act of his scheme. Finally, as the plane was drawing close to the Iranian frontier, the NRO announced, "Attention, people. Target aircraft has begun its descent. The aircraft is now at 4250 feet." It was 0155 GMT, 0455 local.

"What airfields have they got near his current position?" the CIA asked.

"Nearest field is a civil airport at a small town called Zabol. It has night landing facilities."

Zabol! Duffy thought. Wasn't that the place that had figured in those NSA intercepts? To that cloned mobile phone in Istanbul?

On the big display screen before him he could follow the Cessna now banking into a wide turn as the pilot prepared to align himself with the runway. Seconds later a string of lights flashed on illuminating the runway for the pilot. In the predawn light, the images coming down from the Jumpseat satellite lacked the precision they had had earlier when the Cessna was taking off from its German airfield. Now, they had a grayish white cast but Duffy still had no trouble following the plane on its final approach and its rush down the runway.

The pilot stopped his craft, turned around and taxied back towards what appeared to be the airport's administration building. A black Mercedes Benz 190 came into the image heading out to meet the oncoming plane.

"Those mullahs love their Baby Mercs," the Iranian desk man in Langley laughed. "Back in '89 to '93 they bought the damn things up right and left. Baby carriages for the clerics, we called them."

As the car reached his craft, the pilot braked to a stop. The NRO technician brought the image into tight focus on the plane and Duffy watched fascinated as the man in the dark coat stepped from the plane. "My God!" he suddenly half-shouted. "He's fallen down!"

"Don't worry," the Iranian desk-man assured him. "He's kissing the ground and saying a prayer of thanksgiving the way the Ayatollah Khomeini did when he got back to Iran."

He was right. His prayer finished, the Professor stood up and was embraced by the four figures who'd emerged from the car. Two, wearing turbans, were clearly clerics. The other two, weapons slung over their shoulders appeared to be bodyguards although neither was in uniform.

"Pasdaran," the Iranian desk officer ventured. "It's those Revolutionary Guards again."

Clutching his suitcase, the Professor led them into the waiting vehicle. At the airport's exit a pair of machine gun mounting four-by-fours took up covering positions to the front and rear of the car.

The procession sped through the empty streets of a still sleeping Zabol and onto a blacktop roadway heading almost due south through open, largely uncultivated and unpopulated country. Twenty miles from Zabol, the cars shot through another sleeping village as the highway began to climb towards a series of rising ridge lines. Less than a mile into that high ground, the procession turned east on to what appeared to be a dirt road. Almost immediately it stopped at a road block manned by a dozen armed but un-uniformed guards.

"Not an Iranian soldier in sight," Langley observed. "Just those Revolutionary Guards. This looks to be a 100% Pasdaran operation."

"What does that tell us?" Duffy asked.

"That maybe there are some people in Tehran who aren't clued in to what's going on out there."

"Well, those guys in that satellite image sure as hell are."

The guards were jumping up and down in apparent jubilation at the sight of the Professor arriving in his car. Still more armed men came rushing into the picture as the car moved forward. It turned left up a slight incline followed by a tail of wildly gesticulating Revolutionary Guards.

The road led to what looked like a man-made plateau abutting a sharply rising escarpment. A kind of portico projected out onto the plateau from the face of the cliff. It seemed to offer an entry hall of sorts into what was apparently an installation or headquarters which the Iranians had dug into or under the heart of that hillside. Still more men, these unarmed, came swarming out of the portico to surround the professor's car, banging the palms of their hands on its fenders and doors in celebration of his arrival in their midst.

The Professor stepped out into that sea of waving hands and arms. Still clutching his suitcase, he advanced with the dignified stride of a general inspecting an honor guard through those well wishers, solemnly touching his head and his heart in an Islamic salute as he did. Then, suddenly, his figure had disappeared into whatever secret installation it was that the Iranians had scooped out of their mountainside.

Well, Duffy mused, that's it. Our krytrons have reached port.

"Congratulations, Jimbo!" Lohnes chortled from Washington. "Your idea couldn't have worked better."

Duffy was too tired, too drained from the strain of the last ten hours to feel the elation the moment merited. Instead, suddenly he was both exhausted and famished. "I assume we'll be keeping a satellite focused on that site 24 hours a day from now on," he remarked.

"That's a safe assumption. I'm ringing off now to let the White House know our scheme worked."

Duffy stood up. "And I'm going downstairs to that 24-hour cafeteria of yours to get something to eat before I drop," he told the Menwith Hill technician beside him.

"Go ahead. I'll be keeping an eye on this place for awhile."

———

As Duffy began to munch on a cheeseburger in rural England, the man he had followed across half of Europe and the first spaces of Asia was revelling in what he quite justifiably considered to be a triumph of Iranian engineering skills. His engineers, Islamic engineers, had carved a fully equipped nuclear engineering laboratory into this mountainside in one of the most remote corners of Iran. It spanned three floors, one at ground level and two more dug into the mountain's hard limestone sub-surface. Those underground floors were accessed by a pair of elevators and the installation's main entrance protected by massive sliding steel doors which were kept closed when no one needed to enter or exit the lab.

The entire installation was ventilated by electro-static air cleaners so that no particle of radioactive material could circulate in its precincts. Fresh air was brought in from the outside, filtered and kept circulating at a constant 18 degrees centigrade by their air conditioning units. Electric power for the installation was provided by a gas fuelled generator half a mile away and delivered to the site by underground cable.

The Professor's team of nuclear scientists, physicists and technicians, almost all of them trained in the west, had assembled here all the equipment they would need for this, the final scientific step in Operation Khalid. There were row on row of some of the world's finest computers, IBM's, of course, and even a Cray 3X, a machine placed under the most rigorous of U.S. export controls which the Professor had managed to "export" from the Panama Canal Free Trade Zone while it was enroute to what was supposed to have been its real destination in Holland.

He handed his precious suitcase to the 47-year-old MIT trained physicist he had chosen as the chief engineer for Operation Khalid. He did not have to tell him what it contained. He knew. Lovingly, the man lifted the leather case to his lips and embraced it with a fervor another man might have reserved for Sharon Stone.

"Come, Professor," he urged. "I must show you our completed cladding shells for our three plutonium cores." The cladding shells were six hemispheres of finely milled copper which would be fixed in pairs around each of their three cores. On the surface of each were thirty indentations, "lenses" placed at the precise point their studies had shown they would need to be set in order to obtain the maximum explosive yield from their cores.

Engineering those lens emplacements to the tolerance required had demanded weeks of work with the computer controlled and driven milling machines his men had installed in their underground laboratory. They had monitored their ongoing work with lasers, measuring tolerances to less than ten angstroms—a billionth of a meter—a distance so infinitesimally short that even aided by a powerful microscope the human eye could not see it.

The Professor gazed with wonder and admiration at his engineer's work. "By the blessing of God," he said, his voice muted with reverence, "you are going to place unstoppable power in the hands of our Islamic warriors."

He then went to the vault in which the precious plutonium cores extracted from the three artillery shells he'd bought in Kazakhstan were stored. When they had removed them from the shells they had been, of course, in elliptical shape to conform to the configuration of the shells. They had been sealed into an oven, surrounded with inert gas, then melted down and recast into their current, spherical shape. Now in perfectly milled and polished spheres, they were stored in sealed "hot cells" filled with argon gas because plutonium, much like sodium, can react to a moist atmosphere by igniting. That was why, when they were ready to be assembled into bombs, they would be protectively wrapped in their copper cladding.

The Professor beamed. What a triumph this installation was. It had been completed and equipped in barely a year, the finances for it furnished by his secret accounts. The entire project had been run under the strict purview of the Committee for Secret Operations, the knowledge of what was happening here restricted to only a few of the regime's most trusted leaders. None of those meddlesome reformers now clustered around this misguided new president, Mohammed Khatemi, had any idea the place even existed.

Time now to inform the committee that he and his precious suitcase had arrived safely at their underground installation.

His pre-dawn snack digested, Jim Duffy returned to Menwith Hill's Satellite Display Center for a last glimpse of their latest imagery before his drive back to London and a few hours of desperately needed sleep.

"Hey!" the Hill technician monitoring the center said in greeting. "I'm glad you came back. Your office just came up on the secure net. They want you back in Washington as fast as you can get there. Like today maybe."

Macbeth shall sleep no more, Duffy laughed. He turned for a parting look at the images coming down from space of the Iranians secret hide-away. Daylight had come now to that eastern corner of Iran and the satellite's images were clear and sharp. Off to the left on the entrance to whatever it was the Iranians had carved into that hillside were a pair of identical two-story buildings, storehouses perhaps or barracks for the site's Pasdaran guards.

"Look!" he told the technician. "There's some people coming out of the entrance."

"NRO, give me a tight focus on the entrance, please," the technician requested.

It was the Professor, still wearing Duffy saw, that long dark overcoat of his. Must be chilly out there. With an aide beside him, the Professor walked to the center of the plateau in front of the hillside hideaway. He was carrying what looked to Duffy like a laptop computer.

"Son of a bitch! The guy's got one of those new Inmarsat phones!" the technician exclaimed.

"A what?"

"An International Maritime Satellite phone system. You use it to communicate directly with a ground station via a satellite."

The Professor had now lowered what seemed to be the laptop's screen.

"That was fast. Nobody's going to D.F. him."

"What the hell does that mean?" a perplexed Duffy asked.

"You remember that guy Dudayev who was running the anti-Russian war in Chechnya, don't you?"

"Sure."

"Well, he had one of those things. Except he used to talk on it. Too much. One of our birds intercepted his signal and we found out where the guy was standing by D.F.—direction finding, the same kind of technique we used for you here. It was 'be nice to Boris Yeltsin week,' so we passed the information on to our Russian friends who gave it to one of their SU25's armed with laser guided air to surface missiles. They locked in on the signal, fired and it was bye-bye Mr. Dudayev."

Duffy whistled. "Maybe we could do something like that here."

"Only if your friend starts to get real talkative."

Which he probably won't, Duffy thought. But he would be ready to lay odds that what he had just witnessed was the Professor sending out one of those BRAINWAVE transmissions the NSA was catching and decrypting. He'd probably have the text in his hands when he got off the plane in Washington.

BOOK NINE

The Angel's
BLESSING

C ompared to the satellite display centers he'd been in at the National Reconnaissance Office and Menwith Hill, the White House Situation Room, Jim Duffy thought, was a singularly unimpressive place. None of the super-sophisticated electronic wizardry that characterized those other places was present. Instead, they were all seated around a standard, Government issue conference table, on chairs that looked old enough to have been accommodating the august *derrieres* of U.S. officialdom since the Cuban missile crisis. The only hi-tech equipment in sight was a pair of closed circuit TV monitors, neither of which was in use.

What was impressive, however, was the assembly of political and military brain power gathered at the table. Their meeting was formally labelled a session of the National Command Authority. Ask twenty people in Washington what the National Command Authority was and you would probably get twenty different answers. That was understandable. Its membership could and did vary depending on the nature of the crisis it had been called on to address. This morning, the Secretaries of Defense and State, the Chairman of the Joint Chiefs, Duffy's boss, the director of the CIA, and the National Security Advisor were all present. Duffy and Dr. Leigh Stein, the Department of Energy's nuclear weapons designer, had been invited to attend because of the specialized knowledge they possessed of the subject under discussion.

The President had taken the chair. He waited until the last White House steward serving coffee had left the room and the marine guard had shut the door then clanked his coffee cup with a spoon. "OK, folks," he announced tersely, "let's get to work."

He turned to Duffy. "Congratulations, Jim. Your scheme couldn't have worked better—or confronted us with a more serious problem."

"In addition, Mr. President," the head of the CIA interjected, "we are also in possession of a critical NSA intercept bearing on this matter. We've circulated it to all concerned. It was the decrypt of the message Duffy had witnessed the Professor sending from his INMARSAT outside his underground installation.

> In the name of Allah, the Merciful, the Compassionate, may his blessings be upon you, my brother and upon our great enterprise. Our American materials are now safely in the hands of the brother directing our project. He also showed me the exceptional job he and his engineers are doing in preparing our devices to receive these materials as soon as we have replicated them in the number needed. We will meet shortly to draw up the time table for this final phase in the operation but you should inform Brother Mugniyeh that he must be ready to begin implementing his part of our plan within three to four weeks.

"Mr. President," the director of the CIA said when he'd finished reading the text, "our non-stop satellite footage of whatever the hell that installation they've got out there is shows that this man, Professor Bollahi, who was apparently carrying the krytrons, didn't leave it until he came out to send that message."

"Which obviously must confirm the fact that the krytrons are in that installation somewhere," the President observed, laying aside the blown up satellite image of it he'd been studying. "When and from where was the last emission from our transmitter received?"

"At 0300 GMT Saturday, Mr. President," Duffy replied. "Our Jumpseat photo-recon satellite identified it as coming from the car that was driving our Professor from the airport in Zabol to that installation."

"Well, that leaves no room for doubt. That's where those krytrons are alright. Tell me," the President asked, "what happens to our secret transmissions now?"

"They will continue just as they've been programmed to do, one of our krytrons emitting every hour on the hour. Except as long as they are in that underground installation we won't be able to pick up their transmissions."

"Remind me for how long they're going to last?"

"Fifty days."

"So if they come out of there sometime in the next fifty days, then we'll know it, won't we?"

"Not neccessarily, sir. Remember the transmitters we planted in our twelve krytrons were programmed to relay each other. Each one beeps in turn every hour on the hour for 24 hours for five days, then a new one takes over. So whether we could pick up a beep if some of them come back out of that installation either in a bomb or in some other configuration, is going to depend on whether or not the krytron that is emitting at that particular point in time is in the exiting package."

The President digested that remark with minimal pleasure. "So we have no reliable guarantee that we can spot those damn things if they come back out—regardless of what form they come back out in?"

"No sir, we don't."

"I presume we must go on the assumption that the 'devices' referred to in the NSA intercept are those three nukes we're after."

"I think to make any other assumption would be folly, Mr. President," warned the Department of Energy's Dr. Leigh Stein.

The President emitted a weary sigh and glanced around the room. "Anybody disagree with that assessment?"

No one did.

"I think there's a further point in that decrypted text that bears comment, Mr. President," the Director of the CIA noted. "The 'brother Mugniyeh' referred to in there is almost certainly Imad Mugniyeh, the man behind the destruction of our embassy in Beirut and the marine barracks. He lives in Tehran now. They've given him Iranian citizenship and an Iranian diplomatic passport to travel on. If he's involved in this operation, then it is highly likely that what they are preparing is a terrorist strike of some sort."

"Against Israel?"

"Most likely. But it might also be directed at the Saudi oil fields. They could kill a lot of Americans that way and turn the world's largest oil producing area into a radio-active desert for the next 25,000 years or so. Think of the impact that would have on the global economy. And we certainly can't rule out the possibility that they might try to smuggle a device into this country and detonate it in one of our population centers."

"Do you really think such a thing is feasible?"

"I certainly do. The Institute for Strategic and International Studies here ran an exercise not so long ago called 'Wild Atom' that postulated just such an attack. It showed how terrifyingly vulnerable we are to an assault of that sort."

The President dropped his hands to the table top and folded them around his coffee cup. "Alright," he said in a voice heavy with sad resignation. "Before we got into this exercise, we knew they had those three nuclear artillery shells. Now we know where the damn things are. And we have a pretty clear indication that they think they can make them work. Finally, it appears they are ready to implement a plan they've hatched to use them in three to four weeks. So what the hell do we do about it? Does this mean we have to go in there with force and get those nukes? Is there any possible diplomatic resolution to this crisis any of you can see?"

"All of us here in this room have agreed time and time again that the single overriding security concern we face in the post Cold War era is the spread of nuclear, biological or chemical weapons in the Middle East," the National Security Advisor said. "Why, after all, did we decide to attack Iraq?" In that case, however, we were responding to suspicions, well founded suspicions, but suspicions nonetheless."

She took off her reading glasses as though somehow the gesture would give additional weight to the words she was about to utter. "That is not the case here. Here we are dealing with facts, hard, indisputable facts."

She sighed, knowing how unpopular what she was about to say was going to be with some of her male colleagues. "We simply cannot afford to sit around and wait to see what the Iranians are going to do with those devices. We must show the world once again that we mean it when we say there is a line in the sand which we will not allow wildcat nations like Iran to cross. If we are going to be the world's only superpower, we must act as one. We've got to go in there and seize or destroy those damn weapons. Furthermore, I am convinced we've got to do it alone. In total secrecy. We can explain to the world what we have done and why we did it after we've done it, not before."

Her tough, uncompromising words reduced the room to a silence as stunned as it was thoughtful.

"Anybody like to add something to that?" the President asked.

"You mean we don't seek to get the cover of a United Nations Security Council resolution?" asked the Secretary of State.

"That's a disastrous idea, Mr. President," the Secretary of Defense snapped in reply. "The UN's a talking machine. They'll talk the idea to death the way they did our efforts to go after Saddam Hussein. That was a classic example of how not to manage a crisis. We've got to keep this one a total secret. Let it go public and you'll have the French, the Germans, the UN, the Chinese, and the Russians all shrieking at us, 'Stop! Be patient! Don't do anything while we talk nice to the mullahs.' And all the while, of course, we'll be alerting the Iranians to the fact we know what they're up to and increase our casualties when we finally do go in as we certainly will have to."

"Well, how about the allies?" the National Security Advisor pressed.

"The President may want to brief Mr. Blair himself when we're ready to go . . ."

"The French, the Germans?"

A few guffaws greeted the question before the Secretary of State could even address it. "The French won't believe us when we tell them the Iranians have three nukes. They'll say 'it's the Americans being confrontational with the mullahs yet again.' If we go in there, we're going to have to bring those damn nukes back out if we want to make a believer out of Mr. Chirac."

The Secretary of State paused. "The Germans, I think, will display some concern. However, they will not want to let this problem put their mercantile interests at risk. My hunch is they'll tell you: 'Solve the problem, Mr. President. We'll hold your coat for you. Just don't get us involved, please.'"

"And the Russians?" the President asked.

For once the Buddha-like calm of the Secretary of State was shattered. "Good God, no! Tell them nothing! That bastard Putin will be on the phone to Tehran the minute we hang up ordering his Russian technicians out of that reactor they're building in Bushehr—telling the Mullahs what's going to happen. There is only one thing I think we should do diplomatically—prepare a message for President Khatemi to be relayed while we're attacking, assuring him this is not an act of war but a one off police action whose sole aim is to disable and seize those nukes. Nukes he probably doesn't even know are there, by the way."

"There is another, equally serious consideration here, to which the Secretary just alluded, Mr. President—Israel," commented the Secretary of Defense. "The Israelis may not be aware of our success in pinning down where those three nukes are at this moment. But rest assured, they will become privy to this information before very long. This nation has no secrets concerning the Middle East that don't get leaked to Israel sooner or later—usually sooner."

"So what are they going to do about it when they find out?"

"Do, Mr. President? They will act. Without hesitation. With whatever force they think is necessary to eliminate the threat those weapons pose to their existence. Don't forget, sir, Israel's ex-Minister of Defense is already on record as saying publicly that Israel will launch a preemptive strike rather than let Iran develop nuclear weapons."

"How large a nuclear force do the Israelis have?"

"Israel has more nuclear arms than England. They have at least seventy devices waiting for assembly at Tel Nof Air Force Base in the Negev. They have almost as many as that awaiting to be inserted into the warheads of their Jericho missiles in their underground bunkers in the Judean hills."

The President threw up his hands in dismay. "All of which will survive anything the Iranians can do with these three devices. We're talking sheer madness here. Those mullahs can't be crazy enough to attack
a nation armed with a force like that? With—as far as we know—just
three atomic devices in their own arsenal?"

"Mr. President, two of those three devices, one in Tel Aviv and one
in Haifa, would probably wipe out two-thirds of Israel's people. When
the radioactive dust settles, Iran may no longer exist, true. But for all
practical purposes, Israel will have disappeared, too. It's an equation of
madness you and we may not be able to accept, but some of those
fanatic mullahs do. The Israelis understand that. Let them learn where
those nukes are and they will act, believe me."

"Furthermore," the Director of the CIA interjected, "count on the
mullahs to come up with some scheme to point the accusing finger
elsewhere. At the Palestinians, for example."

"The Israelis will never be damn fool enough to buy that one,"
declared the Secretary of Defense. "Although with our capacity to
indulge in wishful thinking, we might."

The President turned to the Chairman of the Joint Chiefs. "Could
the Israelis do it? Could they take out that installation on their own?"

General Theodore "Tad" Taylor took a deep breath, expanding quite
unintentionally his uniform jacket on which rested five rows of ribbons
won during three tours in Vietnam, the Panama invasion and the Gulf
War. "Frankly, Mr. President," he answered "barring their use of a
nuclear missile, which is most unlikely here, I think this operation would
be a bit too big for them. I think they would have to come to us for some
military help like an aircap from the fighters on our Arabian Sea carriers while their troops are down on the ground busting the place up."

"So whether we go after those nukes ourselves or we let the
Israelis do it, we're going to wind up harvesting a whirlwind of hatred
around the world."

"Count on it, Mr. President. It will be another Iraq."

The President rose from his chair and began to pace one end of the
room, hands clasped behind his back, his chin sunk, driven almost,

into his chest, his face frozen into a somber frown. His advisors sat in respectful silence, obviously moved by the deep, personal anguish this debate was causing him. Finally, he stopped.

"And yet," he told the room, "haven't the Iranians been trying to mute the extremes of their policy? Isn't President Khatemi trying to lead them out of their isolation? Looking for a dialogue, even with us?"

"Mr. President," the Secretary of State said, "I don't doubt the sincerity of Mr. Khatemi for a moment. Nor do I doubt that he represents the desires of the vast majority of the Iranian people. What he does not represent, however, is where power lies in Iran."

"Mr. President." It was the Director of Central Intelligence intervening again. "I think for once the CIA's assessment of the situation in Iran and State's are pretty close. Iran is approaching a critical turning point. The hard line mullahs are panicked and afraid. Eighteen years of their regime has left a majority of Iranians disenchanted with the whole notion of Islamic rule and they know it. I think you'll find there are fewer hard line Islamists in Iran today than there are in Turkey or Egypt and the Sudan. And certainly, Algeria."

"We believe Khatemi and his kind are genuinely opposed to this weapons program. But real power, for now at least, is still in the hands of the hardcore of fanatics in the leadership. They feel themselves and everything they stand for threatened. They're anxious to strike back, to re-assert their claims to supreme leadership."

"Well, how do they do it in the face of President Khatemi and his millions of supporters?" queried the President.

"Mao Tse Tung's old dictum: 'Power comes out of the barrel of a gun.' They have the guns, the Pasdaran, their Revolutionary Guard. Look at the satellite imagery of the site we discovered thanks to Jim Duffy here. There's not a single uniformed member of the Iranian military anywhere in sight. It's strictly a Revolutionary Guard operation. And who is behind the Pasdaran, Mr. President? The hard line mullahs, that's who."

"The front for their activities," the director noted, glancing at the legal pad in front of him, "is an organization called the Committee of

Seven. It has nothing to do with President Khatemi's government per se. Four of its seven members are Pasdaran. One of their jobs, by the way is to oversee the collection of the drug money, organize the protection as those drugs go by, make sure no one gets drugs across Iran without kicking into the Pasdaran's kitty. One of the best informed Iranian dissident groups we're in touch with estimates 200 tons of morphine base transited Iran last year, triple what it was in a decade ago. That represents a pile of dough. The other three people on the committee I mentioned are what they call *bazaaris,* financial geniuses who know how to move and invest the money they're making, hide it in accounts they can use to fund programs they don't want people like Khatemi to find out about, such as supporting terrorists or buying these weapons."

The President returned to his seat as he was concluding. "So what impact would a unilateral American operation have on the Moslem world?"

"None of the mullah's neighbors want to live next door to an Iran armed with nuclear weapons, sir, even limited nuclear arms like these. The Turkish military, their political establishment, the Saudi royal family, the other rulers in the Persian Gulf, Syria's Assad, will bless us privately for going after them. Publicly they'll be more noncommittal."

"It's the Moslem masses that will go on the warpath," the Secretary of Defense added. "From Morocco to Indonesia. We'll have a couple of embassies attacked, perhaps some travelling Americans killed."

The President shook his head, the images of such assaults already dancing through his mind. "And suppose we don't act? We wait until they attempt to deploy those things then reveal our knowledge of what they're trying to do? Make it clear that carrying out their plans would bring an immediate, swift, devasting response?"

"What response, Mr. President?" asked his feisty Secretary of State. "We nuke Tehran? Kill hundreds of thousands of perfectly innocent Iranians who in their great majority would have opposed what the mullahs want to do? What kind of a response is that? What sort of a reaction do you suppose that will provoke in the Moslem world? No,

Mr. President, we must hold this thing to the non-nuclear level. Our weapons of mass destruction are useless to us here. As I said at the beginning of this meeting, we've got to go in there and get those weapons and we've got to do it on our own."

"There is another concern here, too, Mr. President," added the National Security Advisor. "Someone, perhaps the Vice President, will have to bring the congressional leadership up to speed on what's happened and keep them fully informed of whatever action we plan to take. However, I would not foresee any problem in obtaining their agreement to action. It's only if we do nothing that they'll crucify us."

The President emitted yet another sigh and turned once more to the head of the CIA. "Any chance of running a covert operation here?" he asked. As he did, a smile flicked across the stern face of the Chairman of the Joint Chiefs, General Taylor. Oh, take this bitter cup away from us in the military, he was thinking. Give it to the CIA. Of course, he knew that was never going to happen, that there was no such thing as covert operations anymore.

It took Duffy's boss three full minutes to explain why: the agency, since Woolsey's days and even before, had been oriented towards technical rather than human intelligence. It had no agents inside the Iranians weapons program and very few inside the nation's government structure. The CIA could provide information to support the military but the days when it could overthrow an Iranian government with a mob of Greco-Roman wrestlers and bazaar merchants were long gone.

The ball, as General Taylor knew it was going to, came bouncing into the military's court. "So," the President asked him, "where do you stand on preparing those force options I asked for last week?"

"Sir, Iran falls under CENTCOM, Central Command—that's Norman Schwarzkopf's Tommy Franks old charge in Tampa, Florida. They've been working on this since you gave the order last week and since Saturday thanks to Mr. Duffy's work, they've had a precise target for their mission and satellite overheads of that target to study. As it happens, the U.S. Special Operations Command, USSOCOM, is down there in Tampa, too. They're looking at the non-conventional options."

"How soon will they be ready to brief me?"

The general barely missed a beat in articulating his answer. "Wednesday morning at ten A.M., sir."

"O.K." Duffy could sense a kind of despairing resignation in the President's voice. "I don't like it. But there it is. We have no choice. We've got to go in there and get those damn nukes. The only question now is how. All hands in here Wednesday at ten for a briefing on force options. And General Taylor, I want that briefing from the horse's mouth. From the men who will have to lead the operation, not a bunch of Pentagon bureaucrats."

———

Night had already darkened the barren hills of northeastern Iran, but inside the Professors's underground engineering lab, the working day was still in full swing. The man the Professor had put in charge of the scientific aspects of Operation Khalid, Dr. Parvis Khanlari, a nuclear physicist with a Ph.D. from M.I.T., spread a black velvet cover over the Professor's desk.

Khanlari was a short, wiry man with cheekbones that arched sky-ward, an anomaly that would have been devastatingly attractive on a woman's face, but was nothing more than that on his. One by one he lovingly placed the twelve EG&G krytrons on the velvet cloth.

The Professor picked one up and looked at it with a bemused air. "Such a tiny little thing!" he laughed. "And to think of all the money we spent, all the scheming we had to go through to get it." He flicked the three wires from the glass bulb of the krytron. "What are these?"

"They're called 'pigtail leads,'" Khanlari explained. "The first one will be hooked up to the battery of the detonator whose antenna will be programmed to receive our pre-set radio signal. When the antenna picks up the signal, it will close a relay which will in turn release a 250 volt charge into that first pigtail lead. When it does, the second pigtail lead will open up the link between the krytron of our firing circuit and the capacitor attached to it. That will unleash a square wave from the capacitor—it goes from zero to 4000 volts in about a nano-second. That's a time span so short it makes the blink of your eyes seem like a lifetime in comparison."

The Professor shook his head with the appreciative awe the contemplation of such dimensions demanded.

"The charge," Khanlari continued, "is then delivered by the third pigtail to the high explosive at each of our bomb's detonators. The firing circuit is so designed that the charge is delivered to each point simultaneously."

"And your plans to replicate these krytrons in the numbers we're going to require are ready? Will you really be able to accomplish that task in just two weeks?"

Khanlari paused just long enough to allow an expression of almost unimaginable satisfaction to enliven his face. "That will not be necessary."

"What! Why?"

"Employing an individual krytron and capacitor at each detonation point was the technique that was employed in the first generation of plutonium bombs. That is the technique that is referred to, however indirectly, in the open literature. But for the last twenty-five years both the Russians and the Americans have employed much more sophisticated designs which allow them to use one krytron and one capacitor for each hemisphere in their bombs. That is the design I now propose we use."

Khanlari, that smirk of self-satisfaction still illuminating his features, told the Professor, "Since you left for Germany, our computers have been working overtime. We have a design that will allow us to detonate each of our bombs with just two krytrons as the Americans and Russians do."

"You are sure of what you are saying? Wouldn't it be better, safer to do it the old way?"

"Absolutely sure. This firing system is far sturdier and more reliable. You see what matters is, first getting the emplacement of the thirty detonators, the lenses, exactly right and then as I said, firing the high explosives simultaneously. Of course, we will also need a third krytron for each bomb to fire off a neutron gun at the moment of explosion."

"What's that?" asked the Professor. It was the first time he'd heard the term 'neutron gun.' "Do we have such a thing?"

There was still no lessening in the intensity of Khanlari's self-satisfaction.

"We do. We purchased six of the from Dr. Gregori Valinovski in Ektarinaburg. He used to work at the old Soviet Nuclear Center Sverdlosk 45. They're desperate for hard currency so they sell them for use with explosives in deep oil well drilling. They are virtually identical to the neutron guns they used in their weapons. Only the casing has been changed."

Khanlari stood up. "Professor," he said, "let's go downstairs to our underground workplace. I can show you down there a scale model of what our finished bomb is going to look like and explain to you exactly how it will work."

Once they'd reached the lower level of the lab, Khanlari led the Professor to a small workroom. Suspended from its ceiling was what looked like a soccer ball sliced in half and stuffed with metal. The M.I.T.-trained scientist pointed to it with the pride of a father indicating his first born.

"That, sir," he said, reverence hushing his voice to soft murmur, "is an exact scale model of our bomb."

The plutonium core was represented by the lead ball cut in two, about equal in size to half a grapefruit. The lead was wrapped, as the real plutonium spheres would be, in a thin layer of copper. Khanlari pointed to the next ring of metal circling the copper.

"This," he declared, "is what we call a tamper, beryllium surrounded by tungsten. And this"—now he indicated a belt of a chalky white substance wrapping the tamper—"is our high explosive, HMX. The HMX is fitted together like wedges of cheese or a layer cake if you like so that together they form a sphere with the inner tip of the wedges fitting snuggly into the detonator points we've predetermined on our beryllium tamper. When our bomb explodes, the tremendous force of our high explosives is going to slam that beryllium into the plutonium core in one momentous blast. It will hold the exploding core together just long enough to let the beryllium deflect the neutrons shooting off from the plutonium back into the core and thus maximize the yield of our nuclear explosion."

The Professor stared in silent wonder at this miracle wrought by his scientists. So much work, so much time, so many resources had been needed and here at last was the culmination of all that, the final flowering of all those efforts. With this, he thought, we can at last destroy Israel and destroy as well the specious, materialistic, sexually depraved American influence spreading its corrupting tentacles through *Dar el Islam,* the Land of Islam. He reached out and caressed the surface of the bomb with the tenderness another man might have reserved for his lover's cheeks.

"And this gun? This neutron gun you mentioned."

"Yes," Khanlari replied. "The key to a successful detonation as I said is the speed with which the explosion takes place and the perfect symmetry of that explosion. The shock wave rolls inward, the metallic plutonium is liquified under its pressure and its density soars. At that precise moment we use our third krytron to fire our neutron gun."

Khanlari picked up what looked like a small piece of metal piping. "This tube is a neutron gun. Essentially, it contains tritium. The krytron releases into the gun that tremendously high voltage charge which causes the tritium nuclei to fuse, to meld together. When they do, they throw off a stream of high energy neutrons."

"The gun"—he waved the tube—"fires that shower of neutrons into the core of the plutonium at the moment of maximum compression to trigger the fission process. The nuclear explosion in other words. The key is in getting that split second timing absolutely right."

Khanlari gazed admiringly at his assembly. Protruding from the top of the ball was the black pin of the antenna designed to receive the incoming radio signal. Spaced below it at equal distances around the circumference of the ball were "witches peaks," the devices housing the capacitor-krytron assemblies, each wired in its turn to the battery connected to the detonator.

The Professor was visibly awed by what he had heard.

"I suppose this means we will be ready to start assembling our bombs shortly."

"As soon as we have tested our firing circuit, probably tomorrow."

"When will our bombs be ready, then?"

"The first should be assembled in a week's time. I would allow a week for assembling each of the others."

The Professor embraced Khanlari, kissing him warmly on both cheeks. "You have justified every trust we put in you, my brother. You and your fellow engineers are the modern counterparts of those great Islamic scholars and scientists of the thirteenth and fourteenth centuries who laid the foundations of so much of the world's knowledge. Thanks to you, tomorrow belongs to us."

———

"As you know gentlemen, I am a firm believer in the Colin Powell doctrine." Lieutenant General Charles "Corky" McCordle, recently appointed Commander in Chief of the U.S. Army's Central Command, paused to allow his words to register as he intended them to on the staff officers he'd summoned to his three story yellow stucco headquarters at 715 South Boundary Boulevard on the grounds of MacDill Air Force base stretching out into the flanks of Florida's Tampa Bay. "Whenever we use force, it should be in an overwhelming manner, against a clearly defined objective, and with an equally well defined idea of what the mission's goal is and when and how it can be terminated."

He paused again and then continued, his tone now somewhat muted. "In this case, however, we have been ordered to come forward and brief the President and the National Command Authority on both a conventional force option and a Special Operations force option. As much as I dislike having those Special Forces assholes wheeling and dealing on my territory, I have no choice here. I am going to have to let them have their day in court in front of the President."

He coughed, then lit up a Marlboro Light, a reflexive indication of his total indifference to the teachings of the American Cancer Society and the mandatory Department of Defense's "No Smoking" signs in his office. "Therefore," he continued, "we must be certain they are on the same page as we are. They've got to have access to the same intelligence, the same satellite overheads that we're getting. The same input, right down the line."

He picked the Pentagon's mission order up from his desk and waved it at his G2, his Intelligence Officer.

"You get down with your counterpart at USSOCOM. I want the two of you to come up with a joint assessment of what the enemy situation is and just what kind of an aircap this operation is going to require and where it's going to come from. Can we run it off two Nimitz class carriers in the Arabian Sea? What kind of cover would that give us?"

"Shouldn't we be thinking in terms of an all-out, preemptive strike to knock out the Iranian air force before we go in there, General?" McCordle's Chief of Staff asked.

"Damn right we should but there's no mention of anything like that in our mission statement. That would be tantamount to an all-out act of war against Iran, and it's very clear the President doesn't want that. What he wants us to do is slam in there, grab those three Iranian nukes and get the hell back out with a minimum of casualties and broken glass. My job is to convince him to do it with overwhelming combat power in the best looking conventional force option we can put together," McCordle growled in the rasp with which two packs of Marlboros a day had gifted him. "We'll also see what those bozos down on the point come up with. We all fly up to Andrews together at thirteen hundred Tuesday and brief the SecDef and the Joint Chiefs in the Tank as soon as we arrive." The Tank was the Joint Chief's command conference center in the outer ring of the Pentagon. "Wednesday morning, we brief at the White House. Let's be sure we get it right, gentlemen."

———

Less than half a mile away, an almost identical three-story yellow building at 7701 Tampa Point Boulevard housed the U.S. Special Operations Command, USSOCOM, the "bozos" to which McCordle referred. Under USSOCOM's umbrella were grouped those organizations that had nourished so much celluloid and news print, the Green Berets, the U.S. Navy Seals and the Delta Force.

This morning the attention of the commander of USSOCOM, Major General Clint Marker, was focused on the Delta Force because, as far as he was concerned, in the event the President elected to employ the Special Operations force option to extract the three nukes from Iran, it was Delta that was going to get the call.

A Delta Force veteran himself, Marker had personally selected the man he wanted to lead the mission if Delta got it, Colonel Charlie "Crowbar" Crowley. Crowley was a quiet, almost introverted 45-year-old, the very antithesis of the Sylvester Stallone image the public expected from Delta Force officers. In fact, the public's idea of a Delta Force warrior, fueled by the imagination of Hollywood's filmmakers, could not have been farther removed from reality. "You could have a Delta guy on either side of you and never know they were there," observed a Ranger veteran who'd often deployed with Delta operators.

The force prided itself on accepting only the best of the best. It took, quite literally, about one out every hundred applicants. They were selected after weeks of rigorous vetting, of being put through a battery of tests designed to measure their psychological ability to function under stress and extreme hardship.

The same rigorous selection process applied to both officers and enlisted men and, once admitted, both were expected to maintain the same high standards. There were virtually no West Point educated officers in Delta's ranks. Delta officers had to be adept at operating outside a formal command structure, something Academy graduates could rarely handle. Officers and enlisted men shared the same mess, the same food, and a saying in the force summed up the relations that prevailed between the them: "When it's time to load the truck, everybody loads."

That philosophy did not always sit well with the officer corps of the regular army and accounted for at least some of the tensions that existed between Delta and its parent organization. The force dated to the moment during Jimmy Carter's Presidency when the German elite strike force, the GSG9 stormed a hijacked Lufthansa 747 in Mogadishu and freed its passengers without loss of life.

"Have we got the capability to do something like that?" Carter asked his National Security Advisor, Zbigniew Brezinski. Of course we do, Brezinski assured the President. Fact was, the U.S. had no such capability, but under Brezinski's watchful eye, Colonel Charlie Beckwith began to set one up. To the ongoing chagrin of Delta Force operators and veterans, the organization's name has always been associated in the public eye with its most spectacular failure, the ill-fated mission to rescue the hostages being held by Iranian student radicals in the U.S. Embassy in Tehran.

The fact that that operation was an ad hoc mission, a grab bag into which a variety of units of which Delta was only one had been thrown, and that it was ordered ahead without a single rehearsal of any sort, was conveniently ignored by the public.

Since then, Delta's actions had never been recorded in the public press but the organization had played a key role in behind the line operations in Beirut, in Afghanistan, and in isolating and later making possible the elimination or arrest of Pablo Escobar and the Cali drug barons. Most recently it had prepared detailed plans for the seizure of Serbian war criminals like Radovan Karazdic, in the unlikely event the leaders of the western alliance should ever develop the political will to go after them.

Still, despite all its post 1979 triumphs, the stigma of its failed first mission continued to haunt the Delta Force. The nagging pain of that memory was reflected in the words General Marker employed handing the mission assignment to "Crowbar" Crowley.

"Charlie," he said, "I think this is the one we've been waiting for all these years."

Crowley began to study the document. On the wall behind was a poster bearing a set of command injunctions, the kind of wall display the military so loved. This one listed the five phases into which Crowley's mission—like all Delta missions—would be divided:

Eyes on Target
Rehearsal
Infiltration
Execution
Exfiltration

Crowley lay down the mission statement, whistling softly as it settled into his lap. "You're right, Clint. Pull this one off and we'll wipe the escutcheon clean for all time."

"I gather there's no time to waste here. I think your operational plan should call for a 'go' in two weeks."

"Tight, Clint, but I guess it's doable. Just."

"Look, Charlie, this is going to be your operation so I'm not going to tell you how to write up your operational plan for the President. I just want to make two points. First, the operation's got to begin and end under the cover of darkness."

"Roger."

"Second, remember our usual time constraints."

Crowley sighed. "OK, Clint. I guess I better get to work on a plan."

The general rose and slapped him on the shoulder. "We're counting on you. I want you to knock the socks off the President up there Wednesday. Make him forget Colin Powell and his doctrine ever existed."

———

"Professor?"

The Professor looked up wearily at Dr. Parvis Khanlari, the scientific director of Operation Khalid. He had not rested since rising at dawn to say his morning prayers. "What is it, my brother?"

"We are ready to test the firing circuit we're setting up to detonate our bombs with a remote radio signal. Would you like to watch?"

"Of course I would. Lead the way."

Once again the two men descended into the bowels of their laboratory. There on a bench Khanlari's electrical engineers had set up a model of the circuit they were about to test. Khanlari picked up something that looked like a cigarette lighter. "Our volunteer bomber will have only to press the top of this device and it will send out a radio signal on a pre-set, very specific frequency to our bomb."

"What frequency?" the Professor asked.

"One point two giga-hertz. The air is full of signals so we chose a frequency that was somewhat unusual. Well away from radio, TV, cellular phones and so forth so that our bomb will not pre-detonate by accident."

"Of course," agreed the Professor, "but we are going to be delivering our bomb or bombs if we decide to employ two of them in stolen cars. Why not wire the detonator up directly to a switch on the dashboard of the car?"

"We feel first, it would take too much time for inexperienced volunteers to set up the circuit, then conceal the wiring so it won't be spotted in case the car is stopped at a checkpoint. And there is always the risk they might make an error. This way we can be sure the bomb will detonate when the signal is sent."

The Professor inclined his head, indicating he accepted Khanlari's reasoning.

"Here"—Khanlari pointed to a black plastic box slightly larger than a pack of playing cards—"is the battery which will fire our krytron circuit when it receives the radio signal."

From the top of the box protruded a black tube the size of a drinking straw. "And this is the antenna," he said, indicating the tube, "which will pick up the radio signal."

"Hosain!" he called, summoning one of his acolytes, then tossing him the triggering device as though it was, indeed, a cigarette lighter. "Go upstairs, open the main door, and go out in the courtyard. When I beep you, press the button."

The Professor waited expectantly as Hosain left the lab. "Tell me," he asked, "is there any danger the bomb or its firing circuits could be damaged if our volunteers have to go over rough roads? Or if it gets dropped somehow?"

"None at all," Khanlari assured him. "Packed properly into a solid container as it will be, it will be a very sturdy device. No bumpy road is going to harm the bomb or its firing circuit."

Khanlari's beeper squeaked out a sound. "He's ready."

He in turn pressed Hosain's beeper. On the esplanade outside, his assistant squeezed the button of his triggering device. As he did, a blue bolt of electric current shot out of the black battery on the test bench. "Perfect," Khanlari announced. "That jolt of electricity you just saw will be shot into the first pigtail lead of our krytrons when the bomb's assembled. We can begin work on that now."

The Professor blessed his words with a smile.

"Come, dear friend," he said to Khanlari. "It has been a long day. Let us take a walk in the fresh air."

The two men marched in silence for a few minutes along the esplanade in front of their installation. "Professor," Khanlari said finally, "there is one thing about Operation Khalid which troubles me."

"What is that, my brother?"

"The Israelis. Their nuclear forces will survive the detonation of our bomb in Tel Aviv intact. Won't they retaliate for our blow? In a terrible, devastating way?"

"Rest assured, my brother, they will retaliate. And with overwhelming force."

Khanlari looked at the Professor puzzled. Was the man foretelling their own death?

"Yes, they will retaliate, alright. On Baghdad. They will destroy Iraq."

"What?"

"The Israelis have one of the best signal intelligence organizations in the world. Department 8200, they call it. They have a listening post on Mount Miron on the Golan Heights where they listen to everything that is said in the Middle East by phone, by shortwave radio, by cellular telephone. Shortly before our bomb explodes in Tel Aviv, they will capture a message. It will be in a code they have broken from a phone they are convinced belongs to the Iraqi Mukahbarat, their secret service. It will leave them in no doubt that it was the embittered followers of the late Saddam Hussein who were responsible for placing the nuclear bomb in Tel Aviv."

———

A crisis that can reduce a roomful of Washington movers and shakers to silence, Jim Duffy told himself looking at the concerned faces around him at the White House conference table, has got to be the mother of all crises. No one was smiling. No one was whispering a confidential aside to a neighbor. They were all just sitting there, as taut and expectant as he was, waiting for the President to arrive.

The President, Duffy knew, was about to order American servicemen out to die in an operation of his own making, without the sanction of the U.N., without the blessing or the knowledge of the nation's allies. It was an awesome responsibility, but then Duffy told himself, that was why people got to be elected President, wasn't it? If your personal anthem is going to be "Hail to the Chief," you better be ready to act like a chief when the chips are down.

The door was opened by a Secret Service agent and the President marched in. He did not, as he usually did, circle the table, greeting each participant in the meeting personally. He went right to his chair and looked at General Taylor, the Chairman of the Joint Chiefs. There was not even the suggestion of a smile on his face. His features were set in an expression as grim, as hardened as that which had been there in those dark hours of the Iraqi crisis. "General," he ordered, "let's begin."

Taylor rose. "Sir, we've prepared three briefings for you. First, the G2, the intelligence officer of Central Command, will brief you on the elements common to both a conventional and a special forces option to go in there and seize those three Iranian nukes. He will also cover the Iranians' ability to oppose our action from the air and our requirements for an aircap to neutralize their capabilities. Then, Brigadier General Jack Blum, the deputy commander of the 82nd Airborne, will brief you on the conventional force option and, finally, Colonel Charlie Crowley of Delta Force will brief the special forces option."

Duffy watched attentively as a major general marched to the head of the table and placed a pair of blow-ups on the easels waiting there. One was an enlargement of a satellite photo of the exterior of the Iranian's secret nuclear installation, the second a map of the surrounding area.

"Mr. President," he began, "let me deal first with the Iranian Air Force. They have four bases within a relatively short flying time of our assault area. They possess a total of 135 combat aircraft. They do not pose a major threat to our attack. Their planes are mostly U.S.-made, over 20 years old, without modern electronic homing and gunnery devices, radar and counter-radar technology. Furthermore, they have been without spare parts for those twenty years. Their pilots are good, but they are under-trained and restricted in their flying time because money is short. They also, as you may remember, have some antiquated Soviet aircraft which Saddam Hussein was kind enough to send them during the Gulf War. We propose to disable the runways of the four air bases nearby but because the Iranians are brave and determined fliers, a few of their fast movers will probably get airborne."

He turned to the blue stain of the Arabian Sea on his map. "To aircap the operation, we propose to station the carriers Washington and the Nimitz here. That will give us 120 combat aircraft available for action both to protect the carriers and overfly the assault area. We will also station a pair of AWACs out of Incirlik Air Force Base in Turkey to pick up those fast movers that do manage to get airborne as soon as they get off the ground. They will dispatch the needed fighter aircraft to the area to neutralize them."

"Our real concern in this operation is going to be protecting our carriers from some lone wolf, suicide bomber willing to fly into one of our flight decks Japanese kamikaze-style. I think that as far as our ground forces are concerned, we can guarantee them a clean overhead while they're busting up things on the ground."

"Any questions thus far?" he asked.

"No, go ahead."

"Right. Next, let me turn to the military situation on the ground. We estimate they have 75 to 100 Revolutionary Guards, Pasdaran, on site, living in those two barracks-like structures. They have a pair of 105 millimeter recoilless rifles at the roadblock giving access to the site, and three anti-aircraft pieces ringing the front approach. The nearest regular army base is at Bandar Abbas, about 350 miles away."

"Do they have a helicopter capacity to ferry troops up to our assault area?" the President demanded.

"No," the G2 answered. "They bought 50 Bell 214 troop-carrying helicopters from us when the Shah was still running Iran. They haven't been able to get their hands on spare parts for 20 years so we estimate less than half of them are airworthy today. They also have a fleet of Boeing 707's they converted into troop carriers in 1992-93, but they'd be flying coffins in an action of this sort. To reinforce by the ground, we estimate they'd require 48 hours given the mountainous terrain and bad roads in the area."

The general shuffled the papers in his hand. He's making it look too easy, it occurred to Duffy. Now he's going to lay the good stuff on us.

"Our concern, Mr. President, is that they will elect to reinforce by non-conventional means. Every mullah in Zabol will rush out of his house shrieking that the devils of the Great Satan are attacking, calling for volunteers. The Revolutionary Guard has secret caches of AK-47's, hand grenades and light mortars hidden in every community in Iran. It'll be Basra all over again. They'll break those out and give them to every 15- and 17-year-old volunteer they can find. They'll probably have thousands of them. Most of them will be slaughtered by our troops but some of them will get through. And they could pose a threat to the airstrip at Zabol which we must control to secure the evacuation of our forces in the event that you elect to go with the conventional forces option on which General Blum will now brief you."

Another general came forward, his trouser tops bloused into the top of jump boots so highly polished that, Duffy thought, you could use them for shaving mirrors.

"Mr. President," he began in one of those parade ground voices meant to shatter glass at ten feet, "the operation we propose will be broken down into three phrases. First, we will drop a reinforced battalion of the 82nd Airborne right onto the target site we've been assigned."

"How many men would that be?" asked the President.

"When you've stripped out the clerks and jerks, sir, about 500. Six rifle companies and an anti-tank company. The 82nd can drop in a significantly heavier force package than the Rangers, the other unit we'll be employing. They can paradrop some 105 millimeter howitzers right there on the site to blow open whatever kind of barrier they've got around the entrance to their installation as well as some anti-tank weapons to cover the ground approaches while the troopers are doing their thing."

"In Phase Two, which we will initiate concurrently with Phase One, we will drop four rifle companies of Rangers on the airstrip at Zabol. Their mission will be to secure a perimeter around the field. Once they have, we will fly in a flight of C47's loaded with armored vehicles. In Phase Three, those vehicles, guarded by the Rangers, will go up to the assault site, evacuate the three recovered nukes, our 82nd Airborne troopers, and any dead or wounded we've incurred in the operation and return them to the airstrip in Zabol where we will then proceed with our aerial evacuation."

"Will you be able to get all your equipment, your trucks back out?" the President asked Blum.

"Probably not. Personnel evacuation will obviously have first priority and loading those vehicles back onto the aircraft that brought them in would almost certainly consume more time than we would feel we could safely expend."

"So that means there'll be a lot of equipment left lying around on the ground for the Iranians to show to the TV cameras of the world's press after our operation" the President pointed out.

"Mr. President." It was the Secretary of Defense. Both he and the Chairman of the Joint Chiefs had, of course, already heard all three briefings at the Pentagon. "By its very nature, this is a big signature operation. These guys are going in there to break things. The operation is going to carry a lot of political baggage, but it will also show the world that for nations like Iran, playing around with weapons of mass destruction is out of bounds. Hopefully the North Koreans will be listening and we will have put a wrap on your Axis of Evil."

"And where will your aircraft be operating from?" the President asked.

"That, sir, is one of the reasons we strongly urge you to adopt this option," the deputy commander of the 82nd Airborne replied. "With aerial refueling, we can run it out of bases in the continental U.S. That means we don't have to press any of our reluctant allies for staging rights on their soil in order to mount the operation overseas. And, sir, let me conclude by saying that by selecting this conventional force option you will reduce the risk of mission failure to as close to zero as it is possible to get."

"Alright," the President said, "let's hear what the Special Operations people have to say."

Duffy studied Colonel Crowley as he strode in his turn to the easel. There was something vaguely familiar about him. Had they met perhaps? In Afghanistan?

"Mr. President," Crowley said after introducing himself. "May I address a question to your intelligence officers before I begin my briefing?"

"Of course."

"How can we be 100% sure that the three nukes we're after are in that Iranian installation we're going to assault?"

The President looked at the Director of the CIA who looked in turn at Duffy. Patiently, Duffy worked his way through the trail of the krytrons and the NSA intercepts. "Where those krytrons are, the three nukes we're after have got to be," he concluded.

"I accept the fact the krytrons are there," Crowley rejoined. "But do you have hard, confirmed intelligence that the plutonium cores are? Do you have an intelligence source who's been in there and seen them?"

Duffy answered with what was meant to be a laugh but came out sounding more like an angry bark. "You're not such a day dreamer are you that you think the CIA has a human intelligence source, a spy, inside Iran's nuclear establishment?"

"I'd like to hope so if I'm going to lead my people in there."

"Well, we don't. But I'll tell you what. I'm 100% convinced they're there. If it'll make a believer out of you, I'll go in there with you right alongside your people."

Crowley eye-balled Duffy. "Haven't we met somewhere before?"

"Afghanistan, maybe?"

"Yeah." The light went on in Crowley's mind. "You're that CIA boss who went into the Parrot's Beak alongside your mooj in violation of Casey's orders. My kind of guy. OK. I'll become a believer and you join the party."

Crowley placed a cardboard panel on the easel. It listed the five cardinal points underlying all Delta operations that had been displayed behind his Tampa, Florida desk.

"'Eyes on target,'" he began. "We love your CIA satellite images. They are first class. Still I want the eyes of my own people focused on the target we're going to assault. At Delta we never trust anybody except ourselves."

"And how do you propose to do such a thing?" asked an incredulous President.

"Tomorrow night if we've been given the go-ahead, two of my operators will jump out of an aircraft at 35,000 feet, fifty miles southwest of Zabol. They'll be under canopy and, using the Global Positioning System, they will fly their chutes to this spot here"—Crowley indicated a point on his map—"five miles from the ridge line facing the entrance to the Iranian lab.

"They'll climb up to that ridge and then dig themselves hideholes on it, line their holes with rubber sheeting and cover them up with brush and weeds over some webbing they'll have. They will live in those holes without coming out, eating, sleeping, urinating and defecating in there, studying every move the Iranians across the way make with telescopes and ANVIS 6 night vision goggles. They will report back to us on what they've observed twice a day with burst radios."

"My gosh!" exclaimed an impressed President. "You've got people who can to do that?"

"Sir," Crowley proudly informed him, "no Delta operator is ever asked to do anything he hasn't already done in training."

"Goodness gracious!" declared an equally impressed Secretary of the Interior. "What kind of men would do that?"

"A couple of weird dudes, sir. Making the magnificent sum of $165 a month."

Crowley turned his attention back to his chart. "Rehearsal," he said. "I have a team out at the Las Vegas test site in Nevada now ready to set up the best replicas possible of the two buildings you see in the satellite photos and the entry to their underground installation. Right down to the doorknobs if we can. Then my assault teams will rehearse and rehearse and rehearse. Anything short of that simply isn't acceptable."

Once again he went back to the security blanket his chart seemed to represent for him in this, the most high-powered briefing he'd ever had to give. "Infiltration," he read out.

"The first aircraft on the scene will be this one," Crowley declared placing the photo of a blackened plane on his easel. "It is our new, absolutely undetectable super-stealth reconnaissance plane, the Dark Star, developed after the Gulf War. This will be its second deployment in a combat situation—Iraq was first."

"There is no way the Iranians will be able to discover that the Dark Star is up there. The plane is equipped with infrared cameras and ultra-sensitive sensoring devices. That equipment can pick up and photograph gun emplacements, moving vehicles, even individual enemy soldiers sleeping in their foxholes or in their guard posts. Every one of their observations is then relayed back in real time imagery to the TV monitors in this aircraft, the V22, which will be carrying the troopers of our assault force. Those men will be able to see on a screen right there in front of them exactly who and what is going to be waiting for them when they hit the ground."

"They will also be relaying those images to a pair of AC130 gunships configured with Gatling guns and 20 millimeter howitzers." Crowley had covered over the photograph of the Dark Star with the photo of another aircraft. "The AC130's will open the engagement by taking out those three anti-aircraft emplacements, the road block leading up to the site and any other obstacles to our assault which the Dark Star has discovered."

"They'll be able to do all that? You're sure?" the President asked.

"Sir, those guys are so good they can put a round in your pocket. After they've finished, none of those Pasdaran are going to be anxious to stick their heads up for a long, long while to come. Which is just dandy because"—he pointed to the word "Execution" on his chart— "that's when we come in."

Now he placed the photo of yet another aircraft on his easel. "This is the V22 which, as I said, will take our teams in. The V22 is a unique attack aircraft. It can carry a 25-man assault team to the target flying at 330 miles per hour as a conventional swept wing aircraft. But—and this is what makes the V22 such a special aircraft—once they reach the target zone, they tilt their wings upward, throttle back their airspeed and become, for all practical purposes, helicopters. They can flutter down to a soft landing on the ground the way a chopper does."

"Now," Crowley continued, "the assault. Since we're not going to be operating in a secure environment, we've got to make our own security. We'll operate on the doughnut principle."

A puzzled look swept the faces of the non-military officials in the situation room.

"Two of the V22's will take in two beefed-up platoons of Rangers, 25 men each, to secure a perimeter around the target area, wipe up anything that's left of their roadblock after the AC130's have hosed it down and closed off all access to the site. They become, in other words, the ring around the hole of the doughnut."

"The hole"—Crowley paused, knowing that what he was about to say was going to stun the civilians around the table—"will consist of three ten-man Delta Force assault teams, one each for those two buildings you see in that satellite photo, and the third to blow open the doors of their installation with shaped charges and go in there and get your three nuclear devices."

"Only thirty men!" gasped the Secretary of the Interior. "But you'll be outnumbered three to one."

"Sir." The tone in which Crowley replied was neither assertive nor brutal. It was simple and matter of fact. "You absolutely would not believe how quickly these Delta Force operators will take those people out. They are excellent shots, the best, bar none, in the world and they excel at killing people. Psychologically and physiologically, they are killing machines. Nobody is going to come out of that installation of theirs alive."

The director of the CIA shook his head, not in disagreement with what the colonel had said but in recognition of the enormity of its implications. "That means Iran will have lost in one swoop all the human, the intellectual resources they need for their nuclear establishment. It will be a generation before they'll recover."

Crowley nodded. "We'll be taking in a digital TV camera so we can send back to you here imagery of the devices we find. That way our nuclear scientists can study them and make sure we're bringing home the right piece of bacon."

"We'll be ready and waiting," Dr. Leigh Stein, the Department of Energy's nuclear weapons designer, promised. "We'll give you copper shielded containers to bring them out in so those plutonium cores won't cause you any problems. Plutonium's radiation consists mainly of alpha rays which the copper will block. It also gives off a few gamma rays, but not enough to be a hazard in the short time your men will be exposed to them."

"Right," Crowley concluded. "Exfiltration. Our V22's will be waiting for us right where they put us down. Our three assault teams will return to them with the nukes, the Rangers will withdraw from their perimeter and we will exit the site."

The President shook his head in disbelieving wonder. This colonel made it all sound so simple, so easy. Was it really possible? "How much time is all this going to take?" he asked.

"Thirty minutes from the time the AC130 gunships open fire to our final lift-off, sir."

"Thirty minutes!" The President clearly couldn't believe the figure he'd just been given.

"Mr. President, this is a surgical operation. No surgical operation that lasts longer than thirty minutes is going to succeed."

"And casualties?"

"Among the Iranians, very heavy, sir. As I said, our Delta operators are the best shots in the world. But more important, they are very, very accurate in their target selection. They know how to discriminate fast when they hit a building. If we go in with the speed, surprise and stealth we want, I believe we will hold our own casualties to a minimum, sir. We'll even make sure you get Mr. Duffy back."

The President stared down at the table in moody silence. He's praying, Duffy thought. Praying he makes the right decision, praying probably for those who were going to lose their lives in the operation. Might not be a bad idea, it suddenly occurred to Duffy, if I got off a quick prayer myself.

Finally, the President looked up and across the table to Crowley. "What," he asked, the hoarseness in his voice more noticeable than it normally was, "is your estimate of the chances the operation you've outlined for us will succeed?"

"One hundred percent, sir. Otherwise, I wouldn't take my men in there."

For the first time since he'd started to brief, the faintest suggestion of a smile graced the colonel's sober features.

"Of course, sir," he told the President, "there's always that old German military saying that goes back to Napoleonic times to contend with—'It matters not how good you are if the angel pees on the flintlock of your musket.'"

The President exhaled and straightened up, his resolve seemingly strengthened by Crowley's briefing. "OK, people," he said. "That's it.

We go with the Special Force option to be executed as soon as possible commensurate with getting the job done right."

"And Colonel." There was no suggestion of a smile on the President's face now. "You make damn sure the angels are on our side on this one."

———

It was the moment towards which the three young men had been working, striving, preparing, praying for weeks, months, in one case, years: the moment when one of them would be chosen to die. All three were under 21. One of them was still a virgin. All were still far from attaining the plenitude of their lives. Yet, in just a few seconds, the sheikh seated opposite them would select the individual who would forfeit the bright promise of his young life to become a martyr for Islam.

Outside the little mosque, adjacent to the Cave of the Martyrs, a chill wind from the north stroked the Lebanese countryside, singing out its appropriately melancholy chords for the ceremony about to begin. Imad Mugniyeh stood off to one side of the little group, waiting to study the reaction on the face of the chosen youth. Of course, as only Mugniyeh knew, when that young man set off for Tel Aviv in his stolen vehicle three weeks hence, he was going to die. No last minute burst of panic, no sudden change of heart was going to alter that.

Unbeknownst to the volunteer, a second, shadow bomber would be following behind him in another car with a firing device of his own, ready to explode the Professor's bomb if the volunteer hesitated to do so. That second volunteer was not a candidate for martyrdom. He was unaware of the real nature of the bomb that was going to be placed in the trunk of the martyr's car—he'd been assured by Mugniyeh he would survive its explosion.

"It is by accepting the virtues of martyrdom that we the weak, the oppressed, strike fear and worry into the hearts of our oppressors," the sheikh was concluding. "The Koran teaches us that those who suffer from tyranny are justified in employing war. Has ever a people suf-

fered from greater tyranny than our Palestinian brothers whose ago-
nies you shall avenge?"

He rose. In his hand was a green elastic headband. On it was written in white Arabic script the words of the Ayatollah Khomeini: "The
martyr is the essence of history." He stepped to the young man at the
left of the line of three before him. Silently, he slipped it around his
head so that its two-inch green swath covered his forehead.

The youth was silent but Mugniyeh saw an almost ethereal glow of
exultation illuminate his features.

"Rise, brave Islamic warrior," the sheikh commanded. He then
embraced the young man as did his two colleagues who, to their
intense regret, had not been selected. Mugniyeh was the last to kiss
him fervently on both cheeks. *"Mabruk*—congratulations!" he
declared.

"Since I was thirteen I have waited for this moment," the youth
replied.

His name was Saad el Emawi and his declaration was not an idle
boast. Like so many of the candidates for the mission of martyrdom,
he was an orphan and the message of militant Islam had replaced the
guidance of a father in his youthful soul. His father had been one of
the bodyguards of the Secretary General of the Hezbollah, Sheikh
Abbas Mussawi, and he had been killed alongside the sheikh in an
Israeli helicopter assault in February, 1992. Saad's mother had died of
a heart attack on hearing the news later on the day of his father's death.

Emawi had thrown himself on his father's bloody, shroud-covered
corpse, swearing that one day he would avenge him. From that
moment on, two centers of gravity had dominated his life—the
mosque in his village in southern Lebanon where he drank deep the
doctrine of radical Islam preached by the village sheikh and his grandmother who forced an education down his reluctant throat, even teaching him to speak serviceable French for the future she'd hoped he
would enjoy in Europe.

So complete had his devotion to the message of his sheikh been
that despite the temptations all around him, he had by choice remained

a virgin, saving the stirrings of his youthful loins for the 72 virgin brides he knew would be waiting to welcome him to Paradise the day he became a martyr.

The sheikh presiding over the ceremony took him by the hand. "Come, my brave warrior," he commanded, leading him out of the mosque into the open field behind it. Cut into its greensward was a freshly dug grave, four feet deep. Beside it, a wooden plank rested on the edge of the hole.

Emawi was ordered to lie down on the plank and fold his arms across his chest. As the sheikh sang out the prayers for the dead, he was lowered into the grave and a second wooden plank placed on top of it. There in the darkness, in the earth's moist embrace, he was meant to feel the caress of his coming death. He lay there trembling, listening to the fading chants of the sheikh's prayer, seeing before him the image of his father's bloody corpse. As he struggled to attain the martyr's serenity, another image plucked at his unfired loins, the undulating line of those 72 virgin brides who would be waiting for him at the moment of his martyr's death.

After twenty minutes in the grave, he was lifted out, the last ritual trial of a candidate for martyrdom successfully passed.

Triumphantly, he was led back into the courtyard of the mosque where, of all people, a barber was waiting for him. He trimmed Emawi's hair then cut and shaved his beard. The snippets of his hair were carefully collected into three bags, one for each of Emawi's three sisters.

They would be given to the three girls at a joyous celebration of his martyrdom 24 hours after his death. His friends would gather around them offering sweets and congratulations on their brother's death. A representative of the Hezbollah would announce to the three girls the pensions they would receive from the organization for the rest of their lives in recognition of their brother's sacrifice. Emawi took a pen and wrote out in graceful Arabic script the message that would be delivered to his sisters along with the locks of his hair.

"May my death in the Holy War serve as an act of purification for me, for all of you, and for the memory of our beloved parents."

A photographer snapped a picture of his smiling, clean shaven face for the fake French passport he would carry on his trip to Tel Aviv. Then a sheikh brought out the clothes they'd selected for his journey: tight black leather pants, Addidas hi-top sneakers, a blue turtleneck shirt and a suede leather jacket from the French store Faconnable in Paris. Outfitted in those clothes he would look like any eager young French tourist on a first visit to the Holy Land.

When those last preparations were complete, the sheikh offered Emawi a Koran. He kissed it. The sheikh then held it over his head. Emawi walked under it for a departing blessing, left the courtyard of the mosque and headed for the waiting car that would start him on the first stage of his final journey, the trip to the safehouse in Jericho where he would await the arrival of the bomb he would drive into Tel Aviv.

Mugniyeh watched him go. He, too, was about to leave on a journey. His was to Zabol where the Professor had called a meeting of the Committee of Secret Operations to prepare for the final steps of Operation Khalid.

———

To the uninitiated, the two Delta Force operators might have looked like a pair of extras waiting to film a sequence for Star Trek. Each wore a Gentex helmet, a full coverage headpiece made of Kevlar which had its own built-in communications system including a microphone and earphones. An oxygen mask was fixed to the helmet with bayonet clips, fitting snugly just below the goggles.

They were wearing three layered sets of full-body thermal underwear topped with a baklava face mask so that not so much as a square centimeter of skin would be exposed to the atmosphere when they exited their aircraft at 35,000 feet. Over all that was a tight-fitting Gortex jump suit. Every bit of equipment they carried from their back packs to their compass consoles in a casing the size of a small taco box, to the rifles configured down the left side of their bodies, was secured and strapped to them by the tightest of fastenings. The shock that was waiting for them was going to be so tremendous it could, quite literally, rip a man's shoes or his laced-up boots from his feet.

Theirs was as challenging, as dangerous an exercise as a man could undertake with a parachute. A decade earlier, it would have been an impossibility. Both men had already made half a dozen similar jumps in training, but no amount of training could ever quell the chill, the tension that always preceded this extraordinary exercise.

Working with the meteorologists at the U.S. Air Force Base in Qatar and their own Delta experts, they had plotted out the direction and strength of the prevailing winds they would encounter in each of the different bands of air they would traverse on their plummet earthward. From those calculations, they had worked out their HARP, High Altitude Release Point, the precise point above the earth's surface at which they would exit their aircraft to take the maximum advantage of the winds aloft on their way to their target.

What they were going to do was, quite literally, "fly" their parachutes, or canopies as experienced jumpers now called them, forty-five miles to their ground target, a flat stretch of land below the ridge line looking across a draw to the entrance of the Iranians secret nuclear installation above Zabol. Their ability to hit their target area would determine whether they would be able to get up to that ridge line before dawn and bury themselves in the hidehole from which they could then study the Iranians' movements.

Their aircraft had flown east over the Arabian Sea, then pointed north, crossing into Pakistan west of Karachi and on into Afghan airspace. Once there, their pilot had only to make this brief detour into Iranian airspace, an incursion so limited in time and space no Iranian radar technician was apt to detect it or pay any attention to it if he did.

A red light flashed on over the aircraft's side door. An enlisted man yanked it open, letting in a blast of air almost 40 degrees below zero Fahrenheit, a temperature which usually left airline passengers totally indifferent when it was announced from the flight deck by their captain but which had a horrifying reality for the two Delta operators about to leap into it.

The first of the two stepped forward and grabbed the sides of the aircraft. I can't believe I'm doing this, he thought, staring out into the blackness. A buzzer sounded. He dove out of the plane head first at a 45 degree angle.

The shock as he hit the atmosphere was brutal. It always was. Exiting, he was hurtling horizontally at close to 600 miles an hour. The still air into which he'd leapt was a wall and at the same time gravity was wrenching him towards a vertical speed of 120 miles an hour, the speed of a body in free fall. Ride the air, he told himself, keep the right body position so you don't start spinning like a top.

It worked. This was a "hay-ho," a high altitude, high opening jump so he quickly pulled his cord and got yet another jolt to his system as his canopy blossoming overhead began throttling down his speed.

He flicked open the clam shell lid of the Silva compass on his belt. It lit up in a fluorescent glow which allowed him to swing himself around to the bearing he wanted while keeping both his hands on the control lines of his canopy. Somewhere in the darkness above him, he knew, his fellow operator was doing the same thing.

As he glided through 15,000 feet, he began to relax in the warming air, once again adjusting his flight path with the indications of his compass. Then the earth was there rushing to meet him. Not exactly a welcome home, he chuckled but at least it was terra firma once again.

His landing was perfect and he managed, despite the weight of his equipment, to remain on his feet. He shed his chute and checked the terrain features around him. He'd confirm his location with his GPS, Global Positioning System, but all the signs seemed to indicate that he'd come down very close to the site he'd chosen before takeoff.

From his pocket he took out a little metal snapping device, a not too distant cousin of the devices the men of the 82nd and 101st Airborne Divisions had used to locate each other after their drops into Normandy on the night of D-Day.

He gave it a snap and heard to his right an answering snap. The two Delta operators advanced towards each other, embraced, buried their chutes and set out through the darkness towards their target ridge line, less than five miles away.

They had familiarized themselves with the topography of the ridge line by studying detailed satellite photographs of its surface. From them, they had chosen what appeared to be the ideal location for their hidehole. It was set in front of a rocky outcropping almost across the draw separating their ridge from the Iranians' secret installation, a site which would allow them to monitor continuously the entrance to Professor Bollahi's underground lab.

A first survey of the site on the ground confirmed to the two Delta operators that theirs had been a good choice, so they set to work digging their hole. Although the overhead satellites had picked up no indication of any human activity along the ridge line, they took no chances. They shovelled out the soft sub-soil as quietly as possible. Noise, after all, travels easily through the stillness of the desert night.

Once their hole was dug, they carefully scattered the dirt they'd scooped from it around the base of the rocky outcropping to conceal what they had done. Then they took a sheet of camouflage webbing and wove into it scraps of weeds and plant growth they plucked from the desert floor. Once they'd slipped into their hole, they would stretch the webbing over their heads as their 'roof,' the final, concealing element of their hideout.

They lined the hole with rubber sheeting and piled in their equipment: long range reconnaissance rations, their burst radio, field glasses, ANVIS 6 night vision goggles, rubber excrement bags, a pair of Belgian made FN30's for use in the final assault on the Iranians installation and two silenced .22 pistols. They were there in case any Iranian shepherds, sheep, cats, dogs, or rats tried to join them in their hidehole. Carefully, they smoothed over the footprints they'd left in the earth around their hole. They were ready to go to ground for days, perhaps even weeks.

"Home sweet home," the team leader announced to his second. "Why don't you get some sleep and I'll take the first shift."

They rolled into their hole, then secured their camouflage webbing over their heads, a gesture the finality of which did not escape either man.

"Ever been in one of these damn things on an operation before?" the second operator asked his leader.

"Hell, yeah. I spent ten days in one outside Noriega's beach house at Rio Hato on the Pacific coast. Had his movements down so tight I could tell you what time he got up in the night to pee. We could have gone in there and snatched him in five minutes. Saved 23 American lives and Christ knows how many Panamanian lives."

"So why the hell didn't we?"

"Don't be stupid. Our political culture wouldn't let us is why. Just like it probably won't let us do this op. Anyway, get some sleep."

While his number two twisted himself into a vague fetal position, the team leader put on his night vision goggles, took up his field glasses and began to systematically study the Iranian installation barely half a mile from his hole. First, he swept the two barracks-like buildings, the area surrounding them and the entrance to whatever their secret installation was. It was 0430. Nothing was moving. No one, as far as he could make out, was standing guard on either of the two buildings. Nor were there any guards he could pick out in front of the main installation. Clearly the Iranians were very confident of whatever locking system they'd installed on those massive steel doors protecting it.

Next he moved his glasses down the access road to the fortified position guarding the entry to the site. There he could see signs of life alright. Slowly, patiently, as he'd been trained to do, he studied the shadows he saw there, trying to establish how many Revolutionary Guards were manning the site in this predawn darkness and where they were. The glow of a cigarette told him where one guard was. It also told him something else. Discipline, at least in this late night watch, was slack.

For the next days he and his second would have one key job: to establish the pattern of existence at that Iranian installation. How many guards were assigned to it? What arms did they have? What was the heaviest guarded part of the installation? When did the shifts change? How? Who slept where and when? Who messed where and when? Who were the leaders? How could you identify them? Who were the slackers? The zealots?

For six hours he peered across the draw, barely allowing himself the time to blink, noting down every Iranian movement he could see, beginning to compile a roster of the Revolutionary Guards assigned to the installation. Finally, he assembled his first report for USSOCOM in Tampa. It began with the confirmation that he and his companion were securely ensconced in their pre-selected hidehole, then set out all his preliminary observations.

He punched the report into a hand held computer that automatically encrypted it for transmission on his burst radio. He loaded the dispatch into the radio, poked it just outside the surface of the webbing covering his hole, pointed it to the compass heading he'd been given for his transmissions and fired it off.

The transmission time required was measured in seconds. The leader eased back down into the snugness of his hole, secure in the knowledge that the device which would allow an enemy to intercept his burst and determine where on the earth's surface it had come from had yet to be invented.

———

Seventy-two hours after that Delta operator had flashed out his first message, Colonel Charlie "Crowbar" Crowley had assembled the elements of his assault force at the Nevada Test Site to start rehearsals for what was now officially baptised "Operation Grassroots." Ranged before him were 30 Delta Operators—that, not trooper or soldier— was the standard label for Delta personnel. He'd already broken them up into three ten-man assault teams. With them were fifty Rangers and the pilots and crewmen of the four V22 aircraft that would fly his men in for their attack and the pilots of the two AC130 Gunships whose firepower would initiate it.

The Army Corps of Engineers, working from satellite photos, had performed in just 48 hours the remarkable feat of building for him a replica of the area his men were going to assault. It was precise down to the location of the Revolutionary Guards' foxholes, guard posts and anti-aircraft emplacements. An esplanade similar to the one in front of the Professor's installation had been scooped out with bulldozers and asphalted in exactly the same way. A rock cliff towered over the esplanade just as one did out in southeastern Iran. A pair of massive steel doors, their dimensions identical to those of the doors fixed to the Iranians' cliff, had been fixed to the surface of the Nevada rock.

Unfortunately, that was where the ingenuity of the army engineers stopped. There was nothing behind those doors except a rock facade because no one had yet been able to determine what lay behind the Iranians' steel doors. They had not been opened in the three days the Delta operators had been observing them from their hidehole. The Iranians entered and exited their installation through a smaller door cut into the base of the steel gates.

It was a gap in his knowledge that profoundly disturbed Crowley. Now he was preparing his assault plan still ignorant of what lay behind those doors.

He glanced at his two visitors, Jim Duffy and Dr. Leigh Stein, and began.

"OK, people, listen up. Our attack will go in at oh-three-hundred hours local, twenty-four hours Zulu. The date will be set as a function of our rehearsals here but in no case will it be later than ten days from now."

He paused to let his men measure just how imminent that meant the operation was, then gestured to the pair of Iranian barracks thrown up for him by the army engineers exactly where the satellite photography had placed them. "These are your standard Iranian army structures. Their design goes back to the Shah's days so we had blueprints of them available and have reproduced them as faithfully as possible. This building here"—he gestured to his left—"houses the 90 Revolutionary Guards assigned to duty out there. For armament those guys carry AK-47's with two extra clips of ammo. Some, but not all of them, carry sidearms."

He shuffled the papers in his hands. "They are divided up into three thirty-man teams, and each works an eight-hour day. Their shifts are eight to four, four to midnight, midnight to eight a.m. The H-Hour for our assault was chosen so that we will have a maximum number of those guards in their barracks asleep when we hit them."

Several of his operators grunted their approval of the wisdom inherent in that decision.

"Their bunking facilities are on the top floor. The ground floor is given over to messing and recreational facilities. Our number one AC130 gunship will open the assault at H-Hour vectoring into the target area at 1,000 feet from the northeast on a heading of 182 degrees. His mission will be to make monkey meat out of that Revolutionary Guards barracks with his 20 millimeter cannon."

Crowley turned to a group of ten Delta operators grouped around their team leader. "You gentlemen in Assault Team One will be on board V22 Number One hovering at 2,500 feet when the AC130 goes in. As soon as the gunship pilot signals to your pilot that he's exited the area, you will drop onto the esplanade here." He indicated a white circle painted on the asphalt of the esplanade. "When you hit the ground, you will exit the aircraft in a column of ducks and assault the building via its main entry port. The two operators leading the columns will precede your entry by tossing stun grenades into the building. You will then enter and your mission will be to terminate any of the occupants of that barracks still standing after the AC130's done its work, roger?"

The ten members of his Assault Team One, apparently unfazed by the notion of attacking a building out-numbered six to one mumbled "roger that" in reply.

Crowley now turned his attention to the two remaining assault teams. "Teams two and three will be on board V22 Number Two. You will hover down alongside the first V22 and land on this spot." He indicated a second white circle on the esplanade's asphalt. "Team Two will have the easy job. You'll rush the big steel gates behind me, set up

HE charges along its base to blow them open if it becomes necessary to do so, then set up a defensive perimeter around your position."

"I will accompany Assault Team Three together with this gentlemen here, Mr. Duffy of the Central Intelligence Agency, who's volunteered to come along with us." He offered Duffy a smile which the agency officer thought contained more than a hint of mockery. "Like all CIA officers, he's received basic military training although in his case"—this time, Duffy could see, humour was writ large in his smile—"it was some time ago."

"Now the residents of this second barracks to my right, forty-two by our count, are apparently the technicans and scientists assigned to the site. Their working day begins at eight a.m. and some work as late as ten or eleven at night. However, at the H-Hour we've selected we expect all of them will in that barracks asleep."

"This"—he held up an enlargement of the CIA's London photograph of the Professor—"is the man in charge. His name is Kair Bollahi but everyone calls him 'the Professor.' As far as we have been able to determine, he sleeps in that barracks along with his co-workers."

Crowley paused to let his audience know he was approaching a critical point in his briefing. "This Professor will know exactly where those three nukes we're going out there to recover are and what state they are in." He gave a questioning glance skyward as though he might be seeking some forgiveness for the action he was about to propose. "We're going to have to invite our Professor to lead us to his nukes."

Now, his eyes went to the ten operators of Assault Team Three. "We do not believe there are any arms in that building so your entry will presumably be unopposed. The first operator in the door will stick his MC5 into the belly of the first Iranian he sees and ask him where the Professor is."

"Suppose he refuses to answer? Or he can't speak English?"

"Terminate him and move on to the next guy you find. These people are scientists. They're educated, not fanatics like the Revolutionary Guards. Put a couple of examples of what happens to people who aren't talkative onto the floor and someone will be ready to finger the

Professor for us. You will then invite the Professor to join you in our effort to locate and seize those three nukes."

"Suppose he refuses?" one of the team operators asked.

"Then that's where Mr. Duffy and I will have to step in."

"And if you two can't convince him?"

"Then I'm afraid he'll have to join the others on the floor and Mr. Duffy will call for volunteers to lead us into that factory of theirs. Or we'll just blow down the doors and go in and get the nukes ourselves."

"What do we know about the state of those three nukes we're going out there after?" asked the leader of Assault Team Three. "Could they detonate on us in their installation or while we're taking them out to the V22?"

Crowley turned to Leigh Stein. "I've brought Dr. Stein, one of our top nuclear weapons designers out here to address your scientific concerns. Leigh."

Stein acknowledged the introduction with a quick nod. "I think I can assure you that, based on our knowledge of what's going on out there, it's virtually impossible that those weapons are operational yet. They can't detonate on you while they're in that installation or while you're moving them into your aircraft."

Stein was observant enough to read the relief—mixed with a healthy ration of scepticism—on the team leader's face. "The nuclear material in those devices is Plutonium 239 in its metallic form. It's a heavy, stable metal which emits gamma and alpha rays in quantities that are not sufficient to be hazardous in the time frame we're going to be working in here. You will, in any event, be equipped with copper-lined boxes to move the bombs in once you've located them. They will prevent any of that radioactivity from escaping."

Crowley took back the briefing. "OK, Rangers," he said. "You will land in V22's Three and Four fore and aft of the protected entrance to the site as soon as the second AC130 has finished hosing down the area. Your first assignment will be to terminate any of the Revolutionary Guards left standing. Then you will establish a defensive perimeter around the entrance to prevent anyone or anything going up there while our Delta teams are at work. As soon as Assault Team Three has loaded the three devices into their V22, the team leader will both fire off a red-green-red flare and inform all hands over your radio net that the mission has been executed. You will be expected to exfiltrate the site within five minutes of receiving that signal. Have I made myself clear?"

As always, Crowley had. He now walked over to the pilots and aircrew of the V22's and AC130's. "Your role in this operation is critical, gentlemen," he informed them. "I want you to work together in the framework of the mission plan I've just outlined to you to come up with an air ops plan that will eliminate any likelihood of a mid-air collision involving your aircraft."

With that, he returned to the center of the esplanade. "Alright, people," he announced, "we will hold two rehearsals every other night until we get it right. The first each night will be a dry run. On the second, the AC130's will use live ammunition as will Assault Team One and the Rangers. The day between rehearsal nights will be neccessary to allow the engineers time to rebuild the barracks after the AC130's have finished blasting them apart. First rehearsal tonight at twenty three hundred hours."

———

Five days and three rehearsal nights later, Crowley took Jim Duffy aside. "We were in and out of there in twenty-four minutes tonight," he noted. "That's as good as it's going to get. We still don't know what's behind those steel doors, though. That's a huge hole in our operational knowledge. Still, as much as I hate to launch an operation without everything I need to know in hand, I think we haven't got a choice here. I think we've got to go."

"I think you're right," Duffy agreed. "What's the next step?"

"We move our men, equipment, and aircraft to Incirlik which will be our forward assault base. It's when we get there that the realization is going to hit these guys that they're really going to do this. Things will get tense then and I hope the President will give us our final OK to move as soon after that as possible."

Crowley grinned. "All presidents love special operations. There's never been one that didn't. They stir up much less flack from the rest of the world because they don't leave a big political signature the way conventional ops do. So I think we'll get the 'go.'"

"And you really think our chances of success here are 100%?"

"Oh, Christ no. Not when we don't know what the hell the Iranians have got hidden behind those steel doors of theirs. Listen, why don't you fly back to Andrews, check in with your bosses, then come down to Tampa Thursday morning and we'll fly out to Turkey together Thursday after lunch at the Officers Club?"

"You make it sound like we're off on a tourist junket."

Crowley whacked Duffy on his knee. "Much better than that, pal. We're off to a surprise party."

————

"Jimbo, for God's sake, call in sick on this one. You've got no business screwing around out there in the desert with those Delta guys," Jack Lohnes pleaded with his old friend.

Duffy, already on his third cup of coffee despite the fact it was barely eight in the morning, shook his head. "How can I do that, Jack? The only reason Colonel Crowley agreed to go in is because I gave him my personal assurance the nukes were there in that headquarters they're going to storm. Besides, you know what? I'm kind of looking forward to going in there with those Delta guys. They've got my adrenalin running."

"Jim, the only reason Crowley and his team are going in is because the President ordered them to." Lohnes office phone rang before he could continue arguing his case. It was the desk officer monitoring the satellite images of the Iranian site in the CIA's Situation Room, 7 F27, a few doors away from Lohnes's office. The National Reconnaissance Office in Chantilly was sending those images to both the agency and the headquarters of USSOCOM in Tampa, Florida.

"Hey," the officer said, "it looks like the Iranians are running a convention out there. Maybe you guys want to come down and have a look."

Duffy and Lohnes were out of the Operations Directorate and on their way to the Situation Room immediately.

"These guys haven't had a visitor since I've been watching the place," the monitoring officer reported as they walked in the door, "and they've had three in less than an hour and here comes number four." He indicated what looked like a Land Rover just clearing the Pasdaran roadblock barring access to the site. "May we go tight on that vehicle, Chantilly?" he asked.

Duffy watched as the car drew to a stop on the esplanade before the entrance to the Iranian's installation. A welcoming committee swarmed around the Rover to greet its passenger. Squinting, he studied the man getting out of the car. The new arrival embraced two of the men and then, touching his forehead and his heart with his right hand, offered a fraternal Islamic greeting to the others.

"Yeah!" Duffy half whispered as the figure moved towards the entrance. "I think I recognize that guy. I'll bet it's my old pal Said Djailani, the Gucci Mooj—the guy who collects their drug tax. I'll bet he's come by to get a look at what all that money he's extorted has been buying for them."

"The other guys came up in baby Mercs," the man monitoring the screen noted. "I figure they must have flown into that airstrip they've got down in Zabol."

"Probably from Tehran," Lohnes surmised. "So this must be some kind of a high-level gathering, alright. What the hell do you suppose it's all about? Do you think it means their program is running into problems?"

"Could be that," Duffy agreed. "Who the hell knows?"

Duffy was concentrating on the figure of his old mooj warrior moving towards the building. So good were these satellite images in the bright, late afternoon Iranian sunshine that he could even see the Gucci Mooj's shadow trailing along behind him. That image brought to mind a Farsi saying he'd frequently heard from his mooj who spoke that language rather than Pushtu: "May your shadow never be shortened."

"It's a shame we're not going in there today. Think of all the shadows we could shorten."

"The what?"

"Nothing. Just an old Iranian saying."

———

Respect. Awe. Reverence. Fear. Exaltation. Hatred. Dr. Parvis Khanlari could read all those emotions writ large on the faces of the members of the Committee for Secret Operations as they gazed down on his first fully assembled and armed nuclear device. The long journey which had begun with the Professor's midnight rendezvous on a steppe in Kazakhstan was almost over. Operation Khalid was entering its final phase.

Khanlari had no intention of giving the men before him a lecture on nuclear physics. None of them would have understood it anyway. What they were interested in was what the bomb could do for them, not how it worked.

The finished bomb, now roughly the size of a beach ball was cradled in the especially built container Khanlari had designed for it, the container in which, under Imad Mugniyeh's watchful eye, it would be smuggled into Jericho on its way to Tel Aviv. The container was the size of a small steamer trunk. Its front was hinged and dropped down to allow the committee members to admire Khanlari's finished bomb. The lid remained to be secured once the front panel had been locked into place.

Khanlari pointed out to his audience the black needle of the antenna which would receive the radio signal to initiate their nuclear explosion. It popped out of the top of the bomb's circular form like a flower stem. The lid would be fixed over that black needle leaving it the only element of the assembled bomb outside the locked container.

Next he indicated the battery which would receive the signal from the radio attached to the antenna. Then he traced three red wires running from the battery to the capacitor-krytron assemblies, one for each of the bomb's two hemispheres and one for the neutron gun, over which the 250 volt initiating charge would streak. Finally, he pointed to the spider web of wires running from those housings to the fifteen detonation points placed on each of the hemispheres and to the neutron gun.

"And just like that, the way it's sitting here right now," inquired an awed committee member, "it's ready to work? To blow up?"

"Yes, but only of course, when our volunteer driver sends it our pre-selected radio signal."

"How large an explosion will it give us?" asked Sadegh Izzadine, the mullah who ran the *Gouroohe Zarbat,* the Strike Force, whose men had murdered Tari Harmian in his London home because he had dared to question the wisdom of Operation Khalid.

"It is impossible to state that with absolute precision because we cannot, of course, test one of our three bombs. To do that would be madness. It would tell the world we really do possess these devices. But all my calculations tell me our bomb will yield between 25 and 30 kilotons."

"Yes," Izzadine insisted, "but what does that *mean?*

"It means that it will explode with a force considerably greater than that of the bomb the Americans dropped on Nagasaki."

"What will it do to Tel Aviv?" pressed Izzadine.

"It will not wipe Tel Aviv off the face of the earth, but its effects will be horrible, absolutely devastating. For the Israelis, it will be a second holocaust."

Khanlari noted the anticipatory smiles on the faces of three of the committee members before him. The others' expressions remained, blank, almost dumb-struck as if they still could not grasp the enormity of the force which now lay in their hands.

"How much time do you need to prepare the other two bombs?" asked Ali Mohatarian, the chairman of the Committee.

"To do it patiently, correctly, taking no risks and being sure everything is done right, five days for each bomb," Khanlari promised. Extraordinary what we have accomplished here, he thought. The men before him could not appreciate what he and his fellow scientists had achieved in transforming three low-yield Soviet nuclear artillery shells into full-scale atomic devices. Too bad. There were scientists in the U.S., in England who could. They would stand in awe—and horror—before their achievement.

"We must allow these brilliant scientists so devoted to our cause the time they need to do their work the way they feel it must be done," the Professor declared. He looked at his watch. "It is close to five o'clock. Perhaps we should go upstairs to my office to begin our discussions."

"Washington," muttered one of the committee members as they all crowded into the elevator that would carry them up two flights of stairs to the ground floor of the laboratory. "Isn't there some way we can get one of those bombs into Washington?"

———

The members of the Committee for Secret Operations had just settled into chairs around the Professor's desk when his Rolex GMT Master 2 wristwatch registered five o'clock. As was to be expected in a man as meticulous as the Professor, his watch was precise to the second.

It was, therefore, at exactly this same moment two stories below his office, that the gallium arsenide chip in the krytron governing the firing circuit on the right hemisphere of Dr. Parvis Khanlari's newly assembled nuclear device emitted its pre-programmed radio signal at 1.50012 giga-hertz. The signal, the first sent out by the chip as it took its turn in the relay schedule set up by the experts of Eagle Eye Technology never, of course, left the confines of the Iranians' underground lab, never stretched its electronic tentacles upward through space towards the satellite waiting there to receive it. Coincidental with the signal flashing out of the chip fitted into the head of the krytron, however, six of the simultaneous side lobe transmissions the Eagle Eye technicians had described to Jim Duffy dropped off the chip. They were all so weak that eighteen inches away from the krytron even the most sensitive of electronic devices could not have picked them up and read them. One of them went out at 1.2001 giga-hertz. The kry-tron containing the Eagle Eye's chip was not eighteen inches away from the antenna of Dr. Parvis Khanlari's nuclear assembly. It was on the right hemisphere of the beach ball sized bomb, exactly ten and a quarter inches from that little black needle programmed by Dr. Khan-lari to receive an incoming signal at 1.2 giga-hertz.

1.2001 was close enough. Dr. Khanlari's antenna picked up the chip's side lobe transmission and immediately recognized it as the sig-nal it had been programmed to receive.

What happened next was the only action in the cascade of events about to begin which the human eye could see or the mind measure. The antenna informed the radio to which it was attached that the sig-nal it had been programmed to recognize had arrived. The radio in turn squeezed shut the electric relay leading out of the battery to which it had been attached. That opened an electrical circuit feeding into the bomb's three firing circuits. The instant it opened, a 250 volt charge of electric current spurted from the battery down the circuit into the three krytron assemblies. The charge activated the switching circuit of radioactive gas in each of the three krytron assemblies which in turn permitted the 4000 volts of power stored in the capacitors linked to the krytrons to burst towards the bomb's thirty detonation points in a square wave with a rise time so short it was on the edge of existence. Although the thirty detonation points were at different distances from the krytrons, the wires carrying the burst of current were identical in length so that all thirty charges of HMX detonated at the same, precise instant. Because of the way the HMX high explosives had been packed into the thirty detonators, the shock waves travelled inward down the cake wedge-shaped charges instead of ripping outward, an implosion rather than an explosion. Their shock wave slammed the outer tamper of beryllium ringed in tungsten inward in one momentous blast, like the pressure of a weight-lifter's fist squeezing a sponge rubber ball. The enormous pressure generated by the blast converted the five kilo-grams of metallic plutonium at the bomb's core to liquid, throwing off a blizzard of neutrons. The beryllium girdle squeezing tight around the bomb, however, reflected those neutrons back into the plutonium, maximizing the effect of the process already underway.

As the plutonium reached towards its point of maximum compression, the third krytron released its 4000 kilovolt charge into the neutron gun. The tritium nuclei in the gun fused, spewing off a hailstorm of neutrons which the gun fired into the heart of the plutonium core.

The result was a chain reaction. It could not have been more perfect and all set off by pure accident by that hopelessly weak, side lobe transmission which had "dropped" off the Eagle Eye transmitter. Plutonium atoms split, throwing off two or three neutrons apiece as they did, neutrons which in turn split at least one more atom, increasing both the speed of the reaction and the energy release exponentially. The whole process was accomplished in a half a millionth of a second, a period so short, it was just a blink in eternity's eyes. It was finished long before the sound of the detonating high explosives had even reached the eardrums of the Iranian technician nearest to the bomb.

Dr. Khanlari and his men had done their work well. As the fissioning of the device that was going to kill him roared to its peak power, it was generating an explosive force of 25 kilotons, well beyond that which had been released by the bomb on Nagasaki.

The first consequence of that was a flood of radiation, the whole spectrum of gamma, and X-rays spreading at the speed of light. Along with them, came the light itself, that awesome glare Dr. Robert Oppenheimer, the father of the atomic bomb, had described as "brighter than a thousand suns." Incandescent heat followed, heat so intense the bodies of the Iranian scientists, technicians, Pasdaran, the men gathered in the Professor's office, were not ripped apart but vaporized, reduced to tiny particles of flesh, blood and bone. They became as one with the molten metal of the lab's equipment, mixed into a radioactive plasma of earth, rock and mineral swirling through the inferno which the lab had become. It was a horrifying and instantaneous fulfillment of the Biblical prophesy: "Dust thou art and unto dust thou shalt return."

Across the draw from the exploding lab, the two Delta operators in their hideholes felt the earth tremble around them. The mountain opposite seemed to shake. "Shit!" the leader thought. "An earth-quake!" Then the metal doors of the lab flew out like kites riding a high wind and a gust of roiling red and black flame rolled through the opening they had left onto the esplanade. Instantly, both men understood what had happened. They had been assigned a "bug out" plan for such an eventuality, head north, loop into Afghanistan, and call for a helicopter evacuation once they were well out of the Iranians' reach.

"We're out of here!" the leader declared. "Do you figure a human can run fast enough to outrun a radioactive cloud?"

Watching the satellite imagery of the scene at CIA headquarters halfway around the world, the officer monitoring the site understood what had happened, too. "Jesus Christ," he gasped, "one of their bombs has gone off!"

Summoned by his call, Jim Duffy and Jack Lohnes literally ran through the seventh floor corridor to the Situation Room. Aghast, they watched a re-run of the imagery of the explosion.

"Can we get a satellite to read the radioactivity that explosion is releasing?" Lohnes asked.

"How about the President?" Duffy said. "Does he know what's happened?"

Minutes later, the National Security Advisor broke into a meeting between the President, the Secretary of Defense, and the Secretary of State discussing how to fund the NATO required modernization of Poland's air force. The four rushed down to the White House Situation Room to watch satellite footage of the explosion. Stunned, horrified, yet relieved, they re-ran the scene three times.

"Where's Colonel Crowley?" the President finally asked.

"Down at USSOCOM Headquarters in Tampa, Florida getting ready to fly out to Turkey," the Secretary of Defense told him.

"Get him on the phone," ordered the President.

"Colonel Crowley," he announced when the Delta officer came on the line, "we're going to stand down your mission."

Even a psychology student taking his first hour of classes could have detected the disappointment in the colonel's voice when he asked, "Why?"

Despite the terrible gravity of the moment, the President couldn't stop himself from laughing as he articulated his reply.

"An angel just peed on the flintlock of the Iranians' musket," he said.

———

Later in the day the President made three decisions as a consequence of the explosion at Zabol. The blast had registered 5.2 on the Richter scale on seismic devices all around the area. Since the region was notorious for earthquakes, the government in Tehran chose to attribute it publicly to yet another quake, this one, fortunately, in a relatively sparsely populated part of the country which had caused limited casualties and damage. Nonetheless, the area was sealed off to foreigners while search and rescue operations were underway.

In reality, of course, neither the Iranians nor anyone else would ever know what had caused the nuclear detonation. The explanation had been lost forever in the horrible conflagration at Zabol. In view of that, the President decided that the U.S. Government would not publicly reveal the information it possessed about what had been going on at Zabol. Instead, he ordered personal emissaries dispatched to the British, French, German and Israeli governments to inform their leaders in secret and privately of what the U.S. knew concerning the Iranians' nuclear operations.

Then he ordered a fifth emissary to the Crown Prince of Saudi Arabia. He was asked to take a verbal message from the President to President Khatemi. The message explained to the Iranian leader what was being attempted in that underground lab, extended the President's personal regret for the lives that had been lost and expressed his hope that, armed with the knowledge of what the radical clerics around him had been attempting to do, President Khatemi would now be able to take full charge in Tehran and guide both Iran and Islam back to the course of justice, moderation and wisdom which had historically been theirs.

His final decision concerned Jim Duffy. "I want that guy given the Distinguished Service Intelligence Medal," he ordered the director of the agency.

"Sir, he already has two."

"Then give him another one. And I want you to give him a new job. I want him put in charge of reorganizing the covert operation capabilities of the agency. Every time I've asked your people to do something for me, they've either failed or told me they couldn't do it. Toothless tigers. We need the means to carry out successful covert operations even more in this crazy new world we're living in than we did during cold war days. Tell Duffy I want him to put some guts back into your Operations Directorate."

––––––––

Jim Duffy turned off Eccleston Street into Chester Square, admiring the line of handsome white stucco townhouses facing the square gardens. In his hand, he clutched a bouquet of yellow roses he'd bought outside his hotel. Almost subconsciously he began to hum in his mind the words to that song he'd liked so much from *My Fair Lady*: "here on the street where she lives." And I'm looking every bit as nerdy, he thought, as the character who sang it. What the hell was his name? Freddy Frightful or something like that.

Ah, two weeks in another town, he thought. A worthwhile reward for the last months and an inducement to the new job they'd given him. Approaching number five, he stopped, startled. Hanging from the wrought iron fence ringing the entrance was a sign—"For Sale. Long Leasehold."

Nancy opened the door herself. "Jim!" she said. "This is such a nice surprise. I've missed all that good advice you'd started to give me. I was counting on your becoming my guru."

"Aren't they lovely?" she declared accepting the roses from his hands. "Shall we have a drink upstairs before we go to dinner?"

Jim mixed apologies along with the drinks. "I'm sorry I dropped off your radar screen without warning," he said. "I stumbled onto something up north that forced me to make a beeline back to Washington. One of the occupational hazards of my line of work."

"Don't worry," Nancy laughed. "Mystery becomes a man."

She took her glass of Sancerre from his hands and gestured towards him, declaring "welcome back" as she did. "Speaking of mysteries by the way, have you read about this earthquake in Iran?"

"I saw something about it in the press, yeah."

"Some of the papers here are suggesting there was more to it than just an earthquake."

"Well, you wouldn't believe everything you read in the press, would you?"

"In London?" Nancy laughed. "Certainly not."

Duffy walked to the windows and looked out at the verdant expanse of the Chester Square gardens. An Englishwoman, straight and sturdy as an oak in Sherwood Forest, was walking her Labrador along its well kept paths. In a strange way, he thought the road to Zabol had started here in this house on that January night, barely four months ago. He owed Nancy some insights, at least into what had happened out there.

"You know, Nancy," he said, turning back to her. "It's best to forget those guys who came here to kill your husband. They're gone. No one's ever going to pick up any trace of them."

Nancy emitted a plaintive sigh. "Yes, I've reconciled myself to that."

"What I can tell you though," Duffy continued, "is this. The men who sent them here to kill him are dead. They were evil bastards. And they died, to a degree at least, as a consequence of a chain of events that were set into motion by something your late husband did—or perhaps didn't do would be a better way to put it."

"Thanks, Jim. That's a much needed comfort. I don't suppose you're going to tell me how you know that."

"Nope. Not tonight anyway." Duffy gulped down a quarter of his drink. "Now tell me about yourself. How are you doing?"

"Just fine since I started taking your advice."

"What the hell does that mean?"

"Do you know the Institute for Strategic Studies in Washington? On K Street?"

"Sure. Everybody does. Why?"

"I heard they were looking for an ethnologue. Someone who specialized in my field. So I sent them a resume and guess what? They've hired me."

"So that's what accounts for the For Sale sign outside!"

"Yes. My poor Tari. It's his last gift. The real estate market's booming here. This house is worth almost four times what he paid for it."

Duffy had settled onto the sofa beside her. So much had happened in so little time. What a rush of events since that bitter cold morning when Frank Williams had pulled up in his driveway to force him out of the Maine woods.

"That's wonderful news, Nancy. You know, I'm not one of those people who believe our destinies are written in the sand or the stars. I believe we write them ourselves. In a strange way these last three or four months have helped me put my life back together again. At the same time they were almost destroying yours. I owe you. I hope when you get to Washington, you'll let me help you get to the point I'm at now."

"Oh, I will, Jim."

A few minutes later they were out in the square looking for a cab.

"Where are we going?" Nancy asked.

"I booked at a place called Daphne's. I hear it's where it's happening."

Nancy squealed out a peal of joyous, girlish laughter, a refreshing sound Duffy had not heard from her before. "Jim, you're unbelievable. You step off an airplane," she said, giving his hand an affectionate squeeze, "and right away you know the trendiest place in town. When I get to Washington, will you show me your favorite haunts over there?"

"Oh, I will. Count on it.

"Promise?"

"Promise."

Whatever is London coming to, the elderly cabbie thought pulling up to the Chester Square curb. A fully grown couple embracing like a pair of teenagers on the sidewalk of Chester Square. Imagine!

ACKNOWLEDGMENTS

As will be clear to any reader of *The Road to Armageddon,* it would not have been possible to undertake the research upon which this book is based without the help, guidance, insights and wisdom of a number of people, experts in some of the areas on which the book touches. Alas, it is not possible to thank them all here for their help because a number of them only agreed to work with me on the condition that their contributions would be anonymous. This obviously applies first and foremost to a number of my friends who are now or who were serving officers of the Central Intelligence Agency or its related intelligence gathering organizations.

For my work on the heroin traffic coming out of Afghanistan, I am indebted to Jim McGivney of the United States Drug Enforcement Administration, Phil Connolly, former head of Heroin Investigation for Her Majesty's Customs and Excise, now with the United Nations Drug Control Program, M. Gilles Leclair, director of the French Central Office for the Suppression of the Narcotics Traffic, Colonel Moshe Roderick, Chief of the Israeli Narcotics Police and Mr. Ray Kendall, the very able Ex-Secretary General of Interpol in Lyon, France. Thanks to them, I was able to work with their representatives in New York, Washington, London, Paris, Amsterdam, The Hague, Nicosia, Istanbul, Ankara, Islamabad, Tashkent and Almaty.

I am also indebted to Bobby Nieves, former Chief of International Operations for the DEA for his wise insights into the international heroin traffic. The problems created by the rapidly expanding international drug traffic are by no means limited, however, to the area of law enforcement. Of grave concern as well is the terrible problem of rehabilitating those who seek a way to escape their slavery to drugs. For help in that area, I am indebted to two very able rehabilitation experts, Dr. Richard Millman, director of the New York Hospital Rehabilitation Center and Dr. Bryan Wells of the Center for Research on Drugs and Health Behavior in London. Through them I was able to meet and work with a number of recovering addicts to attempt to understand the agony and suffering their addiction has brought into their lives. I also owe a debt to my lifelong friend Jim Burke, founder and for many years director of the Partnership for a Drug Free America and his able and helpful associates.

The drug traffic is, increasingly, a global concern rather than a national one and its internationalization is certainly going to become a major problem for us all in this new millennium. I was helped in trying to understand its geopolitical ramifications by Alain Labrousse and his excellent staff at the Observation Politique de la Drogue in Paris. Bill Olsen, director of the U.S. Senate Caucus on International Narcotics Control, was particularly helpful in this regard, as were a number of officers of the department of State and the National Security Council. Columbia's ex-President Ernesto Samper invited me to his nation to work with his narcotics police fighting the traffic under the difficult and dangerous conditions in Columbia's Amazonian Basin.

Last, by no means least, there is the enormous problem of attempting to control the flow of money earned by international drug trafficking into the legitimate banking system. Until there is the international resolve to crack down on money-laundering havens like the Grand Caymans, little real progress is going to be made in breaking the drug traffic. In this regard, Rayburn Hess, the U.S. State Department's money laundering expert and Jack Blum, an ever-wise attorney in Washington, D.C. were of great help.

On the nuclear aspects of *The Road to Armageddon,* I was able to educate myself thanks to the wisdom of Dr. Frank Barnaby, once one of Britain's senior weapons designers, Professor J. H. of the Imperial College in London, David Kay who oversaw the first UN efforts to investigate Iraq's nuclear weapons program and Paul Leventhal, the concerned and able director of Washington's Nuclear Control Institute.

On the thorny problem of Islamic Fundamentalism and the threat it does or does not pose to us in the West, I was aided by long and thoughtful conversations with outstanding Islamic thinkers such as Mohammed Ait Ahmed, Fahmy Hovedi and Saad Eddin Ibrahim in Cairo, Dr. Khalid Duran of the National Strategy Information Center in Washington, D.C. and Dr. Martin Kramer, visiting professor at Georgetown's School of International Studies in the same city.

I was able to supplement my own work on Afghanistan thanks to some excellent research help from Stefan Allix, one of the brightest members of a new generation of French journalists and Anthony Fitzherbert, formerly with the UNDCP program in that beleaguered nation. To ex-Congressman Charlie Wilson and former Green Beret Jim Rooney, I am indebted for their help and numerous, often humorous, recollections of their time working with the Mujaheddin Afghanistan.

I did not choose to visit Iran for research, as a cover story which I wrote for *L'Express* magazine in Paris on the Iranian counterfeiting of the U.S. one hundred dollar bill did little to endear me to the ruling mullahs. I was, however, able to get some very worthwhile insights into events there thanks to a number of Iranians in exile. First among them was her Majesty Farah Diba Pahlevi. I had a long and particularly helpful conversation with Abol Hassan Beni Sadr, revolutionary Iran's first prime minister, at his place of exile near Paris. Representatives of Manoucher Ganji's flag of freedom, the People's Mujaheddin in Germany, and a royalist organization in London all gave me good contacts and helpful advice. Dr. Esham Naraghi of UNESCO in Paris, the author of a fascinating account of the wise but unheeded advice he proffered to the late Shah and his days in the mullahs' prisons, shared a number of discerning observations with me. Bernd Schmidbauer, at the time Chancellor Helmut Kohl's intelligence advisor, a man with much experience in dealing with the Iranian Regime, game me a long and insightful interview. Uri Lubrani, Israel's leading expert on Iran was also very helpful. Two of the actual participants and one of the men assigned to investigate the Iranian's purchase of their small private airfield in Hartenholm, Germany, were of enormous help as I re-created the circumstances surrounding its purchase and employment. They do not, however, wish to be cited here.

I was very fortunate to have the help of a number of experts in some of the more arcane areas I explore in *The Road to Armageddon*. John Kuchjarski, the CEO, Deborah Lorenz, Vice President for Communications, Paul Beech, Director of the Electrical Switches Division and Ray Clancy of the Shannon sales office of EG&G made it possible for me to understand something of the workings of that mysterious little device called a krytron. Matthew Schorr of Eagle Eye Technologies showed me how to bug one.

John Coo, ex-Commander of Operations of the Metropolitan Police's Area Four in London, took me through the steps of a Scotland Yard murder investigation. Glenn Bangs of the U.S. Parachute Association recounted the delights of jumping out of an airplane at 35,000 feet. A very distinguished American military officer who must remain anonymous detailed for me the workings of the Delta Force. To these and all the others who helped me I am indebted and wish to stress that the remarks, judgments, conclusions and errors which the book may contain are my sole responsibility.

I also wish to thank my new publisher and editor, Michael Viner and Mary Aarons at New Millennium, for their help in preparing this book for publication.

Finally, I must thank my beloved wife Nadia who stood patiently by my side during all the long months, bouts of ill humor and anguish, which are the inevitable handmaidens of the creative process.